As The Sun Goes Down

Other books by Tim Lebbon:

Mesmer from Tanjen
Faith in the Flesh from RazorBlade Press
The First Law (audio book) from Elmtree Publishing
White from Mot Press
Naming of Parts from PS Publishing
Hush (with Gavin Williams) from RazorBlade Press
The Nature of the Balance from Leisure Books, forthcoming
Until She Sleeps from CD Publications, forthcoming

As The Sun Goes Down

Stories by
Tim Lebbon

With an Introduction by
Ramsey Campbell

Night Shade Books | San Francisco

First Edition

ISBN
1-892389-08-8 (Trade)
1-892389-09-6 (Limited)

Night Shade Books
560 Scott #304
San Francisco, CA 94117
books@nightshadebooks.com

Please visit us on the web at
http://www.nightshadebooks.com

Publication History

"The Unfortunate" is original to this collection

"The Butterfly" is original to this collection

"Dust" is original to this collection

"King of the Dead" is original to this collection

"Reconstructing Amy" is original to this collection

"Recent Wounds" is original to this collection

"Fell Swoop" is original to this collection

"The Empty Room" is original to this collection

"Life Within" first appeared in *Nasty Piece of Work*, 2000

"The Last Good Times" first appeared in *Enigmatic Tales*, 2000

"Unto Us" first appeared electronically on *At The World's End*, 2000

"The Repulsion" first appeared in *Extremes*, 2000

"Endangered Species in C Minor" first appeared electronically on *Masters of Terror*, 1999

"Recipe for Disaster" first appeared electronically on *Gothic.Net*, 1999

"The Beach" first appeared in *Nasty Snips*, 1999, and reprinted in *Cemetery Dance*, 2000

"Bomber's Moon" first appeared electronically on *Bonetree*, 1999

For Ellie Rose, my little sweetie.

Contents

Introduction
By Ramsey Campbell

One useful and intriguing task for some historian of horror fiction would be to determine when the European approach first appeared in the British field. I have in mind the sort of tale in which the horrors are symbolic and yet convey the sense of dread all good work in the field communicates. Often the horrors are rooted in the minds of the characters and may enact repressed aspects of their psychology, but crucially, they can't simply be explained away as projections from the subconscious. Sometimes they will epitomise some quality of the society the tale depicts. Not infrequently the tale will veer towards surrealism and may even find a home there. Nevertheless the story will certainly be recognisable as horror, for all its entitlement to a place in the European mainstream. Just as Lovecraft and Leiber gained strength from both the British and American traditions of weird fiction, so some British horror authors have acquired a fondness for the surreally fantastic and grotesque that seems to me to have crossed another ocean. I shirk the task of tracing this development and offer it to anybody qualified. One thing I do know, however, is that Tim Lebbon is an inspired exponent of the form.

This much is clear from his story, "Unto Us," which demonstrates one characteristic of this kind of tale — its use of the horror story's orchestration of detail to create an experience more than usually strange and haunting even for the genre. The book goes on to demonstrate Lebbon's range with "The Beach," a story that could have lodged in the *Books of the Dead* series, that ongoing tribute to George Romero — a story told with a succinctness worthy of D. F. Lewis or Richard Christian Matheson. "Dust" demonstrates how at ease he feels with writing science fiction — not true of all of us in the field, I confess — in a grim account of human indifference and cruelty under pressure. "Endangered Species in C Minor" — a European title if ever I heard one — preserves its ambiguity: a study of derangement or something worse? Ambiguity is a key to "Life Within" as well, but perhaps not the only one to this precise portrayal of childhood experience and of its attendant nightmares, both internal and external. By contrast, the swarming vision of "King of the Dead" recalls both Hieronymus Bosch and Clark Ashton Smith without imitating either. Then the book offers a cluster of ghost stories. "Bomber's Moon" is a tale some writers would have told as a novel, but Lebbon needs only a few thousand words to convey a real sense of the power of the past and to spring an impressive surprise. The spectral melancholy of "The Last Good Times" is answered by the redemptiveness of "Reconstructing Amy." "The Empty Room" is an understated study of childhood amorality, while "Recipe for Disaster" is a naked statement of despair. Beyond that there's more than a hint of Lovecraft's cosmicism underlying the human qualities of "Recent Wounds." "Fell Swoop" takes us on an apocalyptic trip, whereas "The Repulsion" is just as effective for the quietness of its Aickmanesque enigma. "The Butterfly" may have a surface of ecological concern, but beneath that is a far crueller vision. Indeed, that darkness informs the longest and most ambitious tale in the book, "The Unfortunate." A harrowing examination of luck and of the arbitrariness of that inescapable presence, it sums up many of the themes in the volume and is worth the price all by itself.

Enough of me! Let me leave you to savour the unique tastes of Tim Lebbon. His work proves that daring and individuality and considerable craft are still alive in the small press. May this book gain him much more of an audience! He deserves it, and the field is the better for him.

Ramsey Campbell
Wallasey, Merseyside
22 July 2000

The Empty Room

I knew Nathan would believe me when I told him that there were ghosts down there. What I didn't know was just how keen he'd be to meet them.

Max had told us about the place. He was a wheezing old git but sometimes he came up trumps. Between passing out from drinking cheap cider, smoking fags made from scavenged butts and scratching his crotch, Max spent his time telling us kids stories of the Old Town. He called it that because the whole place had now been built up, factories razed and new estates constructed to cover the bruises left on the land. This time, Max's story had contained a whiff of truth which we'd wanted to follow up.

An old manor house, he'd said, out in Tempton Woods. He reckoned its owners had once owned the woods as their private estate, but as the family died out and the manor fell to ruin the wilds grew in to possess it. Angry at their years of subservience, he said. Whatever that meant. He'd farted and closed his eyes, and the bottle he'd been drinking from tipped to mix cider with the of puddle of piss around his legs. Disgusting old sod, but as I said he sometimes came up trumps.

"Old Max was right!" Nathan gushed. "But it isn't really haunted, is it?" His eyes held the excited glint of a scared kid who doesn't quite know how scared he should be.

I nodded. "Sure. Ghosts of the woods come here now that the place isn't lived in any more. They spend their nights here because its so dark. Not touched by moonlight, or anything."

The manor was no longer there. Its roof and walls had long

since fallen and been subsumed beneath trees and plants, leaving nothing but a rubble-strewn mound to indicate where grandness had once stood. But there was a hole, like the open mouth of a sleep giant, sheer sides leading down into what appeared to be a basement. Though this was one deep bugger. If I shone my torch down there I could not see a floor, only the jet-black of a deeper hole. Deeper than my light could travel. How far does light travel, I thought, before it stops? Why doesn't it go on forever? Maybe it just gets eaten.

Nathan glanced over at me to make sure I wasn't kidding. I was, but he couldn't see that. "All down there?"

I nodded. "That's why it's so dark. The ghosts eat the light."

"I never heard that one."

"Well, what the hell else do you think they'd eat? It'd just fall out of their stomachs!"

Nathan was quiet for a while as he mulled this over; I could see his jaw tensing and stretching as his brain worked. That's what I'd always loved about Nathan, he was so transparent. And dull. Susceptible. I liked to tell him stories.

What I didn't like was what he did next.

"Come on then!" he shouted, and fell to his knees. Before I could grab at him he'd shimmied backwards until his feet were hanging over the edge of the hole.

"The ghosts — " I shouted.

"I want to meet them! Maybe... " He did not finish but I knew what he was thinking. He'd always been intrigued by the unseen. *Maybe I'll be able to talk to them.*

He went over the edge. I heard him scampering down the walls of the hole, so confident because he expected to strike the floor within a few seconds. More shuffling, and a gasp. Then silence for a couple of seconds... a seemingly endless couple of seconds... before the dull thud of his body impacting far below.

I stepped back and held my breath. For a crazy minute none of this had happened, and I looked around to see where I was. The woods were watching. Roots hunched out of the ground like the ridged backs of petrified swine. Trees stood high and proud, older than me, my house, my parents, swaying contentedly in the breeze as time hurried by around them.

Then Nathan cried out, a faint plaintive plea for help.

My life would never be the same again.

***

"Help me!"

"Nathan?"

"Help me…"

"What? What can I do?" I giggled. The sound scared me but it also felt good, as being scared from a distance so often does. "Any ghosts, Nath?"

Silence, like a held breath. Perhaps he was looking around, trying to see into the dark in case there was anything darker.

"Nath? You alright?"

"Get me out of here!"

Even from the depths his scream made me tremble, a disembodied cocktail of terror and rage. I giggled again and this time it felt even better. My imagination leapt several hours into the future: questions; panic; concern; arms holding me; people crying because I was there, crying also because Nathan was not.

Attention.

"It's dark, I can't see, my leg hurts, I can't even see the sky, the hole bends, it's wet and there's something… there's something moving." I heard a sob and a sniff. "You can have all my Willard Price books if you get me out. All of them!" The promise came from the dark like a whisper from a forgotten genie.

I pondered his offer. All his Willard Price books. I'd never read any of them — my parents thought reading was for pansies, and Nathan never leant his books out — but I knew how much he adored those volumes, how much he took care to keep them in the right order, spines facing out, never bending the covers back too far. He'd read them all at least three times.

I tried to imagine the books on a shelf in my empty room. I'd have to build the shelf myself, of course. I doubted my dad would do it for me. He did very little for me by then.

I also considered what else Nathan would offer if he were down there just a few hours more. His signed Han Solo baseball cap (signed by the actor who played him, of course, not Solo himself)? His pirated copy of *Resident Evil IV*? His… surely not, but maybe his signed Oasis album? Maybe.

I turned and walked away through the woods. Nathan's cries were soon drowned by nature coming to life around me, as if it had held its breath pending my decision. I smiled as a rook took flight and cawed its way across the sky. For want of anything better to do I decided to follow it, and soon I was running along a faint path between the trees, straining my neck with the effort of trying to keep tabs on the bird.

I lost it almost straight away. But as I exited the woods and slumped down in a field, I pretended the bird was still watching me, awaiting my next decision.

✸✸✸

I only went home for a drink. I don't think Nathan even crossed my mind all the way there. It was a ten-minute walk buzzing with plans of where to put the Willard Price books, how to build the shelf, whether to bother asking Dad if he'd help me. There was also a niggling doubt, too, a fear that once the books were in my possession they would be taken away again just as quickly. Taken by my parents and given to poor dead Danny.

Mum and Dad were out when I arrived home, so I went straight up to my bedroom and slumped on the unmade bed. There was nothing there for me. The wallpaper was a ghastly splash of motorbikes on one wall, steam trains on another, the remaining two woodchipped and painted a bright yellow. I'd wanted blue, but Dad had yellow paint left over from doing Danny's room. What was good enough for Danny, he said, was good enough for me. He didn't mean it. He had no intention of hurting me, making me feel inadequate, unloved, transparent. He just said what came naturally, because he was too wrapped up in the past to let the present concern him too much.

My ceiling was a cracked maze of crumbling Artex, years old now and providing home to creepies and crawlies in its myriad splits. The carpet was threadbare, the bed functional... and that was all. Nothing else. No furnishings; no cupboards or shelves; no Airfix models hanging from the ceiling with bubbled glue congealed around the cockpits; no comics splayed across the floor, open at a dozen different worlds.

Nothing. Zilch. Squat.

It was all in Danny's room.

It was an act of worship more than anything else. I see that now, but when I was a kid all I could understand was that my parents stripped my room to furnish my dead brother's. I'd loved Danny, yeah, and I mourned him, but I grew to hate him in a short space of time. Or rather, I grew to hate his memory. Because it was his memory that was stealing my parents away from me.

I lay on the bed for ten minutes that day, considering where the books would look best. Then I thought I got up to go and help Nathan from his hole.

Waking two hours later still on the bed, I realised that I'd only dreamed doing it.

I ran through Tempton woods. For a horrible few minutes I could not find the ruined manor, but then it loomed out of the shadows like a hibernating beast smothered with sneaky shrubs.

I stood at the edge of the hole. And I heard nothing.

✸✸✸

"Nathan!" There was no echo. The hole was a deep wound in the woodland floor, fringed by inquisitive shrubs. The sun found its way into the first few feet and lit up the sides, old brickwork pocked by frost and time, mortar powdered and bleeding down the walls like black tears. Further in the darkness was impenetrable. No light from above, and certainly none from below. No sound either, no hint that down there, somewhere, my friend may be injured or…

"Nathan! Nath! You there?"

It was as if the hole spoke to me. Nathan's voice was lower, grittier, maybe because he was thirsty. That's what I thought at the time.

"There's something down here with me," he said. He was trying to whisper but the old brick basement was an echo chamber. "Something alive, but… It touches me. It reaches out of the dark and touches me."

"Nath, it may be one of the ghosts." At the time I wasn't quite sure why I said it. It was cruel and unkind and Nathan was a friend of mine, but perhaps those Price books just didn't hold the allure any more. Perhaps the Han Solo cap was calling to me, causing vibrations in the Force: *Own me, own me.*

"It's not," he said, whimpering. "You have to get me out. It says it's the king of the dark. It says it'll stud its crown with my eyeballs and make a ladder from my bones and escape." His voice hitched, a fog-horn gasp in the basement's throat. "It says it only likes dead flesh. It'll wait until… until… "

"Nath, ghosts don't eat people," I said. "I told you, they only eat light." I sat down and looked around at the trees, those close in young and still shimmering with their ground-taking victory, those further away older, probably already here when the manor was in its prime. I tried to recall the late-night horror films I'd watched with Danny when he was still alive, the ones Mum and Dad thought weren't too bad for us because they were so old. How do you tell your parents that blood in black and white is somehow more frightening?

"No, not ghosts," I said. "What you've got there is a zombie."

"I can hear it, it's coming, it's — "

"Well, maybe a ghostly zombie. If there is such a thing." I twirled some grass stalks around my fingers and wondered just what was down there with Nathan. A cat or a fox or a rabbit, I guessed. Not a zombie. Surely not a ghost. Surely not.

"It's coming, get me out, you can have all my comic books, all of them, just get me out!"

"And the Willard Price books?"

"Yes!"

"And the — "

He screamed. It was as if the ground itself were crying out in fear. Birds took flight in agitated abundance, other things scurried around the foot of the trees. I stood quickly and backed away from the hole, expecting Nathan's bloodied hands to appear at any minute, his eyes wide and full of rage. Or maybe there would be something else there... something with Nathan's blood running down its chin... something using splintered bones to haul itself up out of the earth...

The screaming ceased. Then his voice again, throatier than before, clotted with fear. "Get me out. Get me out. Get me out."

Nathan had a full set of 2000 ADs, from issue one onwards. His father had given him the early few hundred and Nathan had collected the rest, going to comic conventions and fairs, spending hard-saved pocket money. I'd never been too keen... but I thought how cool they'd look scattered on my floor and arranged across my unmade bed. It would bring my empty room to life.

Nathan had everything. I'd once had something until Danny had died.

How much more would Nathan give me to save him?

I turned and walked away. He must have screamed for hours, because I was sure I still heard him when I arrived home.

✳✳✳

"Have you seen Nathan?"

I shook my head.

"His mother was asking after him. You went out with him this morning, didn't you?"

I nodded. "He went off this afternoon. Said he was going home."

My Mum glanced at me, then back at the ceiling. "You sure?"

I nodded. "'Course."

She glanced down again and smiled a paltry smile. She could

never look me in the eye for more than a few seconds at a time. When I was younger and Danny was still alive, she'd always said we had the same striking eyes.

I went upstairs and found that Mum had made my bed. The room looked even emptier now, maybe because I'd been imagining it scattered with comics, the walls lined with books. I sat on my bed for a few seconds, looking around, wondering just what I was going to do. Darkness nudged at the window. I thought of the king of the dark down there with Nathan, sitting patiently waiting for him to die so he could eat his dead flesh and use his bones for a ladder. I tried to cloth the idea of the king with flesh and bones himself, but I could conjure nothing in my mind's eye. I decided Nathan read too much.

Closing my eyes brought Danny. I remembered all the good times but they were soured, not by his death so much as what had occurred since then. If he were still alive I'd have games to play, models to make, things to do. As it was I had my bed and the darkness behind my eyelids.

I started to hum a song. Whatever I was going to do about Nathan, it would have to wait until tomorrow.

❋❋❋

Later I turned out the light and sat staring out towards Tempton Woods. I concentrated on the shadows spilling from between the trees, trying to see Nathan's screams and taste his fear. Musing upon what such a recipe would drive him to offer me in the morning.

I heard my mother and father go to bed. They followed their nightly ritual of opening Danny's door and going into his room, breathing in deeply as if memories could invoke lost aromas, whispering to each other but, in reality, talking to Danny. They must have run their hands over Danny's old toys, and my new ones turned old by their removal and placing in a dead brother's room.

At the time it all seemed natural to me. I felt something I could not understand — now I realise it was a youthful form of distaste — but their ritual was also my own. I would gaze at the empty walls of my room as my parents creaked floorboards next door, whispered goodnight to Danny and then went to bed. I used to hear them moving in the night, but that had not happened since Danny had died.

I did not go to sleep for a long time. There was a three-quarter moon, by which I tried to make out where I could put the Price books and the comics Nathan had promised me. I realised quite quickly that they would do little to fill my empty room. Rather, their presence would do more to draw attention to the vacuum my life had become.

Perhaps Nathan would need another day or two to decide.

✳✳✳

The next morning was a Sunday. The day of rest. My mum and dad had been sitting up all night with Nathan's parents, trying to soothe them, trying to reassure them, but only making matters worse. The police had spread out through the town to look for him. I said I was going to help them search, and nobody tried to stop me.

Walking into the woods I thought something had changed. It was as if someone had taken something away but I could not work out what; I only knew that it had gone. If Nathan was out of the hole I'd have known by now, but as I neared I knew he was still there. He was screaming. And the woods were silent — that's what was missing. The woods were totally silent. No birds calling, no bushes rustling...

The police had obviously not yet come this far.

"He – elp me. He – elp me." They were gasps more than screams, exhortations pushed past a throat swollen by crying or dried out from thirst. They drifted from the open mouth of the hole like puffs of darkness seeking impossible escape. He screamed between his cries for help, a high, ululating call invoking memories of old Hammer films, virgins fleeing black-clad monsters, camp mummies stumbling blindly at their prey.

I sat at the edge of the hole and listened. His voice was quieter than it had been the day before, as if he were moving away down some subterranean tunnel. Or being moved.

The surrounding trees swung to their own rhythm, undergrowth hiding all manner of unknowns on the forest floor. If I stared up through the canopy at the blue sky I could have been anywhere, not just here in the woods, listening to my friend screaming for help that may never come.

"Nathan," I said.

The screaming stopped. He must have heard me, must have sensed my presence from down in the pit. "Get me out!" he hissed.

"Well — "

"There's something here. It touched me. It... touched me, you know? I can see it even though it's dark. It wants out. It touched me, and it wants out. It's the king. It'll use my eyes to stud its crown, my fingers to pick its teeth. It'll use me, climb my bones, build a ladder from my bones."

"Nath, don't be so dramatic," I said, honestly believing he was going way over the top. Sure, I'd left him for a day, but it wasn't as if he was out in the open where he could get wet, where things could find him. And really, I never believed there was anything down there with him. "Don't believe everything I tell you about ghosts and zombies. It's probably a vampire!"

I giggled and frowned at the same time. Perhaps even then I wondered just what the hell I was doing.

"My leg's broken. I can't move. I'm thirsty. I want my... I want my mum." He began to cry then, useless tears shed in the dark where no one could see them. "And it *is* a zombie."

He cried for a long while, sobs and sighs rising out of the ground and taking flight into the trees. Perhaps, I thought, they sat there watching me, the product of his anger and fear marking and remembering me. I whistled softly. Dampness from the ground soaked through the butt of my jeans. I wondered how wet Nathan was.

"It wet down there?"

Nathan did not answer. The tears continued, but his voice had been stolen by the dark.

I stood and edged closer to the hole, and for a few minutes I was going to rescue him. I tried to spot protruding bricks and other handholds to see if I could make it down into the basement myself, or whether I could guide Nathan up. But then I remembered he'd broken his leg. I remembered my empty room, his books, his comics, mine, and I wondered once again what more he could possibly offer me.

"Nathan, you know your Han Solo cap? And your Playstation?"

"What are you on about? Why's it so dark? It's sitting beside me, it's breathing on me, I can smell its breath. It's waiting... it's waiting for me to die."

"Your stuff, Nath? You'll give it to me? You'll give it all to me?"

"Just help me! I don't want to stay down — No! Don't touch me! Don't, no, no... "

There was no more.

I left Tempton Woods again, strolling through the pine-scented shadows, listening to the sounds of the forest increasing around me as I moved further away from the hole in the ground. I thought at the time it was because Nathan could no longer be heard screaming.

Now, I think maybe it was something different. Maybe there *was* something down there with him, and the woods could sense it, and around the hole they were silent. They did not want to attract attention to themselves.

✳✳✳

When I arrived home my parents were waiting on the doorstep.

The most complicated part was explaining what I'd been doing that morning. I kept it simple. I said I'd gone to look for Nathan in the park, but when I couldn't find him I went for a walk on my own. Along the canal, I said. That lie became my unintentional saviour because I was not allowed by the canal, and my parents' anger changed tack slightly until they were berating me for wandering off on my own. *There might be someone out there,* they said. *Someone nasty.*

I was quizzed by other people, of course, when Nathan didn't show. The police (they went gentle – I was a traumatised friend and they had no reason to ride slipshod all over me); his mum and dad (who reminded me so much of my own parents when Danny had died that for a time, I felt like a child shared between four); friends at school. My reactions were always as expected and no suspicion was aroused.

I never went back to Tempton Woods. I was afraid I'd lead them to him, and consequently to the truth of my crime. Nathan faded in my memory probably at the same time his life was fading from him, down there in the dark.

Nathan's parents did not handle their bereavement like Mum and Dad. His room was stripped and decorated within months, and they handed me many of his things: his collection of books; his comics; his Han Solo cap. They also gave me his signed Oasis album. They said he'd have wanted it that way.

After searching the countryside and the town, the police went into Tempton Woods, scoured the old manor estate, sent their dogs in to sniff out what they were now expecting to be a corpse.

They never found Nathan.

✳✳✳

I went back to the town quite recently on a business trip, but I only stayed for a couple of hours. Max, the filthy old tramp, was still alive, still there, still swimming in piss. I don't think he recognised me, but when I posed a tentative question about Tempton Woods he told me of the haunted manor that lay ruined there.

"Haunted by what?" I asked.

"Take your pick," he said. "Ghosts, memories, guilt. Whatever takes your fancy."

I live in a small flat on my own in London. One room is jam-packed full of belongings, from books to toys to clothes, packed floor to ceiling so that there is barely space for me to crawl in and sit in the armchair squeezed into the centre. The other room — my bedroom — is minimalist to the extreme. All except for a row of books on the wall, a hat on my bed and a splash of comics across the floor. I still have nothing.

I think about the woods. I remember Nathan's screams. I wonder if a thing ever did come out of that hole, hauling itself up on a ladder made of bones, its ambiguous shape impossible in the sunlight.

And I wonder where that thing is now.

Life Within

Simon's mum was waiting for him after school.

"Has she had them yet?" Simon shouted before he reached the car. She swept him into her arms and kissed his nose.

"Not yet. She's as big as a football, though, so it won't be long."

"Can I watch them coming out?" His eyes were full of a frank fascination.

"Gemma will want to be on her own, honey. She'll be hurting, so she won't want us too near."

"I don't want her to hurt," Simon said.

"It's natural, honey, it'll be a nice hurt."

"Was it a nice hurt when I came out of your belly?"

His mother raised her eyebrows. She did that sometimes, and Simon could never tell whether she was pleased or angry with him. "Come on, let's go home. It's summer, kiddo!"

"Yeah!" Simon jumped into the car and secured his seatbelt. Eternity stretched before him, six weeks of sunburn and cool drinks in the afternoon, dens in the woods and hide and seek in the barn on Miller's farm. Today, the future was as bright as the sun.

✷✷✷

"Careful, she might be a bit temperamental," his mum said as they opened the back door. The house was cool, old stone walls sheltering it from the indiscriminate summer heat.

Simon darted to the corner of the kitchen and looked under the worktop, the faint mewling sound reaching him seconds before he

saw.

"Wow! Mum, look!"

Gemma was lying on her side in her basket, breathing rapidly and looking up at Simon with proud, watery eyes. He could hear her breath, taste the warm tang of what was happening in the air. As he watched, the dog arched her neck and licked her puppies, tongue pink and rough on the wet bodies.

A flush of warmth coursed through Simon's chest, and he felt a lump in his throat and a heat in his eyes. He was afraid that if he cried, his mum would think he was scared and send him away, so he swallowed his tears and smiled instead. She knelt behind him, and he sensed her smile over his shoulder. Maybe she was hiding her tears as well. She squeezed his shoulder, and Simon reached up and grasped her fingers, squeezing back.

Gemma whined and Simon felt a momentary pang of fear, a sharp spike catching his heart. The bitch lay down and her side rose and fell, rose and fell with each quick breath she took.

"That's it girl," his mother said, "push, push."

"Push," Simon said, not knowing what it meant but keen to encourage the dog.

There were three puppies, twitching and squeaking on the soft material of the old duvet. They were wet, and Simon felt queasy when he thought of picking them up. They had stuff on them, stretched over their slick fur like the skin of a burst sausage. For an instant Simon though their skin was coming off and he jerked under his mother's gentle hand.

"What's wrong with them, Mum?"

"Nothing, they look fine. They're still got some of the amniotic sac on them, that's all."

"Ani-what?" Simon said, louder now.

"Shh! Look!" His mother pointed without lifting her hand from his shoulder.

Something was coming out of Gemma. It was pale white, glistening, streaked with thick fingers of blood and other, lighter fluids. It looked dirty and gross, but Simon could see that there was something special happening here, something that he would remember forever. Gemma whined as the puppy plopped amongst its brethren, but she stretched over straight away and started licking the tiny creature, cleaning away the stretched skin of the amniotic sac from around its eyes, nose and mouth.

"Good girl, good girl Gemma," his mother said soothingly, and Simon felt a pang of jealousy. She used the same tone with him, when he was ill or shouting himself out of a nightmare.

"Is that it? Are there any more?" Simon watched Gemma, waiting for the next puppy to emerge and hoping at the same time that there would be no more. He had started to shake, but did not know why.

"Don't be scared, honey," his mum said, "there's nothing to be afraid of. She's alright, aren't you Gemma?" The dog looked up at the sound of her name and blinked tiredly. "It's life, Simon. She's just made all those new lives inside her body, and now they're with us in the world."

"Weren't they with us before today?"

"Yes, but they were inside her. They were in their own little world."

Simon looked at his mum and was instantly alarmed at the tears sparkling on her face. "What's wrong Mum?" he said, jumping up and stepping away, as if the very act of crying was contagious.

She shook her head. "Nothing, Mummy's just happy, that's all. What we saw was lovely."

Simon glanced back down at Gemma where she was cleaning her new puppies, saw the scraps of stuff which came off the mewling creatures, watched as Gemma swallowed some of it. He thought he should feel sick, but he didn't. His stomach was rumbling, but it was through the memory of a recent hunger rather than nausea.

"So do they live in it?" he asked. "How do they breathe? What do they eat?"

His mother stood and walked to the sink, filling the kettle and letting the sun dry her face through the open window. "When the puppies are inside Gemma, they have the sac around them for most of the time," she said. "They get their food from it, and they don't need to breathe until they come out. It keeps them alive and helps them grow, but once they're outside, like now, they don't need it anymore."

"What happens to it?" Simon asked, glancing back down to see rolls and clumps of the pale tissue scattered over and between the puppies. "Have you got to pick it up?"

His mother smiled at his childish disgust, opened the fridge to find some Cola. "I expect Gemma will eat it," she said. "Coke?"

"Are we keeping the puppies?" he asked as his mother handed him a frosted glass.

"We can't, honey," she said. "We can't afford them, and Mummy and Daddy both have to work."

"Okay," Simon said, leaping for the back door. The space outside was calling him, the acres of fields straining with six weeks of adventure and excitement. "Be back soon!"

He ran through the garden, ducking under the tyre swing hanging from the dead oak, kicking out at stinging nettles where they poked their heads through the long grass. He knew he had an hour or two before his dad arrived home from work in his rusty old car, a couple of hours in which to submit himself to the spirit of summer. He vaulted the low fence at the edge of the garden and started springing down the road to Miller's farm, the glass of Coke spilling its contents with every step and catching rays of the sun in its brown depths. He wanted to shout, tell the world that this was his summer, his six weeks, his forty-two days. He stopped briefly to put the glass in the hedge, intending to pick it up on the way back but already knowing it would be there for days, perhaps weeks. Maybe it would be there forever.

The farmyard was quiet, dried by weeks of sun, scattered here and there with tired dogs or chickens. It resembled a dusty, silent main street from one the of old westerns his dad loved so much, the silence pregnant with the threat of gunfire and violence. Simon was a cowboy as he ran straight through, heading for the fields at the back of the farm, shouting at the top of his voice and scattering chickens before him like tumbleweed. On his left was the empty barn where he would build complex, awesome dens with his friend Roger. On his right was the cesspit, into which he would throw unwary mice and birds injured by the farm cat, watching them sink with a child's naive fascination with death. There was Sam, the scruffy old farm dog who loved to chase sticks. His head lifted from his forepaws as Simon ran past, lowered it again when the boy continued on his way, no sticks in sight.

Everywhere he looked Simon could see summer waiting for him, spread out like a banquet of enjoyment across the table of the countryside. Every tatty barn, every twist and turn in the path… the whole world, that day, existed for his enjoyment.

✻✻✻

Silence surrounds him. He cannot hear the beating of his own heart. There is no roar of blood rushing through his ears. There are no creaking trees, no snorts from animals on the farm, no secret noises from his parents' room. It is a silence more profound than imagination can conjure, more complete than he had ever thought possible.

He can see only a vague underwater blur. There is a gentle pressure against his body, first on one side, then the other, as if a tide is playing with him, pulling and pushing him within his confinement.

A light shines somewhere, but it is outside, and outside does not interest him. Inside, that is all that counts. Inside there is warmth, safety. Inside, there is life.

He opens his mouth to laugh, but he does not make a noise. He realises that he is held within a fluid. It fills him and surrounds him, and for a moment he panics. He struggles against the tide holding him in place, forcing himself closer to the smudge of light at the edge of his vision. Something appears out of the blur in front of him. It is huge, curved, veined and leathery in appearance. He touches it, and withdraws his hands immediately, the coolness of its surface sending a shockwave into his warm, safe body.

He reaches out again, wincing inwardly.

He finds it difficult to see through the film, even though it does not appear to be very thick. He pushes with his hands and it bows outwards, but it is strong and does not break. He moves his face against the cool surface, ignoring his crawling skin, moving slightly to give himself a better view.

His mother is out there with his father and Roger. They are dead, eyeballs rotting on their cheeks, arms open wide as if in invitation to the birds pecking at their blackened flesh and the small animals burrowing into their stomachs. He wants to turn around, to lose the sight and the memory of what he is seeing, but the tide is pushing him against the wall of the sac now, holding him there to punish him for wanting to see out in the first place. He tries to scream, to tell them that they should have stayed inside where there was life, but fluid fills his mouth and forbids it. He tries to close his eyes, but he has no eyelids.

There is a sudden movement under his mother's tattered dress. She deflates as the flesh of her stomach bursts open. One of the creatures feasting on Roger darts to her and buries itself in the rent.

Simon feels the pressure building, senses that soon he will defeat the smothering fluid that holds in his terror. He opens his mouth, draws in lung-fulls of fluid, and expels it in an explosion of air.

✳ ✳ ✳

"It's alright, honey, alright." Simon could not hold back the tears, even though his mother was rocking him in her arms. His father knelt in front of him, body shielding his son from the night pressing against the window. "You just had a nightmare."

"I'm scared," Simon whispered, and his mother spoke to him in the same tone of voice she had used for Gemma. He tried to push himself further into her chest and she hugged him tightly, stroking his head. His pyjamas were damp with sweat, his hair layered to his forehead in wet tufts.

"Just a bad dream, kiddo," his dad said, ruffling his hair for his mum to stroke down again.

"Did I scream?" Simon asked.

His dad smiled. "Did you! Woke up the whole village, and then some."

Simon nodded, vaguely satisfied. He tried to remember his dream but it was like a faded painting, sharp edges wiped away and the image merged into one mass, one emotion. He was still scared, but thought he would be safe now.

"What were you dreaming?" his dad asked.

"Monsters," Simon blurted, confused and comforted by the lie. His dad gave him the usual assurances that there were no such things, while Simon remembered all the times he had heard his father calling people on television monsters, people who did things to kids or killed other folk in wars. He nodded his head dutifully, knowing without being told that there were no real monsters, only life and death. There was a fine line dividing the two and it was cold, leathery and opaque. It held life in one place, protected it from the terrors that the outside could bring.

He went back to bed but did not sleep. He listened to the sounds of the night, comforted by the blanket pulled up to his chin, fear assuaged by the warmth. The dark was alight with mysterious, secret noises: a creak from the next room when one of his parents turned over in bed; the cough of an animal slinking along the edge of the garden; the howl of foxes in the distance, so much like the screams of babies. Simon imagined being there, alone in the dark, with nothing to protect him but his own dreams.

He heard a sound from nearby, soft mewling noises from the kitchen. He jumped from his bed, suddenly remembering the puppies, the memory driving his fears away. It was dark in the hallway but he could hear Gemma and her pups, and the darkness held a promise. He knew where every loose floorboard lay; knowledge gained from countless midnight feasts.

Simon eased the kitchen door open, jerking it quickly past the half-way creak, flicked the light on and smiled. He hurried to Gemma's basket, knelt down so that he could no longer see the humid darkness at the window and looked in at the pups.

There were four of them, squirming and twitching and whining as they suckled. Gemma blinked tiredly up at him. There was no sign of the amniotic sac; the pups were clean, dark black and sleek where they lay stretched over the quilt.

"Clever girl," Simon said. He reached out to stroke Gemma but withdrew his hand as a growl rumbled from deep within. He waited for a moment before reaching out again, and this time she let him touch her. He tickled her side as her puppies drank. The dog sighed, eyes drifting shut, and Simon felt his eyelids drooping in sympathy. A trace of his dream returned, a feeling of unease more than a memory, but Gemma was warm under his hand. Simon lay down and drifted into a peaceful sleep.

✳✳✳

His dad woke him up in the morning, smiling as the boy tried to stretch the stiffness from his cold body. "More bad dreams?" he asked.

"No," Simon croaked, "Gemma and the puppies kept the dreams away."

His father frowned slightly, the smile now frozen. "Good. Do you want some orange juice?"

"Proper juice, not squash?"

"Proper juice." His dad poured some juice into a glass he had taken from the fridge, handed it to Simon with great ceremony. "Your drink, m'lud."

"Ta." Simon glugged back the ice-cold drink, let out an involuntary belch and laughed at his father's mock scowl.

"Aren't the puppies lovely?" he said. His father turned to the sink and began washing last night's dishes, nodding in agreement. "I wish we could keep them," Simon continued, but his father said the same as his mum — they both worked, they could not afford it. Simon looked down at Gemma and her new family as he spoke, feeling a heavy sadness wash through him like static. The pups were mewling, squirming blindly for their mother's teats.

"Going out today?" his dad said.

"Going to call for Roger," Simon gushed, his attention instantly torn from the puppies by the charge he already felt in the new day. "We might go to the woods to play. He wants to build a den, but I think we might dam the stream and set up all our soldiers, then burst the dam. Blam! Earthquake!"

"Don't go too far in, will you."

Simon tutted and rolled his eyes, laughing when his dad turned around and caught the residue of his expression. "Course not, dad!"

"What time will you be back?" His father did not turn from the sink as he spoke, and seemed to be watching something from the kitchen window. Simon glanced outside, but could see nothing.

"Tea time, I 'spect."

Apparently satisfied, his father flicked some washing-up bubbles at him, then chased him into the bathroom to wash. After he had wolfed down some toast and drunk a mug of lukewarm tea, Simon jumped on his mother's bed to wake her, advance warning for his father who followed him in with a loaded tray. She smiled, Simon laughed, and he barely remembered to say goodbye to the puppies before he ran from the house ten minutes later.

They formed their dam, and they built their den, and a lot more besides. The day had that mysterious quality reserved only for the first few days of any holiday, the stretching of time allowing twice as much to be achieved in half the time. The sun was held back from its travels, the gravity of the boys' excitement slowing its pull to the west. Their ebullient banter, the characters they took on and discarded throughout the day, the whisper of their secret plans, all flowed through the forest to animal ears, startling birds and scaring rabbits down into their burrows.

For the whole day Simon hardly thought about the puppies. He had adventures to make.

✳✳✳

When he arrived back at the cottage, having bid Roger a cheerful farewell, Simon's dad's car was already in the driveway. His mum was sitting in her chair in the garden, and he could smell the tangy smoke from a bar-b-que. She smiled as he ran through the gate, nodded dutifully as he related to her the battles, tragedies and triumphs of the day, all the while guiding him inside to wash and get changed for tea in the garden.

Simon dashed into the kitchen, his proximity to the house bringing back the reality of what waited for him inside.

The puppies had gone. Gemma was sitting up in her box, her muscles tensed as if readying herself to leap at someone. Her eyes were glazed, watery. A steady, quiet whine came from her every time she breathed out. Her ears were up, her nose dry.

"Where are the puppies, Mum?" Simon shouted, happiness slipping from his face like soap. The first tear had cut a brave track through the grime on his cheek, because he already knew the answer.

"Daddy gave them to their new owners, honey. The people came today and took them away. Gemma said goodbye to all of them, it's alright." She went to ruffle Simon's hair but he jerked back.

"I wanted to say goodbye!" Simon shouted, stamping his feet, exploding dried mud over the kitchen floor. "I wanted to see them again!"

"Now Simon — " his mother began, her voice losing its soothing edge.

"It's not fair!" Simon ran to the bathroom and locked the door, glancing at Gemma once more before leaving the kitchen. She looked at him, head high, ears alert, as if he knew where her babies were.

***

He hears nothing, and what he sees is blurred, two-dimensional. He spins around in shock. The tips of his fingers scrape across something rough, but the sensation seems secondhand, a half forgotten memory. He waves his arms and finds that he can control the direction of his movement, steering himself towards the surface. He does not know whether it is up or down. Gravity is redundant.

He feels the liquid throb in his throat, senses the pressure of his containment pressing in on his naked body. His hand catches on something and he thinks it is a stem of seaweed. He shakes his hand, the liquid slowing the movement, and feels a tug at his stomach. When he looks down he sees the cord, waving slowly in the disturbed liquid, one end buried in a raw red wound in his gut.

He panics for a moment, starts to flail his arms. Then he remembers the last time he was here.

He opens his mouth to shout as his movement takes him to the glowing surface, but no sound emerges. He bumps into the stretched skin of the sac, his face pressed to it by unseen hands. He moves slightly to get a clearer view, then winces as light floods in.

Outside, there is no life. It is brighter, true, and there is evidence of habitation. An old, rusty swing. The dilapidated facade of a house, gutters hanging at crazy angles, door and windows smashed and rotting. But the light is dead, suspended in the air like the stale remains of a party, all the laughter dried up. Simon recognises the house as his own, but aged and ruined.

Then his father walks into view, and everything becomes so much worse.

He is expressionless. The man who had read to Simon every night he could remember, pushed him on his swing and taught him to play football, is almost beyond recognition. His face is a half-finished painting, an outline thrown onto paper with no attention to detail.

Simon should be screaming, but the liquid will not tolerate sound. He struggles to punch himself awake within the damping fluid, but his hands are slow, his gaze constantly drawn back to his stumbling father. Curiosity tames panic as his dad reaches into a sack tied to his belt. He takes out one of Gemma's puppies. Simon smiles because the puppy is alive, aware, its ears perked up and its young eyes struggling to take everything in. On the dead canvas of its surroundings, its black fur is a splash of colour compared to everything else.

His dad looks at him.

Simon inhales a mouthful of liquid. He feels a scream bubbling deep within his chest as his father steps across the cracked earth of their garden. The dead man is holding the puppy out in front of him, his face still an impassive mask, the pathetic creature struggling against his grip.

Simon tries to force the scream out, to wake himself up. He knows that he does not want to see what is going to happen.

His father holds the puppy out, grabs its head with one cracked hand and twists. The little dog writhes in his grasp, then its head snaps from its body. There is a wet tearing sound, unbelievably loud as it dissolves the silence. For the first time, there is an expression on his dead father's face. A smile.

***

Simon would not let his dad try to comfort him. Whenever he came near, Simon screamed. His mum clasped him to her chest, rocking him back and forth and trying to stroke away the memory of the nightmare. She shook her head at his dad when he tried once more to reach him, and he left muttering under his breath.

"Daddy killed the puppy," Simon whispered, tears soaking his mum's nightie. She stopped rocking, held him still, asked him why he thought that. "Pulled its head off. Daddy was smiling, he was dead and all horrible like a zombie. 'Cept not so much blood."

"Honey, it was a nasty dream. It must be the heat, it's so hot. Just be glad that all the ugly things you dreamt aren't really here, there's only us and Gemma, and a whole summer holiday for you to enjoy. All the bad things have gone, because you've woken up." She stroked his hair, started rocking him again.

Simon heard the words, but their intended meaning eluded him. They were diluted by the memory of his dream. "I was in a bag. Full of water, except I could breathe. Like the stuff Gemma's puppies were in." Simon remembered the cord at his stomach and his hand stole beneath his pyjamas, but all he could feel was the hot skin around his belly button.

"Anything else?" his mum asked.

Simon remembered the rotten garden, the liquid preventing his scream, his father's smile as he ripped the puppy in half. He shook his head.

"Good. Come on, let's lie down. I'll lie with you a while, until you drop off."

"Love you, Mum," Simon said snuggling down into the warmth between her body and the sheets. "Love Dad, too."

"We love you, honey. Sleep now. You've all day tomorrow to play."

Curled into a warm ball, Simon fell asleep in his mother's arms.

✳✳✳

Simon saw the sunrise. It bled across the wooded horizon as he kicked dew from the grass. He had his hands in his pockets, big trainers on his feet, a chunky jumper holding in his body heat. His parents were inside having breakfast.

Gemma was still in her basket. Each breath came out as a whine. Sometimes she shook, her skin shimmering like ripples in a pond. Simon would sit with her later, after his dad had gone, and stroke her, cuddle her to make the nightmares go away.

He made his way under the apple tree and ducked down as a branch scraped his head. He loved the smell in this part of the garden, a tangy hint of rotten apples and the promise of new ones later in the year. Spider webs glistened between tall blades of grass, dew hanging on them like diamonds, the spiders hunched in their centres waiting for the first flies of the day. Sometimes Simon would look for a fly or a creepy-crawly to throw into a web, but not this morning.

He leant against the fence bordering the garden, seeing how hard he could press his arm against the barbed wire before it hurt. He pushed, trying not to feel the point of pain as a tooth of metal scraped into his skin. He remembered the dream from last night, the feeling of helplessness as the puppy was torn up in front of him. He wanted to cry, but a tear of blood on his arm stopped him. He winced and smudged the redness across his skin to see how long it took to dry.

There was a clump of grass at his feet, rolled up like an old carpet. He kicked at it and saw the perfect cut separating it from the rest of the garden. He pushed with his foot and it lifted wetly, displaying what lay beneath.

Their eyes were shut. They had never been given the chance to open. They were black and slick, as if dipped in oil. Their tiny paws, claws curved and sharp and destined never to feel the clatter of concrete, pointed skyward, or lay bunched beneath still bodies.

Simon gasped. There were no new owners for Gemma's dogs, because they were lying here, dead under a chunk of grass and dirt. He reached down and picked one of them up, disgusted by the coolness of its warm-looking fur. A dribble of water came from its mouth, and he dropped the dead puppy in surprise. It flopped back down among its siblings, head coming to rest atop the back of another.

Simon screamed. There was no liquid to contain his anguish this time, no sac to prevent him turning and running from the terrible sight. The lie plagued him as he ran.

"Liar!" he shouted as he stumbled past the house. "Liar! Bloody, pissing liar!" His mother stepped from the back door as Simon ran through the gate, calling after him. He did not want to stop, he wanted to do all the running the puppies never would, see all the sights they would never see. But he turned, and he saw Gemma gazing around the corner of the house, head down, eyes sad. The tears came.

"You killed them! You killed the puppies, Gemma's babies! Why did you kill them, why did Daddy tear them all up."

His mother moved towards him but he backed away into the road. "Oh honey, Daddy didn't tear them up. He drowned them, babe, before they could even feel anything. They're in water when they're in their mummy's tummy, and so soon after they come out they can't feel anything. They just die."

"But why?" Tears distorted his voice, like the fluid in the sac had blurred his vision.

"We're in the country. Everyone has dogs already. You can't just have puppies running about, they'll worry sheep and — "

"It's not fair! They were alive!" Simon turned and ran, ignoring his mother as she called after him, tears flowing back into his hair. He sprinted across the farmyard, and the barn loomed ahead. Simon ducked inside. There were still piles of last years' hay in the corners, the rest of it mouldy and trodden into the ground by time. He jumped onto one of the stacks and pulled himself to the top.

He sat there, expecting his parents to come in at any moment, afraid of their anger, imagining his father's face with the skin greying and his eyes darkening. The air was cool and unpleasant against his skin. When he closed his eyes the puppies stared at him, accusing him as much as their real murderer. He thought he could hear Gemma whining in the distance. Perhaps she had found the pups.

Maybe she was standing over their muddy grave, growling at his father as he tried to coax her away.

There was something flapping in the breeze from the half open door. It was black, reflecting slashes of light from between the warped boards making up the barn walls. With each wave it snapped at the air like a whip.

Simon grabbed the plastic bag and pulled it over his head. His breath was louder inside, but at least he could no longer hear Gemma's whining. It smelled of last summer, a time when there was only good in the world, when evil wore black hats in cowboy films. His face became warm, and it began to feel as if the bag were filling with a heavy, tepid fluid. He tried to draw in another breath, but the plastic folded into his mouth. He struggled briefly. The terror of the puppies' deaths receded with the light.

He tried to breathe again, but nothing came in. He was safe.

The Buttterfly

You're supposed to have wonderful memories of your mother. Secret things perhaps, but always there, always ready to bandage your fear of the dark, of failure, of life. She brought you into the world after all, struggling and swearing through all that blood and pain while your screaming little body squirmed its way out, holding you in her arms and feeding you even as they sewed her up and put her back together again, staring into your pearly-black eyes with unconditional love. Bonding through nature; the most natural, raw, pure thing there is.

Yeah, right. My mother must have shit me out, then carried on fucking the doctor. Threw me to the floor, no doubt, so that I could suck the dust bunnies in the corners of the room up into my flooded lungs with every gasped breath, every terrified, confused cry from my slippery little body.

Everyone loves their mother.

Yeah, right. Well, not me. Mine tried to kill me. And just take a look at me now.

Thanks, Mum. Thanks for pain. Thanks for misery, and the cold, and stray dogs pissing, and booted feet drunk on power and opportunity, denting my head just one more time before morning. Thanks for stumps that bleed. Thanks for a wheeled wooden trolley that never goes the right way, icy paving slabs, the top of a biscuit tin dented by the edges of copper coins, only rarely stroked with the feathery edges of paper money...

There is one good memory. Just one. She was trying to show me how everything I did had some consequence upon her, how my every action caused a corresponding reaction in her life. It was a way of saying I'd ruined everything for her, I knew that even then, but the way she chose to illustrate this was… well, beautiful. Unintentional, I'm sure, but beautiful nonetheless. It was the nearest she ever came to telling me a story: "Mary," she said, gasping the words through a haze of cigarette smoke, "there's this butterfly. It's in the Amazon. It flaps its wings and months later, there's a hurricane in the USA."

"How?" I asked. "That can't be right." And that's where the good part ends, because I'd doubted her and she said she'd seen it in a film and it must be right. Slap, bed, shut the fuck up.

It's not only what she said to me, or how she said it, but the fact that it made me think. And it stuck with me and is still with me now, *still* making me think. In a way it even helps me past the bad times, because I've turned it around, twisted it to my own means. My version, while a boot pounds into my guts or a policeman moves me forcibly on, is that there's a terrible fate already awaiting these people somewhere down the line. A truck to squash their brains over the road for the pigeons to fight over. A knife in a back alley late one night, its wielder stinking of booze and hate.

One good memory, and not much at that. It's probably made even better because it's the only one. I treasure it and hate her more because of it. There should be too many good times for me to be able to single out just one.

Take a fucking look at me now.

✳✳✳

I noticed the first of the leaves last night. It had been a pretty warm day so I decided to stay where I was in the underpass, hoping that no drunken slobs came by and pissed on me when I couldn't get away from them in time. My arms were aching anyway. It was a long push to the shelter.

At first, in the cloud-filtered moonlight, I thought they were the remains of a pile of shit trampled by a careless foot. They were spread across the paving slabs, darker patches on the dark path. I dismissed them to begin with, but my attention kept creeping back. There was something weird, something fluid in the way they looked, like they were swaying in an absent breeze. Then I nodded off and slept for a few hours, the familiar rank stench of my old blanket surrounding me.

A shout woke me up, or a scream, echoing into the underpass from a darker corner of the town. I hauled myself upright and managed to pull my clothes aside before pissing. Then I noticed the shapes, larger now and more obvious. Leaves. Their stems twisting between cracked slabs, the leaves themselves unfurled in the dark, eager for the sun.

They had not been there yesterday.

They're still there now. The sun has hit them and they've turned already, like a bunch of worshippers following their guru across the baking sky. There's thirty pence in my tin, all coppers, and suits swish and hustle by as fast as they can. Their polished shoes hit the leaves, scrape them against rough concrete edges, crush stem to stone, but they always spring back up. Some of them seem to bleed green sap but the tears heal quickly in the sunlight. I think there's a flower on one of them. Not weeds, then.

I'm cheered, in a way, by the tenacious little plants. I liken myself to them: trampled beneath the shoes of the suits, bent this way and that, always springing back up. But the comparison is just plain stupid. The leaves only sprouted overnight; I've been here forever.

I wheel myself out of the underpass and into the sun, and I cannot help but mimic the leaves and look up. The heat on my face feels good. I love the sun.

It was raining the day my mother tried to kill me.

✳✳✳

A trip to the safari park, she said, with one of her boyfriends in the front of the car smoking and playing his own weird music on the stereo. She bought me some Opal Fruits and told me to shut up and enjoy the trip, exchanged a weird look with the boyfriend then threw us out into the flow of traffic.

Water sprayed up from the motorway and blinded our car, but Mum kept her foot down. Music blasted into my ears from the speakers in the back parcel shelf, twanging my eardrums and conjuring a headache. The noise and the motion of the car made me feel sick, but I knew my life would not be worth living if I threw up, so somehow I held it down. I dropped the sweets and bent down to find them. They'd vanished beneath a seat, but I pretended to be eating them anyway. I knew from experience that my Mum liked it when I was occupied.

She and the boyfriend started talking like I wasn't there, about holidays and flying and fucking on the beach. I tried to turn off and looked out of the side window, counting the cars we passed, wondering what their drivers were thinking, imagining that maybe they didn't exist below shoulder height. Maybe there was only as much as I could see of them and anything else just wasn't there. It's the way I thought about most things, then.

It was often like this, me being left to my own devices. Most kids have Mums who read and sing to them, take time to talk, but mine begrudged feeding me. I'd find myself occupied by the world around me — nature at its finest and most awesome — and I would feel more at home sitting next to a secret pond in the middle of a wood than watching television with Mum and one of her men. So I looked past the drivers and the other cars and out into the countryside beyond. The landscape was still fighting valiantly against humankind's concrete influence.

A sparrow hawk hung above the roadside, waving wings down at its intended victims. I strained my neck looking back to see it drop, but it could not find what it was looking for. It disappeared into the rain and became just another speck among millions. A black, white and red thing flashed by, a badger crushed by careless wheels, and for a moment I was sad. But then I saw some magpies rooting in the corpse until they too were black, white and red, and I was sad no more. They had food for the day. I understood those things even then: that death was a part of living, and life was merely a prelude to the inevitable.

Perhaps that's why I could never feel bad about wishing my mother dead.

"You coming on holiday with us next month, young Mary?" the guy asked.

"No, she fucking isn't!" Mum shouted, laughing and telling him off at the same time. "I'll drop her at Shelly's for the week. She likes Shelly."

As a matter of fact, I did like Shelley. She was Mum's sister, and although she was a small, thin woman with a blackbird's eyes, who did little more than a weekly shop and spend five hours a night in front of the television, she knew how to talk. By that I mean talk with me, not shout at me. Sometimes I thought she was the good side of Mum, but how could I ever tell that to anyone?

I never did get to see Shelly after that day; haven't seen her since. I suppose there's something of a stigma attached to having a sister in prison.

***

There's lots more than usual going on around town today. And what's strange is that people don't seem to notice. Weeds poke stubborn tendrils up between and through cracked paving slabs, and a long creeper of ivy hangs across the post office window like an exotic snake frozen into immobility. In the main street the road is rashed with tiny black pustules, green shoots peering from within the sticky wounds.

Car wheels pass across the bumps, but the shoots are still there.

I wheel myself into the centre of town, thanking the town planners for ramps as well as steps, returning curious glances with a hard glare. Usually this is enough to turn most people away, but those who continue to stare are either the sickos, who laugh and point and jeer, or those who seriously pity or empathise with me. I like to work out which is which before they either laugh, or approach me to chat. Makes me think I can still judge character. Gives me the impression I'm still a part of their world.

I park myself in the covered pedestrian area leading into the main square, near enough to the entrance to be able to observe, far enough in to be sheltered from wind or rain, sun or snow. Some guy in a cheap suit and scuffed shoes passes by, glancing down at me as if I'm the odd one out this morning. Me, some poor wretch with no legs. I'm still human, though I can tell from his eyes that he doesn't think so. If only he could see what he has just passed, because the planters in the square have gone wild. They're overflowing, gushing fresh life out of old topsoil, greenery spraying out across brick paviors like foam. One of them sprouts something so tall that I expect Jack to come scampering down, followed by someone bigger and meaner. But the guy who walks by has eyes too full of the mundanity of his existence, too sanitised by nine to five, two-for-the-price-of-one and the next soap storyline.

He can't see. None of them see. I begin to wonder why I can.

Someone else drops a handful of coppers into my lap and I thank them, not even glancing at their face as they walk away. It will either be embarrassed or pitiful, and most days I can endure neither. So I stare into the square, trying to figure out why the council gardeners have let the planters go wild, but realising at the same time

The Butterfly

that this is not the case, that something is happening beyond my ken and beyond the awareness of everyone else around me. For an hour I itch to wheel myself across to the wild, spilled, still-growing plants, run my hands over their stems to see if I'm the mad one and everyone else is seeing the truth of what is really there: nothing.

But my blistered hands ache and it starts to rain. To go out in this would be pointless, because these are the only clothes I own.

Bob comes by and tries to chat to me, squatting on his way to work so that he can exchange pleasantries and assuage his guilt. I like Bob, I let him blather without giving him the fuck-off stare, and besides, he always leaves me with a fiver. I'm pleased to see him. Today, I can have a bottle for supper.

I try not to notice the crawling things appearing out of the ground and swarming around his feet. Worms first of all, slow and purposeful. Then beetles, black carapace reflecting oily colours. Ants, woodlice, earwigs, emerging not only from cracks but straight up through the solid concrete as well.

Bob reties his shoelace without seeing anything amiss.

"Horrible day, Mary," he says. "You'll get wet if you don't watch it."

"I like rain," I say, because I do. It's the stuff of life, a sign of rejuvenation and the repetition of things. I tell this to Bob but he's pretty shallow really, knows nothing more than kind words and paper money. He's not really here to talk to me, to know me, but to fill in his moral curriculum vitae with memories of how kind he's been. He's too naïve and nice to really blame.

"Hear about the oil spill in Russia?"

I shake my head and feign disinterest, but my heart sinks. Another million square mile of wildlife wiped out by humankind's folly.

Bob eventually gives me a fiver and leaves, unable to indulge me in conversation. He's good at getting the message, bless him. I stay and watch the usual daytime activity: recruiting shows for the armed forces; kids who should be in school hanging around and looking menacing; elderly shoppers spending precious savings on unbranded items so they can keep their pensions for heat at night. By late morning I am again drained of hope, and a familiar mantra echoes in my mind: we've done it all wrong.

Around lunchtime I see a wolf stalking slowly into the square. It looks as lost as I feel.

✳✳✳

When I was old enough to understand the words, my mother

told me that my conception had been an accident. The doctors had failed to tell her she was pregnant, and by the time she knew it was too late for an abortion. Even back-street quacks wouldn't touch her by then, she said. She went on to talk about hot baths and vodka, fighting in pubs and straightened coat hangers. Obviously she'd never had enough of any of them.

Later she told me that she was an accident too, trying to make me feel sorry for her. For a while I felt we were connected by this, in a way that most mothers and daughters could never be. Then I realised that mistakes beget mistakes, and all traces of hope dissipated.

We reached the wildlife park and my Mum grudgingly handed over the entrance fee. "Keep all your windows up," the park ranger told us. My mother grunted. Her boyfriend sat silently in the passenger seat, but I could see that he was twiddling his thumbs. He was a big man with tattoos on his knuckles, faded so much that they were all but unreadable. Once I sat up in bed listening, wondering what my mother read on his fist as it swung at her jaw. It could have been anything, because he was the sort of man she seemed to like. "Let's see the lions!" I said eagerly.

"Shut up," Mum said tiredly. "I've paid for it all so we'll get our money's worth." Later, that comment would come back to haunt me. I'm sure she knew what was going to happen, I'm certain it was premeditated. So what was going through her mind as we drove slowly through the monkey compound, and the gazelle fields? What was she imagining as we passed the elephants and the giraffe?

I hate to think. But I think every night. That sums up my life perfectly.

✳ ✳ ✳

The wolf has paws as big as fists, dappled with blood. Its muzzle and whiskers glitter wetly in the sunlight. It has fed somewhere; good news for the people in the square. It is alone, which surprises me, and I also find it strange when I spot a scrap of cloth snagged on one of its teeth. Wolves are not solitary creatures and they rarely, if ever attack humans.

It pads past a newsagent's and pauses as a huge woman lumbers by with three kids in tow. I can see it sniff at the hem of her dress, growl softly at the smallest of the kids, but there is no reaction from any of them. The wolf walks further, parallel to the shops and heading towards where I sit in the shadow of the buildings. It lifts a leg and marks its territory against a folding notice board exhorting

'SALE! SALE!' as if it has sussed humans already. Then it sees me, stiffens, hackles rising and shoulder blades protruding as it hunkers down. It is no more than twenty feet away.

My breath hitches in my throat and for a while I cannot breathe. A distant clatter indicates another handful of change, and I consider asking for help. But the wolf, anomalous as a rotting corpse in the square, receives no attention from the people there. I can see it. It can see me. Yet it is an oily shadow, shedding the gaze of others, keeping itself a secret.

Who would believe me if I did cry wolf?

It stands then, relaxing its posture as if recognising a member of its own extended family. It stretches its face at the sun and lets out a broken howl, filled with grief. There is no reply above the sound of traffic and bustle and the usual human cacophony, and for an insane moment I want to answer myself. But I'm merely a crippled woman with no life; what do I know?

The wolf darts away quickly, entering a Littlewoods store through automatic doors. Nobody notices the doors opening and closing for the animal, but it proves that another eye has seen it, the electric eye.

I sit that way for several hours, watching in fascination as the square is transformed around me. Like the hour hand of a watch the plants spread across the ground, their movement not visible but still obvious hour by hour. Tendrils of creeper emerge from the flowering mass, scratching at the base of walls then stretching skyward, snaking up the side of the museum and library, entering windows, twisting together and sprouting leaves to hide the ugly concrete.

I try to think of what to do. I can see what is happening, but nobody else takes any notice. People stumble on roots and stems, glance back at the ground and move off embarrassed when they see nothing there. Children are dragged away with bleeding knees.

An old woman trips over a basking snake. As she lies crying in the afternoon sun, shoppers worrying around her as someone phones for an ambulance on their mobile phone, the snake darts forward and bites her stocking-clad leg. It slithers away as a shimmer of panic passes through the crowd, disappearing from my sight in one of the overgrown planters. By the time the ambulance edges into the square the old woman is dead. I hear the words 'heart attack' bandied around, but I do not intervene.

As I said, who would believe me? Who would believe me when I don't believe it myself?

In the late afternoon the offices spew their employees back into the big wide world. And that is when belief and knowledge become two disparate things. I know what is happening, but I cannot believe it, ever. My love of nature, and my willingness to accept its terms, cannot adapt to this. Nature, it seems, is a criminal unto itself, breaking its own unbendable laws.

A woman tumbles on a vine she cannot see and a surge of scorpions scamper across her body, piercing here and there, sending her into a fit. Several people go to help and are similarly stung, one of them jerking away like someone receiving an electric shock, shattering a display window with his head. The crash of glass echoes the screams as other such scenarios are played out around the square.

Here, a man is pinned against a wall by a bear, his head clamped between its massive jaws and slowly, slowly cracked open. Those watching scream, but not because they can see the bear; all they can see is a man whose head seems to be splitting of its own accord.

There, a mother screams as prairie dogs fight over the contents of her pram. She sees her baby coming apart, but not the jaws responsible.

I push with my hands, sending my wooden cart clattering back towards the river. As I retreat my view of the square is reduced in the receding mouth of the pedestrian entrance, until I have only an inexplicable snapshot of what is happening. The sounds still reach me, though. The sounds of a most unnatural rush hour. Or, perhaps, a truly natural one.

One by one, the people are being taken down.

***

I loved the drive through the park, every minute of it. I didn't mind if some of the animals were sleeping or relaxing because it gave me a better chance to have a good look at them. I tried to stare into their eyes, to see whether they were truly happy — back then I liked to think I could connect with them in some way — but they were typically inscrutable. The monkeys scampered across the car, and I had to bite my tongue to stop myself from laughing when they started to tear it apart. Windscreen wipers bent easily in their wiry simian grips, chrome trim peeled back to add to the shed parts of cars glittering along the roadside. Mum swore and cursed and spat, sounding her horn and leaving skids on the road as she pulled away sharply. I closed my eyes then, held my breath, certain that she would run one of them over and leave it steaming in the open. I liked to think she would not do that on purpose, but then I was used to creating my own truths

We ended up in the lion enclosure, and my mother stopped the car at the side of the road.

"Fucking boring," Mum said. She lit a cigarette and half-opened a window so she could flick ash out. She glanced back at me, expressionless, then swapped another strange look with her boyfriend.

He sat smoking. In fact he'd been chain-smoking since we'd entered the park, not saying a word, lighting new cigarettes with the glimmering stubs of old, throwing the dog-ends from the window for monkeys and deer to find and eat. His manner had changed, I knew that, even though I could not see his face. It was in the way he sat there, more upright, stiffer, as if constantly ready to leap from the moving vehicle.

"Fucking boring as hell," she said. "We should ask for our money back when we leave. Or sue them." She giggled; it was a nervous and excited sound.

The boyfriend did not say anything. I could hear the wheezy suck of air as he lit up another cigarette.

"Don't open the door, honey," Mum said.

"I won't." Maybe she was enjoying this. It wasn't often she called me honey.

"I said don't open the door."

"I'm not, Mum."

She turned in her seat, glaring, her face twisted out of shape with an emotion I had seen before but denied. Hate. She hated me. I sat there in that back seat unblinking, uncomprehending. The boyfriend gasped and coughed, then took another drag.

She reached back and flipped the door handle. It opened with a snick, like teeth gently grinding together. From the corner of my eye I was conscious of a lion lifting its head from its paws.

Mum's don't do this sort of thing, I thought.

"Bitch," she said, "bitch, bitch, bitch… " Her lips were drawn tight so the word came out as a hiss. Her eyes were wet but I had never seen her crying. "Help me!" But the boyfriend did not move. All the way through what happened next he did not move, did not turn back to see, did not try to stop her. He just smoked.

She pushed the door wide.

Mum's just don't do this.

I was shocked motionless. Between my mother's curses I heard the grumble of a lion lazily standing up.

But Mum did do this. She did reach out and grab me around the back of the neck, she did twist around and groan with effort as she shoved me from the car.

Mum did do this.

I put my hands out but my arms crumpled beneath me. I struck my head on the road, drawing a smudge of blood from my forehead and nose. I wondered whether this would attract the lions.

I was answered with a roar. Three lionesses had stood and were walking slowly toward me. Mum drove forward, flashed her brake lights at me and parked. She wanted to watch.

I cried out. And the lionesses began to trot.

***

I sit in my favourite underpass. One night I ended up with over twenty pounds here, but tonight it is different. Tonight there are very few people coming through, and those who do are distracted. They frown and gibber and wonder just what the hell is happening, when I could tell them if they'd only ask.

Nature is taking its ageless toll.

There is nothing I can do. I cannot run, because I have no legs. Nobody can run, because it is everywhere.

Around midnight a tiger breezes by. I can hear its fur rubbing along the tiled wall, scratching against the town mural as if erasing it from history. It glances at me, eyes burning bright, but continues on its way. I remain frozen in place, a gasp caught in my throat. This close the creature is massive, eleven feet from nose to tail.

I stay awake all night listening to the town. Normal sounds at first, shouting and jeering and the coughing of car engines. Then noises I have rarely heard before, strange growls and howls, screams of human pain. Then, as dawn stains the smoggy horizon, sounds I could never place because they have never been heard.

In the morning there are two mutilated bodies at the riverside. Screams resound throughout the city; buildings are subsumed beneath flourishing plant life; the sound of running feet is followed by the rapid pad of clawed paws.

Two alligators emerge from the muddy waters, sniff at the bodies and begin to haul them into the river.

***

My mother waited for a couple of minutes, watched as the lionesses paced and sniffed and growled. They came near enough for me to smell their breath, then turned away, staring at the car as if remembering a face. I felt their whiskers scratch my face, but nothing else. I was petrified. Blood dripped from my forehead onto the road. I saw an ant struggling in one droplet. Time was all but frozen; the only movement came from the big cats.

Mum began to shout and curse, but I could not hear the words. Maybe they were not true words at all but a frustrated gibberish, bemoaning the failure of her plan. But where one plan ends, another begins.

It is ironic that, as my mother reversed over my legs, the memory that jumped instantly to mind was of our one good time. The treaded rubber gouged at my skin, then ground my knees into fragments. Blood spurted out across the road, my torso rose six inches from the ground and I pictured my mother, telling me about that unknown butterfly in the Amazon and the effect it could have on the world. She reversed a few more feet, changed into first gear and came at me again. The scream was still trapped in my throat, but white-hot shock was already enveloping me, dulling my nerves and dragging my mind toward the protection of unconsciousness. I wondered what events had been set in motion by this, what would change, as the car passed over my legs once more.

By the third time I was trying to remember who I was, staring across heat-hazed road surface at the lionesses standing a short distance off, sniffing the blood in the air and waiting patiently for my mother to finish running me over.

By all accounts she drove forward and backwards a further three times before she stalled the car. When the park rangers drove in, the lionesses were sniffing at the mess on the road that had once been my legs. Sniffing, pacing around, sniffing again. Never licking or biting or gnawing.

The park shut six weeks later. The animals had started dying, as if in sympathy with my pain. Perhaps the consequence of my mutilation was already being felt.

My mother went to a secure prison. She was mad, they said. My sentence was greater.

✳✳✳

By mid afternoon the town is beyond recognition. I wonder whether my mother is still in the prison; I wonder what is happening to her now. Being eaten by rats? Being attacked by the creeping things living in sewers? I conjure other dreadful images and I hope, fervently, that they are all true.

I once considered forgiveness but decided that it is for the strong, not for the likes of me.

I haul myself across the newly uneven ground, taking an hour to make the five-minute journey to the square. On the way I pass through the deserted bus station and there is Bob, lying dead in the gutter. A dozen big spiders scamper to and fro across his mortified corpse, sucking juices from pustules growing and bursting on his exposed flesh. A flower protrudes perkily from one of his eyes, its petals soft and pink and beautiful. Poor Bob.

The wolf is in the square again, squatting and shitting atop a mound which was once a statue to the founder of the town. It looks at me, then howls.

The tiger is there too, high in one of the new trees sprouting where the library once stood. There are signs of humankind's influence hidden among the creepers and plants like some long-lost Aztec ruin: tumbled walls torn by dogged plant growth; torn books flapping in the breeze, as if trying to impart their lost knowledge to the air; some bodies in the higher trees, pierced and suspended from thick branches like grotesque baubles. And perhaps that's exactly what they are, a celebration of a victory in a war fought for centuries, covert at first, overt at last.

The animals stand there, presenting their triumph for my perusal. They make no move against me, neither do they ignore me. They know I am here, they want me here.

Perhaps at a time like this, nature needs a witness.

Endangered Species in C Minor

As a child, Max spent long summer afternoons pulling the wings off flies, popping spiders' bodies between his teeth and focussing the sun through a magnifying glass onto the soft underbellies of crawling things. Each experience rewarded him differently. Touch, taste and smell all combined to make the experience worthwhile.

In those days, he never thought about death.

When he arrived home for tea his mother would sit him on her lap, ruffle his hair and tell him how much she loved him. He used to think that she knew about what he did and *still* thought him special, but as he grew older he came to realise that this was not the case. She did not know. If she did she would have said. On the surface, though, Max kept up the pretence. He *was* special: his mother said so, and sometimes his father, and Max grew to believe it.

✳✳✳

It was a mantra he repeated every day of his life as he recalled his parents' coffins being lowered into the ground, side by side, as if to mimic their position of death in the shattered car. *I am special, I am special.* If further proof were ever needed, he could show his body.

Different. Special. In his case the words meant the same thing. He was the last of his kind, the end of a line.

Soon, he would become extinct.

✳ ✳ ✳

In the dark, Max found his way by memory. He had crawled along the ditch a thousand times over the last few years, and tonight it was no different, though there were new additions to the fleeting topography: an untied bag of rubbish, stinking of rot and indifference; a shredded car tyre; a dead rabbit, evidently kicked here to die by the impact that had killed it. He sang the song of silence in his mind and mourned the dead creature, but there were plenty more where that one came from. Statistics made the importance of death variable. A billion ants, a million dogs, a thousand people, who cared?

When he died it would be a monumental event, though nobody would notice. He was almost sixty. Not old, but he felt death glaring at him every second of his life.

A car passed on the road and in the borrowed light Max saw the mouth of the culvert. He felt a pang of happiness, knowing that he would soon be with others like himself. Utterly different in many respects — he had no wings or scales or fur or claws — but from one important viewpoint, brothers in the face of imminent death. Endangered species.

The light faded but he was already in the mouth of the drain. Hauling himself through, feeling a dangling root tickle his scalp like a fortune teller loath to see the truth, Max sang quietly. Sometimes he sang for other people, but mostly it was for himself.

During daylight hours the wildlife park was littered with tourists. The clicks of their cameras and the clacks of their voices denied the park its real purpose — to show animals in their natural habitat. Lions yawned, and children thought they were roaring. Monkeys swung from trees to display aggression or sexual prowess, and families trapped in cars — ironically believing that *they* were the ones at liberty — laughed at their simian games. People personified animals, even here, and that was why, for Max, the park was so phoney.

Except at night. At night, when the people had gone home and the air sang with secret calls, the park took on a true elemental wildness. This is when Max liked it best. Cool, dark, mysterious and unknown, sometimes there was a hint of desperation in the cries, especially if they came from the endangered species area. The grunts of creatures dreaming dreams of extinction.

Outside the white Siberian tiger compound he stepped out of his clothes. It was cold, the weather just dipping into autumn, but the cool nip of fresh air invigorated him. He always loved to return to nature.

The tiger paced the bars of her cage, locked up for the night as if the presence of people during the day could control her. She stared out at Max, grumbling deep in her throat, a growl ticking over like a big engine.

Max moved closer to the bars and the tiger stopped her pacing. She stared at him. Breath plumed from her nostrils. Max took another step, sat with his back to the cage and closed his eyes. The cold bars scored his back like teeth. Leaves crunched beneath him, the first sign of the end of summer. He was like a leaf, hanging on tenaciously while all those around him had already dropped. The last two — his parents — had been plucked by the jagged metal of a broken car, not even granted the chance to age and change colour naturally. Soon he would be dead, ignored, cast aside, trampled into the sod of the past. Breaking down to join the rest of history in fossilised inconsequence.

For several minutes there was little movement behind him. Then the tiger seemed to make up her mind. Max closed his eyes and wondered whether today was the day, but fate preserved him for another night.

Eventually he heard the tiger's snores.

✳✳✳

As they opened the gates the rain came down.

Max sat huddled next to his shelter, blanket drawn over his head, legs crossed beneath him. He watched the grim faces of parents as they drove excited kids into the park. The kids were entering an untamed land full of wild animals and vicious meat eaters; the parents were merely offering their cars for the monkeys to wreck.

He began to sing, though few people heard him. Most passengers had their windows up against the rain, but those who had them open a crack heard his voice — strong, sombre, enchanting. It was a voice that they would normally associate with the great singers, not some damp tramp huddled outside a private wildlife park. It was his song of silence, because it mourned the creatures on their way out of existence. Max knew that for some there was hope, but for many — himself included — the point of no return had been reached and crossed long ago. Now there was simply a slow, inevitable decline toward death.

Mary passed by. She glanced from her Land Rover and gave him a tight smile, and Max nodded back without losing track. He slipped in a line about the saviours of the doomed — those who still sought to prevent the inevitable — and he was rewarded with another glance from Mary. Today, she had thought of him twice. She worked in the park, but she had never spoken to him. On dry days, when the gate attendant deigned to chat to him, Max would ask cautious questions about Mary. Sometimes he imagined her examining him, treating him, lifting his cock and gasping, checking his virility, measuring his limbs, staring at him sadly when she realised that there was no hope. He would ask her to kiss him goodbye, and he knew that she could never refuse.

One day, perhaps, he would tell her what he was.

He tried to huddle into a smaller shape, offering less surface area for the rain to soak. He could have sat inside the shelter but then he would not have been able to view the world. He found his own instinct in the matter ironic: he was the last of his kind, but still his mind doggedly sought to flood itself with experience and wisdom, as if to provide race memory for the ghost he would become.

Cars came and went. Max swigged from a bottle of rough wine but drunkenness could never claim him. When he needed to piss he stood behind the shelter and made sure no one could see.

※ ※ ※

The day finished uneventfully. Mary left at dusk without sparing him a glance, even though he sang for her. The gate attendant smiled down at Max in awkward embarrassment as she dropped a pound coin into his lap. Night drew in, and soon the dark inside the shelter was the same as that outside, so Max crawled in to sleep.

He could not recall a single dream from before his parents' death. He had a treasured memory of his mother blinking sudden bright light from her eyes, soothing him as he sweated and cried next to her bed, but he had no idea what had caused the tears. Maybe it was a childish, naïve knowledge of what the future held, dressing itself in the camouflage of his somnolent mind. Now, however, when he was older and more alone than most could think possible, the dreams came thick and fast. They were never pleasant.

He wondered what Mary would make of that were she to examine him. Lying on a table in her room, clean sheets turning grubby beneath his unwashed skin. Her hands pure and dry. Her eyes dulled with clinical detachment. He stared into the dark, wondering what scenes the incessant drumming of rain on the roof would conjure in his mind tonight.

Just as he finally came around to the idea of sleep he heard the fluid hiss of car tyres on the wet road. He took a final swig from his bottle as the vehicle pulled up at the locked gates of the park. The secretive clink of keys merged with the patter of rain, and then a pause, and then approaching footsteps.

Max sat upright and hid the bottle beneath one of his old blankets. A rapping on the corrugated roof echoed his heartbeat.

"Anyone there?" a voice called.

Max leaned forward and pulled aside the heavy sheet covering the doorway. Mary stood before him, arms crossed. Her hair was cut into a functional bob. Her clothes demonstrated an obvious dearth of vanity. Her face looked unmadeup, but it could merely be that the rain had washed it fresh. In the dark, the cautious smile suited her.

"Hi, Max?" she asked. She had never spoken to him before. "I like your singing. It's very sweet."

"Thank you." Max thought of his dreams of her examining him, but he was not embarrassed.

"I drove by with the window open, just in case. Don't you sing at night?"

"Sometimes, but it makes me dream of my parents. So usually I don't."

Mary frowned quizzically.

"They're dead," Max said. "I'm the last one left."

"Oh, I'm so sorry." She turned away, as if debating what to say next with the night. "Would you like to have a look around the park?" she said. "I know you love the place, and the animals. You sing such lovely songs about them."

"Only the ones who are dying out."

It could have been moonlight diffracted through slanting rain, but Max was sure he saw a glint in her eyes.

"That's my interest, too! I've popped in to do some work for a thesis I'm writing about man's involvement with... well, his interruption of evolution. It's... complicated." She waved her hand, dismissing even the possibility of his understanding. "So, would you like to see some of the places the visitors don't usually see?"

Seen them already, Max thought, but he nodded and stood up. "That would be nice."

Perhaps he would sing for her as well.

✳✳✳

"Something I heard you singing caught my attention," Mary said. "That's why I thought you may like a look around. It was something about the last good times?"

"You must have heard that this morning." Max said. Each day his songs were different. They were unique, and once sung they were lost like a sigh in the air. He saw the shadow of Mary's nodding head.

"What does it mean?"

"It was about the animals, and me," he said. Suddenly, something intensely personal was on the fringe of being revealed. He put his thoughts to song, and to explain them like this, one to one, was shockingly new. But it was also refreshing, as if a dark secret were being slowly enlightened by its telling. "It's about what happens when an animal dies out. There must be a last one, you know? The last one of a kind. That one will die away too, and no one will realise what's happened. But its final days are the last good times of its species."

Mary was staring at him, her foot still depressing the gas, the Land Rover grumbling along muddied tracks. "I didn't realise you were so passionate."

"I have reason," Max said quietly. "I told you. I'm the last of a kind."

Max had not expected a reaction. It could be that she was confused by what he had said. Or perhaps she was ignoring him.

"We've got some very rare animals here," Mary said. "I'm trying to save some of them, but it's hopeless. Once you get below a certain number of breeding survivors, a species just isn't viable any more."

Viable, Max thought. How technical. How scientific. He could never use a word like that in his songs. There was no... love in it.

They drove in silence for a while, awkward because they did not know each other. Mary's movements were measured, precise, never wasteful. Max watched her hands grip the wheel, the tendons rise and strain with every slight adjustment, and he imagined them wrapped around a knife. Slitting his stomach from sternum to groin. Opening him up and realising that he had been telling the truth all along, that he was truly different, and that these were his own last good times.

How would she react? Would she gasp? Stumble back, bloodied hands grasping the scream as it exited her mouth? Or would she merely frown with surprise and begin to photograph him for her thesis?

They passed the lake, moon floating on its surface like a rare jellyfish. Animal compounds appeared in the dark, glistening with a million pearly raindrops, black blocks in the night. They were in the secure zone of the park now, the place where food was kept and work was done, the place the public never saw. Max had been here dozens of times.

The white tiger watched as they drove slowly by. Max tried to catch her eye, but she did not want to see him.

"I'm taking you to Death Row," Mary said suddenly.

"Where?"

"The rare house. It's where we keep our smaller animals on the endangered list. Insects, birds, a few small mammals. My office and lab are in there too, at the back. If you like I'll show you some of my thesis."

"I don't think so. It'll be depressing. All those animals, doomed. How can you joke about it, calling it Death Row? They never did anything wrong."

"I don't joke about it, I handle it. And besides, it's not depressing, it's nature. Evolution works through a process of dying and birthing. The weakest die, the strongest survive and progress. Most people don't let themselves acknowledge it, but death is the most natural thing about life."

"Even the death of a species?"

"Especially that." Mary stopped the car and stared at him for a while. "Am I being a fool?"

"What?"

"Bringing you in. I'm being a fool."

Max smiled. "I'm harmless," he said quietly.

Mary smiled uncertainly and opened her door, letting in a sheet of almost horizontal rain. The wet did not seem to bother her. She brushed lank hair from her forehead and glanced back at Max. "So, are you coming?" They were parked in front of a long, low building, pocked with small windows that were each reinforced with steel bars. Whether they were to prevent ingress or egress was unclear.

Max did not want to go. Inside he would see his own hopelessness reflected in the eyes of the doomed creatures. But Mary was looking at him, sizing him up, offering a hard smile. Her throwaway attitude to the gift of life angered him.

"Yes," he said. "I'm coming in."

✳✳✳

Inside was worse than he could have imagined. This was no shrine to vanishing species. It was a lab, pure and simple, with animals kept in small cages, dressings scarring their bodies where parts of them had been stripped away for analysis.

"This is awful!" Max said, aghast. "How can you keep them like this?" He thought briefly of his own situation — the poor shelter, scraps of food, failing health — but he could not ally that image with this one. He lived like he did because he wanted to; he was rich in the mind, if not materially. These creatures had this forced upon them with no say in the matter.

"It's not as bad as it looks," Mary said, and there was a hint of desperation in her voice as if she were trying to convince herself, as well as him.

"Are you trying to save them, or just using them?"

Mary looked shocked. "These are beyond saving," she said. "I'm trying to help, but I can't do anything really. All I can do is study them. It's up to the species to save themselves, and if they don't, maybe that's nature saying they've had their time. They've no free will, and the strongest survive. It's a pity to see them die out, but it's progress in its purest form." A hint of anger edged past the bluster. "I asked you here to see, not criticise."

"The strongest survive," Max echoed. "So the weakest die."

Mary nodded. "I know this looks bad, but what's the point of putting a doomed animal on a pedestal? Better to learn what we can of it before it's wiped out totally. At least then we've got the memory."

"Do you want to remember this?" Max said, and he lifted his sweater.

He showed her.

Only his stomach, not everything else, not yet.

"Max," Mary said, frowning and glancing at his stomach, his face, stomach again. "Don't." She walked quickly to a door in the corner of the room and Max saw a light flicker on. It was as if she had not even seen.

"Don't you want to study me?" he asked. "I'll sing for you if you do." He stared at the open door, shadows shifting in the light cast out from inside. He had upset her. Perhaps she was disturbed by what she had seen, unsettled. Maybe now, late at night, alone, was the wrong time. He changed the subject quickly — asked her whether she loved animals, or merely found them interesting — and the feint seemed to work.

Mary's head appeared around the door jamb, a harsh smile cutting her face, white with teeth. "I love animals. But I love nature more." She ducked back inside without waiting for a reply.

No free will.

Max looked around at the glass tanks and cages, at the insects and birds and scuttling creatures digging themselves into the cover of straw and torn paper. He wondered what they would ask for, given the chance.

He told Mary that he was going to leave but she did not answer. He strolled to her office door and she was looking up from her desk. The computer screen was blank, but her hands hovered over the keyboard. For a second Max thought that there was blood leaking from her fingertips, staining the keys with each jab, but it was only the weak light reflecting from her red mouse mat.

"You were leaving?" she asked. Her hands were stiff. Tendons stood out like spaghetti beneath her skin.

"Yes," he said, frowning. "But do you think I'm special?"

She looked nervously around her little office, as if suspecting someone else of asking the question. She shrugged, nodded, would not catch his eye. "Sure you are. Keep singing."

Max left. He closed the door softly, shutting in the rustles and sighs. Beneath the torrential rain he heard the rapid click of footsteps on quarry tiles, then the tumblers rolling in the lock behind him.

He purposely passed the white tiger's cage, stopped and stared at the magnificent creature where she lay in the corner of the enclosure. He could release her, but what good would that do if she had no free will? And perhaps he really did not want to, because only the fittest survive.

He had never thought of life as a contest.

✳✳✳

Back in his shelter Max sat and listened to the rain beat a white-noise tattoo on the roof, wondering what messages were contained therein. The secret code of nature, perhaps, a cipher of life. If he could only translate, then he would be the fittest.

The muscles of his arms and legs hung limp beneath loose skin. Though he was stronger than some, he was certainly not the strongest. His voice was fine, his mind was potent, but he would need more than that. Nature was not an easy place to live. But unlike the animals on Mary's Death Row, or the white tiger pacing her cage, Max had free will.

He could do something to prevent his own extinction.

✳✳✳

He stayed awake, and several hours later he heard the clatter of the park gates being trundled open. Mary's Land Rover whisked by.

She did not slow down as she passed his shelter on her way home.

He waited until the sound of the engine had been swallowed by the storm. Wind whistled around the corners of the shelter, as if surprised by his thoughts. He found the wine bottle and drained the dregs. It would be more use to him empty than it ever had been full.

With resolve came fear. Max felt the world set against him, a whole history of death looming out of the dark, frowning down at what he was doing, insisting that this was *not* the nature of things. He slipped into the culvert, but even there he was pursued. The wind whipped at his legs, flapping his torn trousers as it tried to gain a grip. Max scurried further in, only realising as he reached the other side that he had been crawling through several inches of water.

The further he walked into the park, the more he felt surrounded by a world unsuited to him.

He found the road and followed it to Death Row. He tried to recall the journey of only hours before, but already that was fading. Mary's voice was still there, her words echoing in his memory, taking on new cadences to form their own strange song. Before long he was singing, imbuing her throwaway remarks with more import than she could have possibly imagined.

At Death Row he reached for the door handle, and fate smiled. Mary had left the block unlocked. Perhaps she had been tired, exhausted from hours of studying dying breeds. What would that do to a person?

There was a bank of switches on the wall just inside the door. Max flipped on a single light and went to the first cage, home to a tiny mouse. It was snuggled beneath some torn paper, but as he lifted the lid it looked up at him. Before today he would have shared in its fear, felt connected to it by its condition. But now it was too trusting, not cautious enough, far, far too weak. It was certainly not a survivor. He held the wine bottle upright over the creature, and even then it did not move. He banged the bottle down and ground it around until he heard the delicate crackle of bones giving way. One less competitor.

He would survive.

He opened the wire-mesh door to one of the walk-in bird cages and entered. As he held out his hand a small, startlingly coloured bird fluttered from its perch and onto his palm. It pecked at his life line as if looking for food. Too trusting. Closing his hand slowly, the dying creature's wings hummed between his fingers. He found its nest on a wooden shelf and killed its brooding mate. There was one tiny egg there, rare in the eyes of some but now, to him, an obstacle to his survival. He picked it up and crunched it slightly between his fingers. Through the crack in the shell, he could make out the dark feathers of a fledgling. He swallowed it whole. Like a hunter eating the heart of his victim, it would slow-release courage and power into his system. He could feel it bleeding already, vitalising him with hope, that elusive sensation missing from his life for so long. It seemed to change the air around him as well as the thoughts flitting in is mind, imbuing it with an underlying brightness, even though the room was still only lit by one bulb. Max rubbed his eyes, but the feel of cooling avian blood on his face disgusted him.

Other cages and tanks in the room began to call out for his judgement. Creatures were stirring, excited by the whisper of breaking bone. In the next tank he found a fat hairy spider and crushed it with the bottle. In a cage there were two vole-like creatures, snuggled together for warmth. He struck them with the bottle and cursed when it smashed. Then he realised that the breaking would aid him, and he slashed the creatures open. With each death he felt hopelessness being driven further out, expunged by the torture of others: nature was, after all, indifferent. He had always known that. The birds had sung as his parents were buried, the flies buzzed, the sheep grazed. If nature cared, surely he would have known some comfort before now. Now, he was making his own comfort.

It took him half an hour to go from cage, to tank, to cage again. Some of the animals began to scream and cry; he respected these more because they were aware of their own need for survival. He killed them quickly. Others merely stared up at him, or remained within reach aim of his smashed bottle, and these he killed quickly as well. They were not worthy of any more attention than he had to spare them.

In Mary's office, clear plastic bottles lined some of the higher shelves. Some were full, others half empty. He flipped the lids from a few and sniffed the fumes, blinking rapidly when his eyes began to sting. They wore warning symbols on their tattered labels. Her desk was paper chaos, only brief shapes of scored timber peering through. The computer sat dark and silent and full of potential, like a book of blank pages. He opened the drawers and shoved their contents aside, leaving rare bloody handprints on files, until he found what he was looking for — an old cigarette packet containing a few lonely smokes and a folder of matches to keep them company. For a second he thought about lighting one, but then he changed his mind. They were bad for his health.

He walked slowly through the dead room and a surprising tear ran a feathery finger down his cheek. So much death here. So many dreams of nature beaten and spoiled by his fury. For a while he felt like a traitor having witnessed the execution of those he had betrayed, but then he emerged into the night the strongest, the fittest, and he was sure that Mary would be proud of him when she returned.

The white tiger stood at the bars of its cage, staring out with weary eyes, watching Max approach. She wanted him to sit at the bars and offer his flesh, but a different man had done that, a weaker one, someone with no regard for himself. For a few seconds he considered not killing her, but then he realised what she would do were she free of the cage. She would make herself dominant by tearing out his throat, relishing every last spurt of his bizarre blood.

He splashed the contents of the plastic bottle through the bars, the liquid spreading across the tiger's flanks like fluid fingers petting her fur. She darted back, startled, then stood facing Max from the centre of the cage. Her muscles bunched, her head lowered.

He lit one match and used it to light the rest. Then he flung the burning folder at the tiger.

It took a long time for her to die. He thought he should feel bad but he did not; in fact, he could not keep the fascinated grin from his face. He felt much the same as he had as a child, when wood lice and slugs had gone about their business in his shadow, unaware of the fate about to befall them. The tiger tried to snap at the flames stripping her sought-after white pelt, but this only gave her head to the fire. She crunched against the bars, as if to push through would be to escape the pain. Max stepped back as the smell hit him.

Eventually the creature lay down at the front of the cage, spitting her last as rain drove beneath the overhang and struck her melted body. She shivered as if cold. Max reached carefully between the bars and touched her hot, sticky back. "Sorry," he said, "but you had to go."

He stared up into the night sky and dared the rain blind him. It blurred his vision, but he could blink it out. Perhaps one day he would be able to see clearly in the dark, breathe in water and fly up to the clouds. Death brought progress, but if you were the strongest — as he was becoming this evening — it did not necessarily have to be your own death that inspired it.

Life, he knew, must emerge from somewhere. He went back into Death Row to await Mary's arrival.

✳ ✳ ✳

When she came he was singing the song of silence.

"Max!" she said. Her eyes were startled wide. She looked out of control, and he liked the idea that he had driven her to this state. "What happened?"

"What did you think of the tiger?" he asked.

"Max, you didn't. Max... why?" She was wearing a T-shirt emblazoned with the motto: 'Kill Blood Sports,' above which the image of a slaughtered fox lay dead across her breasts.

Max giggled between verses. He sang the song of silence but added his own voice strong and loud, because he no longer belonged in the song. Mary seemed not to hear the words, or if she did she could not ally them with what she saw.

"Oh Max, what have you done? I'm going to get — "

"I'm special," Max said. "I'm a mutant, they always told me so. I'm hurt." He clasped his hands to his throat. Tiger blood dripped between his fingers.

"Did you do all — "

"I can hardly breathe," he said, the song dying away from his mouth but living on, ever stronger, in his mind.

Mary came to him, skirting smashed tanks and bent cages, stepping in bloody puddles where the memory of rare life cooled to nothing. "You're bleeding." She bent over and reached out to move his hands from his neck.

He struck out before she could touch him, hitting her across the face, and her eyes flashed confusion as her own blood was added to the imagined blood of the fox. Her experiments may be dead, but a new experiment sought life. Even now, Max could feel its genesis throbbing at his groin. His own triumphant life ached to be released and spread. There was, he wanted to tell her, *always* hope. There was only one point of no return, and that was complete death. He, Max, was still very much alive.

He stood over her, singing once again, his song far different to any she had ever heard. His bloodied hands fumbled at his belt. He finally dropped his trousers and was pleased to see her shock. He was more than ready to begin.

"I bet you've never seen one like this before," he said.

Mary looked at his cock and began to scream.

Dust

*T*he dust would never settle, that was now clear. What was also clear was that we were all going to die. However much food and water there was left, however quickly a rescue mission could get here, it would all be too little, too late. And within weeks of our demise, the sand would inherit our shrivelled bodies.

It had taken less than a day for the planet's gravity to snatch the *Hamilton* out of its wounded orbit, haul it down through the gritty atmosphere and dash it across the dunes. A dozen of the crew had died on impact, three more since, leaving three of us alive. The three unluckiest people in the universe, Kath kept saying, doomed to die terribly, too ruled by instinct to take our own lives. It was ironic that the temperamental motors had kicked in just in time to soften the crash landing. Strange, too, that compartment D, where the three of us had been working together, had come to rest suspended thirty metres above the slow-moving sand surface, held there by the twisted remnants of the ship's spine. It seemed as if fate had left us here to observe us acting and reacting in our final days.

"I'm going to kill myself," Mart said. He stood and disappeared quickly into the shadows, but neither Kath nor I went to stop him. He had done this seven times already — once for each day we had been marooned here — and he always came back shamefaced, though whether at his foolishness, or his inability to go through with his rash proclamation, I could not tell.

"I'm going to check the beacon," Kath muttered. She left without looking back, sliding the door shut behind her. She never looked back, not at me, though often I wished she would.

The beacon was automatic. It should not need checking, and if Kath did find it broken there was nothing that could be done to repair it. Beeton, the engineer, was dead in compartment C. Buried in sand by now.

I knew I should move, do something constructive, but at the same time part of me had already given up. Part of me had given up years ago, the rest following in dribs and drabs. Perhaps it took a disaster like this to fully seal my fate, and reveal my mind.

Another day was ending, a forty-hour cycle distinguished only by the lightening or darkening of the sand and dust storms constantly raging outside. It was like a sea, only slower, waves moving across the landscape, forming, disintegrating, travelling and forming again. An inimical environment, totally forbidding any sort of travel beyond the surviving section of the ship.

We should not even be here.

✳✳✳

Mart did not come back. Neither did Kath. And it was only when I went to see where they had gone that I found myself locked in. Or rather, locked out. Our meagre supply of food and water was all beyond the small room I was trapped within.

My heart dropped, that familiar feeling. I had been victimised, and it was not the first time.

I'd always wanted to travel into space, from the age of five upwards. In space you were weightless, and that's just what I wanted to be. For some reason, I never realised the obvious until I got here; that the ridicule was about size, not weight. I thought that all my problems would go when my weight was evened with others aboard the ship, in the same naïve way that a young kid thinks they'll be part of a gang when they agree to some demeaning initiation. More likely, they'll be subject to an increasing amount of abuse and assault, because they're the gullible kid who'll always do stupid things.

The jibes from the crew were mostly subtle, but always there. Those from some of them bit deep. Jokes about ballast... specially made atmosphere suits... space whales...

Now, however, my problems had gone from bad to much, much worse.

I began to panic. Unreasonable, useless, but still I pounded at the jammed door, pressed my face to the glass viewing port offering a view into the corridor beyond. My breath misted the glass and all I saw was darkness. I could hear nothing from within save the pounding of my heart. It was a silence so total that I only noticed it when it was broken.

Then I heard a noise from outside. Not just outside this room, but beyond the ship. A scratching, scraping sound, like nails drawn across a shined surface, magnified a hundred-fold. It was more than sand blown by the gale, louder, filled with intent. Something trying to get inside, I thought, and I recalled briefly that incarceration of my childhood when all I had *wished* for was for something to get inside. Now, stranded on a relatively uncharted world, I could not imagine anything more terrifying.

"Help!" I screamed, and the scraping paused for an instant. I glanced back at the misted porthole, staring wide-eyed along the corridor, certain I would see Mart or Kath working the manual door lock with a mischievous grin on their face. But they were still not there.

The sandstorm ceased. It was instantaneous, as if a huge wind machine had been turned off, and after seven days of constant buffeting the silence in the ship was dreadful. I heard the final million particles of sand etch their path into the hull, and then nothing. Or *almost* nothing. There was silence except for the scraping, scratching sound, quieter and more restrained now that the camouflaging storm had ceased.

"Help!" I screamed again. "Kath! Mart! What are you doing?"

Kath appeared at the end of the corridor. She swayed unsteadily, one had hovering gingerly at her temple where a huge bruise was taking on a rotting purple sheen. She'd smacked her skull on impact, lucky she hadn't popped her head open, Mart had said. Or unlucky, depending on his mood.

"Kath! Open the door, there's something outside!"

It was very unlikely that she could hear me through the thick bulkheads. My screaming her name was panic more than anything, an exhalation of terror. Yet still she cocked her head to one side, stared around the circumference of the corridor, evidently listening to the scraping and clawing at the hull. She glanced at me through the porthole without approaching any closer. I smiled. Her face remained expressionless as she turned and left.

I shouted an incoherent burst of rage containing no real words. As I slid down the wall my shirt rode up over my stomach, and cool metal prickled my skin. Closing my eyes, trying to blot out the sound by denying myself sight, I retreated into a memory that felt all too new.

✳ ✳ ✳

I was hungry, that was all. I often woke in the middle of the night with my stomach rumbling for food, and the thought of a cookie or a slice of rich cake defeated my subtle fear of the dark and urged me downstairs. I always cleared up after myself, never left a mess for anyone else. Just that one night, I couldn't help it, I was sure I'd seen something in the shadows, and the scream caught in my throat and sucked up the cookies and milk, and they plastered across Dad's new timber floor. The dog barked, bringing a light on upstairs. Dad came down. He'd never hit me in his life and he didn't then. He waited until the next day to punish me.

The cupboard under the stairs was dark and he left me in there for six hours. No food. No water. I haven't liked the dark since. And I hate being locked in.

Some things are much worse than a simple beating.

❋ ❋ ❋

The noise died down to the point where I could not hear it above the beating of my heart.

I stood slowly and checked the contents of the room. Strange how when the door was open, I had not seen the things around me. Now, locked in and trapped, everything was of importance. And everything was useless.

There were six other rooms in compartment D, all of them now controlled by Mart and Kath, but this small dining area — this cell — was devoid of anything useful. There were several empty food sachets on the floor, grim grey remnants all that remained of their contents. The furniture was fixed, the walls bare and bland, no viewing portals other than in the door. There was an intercom unit, but a receiver would need to be picked up from elsewhere for it to work. I could shout as much as I wanted, but if Mart and Kath did not want to hear from me... I was dumb.

Air conditioning grilles pocked the walls, but none were wider than my fist. No help or hope there.

No food. The water beakers were empty. There was a sheen of condensation on the ceiling and walls, but the forming bubbles of water were grey and uninviting. Maybe in a day or two I'd stick out my tongue and scoop them up. Maybe in a couple of days. Not now.

"Kath," I whined, knowing she could not hear me, trying foolishly to reach her via some sort of desperate telepathy. They had obviously made a stark choice. Chances for survival were slim; more likely that two would make it through than three. I wondered how much my weight had swayed their decision — more food for them if a big appetite is left out — and I realised that it had probably been the deciding factor.

Perhaps if I had let my feelings for Kath show, just once, then she would have treated me more as a person.

For a while anger, rage and terror took over. There was little to wreck in that room, but I did my best and worst, kicking the table until it sheared away from the floor, levering a chair from its mounting and decorating the walls with gleaming metallic scars. I lost my mind for a time, sure that in the corners of the room there were shadows, and that in these shadows things were moving. I tried to pulp them but succeeded only in jarring my arms and bruising my hands.

I've seen things in the shadows for years. Ever since that fateful night when my father had discovered me sneaking downstairs for food, splattering his precious new floor with paste-like biscuit, I've seen things at the periphery. At first they terrified me and made me as clumsy as I'd been that night, but over the years I've come to recognise them as constructs of my own inadequacy. There were no real movements and voices in the shadows; I put them there myself. But for those few minutes in that enclosed room, I was a child once more.

By the time the sandstorm had recommenced I was a shivering, mumbling wreck. I'd wet myself and my clothes stank of piss and sweat. I went to the viewing port every few minutes, but the corridor beyond was always empty and sterile, its only features the jagged ends of cables torn loose in the crash.

Still, from outside, a slow scraping noise hid beneath the howl of the sandstorm. A noise with purpose. My father, perhaps, scratching at the wooden door of the cupboard, smiling madly as he waited for the first of my screams.

I sat down in a corner and glanced up at the window of glass in the door. For a moment I was certain that there was an eye there, staring in at me. *Lucien,* my father said, *just a little longer. Just a little while longer.*

I closed my eyes.

※ ※ ※

One day — forty hours — after Kath and Mart had locked me in, the hunger took a fearsome hold. I'd already squeezed any remaining scraps of food from the open sachets, and they had been little more than a tinge on my tongue. I'd licked the condensation from the ceiling, cringing as the salty, gritty water trickled down my throat but determined to keep it down. I'd even spent a few minutes trying to tidy things after my initial destructive fit.

There had been no more moving shadows. I was glad the lights had remained on.

I had never known hunger. From an early age my family had been reasonably well off, and starvation was something that happened in far-away countries to unknown people. I had three square meal every day, with snacks in between... so this feeling was new to me. I knew what it was, of course, but my naïve mind still confused it with less likely options: disease. Had I caught something, was there a minute and complex breech in the hull that had let in some bug from outside? Madness? Was my body rejecting sanity as a defence against approaching death?

I didn't know which option was the least attractive.

My stomach rumbled, spearing my guts with irregular pangs. I looked around again at what I had in here with me and wondered how long it would take to die. My imagination — never my strong point — seemed to find sustenance in my hunger, projecting images of food into my mind. Lavish banquets, simple bowls of soup, all took on iconic forms in my traitorous mind's eye.

I found that standing eased the sensation somewhat, so I walked the limits of the room again and again. Five steps this way, turn, five steps back. My mother had told me that walking was good for the soul; it thinned the blood and set the mind to work, driving away laziness and sloth. I wondered what she would think of me now, were she still alive. A trillion miles from home in one of the most advanced mechanical miracles humankind had ever manufactured, and I was destined to die of starvation.

Perhaps, I thought, it would be better if the life support gave in.

The noise started again without warning. One second there was the rustle of the sandstorm buffeting the hull, then the intimate, secret scraping, like relentless fingernails working at the hidden joins in the craft's shell. Picking, prying, but taking their time, as if they knew for sure that they would eventually make their way inside. There was no rush.

"For Christ's sake!" I screamed uselessly. I ran to the door and looked out along the corridor, hoping to see Mart or Kath coming to let me out, laughing at the cruel joke but knowing I'd forgive them, I'd have to, to not forgive would be to doom us to die enemies and that's something no one could want...

What I saw defied logic. For a full ten seconds I thought I was asleep, or hallucinating, or dead already. Kath was leaning against the door, hands either side of the viewing port. She was smiling in at me as Mart screwed her from behind. Each thrust sent a shimmer across her cheeks. I could see no enjoyment in her eyes from Mart's actions; her amusement came from knowing what she was doing to me.

For the next ten seconds, after I'd realised the unbelievable truth of what I was seeing, I could not tear my eyes away. Kath's expression was a constant rictus grin, though the humour sat only in her eyes. Mart's face appeared at her shoulder. He glanced at me and began gnawing at her neck.

I turned away at last. For the first time I thanked whatever was causing the noise outside, because combined with the sandstorm it drowned out the sounds from beyond the locked door.

I don't know how long I sat with my back to the cool metal. I felt cheapened because I'd had an erection. I vowed to kill the pair of them when I got out, but I knew it would never happen. I could not kill. And I would almost surely never get out.

When I did dare look they had gone. In their place Kath had left an open packet of rations, splayed across the floor to tease me more. I tried to imagine what I had ever done to deserve this, but I knew the painful truth: some people needed no excuse to be cruel or evil. I just happened to be on a doomed spaceship with two such people.

The noise increased in volume, not the constant sandstorm, but the covert grinding beneath it. I cried out again and closed my eyes and I was back beneath the stairs. Fingernails scraped the flaking wood of the door. I did not know whether they were my father's or my own. I looked at the viewing port and saw my long-dead father's eyes, staring in so full of promise and bitterness and rage.

Back with me soon, I imagined him saying, and the words rang in the enclosed room. *You'll be back with me soon, Lucien. You bad boy, you.*

❋ ❋ ❋

The first time he put me under the stairs, I'm sure my father had my good intentions at heart. Maybe there was an element of child-like anger that I'd puked on his new timber floor. Or perhaps being woken in the middle of the night to vomit and tears had upset him more than he let on. I was in there for hours without food or drink, but I was never in any real danger other than from my own imagination. And that, as I've said, was never my strong point. I thought of food and felt safe.

❋❋*❋*

The second time was something far more; he'd started to enjoy it. I'd had two helpings of pudding and forgotten to leave some for my father, and when he came home from work he flew into a terrifying, blinding rage, scooped me into his powerful arms and dumped me among the shoes and coats and old dusters. *Selfish little bastard,* he said as he slammed the door. Through sudden tears I saw moving shadows, but they were only shapes thrown beneath the door as my father paced back and forth outside.

My mother had gone out that evening, making Dad promise to let me out soon. He broke his promise. Instead, he spent the next few hours creeping around the house, sneaking up on the door and rapping on it, shouting, cursing, scaring the living shit out of me and making me scream into the tight, strangling dark. I kicked at the door and begged to be released, but the more I cried and kicked the more he'd shout, unable to hear me above his own screams, his banging at the door cancelling out my own.

He let me out just before my mother arrived home. She was drunk and swaying, gasping alcohol and curses, and she did not notice my tears as she kissed me an acidic good night.

That was only the second time. Following on from that the incarcerations were planned, preventative rather than reactive he told me. I'd watch from my bedroom window as he sought spiders in the garden shed. He'd put them in first, then me. I never did mind spiders, but I always made sure I screamed and thrashed and feigned terror. I was afraid that if I did not, he'd find something far worse to put into the dark with me.

After three planetary days without food, and with only the salty condensation on ceilings and walls to drink, I was in that cupboard more than in the sterile room of compartment D. Shadows flickered from the stuttering power supply and I thought they were spiders scrabbling at the edges of the confined space. I slid across the floor and chased them, thinking of how they would taste, but they were beyond catching. Someone banged on the door and I hauled myself to my feet, stomach grumbling like a lazy old dog denied its sleep. Kath was there, rapping her knuckles on the viewing port until she grabbed my attention, then ripping open a ration pack and stuffing the grey gel into her mouth, laughing, spraying droplets of food across the glass so that there was only an inch between me and it.

Later that day I spent hours trying to grab these droplets, forgetting the glass was there at all.

All the time, the noise from outside continued. I could now

plainly distinguish between the rasping sound of storm-blown sand, and the tenacious, insistent scraping of other things, something whispering over the hull, seeking entry, perhaps to get inside what was inside. I sat in the corner of the room, shouting at my father as he banged on the door and crept around beyond it, holding my large stomach and trying not to imagine whatever was outside getting in, then using the same crackly, clawing sound to eat through my piss-damp clothes and into me, through skin and flesh and muscle…

Mart stood at the door one time, chewing slowly on a fist-full of fruit concentrate, his face expressionless. I screamed and raged and begged and cried, but his eyes did not waver. As he turned and walked away I saw that he was naked, and he had food smeared across his buttocks and between his legs. He looked back once as he reached the end of the corridor, and something tugged at the corners of his mouth. Through distorting tears I thought I saw spiders, and I screamed because I did not want anything worse put in here with me.

✳✳✳

I lost track of time. Hunger does that. It was only after several days of licking condensation from tangy bulkheads that I realised we were all doomed anyway, so trying to stay alive was moot. I laughed at this. Then I crouched and searched the corners of the room one more time for any crumbs I may have missed.

I noticed the sound from outside had stopped. The storm was still raging as strongly as ever, but the noises beneath that had vanished. Whatever was outside had made it inside, I was sure.

I looked around the room, my cell, and at the edges of my perception there was constant movement. In the corners of the room, at the join of wall and ceiling, things were becoming blurred. Junctions became uncertain, bulkheads phased in and out of focus, and before long I was lying in a hazy ghost of what the room had once been.

I did not question what was going on. I merely took it as the final step before death.

Let you out soon, my father said in a sing-song voice. He tapped his fingernails on the outside of the door. *Be out soon. Soon. Bad, bad boy…*

✳✳✳

Some time later —hours or days — I was standing at the

door. Things were still indistinct, and I felt a continuous crawling across the surface of my skin. It was like being immersed in a bath of amoeba, their singular touch unfelt, their multitudinous caress like silk across bare flesh.

Kath appeared at the end of the corridor. She ignored me, hobbling instead to the food packets she'd left there after screwing Mart against the door. She snapped them up, searching through each one in detail, her gaunt face stiff with panic, eyes wide and too big, mouth melted into a painful grimace.

I tapped at the glass. She looked up. There was nothing in her eyes — no recognition or hate, nor any sign of the spiteful glee she'd shown during earlier visits. I'd have preferred anything rather than the look of utter hopelessness I saw there.

Mart appeared and ran to where Kath searched through the torn, evidently empty packets. I heard the bass rumble of their voices as they shouted and fought, but I could not distinguish single words. I watched Kath raking his face with her nails, Mart striking at her temple with one fisted hand and knocking her to the shimmering floor. He kicked her when she was down, aiming for her head, but as she cowered and raised her hands he stopped and walked away.

She stood slowly. I had an impossible and irrational urge to help her, break down the door and tend her wounds, even after all she had done. Shadows were moving everywhere now, and each time I heard my father's voice I was less surprised.

Kath left. She did not look back at me, even then. It was as if she'd forgotten I had ever existed.

I never saw her again.

✳✳✳

I remember little from that moment on. All I can do is to hypothesise.

I survived, as is obvious. Between the time the things from outside got in and the arrival of the rescue ship, must have been at least twenty days. In that time something made me keep licking the moisture from the walls so that I did not die of dehydration. I like to think it was my father, looking in through the viewing port and shouting and cursing, keeping me awake, nudging me from sleep every time my eyes closed and the blurred, shifting surroundings were darkened. I like to think that, and even though I'm sure it's not true, the memory of my father has always been there. So, in a way, he really did save me.

The rescue crews cut through the hull and immediately saw the shifting, shimmering surfaces inside. They used a millisecond burst of radiation to kill off the countless microscopic things lending everything that appearance; our first encounter with an alien life-form, and we fried it. Kath and Mart would have loved that.

Minutes later they discovered me. I was close to death; many thought I was beyond it.

On the way back home they told me that I weighed a hundred pounds when they found me, curled into the corner of a locked room talking about spiders, licking the walls and floor so much that my tongue was bloody and raw. Before the crash I had weighed over two-hundred-and-twenty. My body had eaten itself, and that way I had survived.

I tried never to think about what I was consuming as I liked up condensation from the cool metal.

They'd found Kath and Mart dead in another room in compartment D. Initially, it appeared that both had died of starvation. All food packets were stripped clean, the tenacious, microscopic things from outside having come in, eaten then stayed. Why Kath and Mart's dead bodies were not touched was never explained. Maybe we aliens were too bitter for them.

Kath had started to chew into Mart's leg before she too had died. There were signs that his demise had been somewhat accelerated with the use of a heavy, blunt object. The rescue commander told me this, and in the same breath said that all evidence to support this had been inexplicably lost. Keen not to upset me too much, obviously.

I was too tired to argue.

***

They kept some of the viewing portals open until they were ready for the leap home. As I sat isolated in the medical bay, my withered form punctured in a dozen places by tubes and nanobot injectors, I stared out at infinity.

Looking so far into the past, I could see little more than the inside of a cupboard door.

Fell Swoop

Sometimes when he looked in a mirror, Jack saw someone else.

If he really concentrated he would see himself as others saw him. Subtle irregularities jumped out at him, so familiar that they normally went unnoticed: the scar above his right eyebrow from a stone thrown when he was a child; acne pocks around his cheeks; his left eyelid drooping just a little more than his right. Instant recognition was sometimes a curse. Occasionally it did him good to see himself as a distinct person, a human being... not just as *him*.

He always thought it was simply a matter of perception. He never truly believed that he was seeing a stranger wearing his own face.

He never expected to meet that stranger.

✳✳✳

Something made him open his eyes. A noise, or a sensation, or a smell — whatever, it must have been major. With a nuclear hangover going meltdown in his skull, it was a miracle he could experience or sense anything at all.

Hearing was the final sense to go when you died, he'd heard that somewhere, and now it was the first to return. All he could hear was his own ragged breathing. Vision pulsed in and out with his heartbeat, a slow strobe. At first there was only shadow, and then outlines sharpened and colour found its rightful place. He saw a wall sprayed with graffiti, a pavement smeared with vomit and shit, a naked man sitting cross-legged in the road.

Jack groaned and raised himself up on one elbow, closing his eyes to try to purge his mind of hallucination and pain. When he opened them again the man was still there, hands resting on knees, long hair hanging over one shoulder in a ponytail. His eyes were black and he was staring directly at Jack.

"Wake up," the naked man said. "It's going to be a hell of a day."

"Who are you?" Jack muttered. His mouth felt as though it had been fired with a blowtorch. He felt a sudden urge to piss and scrabbled at his zipper, groaning at the pulsing pain in his head. He managed to free himself just in time, and a puddle of urine spread across the pavement in front of him.

The naked man stood and watched the pitiful display. "How glad I am that I'm no longer a part of you," he said.

Jack put himself away and stood up, slowly, using the wall behind him to support his sodden weight. He tried to recall what had happened last night: an argument with Jane, he thought; a quiet corner in a noisy pub; glass after glass from the end of the bar, and a bottle from his pocket later on. He could not recall the argument, he remembered only her mouth opening and closing, all the bad things she had to say about him bubbling out. He guessed he'd said them right back at her. As usual.

A cloud of shame settled slowly around him. His memories of the night were episodic at best, and in truth he could have gone anywhere, done anything, with anybody. He wondered how many people other than Jane had cause to hate him this morning.

"Who are you?" he asked again. He realised at last that it was daylight and this guy was hanging naked around the streets. He was tall and muscular, fine skin, long hair, big dick… if Jack went that way at all, he'd have to say that he was gorgeous.

And more to the point, he was strikingly familiar.

"I'm who you've always wanted to be," the man said. "I'm who you could have been. You could have been called Rook, so that's my name, if it pleases you."

Jack could not help staring at the man's body.

"Prefer me clothed?" Rook asked. He pirouetted on the spot, Jack blinked, and a second later the naked man was naked no more.

"What — ?"

"No time. As I said Jack, thing will happen today. Lots of things. Shall we go see?"

"I have to go home."

"Home? That odious little house where you live, where Jane is waiting for you even now, the worst rebuke you could ever imagine on her lips? Home is a state of mind, not a place, Jack. Home is where your heart is."

Jack did not answer, could not. He tried to think of Jane but it hurt too much. Even breathing hurt.

"Heartless bastard, aren't I? Come on."

They walked side by side along the street, Jack staring down at his feet, the man striding and whistling as if competing with the birds. It seemed to Jack that the stranger Rook walked without his feet actually touching the pavement, but alcoholic fallout fuzzed his brain and he tried to see no more.

It was only as they came onto the main street, and Jack caught sight of himself and his mysterious companion in a shop window, that he realised why he looked so familiar. Perhaps because Rook's mirror image was all Jack had ever seen before.

The stranger could have been his own twin brother.

"I'll leave you for a moment," Rook said. "There's something here you need to see, it'll give you more of an idea about me. But be warned — however far you choose to run, I'll find you."

Jack watched him turn and step through a wall… not into it, *through* it. And he shook his head and revelled in the bursts of pain, because it convinced him that he was seeing and hearing things. He wondered how such a statement could sound like a threat, a promise and a reassurance, all at the same time.

Alone, he stared along the street at the hundreds of people, milling and driving and aiming themselves to work. He had worked once, many months ago, but then things had gone downhill and he'd used his own bad luck as an excuse to convince Jane to pay his way. For some strange reason she'd agreed. Maybe she still loved him more than he thought. Whatever… they'd been arguing ever since.

You spend all your fucking money on drugs, Jack.
Why don't you go out and get a job?
There's more to life than TV and beer and jerking off all day.
Bitch. What did she know?

Nobody seemed to notice him, or if they did they ignored him, perhaps fearing he may be about to ask them for a handout. He wondered whether any of them had seen the stranger, Rook.

As he went to ask a passer-by, fifty people across the street spun, flipped, screamed and dropped down dead.

For a terrible second blood tainted the air, sprayed and slashed at it like the brushstrokes of an insane graffiti genius, planted on the visual reality of things before gravity pulled it down to the pavement, the road, the upturned, wide-eyed faces.

Then, the screams; the metal on metal as cars crashed; the frightened shouts; a young child pushing at its dead mother; panicked mumblings, smashing windows, sobbing, pounding feet...

... and Jack turned and ran back down the side-road he had emerged from, seeking the sightless, soundless blank oblivion of the previous night.

"I'll find you," Rook had said. The stranger who wore his face.

✳✳✳

Jack ran along the street and tried to dodge the screams. They came from the main shopping precinct behind him, ahead where this side street branched into two, the open office windows above him... they came from all around. In the run-down shops and the low-rental offices, screeches and bangs and cries and groans filled the air with a most unnatural chorus. Jack wanted to add to the noise — he wanted to scream — but he was too short of breath.

He could not run very far. His blood was slow and thick, his breath forced out by the weight of the pain in his head, his limbs, his guts. His arms ached almost to the point of uselessness; even swinging them at his side hurt. Minutes after starting out he was huddled in a boarded-up shop doorway, hugging his knees and whimpering and dying for another piss. *Your time will come,* someone had scratched into the wood of the doorframe years ago. Fresh blood had recently been wiped across the gouging to bring out the words once more. It was so fresh, Jack could smell it.

He felt suddenly sick, and as he leaned forward to puke he fell onto his side.

More screams. More shouts.

He'd seen people dying. He'd seen them dead. Blood splashed across fresh window displays, a string of guts glistening in the early morning sun, a child wrenched from a pram and beaten hard against a wall... with no visible cause for any of it. There had been no madman, no murderer, no knifeman —

— had there?

Perhaps he was still pissed. Still stoned. Maybe he'd taken something from someone in one of the grotty pubs he'd visited last night. He'd had bad trips before, but hell, this one was —

"Hell... oooo!"

He tried not to hear the voice. "Still pissed," he muttered, then he said it again, louder, to muffle the sudden cries of dreadful shock coming from an open first storey window across the street. "Still pissed, get back to sleep — "

"You talking to me?"

Jack started. A face pressed out of the crumbling brickwork opposite.

"I said, you talking to me? Huh?"

"Rook," Jack said, though the man had changed since a few moments before. His face was leaner, his eyes — if it were possible — were darker, madder. His hair was cropped into a clumsy Mohican.

"Who the fuck you think you're talking to?"

"Rook, I…" But Jack could not go on. He closed his eyes. He wished he could close his ears, because then —

"I don't see no one else here."

— he would shut out all this craziness, and when he woke —

"Wake up, you fool," Rook's voice drawled.

Jack opened his eyes.

Rook stood before him, back in his neutral clothes now, his face pudgier, his hair more wispy where it still clung to the pocked scalp.

"Those people," Jack said. "We have to help — "

Rook changed. There was no transmutation, no morphing from one man into another. He simply flipped, like a film moving from one frame to the next. He grew taller, a long coat appeared, and Jack was sure he saw the glint of a gun in the shadows.

"You wanna stay alive, you stay with me."

Rook laughed his way back to himself.

"Oh God, what's happening, what's going on?" Jack could smell his own puke, the rich stench of sweat, the stale miasma of alcohol and cigarettes. They repulsed him but they were smells he recognised, so he hugged them close. Rook was people he recognised, as well. His favourite characters. The actors he'd wanted to be, when he'd had anything like ambition left in his heart.

How could he know?

"Oh Jack," Rook said, and a note of sympathy crept into his voice. "It's the end of the world. Face it."

"Who are you? Are you doing all this?"

Rook looked genuinely offended. "Of course not! I'm here to help you. Give you a little time. Guide you through as best I can."

"But what…" Jack could find no words.

"…am I?"

Jack nodded.

"I'm… I'm your guardian angel. Your fairy godmother. Your lucky charm. Your black cat and chicken's claw and piskie, all rolled into one big fat me."

"But you're… you're me."

Rook shrugged. "Well, I look like you, granted. And there are other… distasteful similarities. For instance, I am well aware of the sordid little acts that you passed your time performing last night. But at this present extraordinary moment in time, I smell much better. Now follow. Places to go, things to see." He smiled. "You may be surprised."

❋❋❋

Rook walked and Jack had to follow.

There were sirens now, blaring from the distance and bringing an upset sense of normality and control to the terrible scenes. But still he heard screams and sobs and the disbelieving words of a hundred people mixing in the air, a soup of terror, tainting the bright morning with fears that should never exist. That *could* never exist.

"What the hell's happening?" Jack asked, but Rook merely giggled theatrically and strode on. "Where are we going?" Again that affected shrug, a twitch of the shoulders that changed Rook's coat into a cloak and sent it shimmering in an invisible breeze.

Jack reached out and grabbed the man's shoulder. He felt fingers digging into his own shoulder as well, but he could not turn around to see who had a hold of him, he simply could not. Because Rook had turned and was staring at him, and it was like looking into a mirror. It was not a flattering mirror, this one, certainly not one that would tell him he was the fairest of all. It threw memories back at him, things he had wanted to forget for so long: a stinging palm from where he had slapped Jane; the sinking shame of seeing her sprawled on the floor in a nightclub, his hand still extended from the push; the warmth of splashed blood on his chin after he had accidentally mashed her lip into her teeth —

— *accidentally? Really Jack? Accidentally, are you sure?*

… and the voice was Rook's.

"Accidentally, Jack?"

"Of course it was an accident!"

"Ah," said Rook, turning away again. "Look, there's dear old Piccy!"

Jack saw a man jogging along the street, long hair flowing behind him, his face a determined frown.

"Can you see it following me?" the man screamed, but he said no more. One second his throat was stretching and twisting around his own particular dialect, the next it was spread across a baker's window, speckling Jack's view of the cake trays with a strawberry redness.

"Oh Jesus!"

"No, just Piccy. Hi Piccy!" Rook shouted.

The man was still twitching on the pavement. Jack hoped — in fact, he *knew* — that this was not who Rook was referring to. On the windowsills above, pigeons cooed in interest at the mess they saw below them. Thankfully they were biding their time. As Jack looked closer he saw something... something dark but not a shadow, more a stain upon his vision. It held the vague shape of a human. It kicked the dying man in the chest. He groaned. And then it was not there any more, and Jack was unsure whether he had even seen it at all.

"I'm going mad, " Jack said.

"No, in fact, you're more sane — "

"Going mad and I'll wake up and I'll be in bed, hungover and a little worse for wear, maybe with someone in bed with me, what's her name? God what's her name? Let's hope I remember in time, nothing more embarrassing — "

"Earth calling Jack! Hello, reality check, Jack!" Rook grasped his cheeks roughly, squeezing until the bones in his face felt ready to crunch and crumble. He spoke directly into his mouth, and Jack could taste his breath. It was sweet. It was succulent. It was rich and potent, not sour and rancid as he had expected. Perhaps this man really was a guardian angel, if rather different to what Jack could have ever imagined.

"Who's Piccy?"

"That dead man. And his murderer. Bit of a demon, really."

"You were *waving* to him?"

Rook looked thrown for the first time in the few minutes that Jack had known him. His confident outer coating slipped a fraction to show the potential of turmoil beneath, like a sheet of thin ice covering a boiling lake. "Don't ask about what you can't understand," he said at last, and he turned and stalked away.

Jack followed because he did not know what else to do. He tried to think of Jane but it hurt too much, he had hurt *her* too much, and she had hurt him back by threatening to leave. His arms still ached. His hands stank of cigarette smoke and pine forests. He tried to breath deeply but the fresh air twinged his hangover. He told his legs to stop... but he kept on following Rook.

He truly did not know what else to do.

✳✳✳

They came to a small park surrounded by tumbled walls and overturned refuse bins, the trees more used to drunkards' piss than lovers' knives. Rook appeared keen to enter, and for Jack it was respite from the terrible sights in the streets all around. Panic and chaos had settled down over the town, and while the ambulances and police cars flitted to and fro, still a great sense of disorder tainted everything. Normality had slipped, dead people lay everywhere, nightmares now lived in daylight. In one place, blood flowed along a gutter.

But the park, though no escape from the noise and the shouts and screams, offered some shelter from the sights. Initially, at least.

Rook led him straight to its centre, where four stone benches were arranged around a central statue. Jack thought the image was of a soldier from one of the wars, but on closer inspection it could just as easily have been a miner, or a sailor, or a person who was meant to look like someone else. He searched for a plaque, but there was none. He had been here many times before, but he had never paid this monument any attention. Just like any town dweller, he rarely looked up.

Rook leaned against the statue, raised an eyebrow and nodded at one of the benches.

Jack looked. There was a shape there, insubstantial but defined. It was a man, long hair flowing in an unseen breeze, his face moving like heat haze, distorting the rose bed behind him.

"Keene," Rook said, "long time no see."

Jack heard no reply, but he did sense some subtle communication. It felt like a fly trapped in his ear, struggling to get out, beating its wings against his drum as it described impossible, mad circles around and around. The shape was looking up at Rook. A shadow twisted where its mouth should be, a hole in the air.

"Really?" Rook said. "Wow! And I thought I was having fun with this one!" He nodded at Jack. "I'm just taking Jack here to see his."

"See my what?" Jack asked.

The fly began to laugh.

"Over there," said Rook, "is another body. Come on, I'll show you." He reached out quickly, grabbed Jack's shoulder before he could turn away, almost dragged him between two of the benches and behind a wild stand of shrubs.

There was indeed a body there, freshly dead, blood still flowing from an open artery in its forehead. Its eyes had been removed. "Only the good die young," Rook said. "You believe that? Well, it's bollocks. This man was not good — "

"How do you know all this, unless — ? "

Rook raised a hand, palm out, a silent 'shut up'. "As I say, this man was not good. A year ago he punched his wife, six months ago he stole from his mother. He could have been better. He could have been someone valuable to society, someone with ideas instead of hatred, positive thoughts instead of rancid dreams. He was a dreamer, you know; he had such dreams! He could have been a philosopher. And now… now, he *is* that person for the first time. He's Keene, as Keene has never been before. Death, my friend Jack, becomes some people."

Jack stared down at the body. His hangover kicked at the base of his skull as the sun revealed itself, and he tried to think again about last night. Vodka, he thought, he was sure he could still taste it under his tongue and in his teeth. But what else? What else had left this sour taste in his mouth?

"So," he said, "I suppose you'll tell me… is this the Keene who's sitting out there?"

Rook raised his eyebrows, mouth dropping open in a feigned show of admiration. "My Jack, alcohol hasn't totally pickled your brain after all!"

Jack glanced back at the square of seats and that uncertain statue, trying to see the wraith that had been sitting on one of the benches. All four stone seats were empty.

What he did see, though, was that the statue now resembled something inhuman… or something more than human. It held a perfection that he could not quantify.

Jack closed his eyes. "We have to tell someone about this body," he said. "Why did you show me? Why show me a ghost? Why bring me here to…?" He trailed off because his thoughts were leading in circles. Ever-decreasing circles with madness at the hub.

"No ghost," Rook said, "just a truer reality. I'm keeping you from yours for a time. Feel honoured. You're seeing what most people never will. Follow me, Jack."

And of course, like all the best rats, Jack could do nothing but comply.

✳✳✳

The streets had changed.

There was the slew of bodies, cut down by some grotesque random harvest, and the people attending them and crying over them. There were cars parked kerbside or buried in shopfronts, some of them with bloodied shadows pressed against windscreens, other still burning or sitting with open doors, their owners fled some-where else to die. Not normality, perhaps, but something under-standable, identifiable.

But there was also something wrong with the buildings.

A pub on the corner of two streets — perhaps one which Jack had frequented the previous night — was out of focus. Whichever angle he viewed it from, however much he winced or stared or rubbed his eyes, all lines were losing definition and hard edges were softening. He could almost see the clarity of the place being stripped, and here and there misplaced shadows clung to the walls, like patches of wavy moss.

A takeaway had slumped down without any of its structure cracking. Its sign was bowed out but the words were not distorted, and its window, although not broken, had taken on a shattered edge. Birds flitted in and out with cold chips in their beaks, passing through the glass and leaving tiny ripples in its previously solid surface. It moved like flesh, shook like a face being struck with an open palm... Jane's face, his palm.

"Things are looking much better already," Rook said. "Don't you agree? Yes indeed." He bent down so that his nose was inches from Jack's. "Things are moving on apace, my friend. Come on, let's hurry." Then he looked up at the sky, smiled and said: "Oh-oh, hang on a minute. Here comes another one!"

Jack was watching three firemen trying to extract a body from a crashed car. Two of them dropped down dead — one with his head twisted on his shoulders, the other with ribs shattered and protruding through his uniform like blood-streaked ivory.

The survivor stood there for a long time; looking, staring, not seeing. Shadows buzzed him. He seemed unaware of them.

More shouts. A car crashed somewhere across the river and a pall of smoke puffed up into the still air. On the town bridge Jack saw a dozen people drop like felled wheat, a dozen more run to their aid in shocked silence or with a useless shout. Others wandered aimlessly, talking into thin air, looking around them as if surrounded by phantoms.

The bridge parapet lifted slowly into the air, solid metal sheets splitting in equal patterns and stretching as well, opening up into metallic rose sculptures, the road bowing in the middle and rising to mimic the transformation of its surroundings. The bland grey metalwork took on new, wonderful colours — oily green and blood-red and the brightest, lightest blue Jack had ever seen, the blue of a ten thousand year old glacier — and it was gorgeous.

He could never have imagined anything like this. In his wildest dreams, in his most ambitious youth, he had never dreamt of anything as wonderful, nor as beautiful as this.

He stumbled back against a wall and felt it move beneath him. He spun around, his brain seeming to lag behind, and stared at...

into the eyes of… something was on the wall, a shadow, a blip in the sunlight, hands scraping at brickwork and turning it slowly, impossibly into something else. The bright red bricks faded to an oaken brown colour, their aggregate lengthening into bark strips. Jack backed away and looked up at the windows as they deformed, the roof where it buckled and changed colour from a bland slate-grey, to a vibrant leaf-green. It was a building made of trees, not simply constructed but grown.

Rook nudged him. "Always wanted to be an architect, didn't you?"

"How did you know?"

"It's easy when I'm you."

Jack did not acknowledge him. He was too aghast with what he was seeing, the change being wrought over his surroundings. Some of it was slow — the bridge was still lifting, its metal flanks still stretching and warping into fantastical new shapes — some of it was fast. The shopfront changing to wood. The corpse in the gutter, flowing and melding, becoming a part of the ground even as he watched…

"Let's go!" Rook said once again.

"I'm not going with you." Jack backed away, expecting Rook to leap at him, grab him in a headlock and drag him along the street. But the tall, weird stranger *(but he's not really a stranger, Jack, any more than that person you sometimes see in the mirror, the real person behind your familiar face)* merely stood and watched him go, a quizzical smile on his face.

"Jack, you have to."

"Why? It's written, is it? Is that what you're going to tell me: I should follow you because it's written?"

"No," Rook shook his head. "I just thought you'd want to know what's happening to Jane."

Jack paused. Talk about a loaded comment. He could see something behind Rook's surface expression, but he didn't know exactly what it was. He wasn't at all sure he even *wanted to* know.

"Duck!" Rook shouted suddenly.

There was a shimmer in the air, a vibration with no noise or feeling, a certainty that something was happening. More screams… more shouts… in a greasy spoon café across from where they were standing, several people were thrown against the window in bloody red abandon, their dead expressions sliding down the glass, wide white eyes blaming Jack.

"You're enjoying this!" he shouted. Rook was smiling, he'd always been smiling, even behind his frowns and strange impressions.

"Yes, of course," the tall man said. "It's my time. That's why I'm guiding you around for so long. Hey look, bet you could never have designed that one!"

Jack looked to where he was pointing. A building he had never taken any notice of before — a council office, he thought — was bulging at the seams. There were several dead people on the pavement near its main entrance, and as the brickwork expanded so it shoved them aside, crushing them under and smearing their corpses across the crumpling pavement. Jack felt sick but he was also amazed, enthralled in what was becoming of things.

The building started to contract again... then expand... contract, expand...

"No need for plumbing or heating in a living building," Rook commented.

Jack shook his head. *No. Impossible.*

"Oh, I think we should go," Rook muttered, his expression suddenly serious, his hands reaching out for Jack. They kept reaching, past any chance he had to defend himself against them, into his personal space, around his neck, squeezing —

Rook backed off with what looked like a great effort.

Jack gasped.

"Let's go and see Jane," Rook said.

Jane. Jack had a lot to say to her, even now. A lot to apologise for. Things were changing. Things *had* changed. Now, more than ever, they would need each other.

But this was all impossible, he knew that. He was drunk somewhere, sleeping under a bush or in a gutter or in a cell, pissing and shitting his pants and being pathetic. Nobody was dying. Buildings weren't changing... buildings weren't *breathing*, for fuck's sake!

"Quickly!" Rook said. "I can only protect you for so long." He started to run.

Jack had seconds to decide; it took him only two before he followed. He'd always been weak, a sheep, a feeble man with no real control over his own life or ambitions. He knew that and accepted it, even though it had never made him proud. Now, he felt more wretched than ever.

Jane, he thought, *what did I do?* He rubbed snot from his nose as he cried, and he smelled pine forests and piss.

✳✳✳

Whatever change was occurring it had yet to reach his street.

Rook muttered and mumbled as they walked, most of it inau-

dible, the bits Jack did catch confusing and frightening. He spoke of
new orders and dead people and a time for change. Jack had seen
corpses and change this morning — new orders, he did not want to
know about.

The street brought back bad memories. He had obviously left it
yesterday in an effort to flee the row he and Jane had had, the violence he may have meted out to her. He wondered what she would
say at his appearance now, especially with the strange Rook leading
him on. He hoped she could forgive. He looked at his hands and
wondered what they had done.

Alcohol bled his memory, like a leech used to suck out bad
blood. He craved a drink even now. He craved forgetfulness on a
larger scale. In a way, he wanted to be that stranger in the mirror.

"Well," Rook said, "here we are. At last." He looked strangely
at Jack, a glimmer in his eye that Jack could not identify.

"Jane!" Jack called. He walked forward. The house looked
quiet, still. There was no movement across its masonry, no dip or
rise in its roof, no change of colour. He almost believed he'd never
seen those things just now — not only believed, but sought to
convince himself of this belief — but then he saw the evidence,
even here.

Above the house, rising in the distance, stood a solid tower,
transparent and as wide as a football field. People launched themselves into the air from its heights, fell and then drifted back up and
out. Gossamer wings reflected sunlight like oil on water. They
spiralled up and down, catching the thermals and apparently denying
gravity when there were none. One shape plummeted straight up,
disappearing into the clouds before swooping back down, wings
glittering with moisture and ice.

"What...?" said Jack.

Rook spun on his heels and he was naked again, his back ridged
into two spines, each split down its length and betraying the odd
protruding feather here and there.

"Angels?" Jack whispered.

Rook shook his head. "Of course not, fool! We just like flying,
every now and then. Hurry up, now, I'm only giving you a little
more time."

"What do you mean?"

"Time. I'm giving you more time. I can only hold back...
protect you... for so long, you know. Go in. Find Jane. Make your
peace."

Rook was changing, subtly but certainly. His nails were longer.
His face was narrower. His eyes had lost their humour, and that

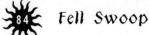

worried Jack most of all.

"Jane!" he called.

Someone walked out of the house. At first he thought it was Jane and he went to go to her, but then he held back . The person — the thing — had Jane's features for sure, but Jane had never had teeth that long. Jane had never possessed fingers so strong, so gnarled. Jane, Jack was positive, had never had scarlet skin.

Rook and the new woman exchanged a few quick, incomprehensible comments. He laughed. "Well," he said to Jack, "seems you had quite a row last night. Pity you couldn't remember, because then I would have known too and I could have spared you… well, so much heartache."

"You bastard!" the thing on the steps spat. Jack was not sure whether the comment was directed at him or Rook. Rook's laughter answered for him.

"What?" Jack asked. "Where's Jane? I need to see Jane?"

The scarlet thing's eyes opened slightly.

"Will you let him?" Rook asked. "Just let him see? He's a little hungover, you see."

"But you know what — "

"Only briefly, and then I'll finish it. I've kept him for too long as it is."

It nodded.

Jack ran up the steps and past the scarlet thing where it stood in the doorway. It had Jane's eyes. It even stood like Jane, one knee bent, one hand on one hip.

"Jane!" he called. "Jane, you alright?"

But coming back into the house — his house, his books scattered around, his clothes strewn in his own untidy patterns across the floor — brought back more of last night. Things he did not wish to see, because they were shameful. Then other things, things he had no wish to recall because they were too frightening. Too damn frightening.

— arguing, fighting, into the bathroom —

He ran upstairs.

— she'd already run a bath, they were due to go out —

He shoved open the bathroom door.

— she had yet to run any cold, it was scalding —

The air in the bathroom carried a hint of pine forests. Jane had liked bath salts. Soothed her aching muscles, she always said.

She was lying in the tub, fully clothed, her skin branded pink by the once-hot waters, dead. Bruises on her throat. Face submerged. Mouth open in a wet scream. Eyes wide, still seeing the final terror.

Still seeing Jack.

His hands began to sting with the memory of them closing around her throat.

"Oh no!"

Rook suddenly stepped through the wall, trod on Jane's corpse and stood next to him.

Jack turned to run, not only from the awful deed he had done, but from this thing as well. It meant him no good, he knew that now, it had been playing with him, not saving him. Like a cat with a mouse before it delivers the final, fatal blow...

Within a blink Rook was blocking the doorway. The disturbed bathwater swilled behind Jack, as if Jane were still alive.

"And now," said the tall thing with Jack's face, "I can make good all the potential you ever lost, wasted or forgot." It reached for him, ripped open his shirt, hissed. Its nails were long.

Jack's chest was vulnerable.

And his heart, as he had always known, was weak.

Recent Wounds

Martin craved the truth behind reality. It terrified him but, like most people, he was fixated by his greatest fear.

Truth hurts, the saying goes, and it was never more true than in this case. Like an old indiscretion, the obsession came between Martin and his wife, Kerry. Whether she knew it or not — and often, she did not — most of their arguments were rooted in her husband's search.

"You're not going to those horrible woods again, are you?" It was stated as a question, but intended as a reproach.

Martin shrugged it off and pecked Kerry on the cheek. Their relationship had become one of word-sparring and complexities which they both became lost in. "Only for an hour or so. And they're not horrible, they're nice. Peaceful. You really should come with me, sometimes. It's not muddy in there anymore." He didn't really want her there, and he was glad when she turned back to the television without answering. Once, they had made love in the woods. That was when they had been in love, not simply each other's bad habit.

Martin pulled his walking boots on at the front door. He caught sight of himself in the hall mirror and smiled. At least he still had a friend somewhere. Sometimes he wondered what his reflection was doing when he could not see it.

"Don't be late, I've got to be in work early tomorrow." Kerry's voice was flattened by the television. She couldn't even be bothered to turn her head to look into the hallway as she spoke.

"I won't." He shut the door gently, the act as potent as a slam.

Once, Martin had sat in the woods for over an hour while a stag deer wandered through. It had rubbed its antlers on trunks, scratching white wounds into bark as a signature of its presence. He had watched as it stood still, staring between the trees for minutes on end, perhaps seeking the same truth as Martin; the knowledge lying camouflaged beneath a bland world perceived by untrained senses. In some places this truth peered through, offering itself up for inspection. That day, watching the stag, Martin had been sure that he had it. A moment of epiphany had brightened the air and made colours, smells and sounds so intense that his senses began to scream. Even when the animal had finally taken fright and fled into the shadows, Martin shook with the clarity of the experience. His life up until then had been lived in sepia and monotone.

Upon leaving the woods the sensation had dissipated, fading away like the dregs of a dream. By the time he had arrived back home, all things were hidden from him once more. Ever since then he had been seeking those lost feelings.

He entered the woods over the stile at the bottom of his lane. A familiar anticipation grabbed him and quickened his step. He walked across the rickety bridge spanning the stream and passed between the first of the trees.

Eager to seek out the secrets therein.

Ignorant of the fact that, sometimes, a wild obsession with truth can gild lies with the gold of revelation.

***

Dark was already growing beneath the trees. Martin paused, breath held, listening to the myriad whispers of a million wood ants going about their business. Ahead of him a shadow shifted on the ground, a huge nest writhing with to-ings and fro-ings. He poked it with a stick and did not mind when several ants ran up and stung his hand. He shook them off and continued on his way.

Shadow hid the sources of sounds, making them more mysterious. Evidence of activity lay everywhere: dark holes in the forest floor; paw prints quivering with water; paths worn by countless generations of footsteps, both animal and human. It was dark, but Martin was not afraid. He had been here many times. He knew that the forest it would never hurt him.

He was surprised when he came to the stone circle; he did not think he had walked that far. The woods were deceptive sometimes, all sense of scale and direction smothered by their pine depths. He tried to make out the setting sun but the sky was hazed with cloud, and all around the softly fading illumination was the same. Beneath the trees, light wavered with every ghostly flicker of leaves. The stones were speckled pale grey with waning sunlight and dark green with moss. The circle was imperfect; some stones had tumbled into time, others were pocked and chipped where people had tried to leave their mark forever. Vandalism never existed on the stones for long. Once pierced, their surface sucked in moisture and frosted out the names of those daring to presume their own immortality.

The highest standing stone came up to Martin's chest. He had often sat at the centre and tried to see a pattern, a shape, a relevance, but sometimes he thought that nature was playing with him, and had placed these markers here as part of some endless cosmic joke. The thought came often, and far from depressing Martin it comforted him. It made his lack of success seem understandable rather than pitiful.

He'd try explaining this to Kerry, but she would only look at him as though he were mad.

Martin leaned against the stone and it moved. A lump of it came away in his hands. The forest fell silent for a moment, but it could have been the rush of blood through his ears excluding all sound. The lump was larger than his fist, smooth and weathered on the outside but ridged and pointed on the inside. Excitement punched him in the chest. He almost went to throw the chunk down — lob it into the shadows to scare some life back into the place — but when he looked up the trees were moving again in the soft breeze, and as if agitated by his attention the forest sounds erupted once more. They did not begin from nothing, but came instantly into being.

The rock was cool in his hand. The surface exposed by the break was rougher than he had originally thought. He could not see properly in the fading light, but he was sure that there was some design to the corrugations. That was plainly impossible, but it had also been hidden, and he had spent his whole life searching for hidden things.

He touched the bare rock with the fingertips of his left hand. A thrill jarred his arm, like the low thud of an electric cattle fence, and once again the woods were silent. This time there was a threat in the air, not just an absence of noise, and Martin looked up into the canopy with trepidation for the first time. The branches still swayed in the breeze, looking like giant python heads trying to mesmerise him into inaction. It was suddenly darker than it should have been. Fingers of cloud flitted high in the atmosphere, keen to pass quickly over this place and reach safer climes.

Martin dropped the rock. The thump of it landing on the soft ground came long seconds after it should have.

A dog barked. A man passed by, using an old branch as a walking stick, throwing a guarded glance as Martin slumped to pick up the rock.

"Lovely evening," the man said.

Martin straightened, nodded.

"You all right?" It was the old man who lived down the street, his dog a basset with jowls matching those of his master.

"Fine," Martin said. "Just enjoying the peace." He had not meant it as a rebuke, but the man raised his eyebrows and threaded his way quickly between the trees, obviously offended.

Martin made his way home. The woods were back to normal, full shadow blossoming from the secret places beneath trees as the sun finally touched the horizon. Kerry was in the bath when he arrived, eyes closed, enjoying the intimate tickle of warm water. More intimate than the two of them had been for a while, at least.

"Hi," he said.

"Nice walk?"

"Yeah. Saw old Jangle with that daft dog of his."

"I like bassets," Kerry said without opening her eyes. She sighed and shifted, causing bubbly waters to break across her body. .

"I'm going to sleep," he said. "Tired. I think I went further than I intended." Kerry murmured something. He cleaned his teeth and went to bed, and he did not see his wife again until morning.

✳✳✳

Martin felt ill. He had not taken a sick day in years, but a stab of guilt still speared him as he telephoned in and gave the wry excuse: "Stomach bug." In truth, he could not really describe what was wrong. He felt unsettled, distant, removed from his surroundings... but that would not have sounded very convincing.

Kerry had left for work at around seven o'clock, the drive into the city stealing an hour from either end of her day. She had pressed her face against his cheek, lips hardly moving, more a head-butt than a kiss. He had watched her pull away, and wondered for the millionth time how things could have been different.

Years ago, they only had eyes for each other. Now Kerry's eyes spoke volumes, mostly contempt. She never hugged him anymore and her smile was usually one of acceptance rather than allure. Sometimes, he wondered why neither of them ever suggested things be taken further, but perhaps there was still something there, a hope buried deep like forgotten treasure.

Martin trundled downstairs and jumped as post exploded through the letter flap. A bill, a guaranteed colossal win, a postcard from one of Kerry's friends in Italy. Sheets of paper coated with lies. If only truth would come with the mail.

***

Kerry arrived home at six o'clock. After a cursory chat, Martin retired upstairs to his study. It had been calling him all day, but something had kept him away. There were always other things to do: make a sandwich, watch the news, browse his collection of books and rearrange them needlessly. And all the while, at the back of his mind, was the rock.

It lay in a nest of crumpled newspaper on the desk, like something without a home. In the light it seemed less extraordinary than it had when he could not see it. Just a rock, outside smoothed by the slow breath of time, rough and broken inside. He picked it up, took it to the window and opened the curtains. Under natural light it was different again, the edges sharper, the fractured face more ordered than a shatter should have been.

Much more ordered. Surely there was some design there, a conformation of edges, more regular than a random break? He flicked at the ridged stone with a finger, cursed as one of the sheer points opened his skin. He stared at the cut as it began to bleed. Stone dust welled up in his blood and ran around his finger. He put the injured digit to his mouth and sucked at the tiny wound.

Part of it looked like the capital letter 'A' inverted, Martin thought suddenly. Or a beaker half-full.

He fetched his toothbrush from the bathroom and sat at his desk, clearing more stone particles from around the figure. He blew lightly, hardly noticing the grit speckling the old oak surface, scratches waiting to happen.

"The news is on," Kerry called from downstairs.

His answer was sharper than he intended and she said no more. His stomach settled from the shock and he sat back, frowning at his handiwork. There was a second symbol, resembling a half-moon, or a pig, or a scythe. Hell, it could have been anything. He brushed lightly with the toothbrush, the sound of bristles on rock a soporific whisper. He ran his fingertips across the first shape, and the one newly revealed.

Later that evening his sickness lie returned to take vengeance upon him. He rushed to the toilet, fell to his knees and was violently ill.

✳✳✳

In bed that night, Martin was certain that he did not sleep. The next morning, he struggled to convince himself that he had. Nothing else could explain what he had seen. It must have been a dream.

The bedroom window bowing inwards. His surroundings impossible to view, obscured by more than the night. The constant thought that someone was staring at him through drawn curtains, the certainty that should he open them there would be faces there, with wide mouths and sharp noses, but no eyes. Still, they would see him.

What he heard, too. A thumping at some distant wall, like the heartbeat of the house audible only during the barren night. The whisper of many voices, or the rushing of blood in his ears. Kerry's breathing next to him; peaceful, undisturbed. His own screams.

It had to be a dream.

✳✳✳

He spent the next day ill in bed, his fabricated malady of the day before still haunting him. Kerry went to work preoccupied, leaving him a glass of squash and an empty paracetamol packet like the detritus of a suicide. She had spent longer than usual in the bathroom. Martin wondered whether she felt ill as well.

He was sick, he sweated, he slept. He hardly moved all day. He kept the curtains closed, cursing the sun when it found its way through the join and threw a bar of light across his eyes. He dreamed of the rock, and of picking at it with bloodied fingers.

✳✳✳

That evening he was feeling better. He made dinner while Kerry sat staring at a blank television screen. He wondered what images her mind was playing upon it.

"I'm pregnant," she said.

It felt as if gravity had suddenly increased. Martin struggled in from the kitchen and sat heavily on the arm of the settee. "Are you sure?"

Kerry nodded, her gaze steady on the dead screen.

"Well, great," Martin said, but he could not clothe his voice with the enthusiasm he knew he should feel. He went to touch her arm, but ended up patting her like a pet and standing again on shaky legs. "Let's have some wine to celebrate."

"It's due in February," she said. "I'll go to the doctors soon, have it confirmed. Antenatal classes, and stuff. Have to take chloric acid. Guess I've just given up smoking." She looked up at him at last. "That is, if you want it."

Later, in the study, Martin realised that what Kerry was carrying inside her was closer to the mystery of things than any bit of rubble or scenery he could ever hope to see. Life was emerging within her womb, a heartbeat waiting to happen, a blueprint of what would soon be their child. The greatest mystery was staging itself right next to him, could he but see it. It was miraculous. He should be ecstatic.

He went back to the stone. He used a small paring knife and a fresh, softer toothbrush. He felt like a surgeon laying open a wounded heart, peeling away the outer layers to see what no one else had ever seen before. A secret waiting to be told.

He smoothed his fingers across the images standing proud of the rock.

✳✳✳

This time, the window would surely break. He was certain he could hear the glass straining and cracking, but it may have been claws on concrete. There was more chanting in the distance, or hoarse whispering nearby. He turned to Kerry, but she was already staring at him, eyes open in a blank mockery of death, as if painted onto her closed eyelids.

Walls bowed in, changing their planes and spilling him onto floor. He dug his fingers into the pile to prevent himself from tumbling up the wall and smashing into the wardrobe mirrors, scraping himself raw on the ceiling Artex. Beneath the floor, something thumped at his body. Like a huge heartbeat. Or something trying to break in.

✳✳✳

"You were twitching away in your sleep last night," Kerry said. "Arms and spittle everywhere."

"Why didn't you wake me up?" A memory of Kerry flashed by, but he could not ally it with his wife now. Martin thought of distant heartbeats and dead eyes.

She shook her head. "I tried, but you mumbled something about the walls then stopped. Maybe you're getting the decorating bug, now we've got junior on the way."

Martin smiled past a mouthful of Sunday morning cereal, but

his expression mirrored his wife's sarcasm. Sometimes they could go on like this for days, both acting their roles, both knowing what the other really thought. He often wondered whether this was one of the reasons for their failing marriage; they knew each other too well. A more unsettling idea, entertained in his darkest days, was that he only *thought* he understood Kerry, whereas she knew him completely.

After ten minutes of subtle verbal combat interspersed with uncomfortable silences, Kerry held up the white flag. "Marty, don't forget we're going to D and B's tonight for dinner. Let's have a good day today, go for a walk or something. Have a talk about some things. The baby, the future. Us."

"Us?" He spoke with acres of scorn in his voice, but he could not un-say it. He finished his cooling tea instead, stood and wandered upstairs. The rock sat alone and aloof on his desk. For a moment he was afraid to approach it. He remembered the thrill he had felt in the forest, caressing its coolness for the first time, and a sudden idea urged him back downstairs.

"I'm going for a walk," he told Kerry as he passed through the kitchen. "See you later." He did not even give her a chance to accompany him. He felt bad about that, but the fresh air soon washed his guilt away.

✳ ✳ ✳

The woods welcomed him into their shadowy underside. Water-filled footprints showed where others had walked their dogs that morning, and for a moment they all looked as if they went only one way: into the woods, with no trails coming back out. But the mud distorted things, and soon Jangle approached with his imitator bassett. The man fired a curt nod at Martin, nothing more. Martin barely smiled back.

He often found the woods more unsettling during the daytime than at night. At night if he could not see something, it was due to the darkness. During daylight hours, if something was out of sight it was because it had hidden itself away. Not wanting to be found.

He found the stone circle, though it seemed to take him longer than it had the last time. He walked a complete circuit, trying to recall which rock he had taken the split portion from, but the surroundings were so different in the light. A breeze whispered through the trees as he stepped into the centre of the circle, the forest sighing at his intrusion. He looked up. It seemed that the trees met miles above him, high branches touching like the fingers of tentative lovers, or the blades of slow-motion duellists. Birds shrieked, but he could not see them. He approached every rock and ran his hands over the surface, feeling for the rough patch, his vision blurring as if assaulted by sand.

Mould coated the rocks, spotted with bird shit. No fresh wounds. No recent breaks. He found a thick stick and struck at the standing stones, gently at first, then violently, trying to break away loose shards. To expose the origin of the rock he had at home, in his study, spelling out some hidden truth in the scar tissue of its yet-to-be uncovered message.

Nothing happened. Martin thought that night was suddenly drawing in, even though it was still morning. Shadows dipped from branches like ethereal bats, expanded out from holes in the forest floor, seemingly stealing his vision but actually there because of its failure. He wondered whether mould spores could poison the eye and induce blindness.

By the time he arrived home, Martin was running one hand along garden walls to guide himself. He looked down at the pavement to avoid not recognising anyone. His heart was steady in his chest, belying his panic.

✳✳✳

Kerry bathed his eyes with cotton wool balls soaked in Optrex. After several stinging minutes he told her he felt a little better, even though everything was still a blur. He spent the afternoon sleeping on the settee, dreaming vividly of things unseen. As evening came, he asked her to drive.

Debbie and Bryan lived in a cottage several miles away. Lanes twisted and wound their way there, passing little-known farms and hillsides normally only seen from a distant road. Twilight followed on their tail.

They had been good friends with Debbie and Bryan for many years, regularly visiting each other's homes for dinner and drinks. It was an undemanding friendship, needing only a monthly meal and chat to survive comfortably and satisfactorily for both parties.

The evening was a complete disaster. They were late, for a start. "Dinner's on the table!" Bryan said, answering the door before they knocked. "Hurry! Pasta, so we couldn't keep it hanging around." He kissed Kerry on the cheek, clapped Martin on the shoulder. Debbie looked as gorgeous as ever, even though Martin's sight still dulled sharp edges, and he resigned himself to another evening entertaining shameful fantasies about his friend.

Food eaten, cigars clogging the atmosphere, Kerry decided to start drinking. "But I can't drive," Martin said, trying not to whine. "My eyes."

"Get them fucking tested," Kerry countered, then giggled herself into a second vodka and orange. Bryan grinned with her. Debbie merely smiled, nonplussed. They were good friends, but too cosseted by their own affairs to appreciate the intricacies of other people's.

Martin blinked, fogging his vision even more. Things closed in around him, a similar sensation to being drunk: his body weightless; an absence of peripheral vision; a dull thumping at his ears, insistent, painful, though he could not identify its locus. None of the others seemed to acknowledge its presence, but perhaps they could hear it and were simply feigning ignorance.

"Debbie has just finished her Open University exams. Haven't you, Debs?" Bryan raised his wineglass at her in a half salute. Debbie smiled and went on to tell them what she planned on taking next year, but for Martin the words fused into white noise, then nothing. All of his attention was focussed on her face, how it moved, the gentle stretching of her cheeks as she blinked, the crow's feet, the long lashes. Her blinking appeared to remove her eyes, not hide them. Sometimes Martin blinked at the same time, and that was when he saw the most: a flash, less than a single frame on a film, but an image nonetheless. Debbie's face, with only a blank spread of skin where her eyes should be. Blackened, chipped nails on long fingers, clinking nervously against her wine glass. Another blink, and it was his friend again. But now she was so much less attractive than before.

"What do you reckon I should do?" Debbie asked him suddenly, drawing him in from a hazy distance.

Martin frowned, blushed, shook his head. "Sorry?"

Kerry snorted laughter and sprayed a mouthful of red wine, spattering her dress like careless blood.

The evening aged, following the wine. Most nights when they came around, Bryan would pull out some exotic bottle procured from an overseas source. Martin hated red wine and he thought Kerry did too, but this evening she put away three glasses with ease. Martin wanted to ask her to stop. She was pregnant with their baby. By the end of the evening, when even Debbie and Bryan could perceive problems, she was pissed enough to tell them the news.

They would have acted pleased, Martin was sure, if they had gleaned the slightest evidence that he and Kerry were pleased as well.

As it was, the announcement effectively ended the evening. Bryan ordered them a taxi and Kerry fell asleep on the back seat.

Martin rested his hand on her stomach, endeavouring to imagine the amazing thing inside, and stared out at the night. He tried not to look in the rear-view mirror, because the driver had no eyes.

He closed his own eyes but did not see less.

*** *** ***

He put Kerry to bed, running his hand across her bare stomach. The key to his obsession lay within, he knew, all the mysteries of life already begun. Reproduction, so close yet still so bemusing. A heartbeat soon, starting from nowhere at signals far too subtle for the mind of humankind to contemplate or understand. The merging of seeds and the dividing of cells and unlike so many people, each cell knew its place. If ever something begged the title of miraculous, this was it.

Yet in his mind's eye, inside Kerry there was only a rock. Peppered with the dust of ages, but still corrugated with words of wisdom from beyond the petty span of humanity. "My baby," Martin muttered, tears wetting his cheeks. "My baby." This time the words were a plea. But Kerry was sound asleep, and he was too weak to listen to himself.

He went back to the stone.

*** *** ***

The sounds of the night told him how late it was; the mournful child-like cries of mating foxes, the screams of feuding cats. He scraped and chipped, blinking away dust as it scoured his eyes. As he uncovered each strange design, he sought its like in books. Each was unique, undocumented anywhere. When he closed his eyes against the sting of the dust, he could almost see their hidden message.

He fell asleep over his desk and the dreams came easily. His study walls bowed inwards and disappeared altogether, as if twisting away from the dimensions of the senses. There were tall grey shapes waiting behind the walls, not seen but imagined, raising spindly arms to a black sky, mouths hanging open at the whim of their unheard screams, eyes utterly absent. Their fingers were tipped with long, pitted nails. Their backs, chests and stomachs bore parallel slashes of livid scar tissue. His perception of space began to spin, bruising him against his own nightmare.

He was back at his desk, brushing at the stone once more, unaware of having woken. The last letter emerged from the rock, the final symbol in the message he felt so close to comprehending.

He made a cup of coffee in the kitchen. He breath was fast and shallow, as though he were sexually aroused. He felt certain that he was on the verge of some great knowledge, the revelation of a truth previously hidden, an understanding of all things at all times. And he would be the first to know. It was dark outside, but he was not scared. Inside was what frightened him.

He looked in on Kerry briefly before returning to the study. It was almost four in the morning. The lightbulb died with a clink, but Martin sat at his desk anyway. He closed his eyes, sighing with the comfort of sightlessness, the freedom of imagination. His fingertips became the focus of his senses, the receptors for whatever was about to come.

He ran his fingers across the symbols in the rock, left to right, three rows. As he did so the images rushed in. The blind shapes of an unknown, ancient race, a smooth span of sun-browned skin where their eye sockets should have been. Their arms raised high, in worship or an attitude of attack. Teeth suddenly long and exposed in wild, red grins, thin limbs flailing as they propelled themselves at him like monstrous spiders.

Martin's eyes snapped open, but he was blind. His eyeballs burned, a ghost pain because they were no longer there. He reached up and felt a cool layer of skin across his eye sockets, like stretched muslin. It hurt when he touched it. He tried to shout out in panic, but a sudden disturbance from downstairs stole his voice. Glass broke, wood splintered, followed by snorting gasps as hunting things crept upstairs. He reached for the rock to use it as a weapon, but it was no longer on his desk. He called Kerry's name, but more violent upheavals from their bedroom drowned his cry. He heard her shout, then her screams. Wet screams.

The truth clutched at Martin's heart, the realisation that he had been a slave to lies, and that the real wonder of things lay in the future of his unborn child. A future he would have shaped and nurtured, had he given himself the chance.

Silence reigned once more, as sudden and terrifying as the noise. Then the multiple sounds of claws scraping across wallpaper. The pad of feet unused to carpet, guiding their owners to Martin.

As he felt the first touch of cool hands, at last he saw.

The Repulsion

As they rounded a bend in the road and the whole majesty of Amalfi was laid out before them, Dean knew that it was over. He grabbed Maria's hand and she squeezed back in surprise.

It was their second attempt at loving each other. Dean had the feeling that trying to make it work again would be like buying a new version of a favourite shirt — the original would always be special, however much the second looked, smelled and felt like the first. They had been travelling for ten hours and each time he glanced sideways at Maria, he knew her less.

The minibus wound its way down the cliff road, the driver tooting at nothing, other horns blaring in response. Mopeds chased each other through the traffic like dogs in heat, their drivers cool in shades and shirtsleeves. Pedestrians took their lives in their hands and walked along the roads, bending sideways and holding in their stomachs to allow for wing mirrors.

"Busy place," Dean said. Maria glanced at him and smiled, but she did not reply. He caught a whiff of her perfume, mixed in with the stale scents of a dozen hours of travelling. Obsession. It gave him a headache.

When they had been on holiday before, the arrival at the resort and the discovery of the hotel was often something of a let-down, an anti-climax propagated by tiredness and dislocation. Today, however, it was not the same. Maria waltzed into the hotel ahead of him, her jaunty step raising a nostalgic desire rather than the real thing. When Dean reached her with their suitcases she was chatting to the woman at reception, laughing, joking, excluding him even more. The woman looked at Dean and smiled sadly, as if she could see through the charade.

"Please," she said, "leave your bags here. They will be brought up to you. We have a lovely room for you, sea view, balcony with a wonderful romantic view of the town and harbour."

Dean smiled at Maria, and she smiled back. "Okay?" he asked.

"Yep. Here at last. At last." She followed the woman.

Their room was big, sparsely furnished, floored with old marble and opening out onto a large balcony. The doors were already clipped open, outside table set for a meal as if the previous residents had only just left. Dean could smell them in the air: a hint of aftershave; the incongruous scent of pine shampoo. He tipped the receptionist and fell onto the bed, burying his face in the pillow, breathing in deeply. Old smells; soap powder; dead dreams.

"Shall we go out, have a look around?" Maria asked.

Dean was tired and jaded and suddenly, for no apparent reason, he wanted to be back home. Hopelessness rumbled in his stomach, tingled his skin.

"Dean?"

He nodded. "Sure." He sensed her perfume again. It smelled like someone else had bought it for her, and he knew that they had already failed.

*** *** ***

The road took them past the front of the hotel and down to the town square, where it sat facing the ocean; hundreds of people, tourists and locals alike, sat outside cafes and bars doing likewise. Waiters buzzed them like black and white bees, balancing impossibly large trays on unfeasibly splayed fingers.

Dean suggested a beer, but Maria wanted to get away from the tourist areas immediately. He followed her lead, wishing they could be walking side by side instead of in single file. As he was not holding her hand his own ached for something to do, so he lit up a cigarette.

"Thought you were going to give up on this holiday?" Maria said, glancing back at the sound of the match popping alight.

"Thought we were going to be together this holiday," Dean retorted. He tried on a smile to take the edge off his voice, but the damage was already done. Maria shrugged, turned and started towards an arched walkway between two shops.

As they strolled, the streets began to lose themselves in darkened alleyways. Washing overhung the paths like sleeping bats, dripping soapy saliva to the ground. Traffic argued at roundabouts, and the sea purred onto the beach, constantly, relentlessly. Between buildings they could see up to the cliff tops, where ruined churches or Saracen watchtowers commanded wise old views of the sea and town. The whole place oozed history, wallowing in its past; each slab in the path possessed a million untold stories. And it was hot. The sun splashed from whitewashed walls and twisted its way behind Dean's sunglasses.

They saw only locals, as if this were the real Amalfi and the chaos of the square was there only to appease marketing managers at package tour operators. Sometimes the people they passed would nod a curt greeting, other times Dean felt unseen. They walked for twenty minutes without emerging from the warren of alleys and paths. Steps led up and down again, and more than once Dean was certain that they had crossed their own path from a different direction.

It was strange how the wonder of the place touched them individually and distinctly, as if its magic sought to emphasise the bad air between them. Sometimes it was almost physical, an impenetrable barrier forcing them apart like similar magnetic poles. Amalfi had so much to offer; Dean and Maria took their fill of different things.

"I'm hungry," Dean said. "Airline meals don't do much to fill you up. Pizza?"

"If you like." Maria stopped and leant over a fountain, its outlet concealed in the groin of a five-hundred-year-old stone boy. Damp circles had marked her blouse beneath her arms, and a haze of perspiration clung to the fine hairs on her top lip. She used to sweat like that when they were making love.

They turned around, and it seemed natural for Dean to lead the way back. At some point — he could not really tell when — the echoes of two sets of footsteps turned into one. When he looked over his shoulder Maria had vanished.

"Mi!" It seemed all right to use his familiar name for her now that she might not hear it. "You hiding?" He walked back up the path, glancing at closed doors. When he looked between buildings he could no longer see the cliffs; now, there was only sky. A flight of worn stairs curved down from higher up and he could hear hesitant footsteps descending, but their owner never arrived.

Street noises appeared from nowhere, and within a few strides he found himself back at the edge of the main square. He glanced back, confused, and then he saw Maria sitting on the steps of the huge cathedral. She stood when he approached and walked back towards their hotel, hardly acknowledging his presence. He was sure that if he were to stop and sit down for a drink, she would walk all the way back to their room without noticing.

"Maria," he called.

She waited for him, running her hands over strings of red chillies hanging outside a shop. When she looked up her eyes were hard and distant.

"Where did you get to?" Dean said. "I was worried."

"Why?"

"You vanished. One second you were there, the next I couldn't find you."

"I was behind you all the time," she sighed, turning and walking away. She had not even tried to hide the fact that she was lying.

By the end of that first afternoon, when they returned to their room to get ready for dinner, they were strangers. Maria went into the bathroom and closed the door to shower and change.

✳✳✳

The food was fantastic. Throughout their several years together, Dean and Maria had always put good cuisine at the top of their list of priorities when choosing their holidays. If they wanted a beach, it would have to be near a good restaurant. A hotel, though it may have health suite, rooftop gardens and apartment-sized rooms, was only as good as its chef.

Dean ate without tasting. He was thinking of those few minutes earlier in the day when Maria had been lost to him, trying to analyse his emotions and convince himself that he had been scared, not quietly, selfishly pleased. They had come here to be together, but alone was much more comfortable. Even now Maria's mind was far beyond these four walls. Dean could see it every time he looked at her.

When a waiter trundled over with the sweet trolley Dean was subject to a sudden, weird moment of utter optimism, one of those rare flushes of rapture that strike all too seldom and are as difficult to keep a hold of as a lover's gasp. He smiled, tapped his fingers on the table, glad to be alive and confident that everything was going to turn out all right. He looked at Maria, grinning, and he was about to tell her how lovely she was when she spoke.

"Have you ever come face to face with yourself?" she said. "Ever really seen yourself from someone else's point of view? It's the most humbling thing I can ever imagine."

Dean felt the moment leave him, bleeding away like blood from a stuck pig. "Are we going to really try this week?" he said. "I mean, really? Look at this place, Maria. It's our perfect holiday. It's as if we were drawn here to... give it one last go. Are we?"

Maria shrugged, stared into her glass of red wine as if trying to define a truth in there. "Maybe some things are more important," she said.

"Where did you go today? Before I found you in the square?"

"I want to go to bed," she said suddenly, and Dean was shocked by her paleness. "Take me to bed." On any other occasion — weeks, maybe months ago — this plea would have stirred him in other ways. Now it merely made him afraid.

They went up in the rickety lift and Maria waited for Dean to unlock the door. She leant against the wall in the hallway, fingers splayed against the cold plaster as if reading its history. She did not even undress before flopping onto the bed and stretching her way into a deep sleep.

Dean opened the doors and went out onto the balcony. The thought of going inside and lying next to Maria, perhaps naked, perhaps with love in mind, now seemed alien and foolish. However much he tried to convince himself otherwise, their relationship was still a shadow of its former self, and coming here could have been a big mistake. If there had been some serious misdemeanour it would be simpler, but in reality it was simply a matter of things growing stale. Neither of them wanted to be the one to finally pull the plug.

He lit a cigarette, inhaled deeply and watched the smoke haze away in the dark, picked up briefly by the lights from the harbour. It was a noisy night in Amalfi, straining scooter motors underlying the aimless car horns that seemed to spring out of nowhere, and unknown conversations were shouted through the dark. He could sense rather than see bats jerking about in the night, dipping and weaving like points of black light thrown from a negative torch. From inside he heard the toilet gurgling its displeasure at someone flushing elsewhere in the hotel. Outside again, a splash as something fell into, or jumped out of the water down below, confident of safety under cover of night.

He stood to go to the loo. The cigarette had burned down and fused itself to his two fingers, but he felt no pain. In the bathroom Maria stood before the full length mirror, naked, a breast in each hand. Her nipples were pink and risen, as if recently pinched.

"Have you ever come face to face with yourself?" she asked, turning to look at him. Seconds later her reflection followed suit. Its eyes were not her eyes. They were eyes painted by a bad artist, unable to follow him around the room, shallow and soulless. "Am I asleep?" the reflection said. "I've pinched, but I don't wake up."

A pain in his fingers pinched Dean and jerked him from sleep, and for a couple of seconds he did not even know which country he was in. He dropped the cigarette butt and stomped it to death, hissing as he felt the blister already rising on his index finger. Shaking, he went in from the balcony and shut the doors, locking out the night. Maria was naked on the bed, covers screwed around her waist. Her nipples were soft and pink.

After running cool water over his fingers Dean stripped and climbed into bed next to Maria. There was no warmth to share with her; not because she was cold, but because he could not imagine cuddling as they once had.

❊❊❊

The next day they were booked on a boat trip to Capri; Dean had thought that exploring together may encourage sparks from the dying embers of their love. Now, the most he could hope for was a smile for old times. And he realised, in a moment of shocking clarity, that he really didn't know Maria that well at all. He was unaware of her past, other than what she had chosen to tell him. If she had problems, maybe he had not even discovered them yet. If she had always wanted to come here, and she did not want him to know… then he never would.

Maria rose late and readied herself as if still half-asleep. They had breakfast brought to their room but Dean ate it alone on the balcony. He kept glancing into the room at Maria, watching her move slowly across the marble floor as she searched both suitcases for some elusive item of clothing. She looked up, saw him staring and smiled, a vague twitching of the lips which was still better than he had had all day yesterday.

He went back to his strong coffee, unsettled by the notion that she had not been smiling *at* him at all, but *past* him.

They were already late when they left the room. Dean was a constant ten steps ahead on their walk down to the harbour. He glanced at his watch every few seconds, trying to will the minute hand back fifteen minutes to before the time when they were due to leave. Passing through the square they heard the hooting horn of a boat, and a huge catamaran turned gently away from the pier.

"Come on!" he shouted, hurrying towards the boat, knowing already that they had missed it. He slowed and stopped, aware that dozens of people watching him. "Have a good time," he muttered, then turned back to Maria.

She was standing with her back to him, facing into the square.

She brushed hair back from her face, her short dress stretching around her hips as she did so. She was a beautiful woman, but now Dean felt only a nebulous anger, and a certainty that she had made them miss the boat on purpose.

"Well," he said as he approached her from behind, "looks like we're stuck here today. You could have just said you didn't want to go."

"I thought it was obvious," Maria said. "Besides, now we can explore the town in detail. We only scratched the surface yesterday."

"Didn't you want to see Capri?"

Maria shrugged. "Maybe. But we're here now. There's so much history here. Can't you feel it? Can't you breath in the old times? I can almost see them... Come on, Deano. We can still make a day of it."

It was the first time she had used her nickname for him since they had left home yesterday morning, and it went some way to quashing his disappointment. But as she walked on ahead of him, heading for a shady corner of the square, he could not help scrutinising how she had said it. The more he replayed it in his mind, the more he became sure that she had forced it to make him happy.

He felt used, manipulated, putty in the hands of an imaginative child. He wondered what shape she would twist him into next.

They came to an alley leading off from the square, so hidden beneath the old buildings of the town that it would never be touched by the sun. A sign screwed to the wall above said *Follow the ancient steps'*, the script gnarled-looking where decades of heat had chipped the paint. The path curved out of sight no more than a dozen paces in. Without looking back Maria walked on.

For an instant, Dean considered not going after her. He would go back into the square, buy a beer, sit down and light a cigarette, watching the world go by as he waited for Maria to return. Then the moment passed, and Maria was little more than a shadow moving away from him. He followed.

"It's a beautiful place," he said, not really believing himself. Maria mumbled an incoherent reply. "I wonder who lives back here?" He did not want to know, and again there was only a vague response from Maria. The walls were swallowing her words.

He was looking down at the path most of the time, making sure he did not trip over a loose stone or step in the occasional splash of dog mess. He should not have been surprised when he looked up to find Maria no longer there; should not have been, but was, because there was nowhere she could have gone.

He thought about going back, but feared he may be nearer the end of the path than the beginning.

Smells and sounds pulsed in and out, as if Dean were moving to and fro in reality. He guessed that it was some strange quality of the maze-like construction of this place, that even sound and scent would become momentarily lost between buildings. It became darker still and looking up he could see eaves reaching across the alley like long-lost lovers craving a final touch.

He turned a corner and suddenly found himself back with civilisation. Soon he was among people again, standing at the edge of a one-way street used by loud two-way traffic, happy to hold back and watch the hustle while he gathered his thoughts. He had found no ancient steps. Indeed, there had been no steps in the alley at all.

No side-alleys, either.

No open doors.

Where had Maria gone?

He felt a rush of unreality blur his senses — a mixture of nausea, dizziness and the urge to giggle at the absurdities around him. He sat down at a table and barked a laugh when a menu was forced into his hands. There were three women chatting away at the next table, oblivious to the noise around them, and when he strained to hear what they were saying he could not identify their language. It could have been a new one. The waiter wafted by with a casual glare; Dean ordered a pizza for appearance sake, a beer for his throat and a red wine for Maria. Then he waited for her to come back to him.

He was finishing his unwanted meal when she scraped back a chair and sat down. She did not reach for her wine, but sat there staring through her fringe at the ground.

"Maria," he said, "where have you been? I've been worried."

"I doubt that," she said, but there was no reproach there. It was merely a statement of fact. Her mouth twitched, as if haunted by the memory of a smile.

The three women had been replaced by a short, athletic-looking American, sitting with her back to them, mobile phone pressed to her ear like a field dressing. "I'm concerned about what will happen if I come home right now," Dean heard her say. "I worry about the kids. I don't want to subject you to the strangeness I'm going through right now."

He turned back to Maria and stroked her arm, but it felt as alien as kissing a bus driver on the cheek. He withdrew his hand, embarrassed, sure that everyone in the street would see through the sham.

"Shall we go back to the hotel?" he said. "Or another walk. An ice cream?"

"All right," Maria said and, not knowing which suggestion she had agreed to, Dean followed her into the thronging street.

The American woman had left, apparently without paying. The waiter seemed unconcerned. Her table was already set for the next customer.

✳✳✳

They spent the rest of the day by the pool, not talking, lying back and letting the sun slowly burn their skin. Dean tried to read but he could not concentrate. He kept glancing sideways at the woman he had used to love, watching her chest rise and fall with peaceful breaths, certain that behind her glasses her eyes were wide open. Her skin remained pale.

Maria had always been lively, inquisitive, sometimes too much so for Dean. He was happy to sit in and watch the television, open a bottle of wine, cook a nice meal. Maria would want to know who the director was, find out where the wine came from and search out an alternate recipe for whatever they were eating. He'd often tell her to sit back and enjoy, not worry about things. Loosen up.

She had loosened up now. She was so loose she was almost flapping in the wind. She was not the Maria he had used to know, but then that Maria had been leaving him for a long time, so that did not trouble him so much. What troubled him was that she was becoming a woman he had *never* known.

Later, at dinner, Dean tried to catch Maria's attention and smile, attempted to edge her into conversation, but all talk was one-sided.

They went straight to their room after the meal. Maria laid on the bed and seemed to fall asleep instantly. Dean bent over her and lowered himself to within kissing distance, trying to breathe in her scent, recall when they had used to kiss. But her breath was insipid and untainted, and as light as a sigh hitting his face. Her perfume only gave out a ten-hour staleness.

He stayed that way for a while, hoping she would look up at him, but there was no movement beneath her ivory eyelids.

Eventually he moved out onto the balcony and lit up a cigarette, closing his eyes and enjoying the light-headedness of wine and nicotine. He listened to the sounds from the town, trying but failing to pick out single voices.

Three cigarettes later, when he went back into the room, he was not surprised to find it empty. Maria had not even worn her shoes when she left; they lay on the floor next to the bed, looking as if they had never been worn.

✳✳✳

Dean curled up on the bed. Maria had gone of her own accord, of that he was sure. He was also sure that he had let her go too easily.

He slept within minutes. A loud, insistent thump echoed its way into his dreams; a door opening and shutting deep inside the hotel, or perhaps a trapdoor. Voices mumbled in distant rooms, or from somewhere else entirely. Footsteps forever promised to suddenly increase their volume and darken the strip of light beneath the door. It was a night pregnant with the promise of something happening, but in the end potential was aborted. Dean slept long and deeply, and when he woke up the sun was shining through the still-open balcony doors.

Guilt grabbed him and would not let go. Maria had not returned, her suitcase still lay open, its contents hauled out like luggage intestines. She could be anywhere, she could be in trouble.

She could be nowhere.

Have you ever come face to face with yourself?

Without changing or washing Dean hurried from the hotel, hardly sparing a glance for the surprised receptionist. He almost ran down the road, and he was glad that the bustle of the rush hour camouflaged his concern. The place felt even more impersonal than it had the previous day, but he put it down to being alone. Even though he and Maria had really had no hope at all, at least they had been in each other's company. Their time together may be doomed, but the past still held a charge. They would always have a history. There would always be a story to tell.

He found himself in the corner of the square without really thinking about where he was going. 'Follow the ancient steps' the sign said, and within thirty seconds of entering the alleyway, he had found them. They had not been there before, he was sure, but everything lately had been all a-tangle, and he could so easily have missed them the first time. They were dusty and cobwebbed with underuse, the shadows beneath their risers soupy with age. Dean started up them without hesitation, subconsciously sniffing at the air for Maria's perfume but knowing it had changed beyond his ken. Even if he did find her, it could mean nothing. She may be where she wanted to be.

He came face to face with himself. His double was as shocked as he, and they both raised their hands in fright. His opposite's eyes were sunken, full of a deep-set hopelessness, but then he realised that he was facing a mirrored door. He felt foolish, even though he was alone. Alone, but perhaps not unwatched.

The steps ended in a courtyard. The sun was almost directly

overhead, but the area was still swathed in shadow. It was timeless, echoing with sighs uttered centuries ago, its walls bathed in history and stained by it. The graffiti of ages, chips and cracks and the words of eloquent vandals. Shuttered windows stared down like the closed eyes of the dead.

Maria was there... but she was not. Her perfume hung heavy in the air, fresh and vibrant. He knew what she was thinking, though he could not see her. He knew, suddenly, of the times before they had met: the hurried drug-taking in train station toilets; the bursts of temper at her parents, unreasonable but more intense because of that; kicking her pet dog when it had stained her carpet, kicking until it bled. He knew her mind in more detail than he ever had, and this made him sad. Now, of all times, he could try to love her fully. She had what she wanted, and he was glad, but it also made him sorrowful. It meant that they had failed. Their time together really was at an end.

He turned and fled, coolness stroking his back as he staggered down the dusty steps. It felt like fingernails of ice piercing his skin, leaving him an invisible scar to remind him of where he had been, and where Maria remained. He would always be troubled by this place but he hoped, selfishly, that in his dreams he would somehow lose his way.

He saw no mirrored doors.

And as he arrived back in the square, he knew that during the loneliest of nights he would find those steps once more.

Unto Us

James never wanted to knock the two rooms into one. It was a job he had been avoiding for a long time, but then a free weekend crept up from nowhere and stabbed him in the back. He could find no excuse, and even though Beth had not been downstairs for three months, she would soon realise the truth if he prevaricated any longer.

So he set to work with the sledgehammer and pick, hired a skip for the rubble, taped polythene over the doors to keep the dust from escaping to the rest of the house. It still found its way upstairs, of course, giving Beth another reason to complain. But James took little notice, said he was busy, said if she wanted the fucking job done she could just fucking well put up with a bit of discomfort for a while.

He was a heartless bastard sometimes. She was so angry she had another fit, and he had to sit with her for two hours while she came back down.

***

When James found the body in the wall his mind would not accept it. It was one of those unreal, surreal situations; even though it was obvious what he was seeing, the 'never-happen-to-me' traitor in his psyche denied reality. So he put the little corpse to one side for ten minutes, made a cup of tea, then he sat heavily onto the sheet-shrouded settee and stared at the mummified package. Dust drifted up and obscured his view. Even now, he thought, it could be something else.

"James!" Beth took that moment to call. "I need a drink."

James thought it may have been a girl, once, though it was barely larger than a newborn baby. He could look and see, he supposed. Maybe it would crumble at his touch. Perhaps it would turn to dust, leaving him to get rid of it with the rest of the rubbish.

"James!"

"Coming!" He grabbed a glass of water from the kitchen, peeled back the polythene from the dining room doorway and trudged upstairs. It was a trip he had made a million times for Beth, and one that rarely held happiness at the end of it. Even when he reached her room and she threw back the covers — an invitation to screw her — there was hardly any pleasure.

This time, Beth was sitting up in bed for the first time in several days. She smiled at him, a skid-mark of lipstick. James cringed inwardly but forced the smile back. The lipstick was as much use as new doors on a burnt out, collapsed house. Beth would never have any takers other than him, and for that he only had himself to blame.

"Hello honey," he said.

"James, I need a drink. Not water. I want some wine."

"You know you're not supposed — "

"I'm not supposed to have wine because alcohol can bring on an attack and every time that happens I'm one step closer to death and that's the last thing you want to see, me lying here dead, well, sometimes I feel — "

"I'm thinking of you. Dr Finch said you mustn't. I can only listen to what he says — "

"For my well-being?" she asked, eyes blazing from a face that had lost its fire years ago. Even her ginger hair seemed duller than ever before. "You're my husband, though sometimes I'd never guess it. Don't you know what's good for me, now and then?"

"I've got you some water." He held the glass out to her, noticing the scum of dust on its surface.

"I only ever wanted a baby," she said, face crumpling into tears.

James could not avoid frowning. She saw. She always saw. But she continued anyway.

"Just a baby. One to call my own. It's not fair I'm ill, not fair they can't find what's wrong with me, and it's not my fault! Why should I suffer if it's not my fault?"

"Beth," James sighed. "I'll fetch you a glass of wine, but I'm covered in dust. And there's something — "

"You finished that room yet?"

James knew that even if he had, Beth was unlikely to see it. She hated to move from her bedroom, let alone come downstairs. If he ever did finish it, the chances of her seeing it were remote. But she had to feel that she had some control over the running of the house. She had been that way before she became sick and she still was now, and even though James liked to tell himself that it was he who ran the home... truly, he knew that was not the case. It was Beth. It had always been Beth.

He fetched her a glass of wine, made the journey again for a plate of cheese and biscuits, and again for a slice of cake. By the time he returned to the wreckage of the dining room he had almost forgotten about the thing he had found. The corpse.

The child.

It *was* a child. A baby. It was as light as a feather because it was all dried up, and the life had gone from it years ago. Many years, he thought, it had been here for a long, long time. The wall was held together with black mortar, crumbling and loose with age. The bricks were fragile. Whoever had buried their child inside this house had surely passed away long ago. The dead were beyond the law. The dead, too, were beyond help. No good would come of reporting this. An investigation, police, reporters, an unmarked grave for someone long gone and forgotten.

And Beth. Her heart would break, because she had become ill before they could even try for a child. To discover that there had been a dead one here in the house all along...

He could not throw it in the skip. It would be found. A dog, perhaps, sauntering into its master's house with a crumbling gift in its slick jaws...

The garden, then. He would burn it.

But the smoke, the flames, the fumes... Beth would sense them, if no one else.

Then part of it crumbled under his nervously prying fingers, and he had a fine idea.

✳✳✳

He used the end of a brick to crush the final pieces of bone. Then he piled the dust into his pockets and ripped open the seams. His walk around the garden that evening was a great escape, a cigarette in his mouth, his hands working the gritty dust through the holes in his pockets. Its whispering journey down his legs felt like fingertips tickling his hairs, uncomfortably familiar.

That night Beth wanted sex. It was their usual harsh affair.

Later, James went into the spare room, but he could not sleep.

✳✳✳

He went into town the next day to buy food. He also thought he may invest in a new pair of trousers, his old ones were… well, ruined. They were already bundled into a bag and buried it in the skip, piled beneath chunks of old brick and a layer of black dust.

Beth had been nattering on that morning about the wonderful sex they'd had the night before. James had forgotten it already, but Beth talked of babies, redefined love, reinforced vows. After sex she often made him put a pillow under her rear, to elevate her lower torso as an aid to fertilisation. The fact that she was sterile never seemed to get in the way of her wretched fantasies, and James had long since ceased trying to talk to her about it. He had merely nodded and smiled and said he would be back soon. And yes, the rooms were nearly done.

Next, she'd said, he could turn the spare room into a nursery.

He'd had a fleeting image of a freshly painted room with bunnies and mobiles and Winnie the Pooh wallpaper, a shrivelled and desiccated child in the shiny new cot.

In the underpass on the way home his eyes were drawn to graffiti veining the walls. *Martha fucks, call her now* and *Dennis is gay* and *Janey takes it in the ass.* Alongside these crass statement were crude drawings of sexual organs: huge cocks spurting gallons of semen; vagina yawning open. All sexual, even the signatures of the so-called artists were underlined with phallic symbols or nude women, or other indefinable, more disconcerting images.

Except one. *Woke up this morning, my baby was gone,* it said. James scratched at his legs and wondered who had written it. The paint was jet-black, not yet faded by time or wind, or worn by couples rutting against the tiles. It was new.

He passed by the sprayed words and wondered whether they were still there when he was not looking. He glanced back and saw them shouting into the dusk beneath the road, then looked away again. It should not matter whether they were there or not when he was absent… it should not matter, but it did.

He called into his local pub for a pint on the way home. Once he'd had a close circle of friends here, but they had all moved on to other pubs, other friends. He did not hear from any of the now, not since Beth had turned really bad and he had begun spending more time at home to look after her. At the start they had told him he was going strange, and now he supposed they had been right, in a way. At the time he had asked them what the hell they would do if their wives became ill. Now, most days, he wondered just what *he* was doing.

Beth was asleep when he arrived home, so he used this as an excuse to sit in front of the television with a beer instead of working on the house. It began to rain. He thought of dust filtering down into the soil, fertilising the ground with dead flesh, and when he drifted into an alcoholic sleep the roses he saw growing there were bright red, dripping stale blood from icy thorns.

✳ ✳ ✳

James worked at a pub in the town for two afternoons each week. The time away from Beth seemed to recharge his batteries, but the feeling was false. He was not reinvigorated, more temporarily resurrected, like a dying battery placed on a radiator to urge a final spurt of life. It never worked for more than a few hours, and the days between shifts were long and hard.

It was not that he no longer loved Beth. He was certain he did, in a deep place that her illness had done its best to shut off. It was more that he no longer liked himself. He had become an automaton, one with a heart that revelled in depression, and an outlook drained of hope. Beth's illness may be non-contagious, but he was dying from it as surely as she.

On the Tuesday following his discovery of the body — days after the dust of its remains had been washed down into his lawn — a pain in his stomach drove him into the pub toilets on several occasions. There were four cubicles, all of them spotlessly clean, inspected several times each day by the head barman. James hated using the toilet in public, and he always chose a cubicle on the end so that there could only ever be one person next to him. He would normally wait until he was sure he was in there on his own, but this time he was truly out of control. He was lucky, though, on the first two visits — no one else was in the toilets and he could relax and allow nature to take its course.

The third time there was only one cubicle free. James rushed in and dropped his trousers and boxers, unable to believe there could be anything left to come out. He tried to hold on but whatever had upset his stomach would have its way. He buried his face in his hands and groaned as he heard a stifled giggle from another cubicle.

At least he could wait in here until they had all gone. At least they didn't have to see him.

He glanced up at the back of the door. *Cradle Snatcher!* the words said. They had been carved into the metal with some sharp implement, and then smeared with shit. The words were brought out in filth.

Cradle Snatcher! It could apply to anyone, could have been written by anyone. It may have been here for days or weeks, the smear of shit only now revealing the words. James could not help thinking of bones crumbling to dust and the feel of dried flesh disintegrating beneath his touch.

He finished up and rushed from the toilets, not even stopping to wash his hands. "I'm feeling very unwell," he told the manager. Already his stomach was making more warning noises.

The manager told him to go home, James left, and on the bus journey his knuckles whitened on the seat as he struggled to keep control of his bowels. There were words scrawled across the rear of the seat in front of him, he was aware of their spider-trail design, but he did not look too closely.

When he arrived home Beth was ready for him.

"James, I need a drink. And I've wet the sheets... I'm sorry, honey, but I've done it again."

"One minute," he shouted. The toilet door had barely banged shut before he was straining and groaning again.

Bent double with the pain, he saw patches of dry skin on his legs, bubbled like burnt cheese. When he touched one it burst. Only dust came out.

✳✳✳

"I think it might have happened last night," Beth said. "I really think it might."

"Must have been something I ate." James heard her but he could not bear to reply. If she hadn't come to terms with it by now, she never would.

"I think I can feel it. You know, some women know from the moment of conception? I really think I can — "

"Had sausages and chips last night, can't have been that. Can it?"

"James? Are you listening to me?"

"Maybe it was the cheese I had for supper. Gone off."

"James." Her voice had changed, from whimsical to stern. It amazed him how she could shift her moods from one extreme to the other without passing any intervening stage.

"I heard you," he said quietly. It would not be a good idea to ignore her any longer, not when she was like this. She might have a fit and he truly did not think he could manage that at the moment. He may just walk away and leave her there, dribbling and pissing and straining so much that the veins stood out in her neck and on her forehead, knee joints locked rigid, eyes rolled up...

"And?" she said. "What do you think? Aren't you happy for me... for us? It's what I've always wanted, it's what I've lived for, and then all this happened... all this terrible stuff, me being ill... and you're not even pleased for me?" She was crying now, but they were strange tears, stage tears. She was angry, not sad.

"I should get back to the dining room."

"James!"

"Honey... Beth, I'm happy for you, if that's what you want. You know — "

"You never wanted to give me a baby! Even when I was well, you never wanted it! Now you keep me all wrapped up in this stinking room while you're off gallivanting around, doing what you want to do!"

"I spend my life doing what *you* want me to do!" he shouted, and he knew that was the end of the conversation. Shouting just once would ensure that he could not get another word in, placatory or otherwise. So he turned and left.

Beth's screams, her shouts, her curses strafed his back as he walked downstairs. And one phrase cut in and burrowed under all the defences he thought he had built over the years.

"Give me my baby!" she shouted. Over and over again.

He shoved the sheet of polythene aside, slammed the door, taped the plastic back around the frame and flopped down onto the covered settee. He could still hear Beth shouting, but the words themselves were blurred by their passage through floor, wall, door. Their tone was evident, their meaning not so. James closed his eyes, breathed in the stale dust of the room, scratched at his legs. They were itching like old scars trying to remind him of their existence, an annoyance rather than a pain. He wondered whether he'd picked up an infection in the pub's toilets. Perhaps it was a sweat rash — he was not used to physical labour.

He edged around the truth like a lion circling its prey. Dust, he thought, old bone dust from somebody forgotten, long gone.

But were they really forgotten?

Cradle Snatcher!

He opened his eyes and stared at where the wall had used to be. Now he was looking straight through into their living room. The hole was still rough around the edges and not quite the size he had intended, but the place where it had been — the place where the baby had been — had changed. He had changed it. All it had taken was a sledgehammer and a pick.

Unto Us

Beth was still ranting, but he thought the strength was going from her voice. That was good, a gradual wind-down was good, because it meant she was not having a fit, and *that* meant that he would have no shitty sheets to wash or puke to clear up.

He went outside to let her charge fizzle out. Once in the garden, he decided to stroll down the street, only as far as the corner shop, then he would come back. Once at the corner shop, he walked along the next road. And at the end of that street, the park looked inviting. His walk set him thinking about the old lady who had lived in the house before them. The estate agent had said she'd been found dead in there, but over the years since they'd moved in, James and Beth had heard local legend whispering of her at parties and in shop doorways. She was a sad, lonely old woman, it said. Not very sociable. One day she had gone for a walk and never found her way back. Her body had been found on a heavily wooded roundabout, badly decomposed, many years later.

In the park James made his way to the bandstand, a place where he and Beth had kissed on their first date, made love on their third. It had always been a mystical place for him: initially, it was where he fell for the love of his life; lately, as perceptions shifted, it was where his life had begun to end.

How things change.

As he sat on the bandstand, dangled his legs and thought about Beth — good thoughts, bad thoughts, indifferent thoughts — he became aware of someone shouting. It was in the distance, a raised voice almost too far off to hear. He looked around but he was alone, not even a dog-walker or a courting couple shared this part of the park with him. But he could still hear the sound, like someone screaming a mile away, screaming just for him, and slowly the words were taking shape. Repetition was revealing the distant message, like a song lyric made out after dozens of plays. Six words:

You took my one and only.

As he recognised the words he saw them, sprayed across a retaining wall at the edge of the band area; and as he saw the words, so the shouting ceased.

He shook his head and tried to decide whether he had really heard the voice at all.

You took my one and only!

James knew it was for him, it had to be for him. He thought of dust settling into voids in the ground and his legs began to itch... and the exclamation mark, that had not been there seconds ago. He blinked.

You took my one and only, you bastard!

Unnerved, James stood and backed away across the concrete expanse. He kept his eyes on the sprayed message, and though it seemed to shimmer under his gaze it did not change. Not until he stumbled and nearly fell, glancing down to see what had tripped him.

You killed my one and only, you bastard!

James turned and ran. As soon as he presented his back to the graffiti he heard the shouting voice again, a long way off but the words very plain. The ever-changing words.

He only lost them as he left the park.

Outside the corner shop he doubled over and vomited violently into the gutter, his breakfast followed by a dozen dry-heaves. Nobody came to help. Maybe they thought he was a junkie.

As he let himself into the house and heard Beth's soft snore from upstairs, he wondered what the words on the wall were saying now.

✳✳✳

Night came. James sat in the kitchen. He was watching the lawn. He was wondering what would grow out of it over the next few days.

It was too late to tell anyone, he was sure of that. Besides, without a body he would be taken for a crank. And the last thing Beth needed was heartache like that. She was ill, very ill, and he had the occasional dark moment when he guessed that her time was short. In the very blackest of moments, he actually prayed that this was so.

His throat was still burning, singed by his own stomach acids. He had puked several times that day, managing to hide it from Beth by doing it downstairs and washing it into the kitchen sink. He no longer needed to poke it through the plug hole because there were no more lumps. He could not keep any food down.

Beth had slept all afternoon, and still slept now. The doctors had said she may feel lethargic and jaded much of the time, but James still thought she slept mostly to escape reality.

He wished he could sleep as well, close his eyes and drift away, forget scrawled messages on walls and doors, let concerns about his discovery wither in the realms of sleep and be lost when he woke up the next day. He tried, but sleep did not come. So he sat watching the lawn.

In the distance, beyond the howls of cats and the secretive rustling of things beneath hedges, a voice came from nowhere. James had to listen for a very long time before he could make out what it

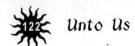

was saying.

Murderer! I know where you live.

✳✳✳

Next morning, those words were scratching into the window of the corner shop. They had been scored in so deeply that when James reached out to touch them, the window came apart under his hands.

He turned and ran back home.

✳✳✳

"You've cut your arm," Beth said. "Here, let me see." She held out her hand and James saw how long and thin her fingers were. It was like being touched with a bunch of sticks.

"I feel faint," he said. He sat on the edge of her bed and let her examine the wound, but he did not tell her that he'd been feeling this way all night.

"How did you do it?"

"Someone broke Macey's window."

"While you were there?"

James nodded. "A brick. Came through the window."

Beth twisted his arms this way and that. "It's not that bad," she said. "A bleeding scratch more than anything."

"I still feel faint."

She smiled then. It could have been coy, but her hollowed cheeks turned it into a grimace. "I'm feeling a little queasy myself. I think it may be morning sickness."

James nodded. He could not face another argument, not now, not when he felt so bad. He was burning up, his throat was so painful he could hardly swallow, his tongue was a stone in his mouth. And the sores on his legs were now open, doing their own little bit to vent his juices to the outside.

"Did you hear me, James?"

"Yes, I heard you. Morning sickness." He looked into her eyes and tried a smile. It seemed to work because she smiled back at him, revealing gums bruised with infection and teeth too big for her wizened features.

"Have you thought of a name yet?" she asked.

"What?"

"A name for our baby. If it's a boy I like Samuel, if that's alright with you."

James stood and swayed as a sense of dislocation enveloped him. Beth's voice receded into the haze, and when it came back it was muttering words he did not want to hear. *Murderer! I know where you live,* she said, and *You killed my one and only.* James glared at her through countless spots flowering before his eyes, and the words did not match the shapes her mouth was making. They matched her eyes, though. Eyes full of blame.

James needed to sit down again. Vertical and horizontal competed with each other and he could feel blood thickening in his thin veins. He would not sit next to Beth, though, not when she was like this. The words still came, mismatched to whatever she was saying, and now the voice was closer still, so close that it no longer needed to shout.

It was not Beth's voice.

"I've got to lie down," he said, or thought he said. He could not feel his mouth move. He went for the door but arrived at a wall, feeling the bumps of woodchip prick his hands with bright points of flame. Everything seemed to hurt now, and he wished he would faint to remove himself from the pain, the voice, the terrible words it was saying.

He made it into his own bedroom and thought he felt a little more in control, but then he made the mistake of looking from his window. The house directly opposite had been vandalised, a message gouged into its brickwork so deeply that in places he saw the white flash of cavity insulation.

I'm coming for you, child killer.

As soon as he saw the message the voice stopped.

He ran downstairs. He could hear Beth shouting, but he did not listen. He did not want to understand, because he heard her talking of babies, and fate, and how he had side-stepped his duties. He burst through the dining room door and something wrapped itself around him, trying to smother the life from him with a cold caress. The polythene sheet. He stepped past it and closed the door against Beth's shouts. The sheet fell back across the door, but it could not drown his wife's voice.

The messenger was coming for him, but there were other things it could find when it arrived. Its baby, perhaps, reformed and replaced. A mistake he would say. But first he had to find it.

It was cold outside. Wind whispered in the trees at the bottom of the garden, but James could hear no words in their mumblings. He knelt on the lawn, feeling dampness soak into his trousers and calm the itching there for a time. It was hard to focus. It may have been bad light but his eyes were dry, his vision twisted out of shape. He felt among the grass with his fingertips, snatching up anything that felt stony or sharp, inspecting it and discarding it over his shoulder when it was not what he sought.

It took ten minutes to find the first piece. No bigger than his little fingernail, the white bone shard was dim and pitted in the light. James placed it carefully in his pocket and continued his search.

It began to rain, but when he looked up he saw that there were no clouds.

The trees increased their discussions, joined now by another sound. A distant sound, but one closing quickly, its words so full of impotent rage that James could not discern their meaning. He scampered frantically across the lawn, pocketing pieces of stone and dead dried beetles in his haste.

A loud *thunk* stopped him in his tracks. It had come from the trees, and though he recognised the noise he could not place it. It came again: thunk! He looked down the garden and saw something damp and bright, something exposed that should not be exposed.

As he watched, the something was slashed again into a shape. A letter 'D', carved into the living flesh of a tree.

Other thuds came, and as they did so the shouting lessened. A further message was being given, perhaps a final message. James did not wait to see what it said.

In the house, Beth no longer screamed. Asleep or exhausted, James did not care. He slammed the back door, engaged the bolts, locked the deadlock.

He panted, each breath stinging his chest. Sickness threatened, but there was nothing left to bring up. His fingernails were pale and one or two of them had crumbled. His legs were itching more than ever, and he could not prevent himself from scratching furiously. He felt the cool kiss of blood meeting air as it ran down his shins.

He took out the gritty pieces from his pocket and scattered them on the ragged floor where the wall had been. He began to cry helplessly because he knew it would not be enough, could never be enough. He was a cradle snatcher and a child killer.

Something arrived. He sensed the garden contracting as it was filled, and seconds later the windows of the house shook as gouges were smashed into the patio stonework. James went to the window and peered out. The letters appeared as he watched, three feet high and written with a furious hand.

D, then and I, and an E, then a D again... I... E.

"I'm sorry!" James shouted. He realised that he was defending himself for the first time, only now comprehending that he was blameless, an innocent party. Beth may not agree — she surely would not — but he had never meant any harm. "Leave me alone, leave me, I'm sorry!"

He picked up the sledgehammer and backed away until he was standing against the wall.

Something smashed into the windows, popping holes in the glass like bullets, ricocheting from the walls and clattering to the floor. Bone shards, he saw, splinters of the corpse he had crushed and spread about his garden. They were not still, even inside. They twitched and skittered across the bare floorboards, seeking the other bits he had recovered himself, dancing with them and singing a hollow bone solo beneath the cacophony from outside.

In seconds, a tiny partial skeleton was squirming on the floor.

The dining room door opened. Something came in, something thin and witch-like with bloody outstretched hands, leaving exclamation marks smeared across the polythene. A ghastly croak came from the figure, matching each impact of the invisible hand on the patio stones.

James swung the hammer. Its contact matched the final crack from outside. His arms jarred.

Beth slithered out from behind the heavy polythene sheet. Her head rubbed down its length, leaving a gruesome trail behind. Her hands were already bloody, as was the back of her night-gown, bloody and wet and all his fault, it was all his fault —

As his wife's ruined head struck the floor, the crashes from outside began again. They sounded different now, because they were against the walls of the house. Windows smashed upstairs, bricks showered in as holes were punched through old masonry.

The baby skeleton turned on its back. It was incomplete, but the gaps and spaces did not seem to matter. A terrible attraction held it together. If it had possessed eyes, it would have been staring at him.

James shook his head and shouted and cried. He was being given a final message, but he could not read it.

The noise stopped suddenly. In the utter silence he could hear only his own laboured breathing, and the steady *drip drip* of his wife's blood falling from the polythene sheet.

His wife...

She moved. Beth pushed herself up onto all fours, raised her head — there was blood leaking from her eyes, her skull was a shattered wound, sludge leaked from her head and pattered to the floor — and looked at him.

Whatever had been making the noise outside, was now inside.

"You can never know the strength of a mother's love," the corpse said.

And then it stood.

The Last Good Times

Something kisses me awake. No one has touched me like that since Josh died. I have been waiting for this for a long time.

I open my eyes and cast my dreams aside. It has been a long, hot summer, and my curtains are flowing gently in the warm breeze. The world outside is silent. There is that faint contact again, a cool breath against my exposed neck. I sit up quickly, the sheet clammy and damp against my breasts, and see the shimmer of something moving silently across the room.

It stops by the window. I have been expecting him, but still it comes as a thumping a shock. I know it is happening everywhere, but I had never really thought it would touch me. The sheet drops, revealing my nakedness, and I snatch it back and clasp it under my chin. I see the absurdity of this act — he has seen it all before, and he's not really here — but like a child holding a blanket over its head, the sheet will keep the nightmares from me. Though, I wonder, will it keep me from nightmares?

"Josh?" I say, my whisper a shout in the silence. The shape does not move, and there is no indication that he has heard. I remember him as he was: bright, cheerful and strong; ready for romance, but never for marriage. Now, I can literally see right through him.

He moves to a chair and *flows* into it. I'm glad that as yet, I cannot see his face.

"Josh," I say again, but I know it is useless. He is dead and cannot do, or say, anything.

***

"Josh came back to me last night."

Hel is silent. Then she reaches across the table and touches the back of my hand. "Oh Rena, I'm sorry! Oh God." She looks away from me, avoiding my gaze or hiding her own. Perhaps she feels a selfish relief. I can hardly blame her.

"It may not be so bad," I say.

"I knew it was about time, now," Hel says, still not looking at me. "But I was hoping against hope... praying you'd be spared."

I shrug. "Why should I, when it's happening to everyone?"

I look around the restaurant at the people gathered in quiet huddles, both alive and dead. In the opposite corner there is an elderly couple, eating a lank salad and trying unsuccessfully to ignore the wraiths sitting beside them. I can see the ghosts' faces, but they are expressionless. They simply stare at the diners, as if jealous of the bad salad or covetous of the age they never reached. They look like faithful pets, patiently awaiting scraps from the dinner table. The woman mumbles something to the man, but he merely shakes his head without looking up, eschewing the comfort of eye contact. The movement causes a faint flutter of animation amongst their erstwhile relatives. One of the ghosts is wearing a wedding dress. Another sports a split throat.

"What are you going to do? I mean, if he's around forever... you know...?" I love Hel dearly, but she thrives so much on drama and disorder. She seems to have an emotional non-return valve, which lets in all the sorrow there is in this exhausted world, but exudes only a morbid curiosity of what is happening. Perhaps, I have often thought, she is lucky. Maybe this is her defence mechanism. I wonder what she will think when she gets an eternal visit, but quickly dismiss the thought. It's too hard to bear.

"What can I do?" I say.

"Where is he now?" Hel glances over my shoulder, as if expecting to come face to face with the bland visage of my dead boyfriend.

"He was sitting in the rocking chair in my room when I left," I reply. "They say it takes a few days before they tag on fully. For a while they just hang around the place they come back to. They say... they say it doesn't take long." I feel tears threatening, but I bite my lower lip and attack my lunch with a fork. The old woman looks up at the sudden clash of cutlery on crockery. I glance at her, but see only the curtain of ghosts surrounding the table.

"Oh." Hel can say little more. I am glad.

"So, if you're a real friend, you'll take me out tonight to get me horribly drunk and seriously laid." I grin at her astonished expression, gulping down my remaining wine like water and refilling the glass to the brim. "Maybe not the laid bit, but drunk at least. It's like… " I trail off, feeling a welcome melancholy trying to melt its way into my feigned jollity. "Remember our holiday in America? In 1999? The Americans were getting ready for the millennium celebrations and we caught the fever. It was a time of… impatience. Baited anticipation. The whole two weeks we spent as if they were the last good times left to us on Earth. We rushed everywhere, drank everything, ate like hogs. It was like the world was coming to an end, and we had to cram everything in before it all went up in smoke."

Hel smiles, but her voice is far from cheerful. It is full of a sad nostalgia. "Oh yes, I remember it well. They say, you know, that this is the end anyway. Why don't we feel galvanised into action now?"

I shrug. "I do." But I am lying, and I know how apparent that is to Hel. "He's back there, waiting for me… " My face begins to crumple, the tears finding their way out at last. " …waiting, not saying anything, not thinking anything. Just sitting there… " Hel grabs my hand again, and it is as if her show of concern crushes rage from me. "I loved him, Hel," I say, perversely pleased at the past tense. "I loved him, but why can't he stay dead?"

I receive a few looks from others in the restaurant, but no one comes to help. The old couple do not even turn to stare. Nowadays, people are all too used to seeing tears. It is ironic that public grief has become more private than ever.

✳ ✳ ✳

Hel walks me to my front door She will not come in, and I cannot ask her to. It's not fair. I have to face this alone, like billions across the globe, grimace and bear the impossibility of what is happening. But any false confidence I had — any calm acceptance planted by the fact that this was widespread, endemic in the new world — vanishes the second Hel turns her back on me.

"Tomorrow, then?" I call after her.

She glances back over her shoulder; I can see the terror she holds for me. It makes me feel worse.

"Damn right! Tomorrow, at seven. We'll paint the town red."

I think of blood, flowing in the gutters and clotting the drains like the clogged veins of a dying world. No blood inside; no risk of a mess here; just Josh, beautiful dead Josh, sitting silently and waiting for me to come home, waiting for the time when he will walk with me, and never be away from me again.

Can a ghost be haunted? Will this eventually be a world haunted by tortured souls, haunting tortured souls? It is a pathetic image, and I almost smile. But I frown instead.

I slip the key into the lock, push the door open and rush upstairs, all without thinking. The landing is dark and I leave it that way, preferring a fear of what *may* be there to a dread of what is. I hear the remote thump of music from downstairs. Strike, the guy who lives there, had his whole family come back a month ago. Maybe he thinks the volume will drive their staring faces back into the darkness. It may work for him, but it doesn't make it any easier for me to sleep. I am beyond complaining.

I open my door. It's dark inside, the curtains still closed from this morning when I had fled in a panic. I know what I will find, but perhaps if I step quietly, hold my breath, avoid the creaking floorboards, Josh will not hear me.

He is still sitting in the rocking chair, denying its purpose with his inertness. He looks up as I enter the bedroom. His eyes follow me to the bathroom cubicle. There is nothing there — no intelligence, not a hint of rationality — but still, I wonder what he's thinking.

I sit on the loo and let the pressure on my bladder go, crying into clenched fists, listening for the soporific creak of the rocking chair. We had made love in it once, two summers ago when the temperatures were breaking records yet again and we had to sleep with the windows and curtains wide open. The moon had been full, the time of the wolf, Josh said. He'd chased me around the small flat until we ended up in the chair, and we'd let the motion do its work as the moon bathed us in borrowed light.

I look up and gasp. Josh is standing before me, his body split down the middle by the wall of the cubicle. An honest childhood concern comes instantly back to haunt me — if a ghost can step through walls, why doesn't it fall through floors? Why isn't Josh joining in with Strike's musical explosion downstairs right now, mixing with his own kind, mingling with the dead?

"Josh!" I sigh, trying to cry some more because the tears will blur my vision, and I do not want to see. "Josh, why come back? Won't you ever leave me alone?" I expect no answer and I receive none.

I finish in the bathroom, exit the cubicle, trying desperately not to touch him. I'm afraid that I'll go *through* him. The bed creaks as I sit on it, but not when Josh does. There is no depression in the sheets beneath him, no sign at all that he is here: no breathing; no smell; no swish of air as he moves. Only his image, sitting blandly next to me, looking at me with empty, blank eyes.

I wonder whether I would know he was here were I blind? Are the sightless the lucky ones, now?

"Oh Josh, I've missed you," I say, but I can see no change in expression. I lie down and he moves back to the rocking chair. I close my eyes to sleep, but this is when I see him most clearly. In memories.

✳✳✳

"Never understood how they got planning permission for this place," Hel says. We are standing in front of The Slaughterhouse, the most popular nightspot in town. Its facade is adorned with two great meat hooks, twelve feet long, crossed above the entrance like swords over an ancient mantle. Drops of neon blood fall continuously towards the heads of those below, stopping just above the doors before blinking out and starting again. The name itself is splashed in great, glutinous letters designed, apparently, to resemble internal organs. To me, they look like Christmas decorations turned nasty.

"I haven't been here for a long time," I say. We've already had a few drinks and my head is buzzing. I'm still flushed with the relief I felt when Josh did not choose tonight to leave the flat with me.

Hel is hanging onto my arm, both for companionship and mutual support against the effects of inebriation. "It's not changed much," she says. "The wine's still piss, the carpets still stick to your shoes and the music stinks."

I grimace. "Now you've reminded me, maybe we should go somewhere else?" She hugs my arms and grins at me, shaking her head. It may be a dive, but we spent some good times here when we were younger. Josh came, sometimes.

"Added bonus that they don't let anyone in with tag-alongs." Since the ghosts started to appear, The Slaughterhouse has maintained a policy of allowing only the 'unaccompanied' entrance. At first the rule was regarded as the worst type of prejudice — as bad, people said, as allowing no entry for gays or blacks. But as the plague of wraiths took hold, the club became a refuge. Other places adopted the same policy, but The Slaughterhouse reaped the benefits.

"Clientele must be shrinking," I say, but Hel does not reply.

We are cocooned within a warm mass of people, mainly younger than us, but there are also a few older, haunted faces in the crowd. Perhaps they're here to do what we're doing, having a final fling before their lives change forever. For once I revel in the press and the crush of the throng, pleased that there are no fleeting shapes to remind me of Josh, no sad people trying in vain to avoid the apparitions which seem attached to them by some insubstantial string.

We eventually squeeze through the single door into the club. Hel does her best to affect a vacant stare — it's a sick joke and I can't help but giggle — but one of the bouncers confirms her flesh and blood status by pinching her rear. She frowns up at him, trying her best to feign indignance, even though I can see she is enjoying the attention. The bouncer smiles blandly and looks away.

Hel has rarely become involved with men since her son Toby drowned in the bathtub six years ago. He was one year old. We've hardly ever mentioned him, especially since the tag-alongs began turning up a few months ago. The very idea of him sends Hel into paroxysms of terror. His death — indeed, his short life — is a pain beyond bearing. I rarely even think about him myself, lest my thoughts tempt fate and Hel rings me in the middle of the night, a tear in her voice and a familiar shadow at her back.

"That big monkey pinched my bum!" she shouts through the haze of music and stale smoke.

"Yeah, you hated it!" I shout back. She squeezes my arm and heads across to the cloakroom. I keep my jacket with me. Josh bought it for my twenty-fifth birthday, two years before he died. I cannot risk losing it. I wonder what he would do if I did. I wonder how he would look.

Hel reappears at my side. "Stop thinking about it. We're here to have a good time! We're going to get painfully, vomitously drunk!" The music dies down just as Hel shouts, and we stand in the middle of one of those uncomfortable moments when we are the centre of attention. I start to giggle, feeling Hel shake as she struggles to contain her own mirth — then, like a sudden storm, the laughter comes.

The music cranks back in, the volume slips up a few notches. I can see a boiling, colour-soaked cluster of dancers through the acidic clouds of dry ice and stroboscopic lights, turning the whole dance floor into some nightmare vision of Lovecraftian proportions. I read a lot when I was younger — not so much lately, not since Josh died and the ghosts came to bring the supernatural home to us — and I imagine multi-coloured sucker-less tentacles reaching out, delving into the dark corners of the club and pulling courting couples and drunken kids screaming into its pulsating mass. As if grabbed ourselves, Hel and I plunge into the throng.

The night becomes a fusion of sound, smell and sight, a bastard product of effects and music to attack the senses and purposely disorientate. Hel and I dance for hours, sweating and gasping for every breath but enjoying the impersonal abandon with which we twist and turn between the other dancers. We take it in turns pushing our way to the bar to grab drinks. They don't last for long.

There is a feeling here that I have never experienced before. It is a frantic, almost self-destructive eagerness to merge with the music, a blending of all thoughts and senses into one violent act of expression. I am drawn into it and soon there is nothing but the atmosphere of the club, the assault on the senses, the press of strange bodies against mine, sweat flying, hands grasping. There is a realisation of exaggerated freedom, I can taste it in the air as if exuded from the wide eyes and dripping pores of those around me; a liberation from the confines of outside, where autonomy has little meaning now. I lose sight of Hel as she disappears across the floor, carried between gyrating bodies. She is smiling maniacally and waving her hands at an invisible enemy attacking her from above. The music increases in volume until it is more than simply a sound — it is a wall, a solid vibration closing in on me, encouraging me to climb its pounding surface and punch my way to the top, from where I will be able to see everything. I strike my hands upward, screaming incoherently. Hands reach for me, but in the crush of bodies I cannot tell whose they are or which direction they come from. Callous fingers bite into my left breast, but the pain melds into the sensory overload that is still rippling through me. I shout, losing my voice among the flashing lights. The hand leaves my chest and reappears elsewhere.

Josh.

Josh is here.

He's reaching for me and I'm ignoring him.

I stop dancing, realising how much damage I could have done. My nose is bleeding and white-hot, my top lip swollen and stiff in a parody of patriotic pride. I spin around, sure that Josh will be here, equally certain that I will not be able to see him in the ruckus. Having lost the spirit of the dance, twisting bodies bump and nudge me to the edge of the floor. I move off gratefully into the shadows, away from the explosion of hypnotic light, all the while looking behind me and expecting to see Josh standing there. But I am wrong.

In the depths of the club, where the flashing lights fail to enlighten, darkness courts privacy. I wander across the sticky carpet, dodging overturned chairs and unconscious people merged into the grim background. There is a full bottle of water on a table and I take a healthy gulp from it, hoping its owner is not watching. I stare into the gloom, wondering whom I am seeing, who can see me. There are shadows in shadows, outlines of things that may be people moving with shivers that could be ecstasy, or agony.

I move past a pillar. Hel sits exposed in strobe, a glass in one hand, her head in the other, her shoulders and arms shaking with dry sobs. Sweat still glistens on her bare back from her manic dancing. I can see that her glass is empty, but every so often she mimics taking a drink. Perhaps the mouthfuls of air are helping purge her of self-reproach, but there will always be a hangover. She looks up and a trail of coloured lights marches across her face, changing her from red-faced demon to yellow-faced doll in a blink. Her eyes, strangely, do not catch the light, but glisten with their own sorrow.

When I was young, I thought the world renewed itself every time I blinked. For that split second, the controllers — faeries, goblins, giggling deities — went to work and cleaned things up, hiding the badness away and preparing the beauty again. The strobe provides a false blink, a pseudo-flash of sightlessness. But I see no controllers, and Hel carries on looking scared. In one thought, I curse and mourn the childish naivety that never really leaves anyone.

"Hey, what's up?" I sit next to her, nudging a loose-limbed drunk along the settee. Music still blasts away behind us, like a distant artillery exchange.

She shakes her head and tries to smile, but it turns into a grimace, which I have to hold. Silent, bitter tears flow across the back of my hands. I tilt her head and kiss her on the forehead, tapping her cheeks gently as if to force in some joy.

"Oh Rena, I'm sorry. I know what a night this is, what we're doing here. I'm really sorry. I know it's your last night on your own. Maybe." I could see that she was struggling with unalloyed guilt, but I felt too bad for her to really come to blows with my own situation.

"Tell me what it is, Hel," I say. I have to shout; they have notched the music up for the final hour. I can smell pot, and the warm-acidic haze drifts between us. The drunk on the bench has lit a joint, and he is trying to prop himself on one elbow to take another drag. "Come on, talk to me. This is all happening to you, too, you know."

Hel nods. "But it's you, Rena. I'm going to lose you! He's going to be there every time, now… Josh is going to be watching us all the time."

"Josh is dead."

Hel shouts louder than she has to, and that scares me. She has never shouted at me before. "It doesn't matter any more! That makes it all worse, Rena!" Her face creases again, but she does not cry. She's all dried up. "He's dead, yes, but he's going to be with you forever. And I'm going to lose you to him, because you won't want us to go out when he's sitting there, staring… And Toby… "

I begin to shake. It's cold — someone has opened the fire escape doors — but I shiver more from a slowly dawning dread. It creeps through me as if my stomach has been its hiding place for so many years, finding its way into veins and tendons and bones, forcing its way into my eyes. My vision blurs, Hel's face suddenly drops as she sees herself reflected in me. I turn away, reach for the joint the drunk has dropped. The tip is still wet with his spit, but I do not care, I take a huge draught and hold it in for thirty seconds.

When I look back at Hel she has the ghost of a smile on her face, though I cannot tell whether it is an image of a past expression or one that never really existed at all. "I hope, when Toby comes back, he'll recognise me," she says sadly. I understand the words without really hearing her, as if the smoke I exhale is insulating us from the thunderous music and the repugnant truth.

I shouldn't laugh, but I cannot help it. I wonder briefly why the hell people smoke this stuff, then I stand and feel my head swaying around the world. A stool tips and tilts and spins around to the ceiling, then back to sit on its own floor bolts. The drunk wakes and stares around for his joint, smiling at me with cheerful camaraderie as he sees me taking back the last lungfull, fingertips burning, throat smarting.

"Come on!" I shout. Hel stands and I grab her arm, hauling her back onto the dance floor before I've even thought of letting go of the scorching stub.

We dance to the end of the night. Minutes before two a.m., a group of people sneak through the fire exit and flow onto the dance floor. They have their dead relatives with them. There is shouting, punches are thrown, and an angry stampede makes my head spin with inconsistencies — I see a girl run through a boy, a man standing half-in another. The dope makes me smile, but inside, where sobriety always knows the frank truth of things, the sadness is swelling once more.

Eventually, we fall from the club with a flood of other people who had paid to forget. Cold reality hits us hard, cooling the sweat on our bodies and the rebellion in our hearts. There is little conversation.

Hel and I move quickly away from the crowded club entrance,

keen to distance ourselves from whatever ugliness there may be when the gatecrashers emerge. We stumble through quiet streets, and once again I am aghast at the change in things. There are still lots of people about, walking arm in arm, patrolling in groups like meer cats, but conversation is down to a minimum. There is the occasional shout but, ironically, it is nearly always directed at a shape which cannot talk back.

I walk Hel home and we hug outside her front door. She has said little since leaving the club and she does not speak now, but I try to catch her eye and let her know how I feel. I think she knows, anyway. Any friend as close as Hel should always know.

"See you," I say as she swings the door shut. She nods, staring over my shoulder as if imagining herself there. The door clicks shut.

I do not want to go home. As I walk away from Hel's house I come to realise how strained I have been all night. Being alone feels good. The weight of company has been lifted from my shoulders and I am my own person. I am still drunk, and a little queasy from the dope, but the feeling is nice. Real.

I head on impulse towards the park. It is where I used to play as a child — exploring the stream, keeping tadpoles, watching the boys act tough at football — and it is still one of my favourite places. To me it is timeless, regulated only by the buds or leaves on the trees, the frost or cut grass clinging to the slopes above the playground. Tonight, in the dark, it could have been anywhere.

The gate is open. I walk a little way in and before long find myself at the small circle of stones, placed here eighty years ago when the park was first formed and mythologised ever since by the local children: devil worshipping, virgin martyrs, alien landings, all have occurred within the circle at one point or another, many of them reenacted by serious-faced kids and giggling teenagers.

I wonder if there were ever stories about ghosts. Try as I might, I cannot remember.

I sit on the flat slab in the middle of the circle and exhale slowly. I do not breathe for a few seconds, relishing instead the unpolluted sounds of the night, and the breath of the sleeping planet sighing gently through the trees. This must be what nature sounded like before man came. I feel calm, serene, the darkness washing through me and purging any dregs of sadness away into the night. Here, memories hold sway, courting loneliness and twisting it into a pleasing melancholy, like a dull pain that borders on pleasure. I can look inwards without the constant threat of a voice forcing me to look without. It reminds me that I'm alive, active, a moving cog in the engine of the world.

A philosopher said that happiness is not a given gift to humanity, but something we have to earn. Our natural state is stress and conflict. Now, I feel that I have earned a moment of happiness, and I let the feelings envelop and bathe me in their curious energy. I am enjoying the loneliness, revelling in the solitude, though try as I might I cannot forget the reason why.

They say that the dead have come to us because we are removing ourselves so far from death. Medicines, research, all combining to drive death further away. We're playing God. We're averting nature.

They say we've brought it all on ourselves.

I sit there for a long time, eyes open or closed, dozing or simply letting the night happen around me. At some point, when I see the first taint of light in the east, I head home.

※ ※ ※

I'm dreaming of being kissed all over. Josh is smiling down at me, his face sunburnt and happy. It is our first holiday together, and his eyes have never been so full of life. He kisses my throat, my breasts. He glances up at me and dips his head lower, as his eyes split and let out a stream of real light.

I jerk awake, squinting against the sunlight slanting in between my half-drawn curtains. Josh is still in the rocking chair, and his head turns slightly as I swing my feet from the bed. My skin crawls as I wonder how much of what I had been dreaming was purely imaginary.

I stand and dress quickly, trying to ignore my thumping hangover. I glance back at the rocking chair, desperate to see sense in the pale shadow of Josh sitting there, but his is an insoluble puzzle. When he was ill, dying, we did not have the money to buy the expensive cures. Life had become a commercial consideration.

There are a few people in the street below, most of them followed by ghosts. One of them, an old man with a zimmer frame, has six trailing him, ganging around him like piglets to a swollen sow. I wonder if he really cares.

I try to ring Hel, but there is no reply.

I make myself some breakfast, boiled eggs with soldiers to give me a taste of childhood. A huge mug of coffee steams away beside me as I eat. Josh seems content with sitting in the rocking chair, and as the steam obscures the view I can almost imagine I'm on my own.

I 'phone Hel once more. I leave it ringing for a ridiculous

length of time, willing her to answer. Nothing.

I am dressing to walk around to her house when I feel something beginning to happen. The air is suddenly still and staid, as if I am living in an old sepia-tinted photograph. I sit carefully on the edge of my unmade bed, struggling to hear something, anything, from outside. In the distance there is the steady drone of an aircraft, the tone of its engines shifting as it passes overhead. I feel a sudden, immensely strong nostalgia for childhood, the joys of youth, sunburnt summers and ice creams in the park as the sun sinks. A simple time. A time when worries were not real, where adults took the blame and kids merely dealt it.

Then, I see a hint of an expression flit across Josh's incorporeal face. His eyes widen; just a fraction, but they remain that way.

On the floor next to the rocking chair, Hel appears. She slips into existence in the blink of an eye.

"Oh Hel!" I sigh, because she is dead, and because in a way I was expecting it. She is dead, and she is with me again, and now she will be with me forever. I really don't think I can stand that look of desperate guilt branded onto her face. And I know I can never come to terms with the pale, fleshy lips of the fresh cuts on her wrists.

I run from the flat, realising that I am betraying our friendship by fleeing but also resenting what she has done to me. I sprint along the pavement, dodging the occasional stroller but running straight through the ghosts that accompany them. I enjoy the stitch prickling into my side, deliberately pound harder as my knees jar and send slivers of pain into my brain. I am revelling in the momentary freedom I still have, while those around me trail ghosts and wraiths like echoes of themselves. People look at me, but they do not offer help or words of comfort.

I reach the river and lean against the railing, staring down into the swirling muddy waters below. Years ago, even before I met Josh, I had fallen into this water during a drunken prank on the nearby bridge. The cold and the terror sobered me instantly, and for a few minutes I was sure that the mud was going to suck me down. It was the first time I had confronted death. I wonder why I cannot feel the mud sucking me under now.

I sense someone standing beside me.

It is Josh. He has come with me. He has come to stay.

I turn and walk away. Josh follows. I walk for hours, shaking, constantly aware of the shimmer in reality that marks Josh's presence next to me. I expect people to stare, but most of them have their own problems, and those who do glance at me see nothing remarkable.

I am surprised at how I feel; an incredible sadness at Hel's death, but I know she is still here, in whatever weird way the ghosts can be said to be here. And having Josh with me brings a remote sense of comfort. I recall the previous night like a dream, sitting in the dark park and loving my solitude, and realise that I am lonelier now than I have ever been in my life. The feeling is shocking, but somehow comforting; proof perhaps that adaption is humanity's natural state, not conflict and stress.

I see a couple leaning against the wall of a pub, kissing, holding onto each other so tightly that they surely cannot be breathing. I pause and watch, jealous of their freedom but not hating them for it. Josh stands next to me, and though his gaze is set in the familiar million-mile stare, I hope he is watching too. Perhaps, he is remembering.

The couple lean from the wall and walk away, and as they do so a ghost emerges from the brickwork and follows them. I laugh out loud, realising what they had been doing, realising also that there is always a way to discover happiness in a sea of depression, however temporary that happiness may be.

I walk through the town, and on the way home I pass through the park. There is someone sitting within the stone circle, staring into the distance and thinking he is alone. But, as yet, he has no idea of what true loneliness is.

King of the Dead

K ing Kofar of Blede had never had cause to fear his three
wizards. True, they came from the dark mountains of Cratey,
where necromancers practised their grave art with lofty abandon.
But they were also loyal to their King, grateful for the gifts he chose
to bestow upon them, eager to use their skills to beguile the most
beautiful women into their chambers. They thought he turned a
blind eye, but the King could never be blind — he had at his dis-
posal the crystal from the old crone Creetha.

So he spied upon Lewis, Cerniss and Trakiss from time to time,
ensuring that none of the dark arts crept back into their repertoire.
He saw them coaxing women to their beds, but he saw also that they
were not unkind to these women, so he let them be. He even
perceived the occasional shadow of insanity pass across their features as they stared into the dusty corners of their rooms, perhaps
recalling their deathly times in Cratey.

Kofar knew that they had suffered terribly at the hands of other
necromancers; their souls torn out, opened up to the dead and thrust
back into their unsuspecting bodies. They had been purged of the
affliction, in time, but the dead left a trace, like berry juice on a
wooden plate. Their souls were stained.

He never feared them.

＊＊＊

Fear was held in reserve for other things.

On the day that Blede fell, that fear was realised even before the

King awakened to the tepid sun. In his dreams the sea came to kill them. Its water turned into a forest, branches spiked with living weapons cruel and inimical to human flesh. The trees marched in relentlessly, sending scarlet breakers ahead. When they broke on the shore these waves screamed, sending the fear of death into Blede's cowering population.

At some point, the dream changed into waking. The breeze was cool on his skin as Kofar stood on the palace balcony. Cerniss knelt beside him, eyes closed, tongue extended to test the air.

The old wizard gasped. "Death!" he said, spitting putrid green saliva from his mouth. He scraped his tongue with his nails, gouging bloody furrows. "Death, my Lord. Death from the sea. A fleet of death, coming for Blede."

And even though the King knew that Blede was well defended, virtually inaccessible, a rock on its own in a world fast dying, he was afraid.

"Wake Lewis and Trakiss," he said. "Tell them to send their women away. Tell them to meet me here, now."

Cerniss nodded, closed his eyes and spoke to his fellow wizards.

From the balcony the King could just make out the sea, a hazy, distant border between land and sky.

It had changed.

It was no longer flat.

All along the horizon, spikes sprouted from angry waters. The masts of a thousand ships.

✳ ✳ ✳

Blede was much more than a town.

It had started life as a collection of haphazard huts on the sea's edge, home to sailors and traders, and those certain that there were better things across the sea. They had explored the coast in both directions, finding isolated communities which were prepared to exchange goods for goods: food; clothing; weapons, both conventional and magical, though those last had been waning for centuries.

These traders had returned to Blede time and again, secure in their little enclave, happy that they could protect themselves from attack and pillage. Because Blede was unique: it was an island, yet not an island; set apart, yet still a small part of the mainland, bathed by a livid sun, serviced by streams and tributaries that still managed a bare trickle. It sat on a huge spit of land, five days' horse travel in each direction, connected to the mainland at low tide, isolated at high tide.

And so the life of Blede was governed more than most by the sea, and the moon, and the symbiotic relationship between the two. As the traders and sailors travelled farther afield, the settlement grew. In the early days, when the sun was still kind and crops could be grown in the rich volcanic soils, the ruler was the best farmer. Later, when the roots of plants rotted in foul soil, the ruler was the greatest trader.

Now, with their island dead beneath them, the million people of Blede looked up to Kofar. He had been made King when he brought the wizards. And he had brought the wizards because he wanted to be King. He was the moon, Lewis, Cerniss and Trakiss the tides.

The people were happy with that.

✳ ✳ ✳

The main port of Blede huddled on its western shore, hundreds of buildings surrounding a natural bay. There had never been any successful attempts to land on Blede from the sea. The two attempted invasions that had been thrust upon them — a band of necrophiliacs from the distant Isles of Sod, and the insane dispossessed of another diseased land — were successfully repelled. The rotting hulks of the fleets still formed an effective reef a mile out from the port, a home to all manner of strange creatures, many of them existing only here.

Now, something else was coming.

At first, it looked as if the sea was unknitting from the sky. Curious people left their homes on the hillsides surrounding the port and ventured higher still, to the summits of cliffs. Others remained at the harbour, chatting nervously, trying to cover their unease with bland banter.

The wait was long. For hours, the strange line barely seemed to move. Various theories abounded, from the stubble of a god yet to reveal himself, to a massive tidal wave, to a forest of mould possessing even the ageless waters. No theory held any hope; each was apocalyptic; each spelled their end. And so the mumblers of these ideas congregated in the harbour bar, and poisoned their stomachs with some of the foulest liquor available, sure that they would never live to regret it.

They were right, in that sense. But in another sense, they were so very wrong. Death does not forgive. Death remembers. And when death is deceived, its retribution is harsh indeed.

Soon, the sea began to react to whatever was creeping across its surface. In front of the petrified observers the harbour level dropped, lower and lower, until the ships were bogged down in a sea of mud. All manner of strange creatures died in the weak sunlight. The waters drew back as far as the wrecks of those failed aggressors from so long ago, exposing the corpses of ships, stirring the remains and giving flapping, skeletal arms the semblance of life.

Then, the ocean returned. But its colour had changed. Instead of the salty green they were so used to, the port people of Blede saw a red wave thundering towards them, twenty feet high, roaring and screaming as though it were the life-blood of the planet itself, spewing forth from some terrible rent in its surface.

At that moment, those on the cliffs knew that they had made the right decision.

Those at the harbour knew that their end was nigh.

The drunks in the bar looked from the windows, nodded wisely and took another drink.

The wave scooped up the remains of the ancient fleets before it ploughed into the harbour. It smashed the ships of Blede into a million shards, arming itself with more death-dealing shrapnel as it struck the harbour wall, leapt over with a scream too loud to call merely a noise — this was a solid thing, a wave sent into the air to shatter eardrums and rip skin from flesh — and pummelled the port to smithereens.

The streets gushed with bloody waters, flowing liked opened veins. Screaming and drowning bodies bobbed and rolled in the deluge, their own skin and flesh split to add more redness. Buildings collapsed under the onslaught. The scream continued, thumping up and out, pounding shockwaves deep into the land and sending people stumbling and falling on the high ground above.

Slowly, the waters calmed and receded. The scream did likewise, but it left an echo in the minds of those who had heard it. Ears bled, bodies shook, fingernails popped from their mounts, hair fell from scalps as the memory drove a thousand people mad.

By the time the sea was back to its usual level, the port was no more. It had been scoured from the land. Blasted from existence, leaving only the roots of buildings behind. There were few bodies; bits of bodies, yes, already attracting flies and disgusted, fascinated glances from the survivors on the cliffs. But none whole.

On the hillsides, where the very tip of the wave had reached, the rotting hulks of the ancient fleets settled slowly into unrecognisable mounds. Here and there, a skeletal hand protruded from the mess, laying a defiant touch on the land it could not win aeons ago.

The survivors were discussing whether or not to venture down to the port to look for survivors when a shout went up.

"Look! Out at sea! We're doomed, we're dying, we're dead already!"

The horizon had closed. Masts marched solidly toward Blede, like a line of soldiers confident of victory. But these were no normal ships. Each was different, a varied armada of nightmares. Each ship was alive, bearing eldritch masters toward their destinies; every sail was a flap of skin or a stretched wing; every crew member held tightly onto squirming weapons.

Nowhere was there the glint of steel. These tools of destruction were more advanced than that, closer to nature, nearer the land of their making. These weapons had teeth and claws and blades, poison fangs and venom launchers, spines and acid sacs, flaming eyes and ice-cold vents. And the warriors spoke to them gently, coaxing them into a rage, never once taking their eyes off their quarry.

Blede.

The undefeatable was about to fall.

The survivors screamed, but as if to drown their exhortation of terror, a second wave rose up and bore landward.

***

Each in their own way, the wizards could see further than mere senses would allow them. Today they were all terrified; pale as death; shaking in their leather boots. Their thumping hearts beat a concerto of fear.

Cerniss sat with eyes closed and tongue out. His frown was so pronounced that it sought to rip skin from his skull. His body shook so much that Kofar was sure he heard bone scraping against bone. The wizard's tongue pricked at the air, stealing knowledge from invisible currents like a frog catching ghostly flies.

Lewis' eyes were open, but they saw something far more dreadful than the bland grey walls of the King's chamber. They sparkled with an overt madness; the oldest of the three wizards stood at the abyss of utter lunacy. His long black hair squirmed across his shoulders and around his neck, as if trying to escape the horror its owner was viewing.

And Trakiss held the air in his huge hands. His fingers twitched like individual snakes, jerking back from whatever they touched, transferring a vibration along his arms and into his body. His bald head shone with sweat.

"Tell me," the King commanded.

"We're all going to die," Lewis said. "There is no hope against damnation. The worst of the worst has been visited upon us, for whatever reason, and I see no way out."

"Trakiss?"

The hairless wizard tucked his hands into his armpits. "Lewis is right, sire. There is no hope. Terrible. Terrible!"

"What is it?" said the King. "What can be so terrible? How can it be so hopeless? This kingdom has *never* been invaded. We can hold them back. We must."

The three wizards exchanged glances, and for the first time Kofar truly feared them. Not as people, but as magicians, as things that could destroy him instantly, at a snap of their fingers. He had always believed loyalty an adequate shield, but now, when all three saw doom looming, what was to stop them from destroying him and fleeing?

"We can show you," said Lewis.

"But I have no magic about me," the King said. " I never have. That's why I brought you with me to —"

"You have Creetha's crystal," Cerniss said. "With the power in that, we can show you what will take your kingdom. It will do no good, of course, but —"

"Then show me, now!" Kofar shouted. He was hardly surprised that they knew of the crystal — they were magicians, after all.

The three wizards stood and bowed as the King brought forth the crone's gem. They cringed inwardly, because they knew the crone of old. But they also knew that the crystal was now in the hands of an honest man. There was no danger from the King today. Today, the danger came from elsewhere.

"We will show you," said Lewis, "but you will despair. I warn you now, because that is what I am here for. You will despair. There is no magic we can cast against this terror."

"I need to know," said Kofar. "I had a dream. I need to know."

The three wizards cast spells, whispered and imagined secret incantations. It took longer than it should have, so disturbed were they by what they had seen, felt and tasted. But eventually the crystal began to glow, and Kofar stared inside.

And then he began to scream.

✳ ✳ ✳

The invaders poured ashore.

The hallowed ground of Blede was trodden by all manner of

feet, claws, icythoid limbs and stumps. The ships howled as their passengers disembarked, squirming in the blood-red harbour, scraping themselves against shattered stone as if trying to drag themselves onto the land. Like contagion entering a bloodstream, the invaders spread out from the port. They found no living victims, but when one of them did come across a body they would wreck it, taking great pleasure in the eruptions of thickening blood as they let their living weapons rip it, scrape it or chew it to pieces.

After each ship had disgorged its passengers, two more would set upon it and smother it into the harbour depths. The victim would put up a token defence, but always they would lose. Each ship was huge. Some of them resembled malformed whales with teeth the size of people. Others were communities of smaller things welded together with an obsidian, bone-like substance. One barely touched the water but floated above it, inflated gas bags either side of its myriad mouths giving buoyancy.

The warriors, once landed, paid no attention to the brief battles behind them. They had no need of the ships now that their feet could once again kiss rock.

They were here to stay.

They rapidly fled the town, swarming up the hillsides, heading for the higher ground and the heart of Blede. Under the baleful glare of the midday sun, the invaders spread like a tumour. There were so many of them that the ground was barely visible. Their stench reached inland before they could even be seen, the reek of rot, the stink of the sea. As the first of the warriors reached the port militia where they had already dug themselves into trenches and bolt-holes, ships were still landing.

The militia numbered several hundred. They had watched the destruction of the port from the cliffs, then retreated as the first of the aggressors' ships docked. Half-mad with what he had seen, their lieutenant still served admirably. He sent messengers inland, and the grateful few set off at a run, sorry to leave their friends but glad that they could flee the horror.

For horror is what they saw:

Horror, mounting the hilltops and swarming at the trenches; horror, gasping fire ahead of them to singe the eyeballs from lookouts; horror, launching strange living arrows which squirmed past shields and buried themselves in throats.

Horror. Living, breathing, slashing and gashing; cutting, stabbing, smashing and crushing; eating, chewing, ripping and gnawing at terrified bones, sucking out the fear and revelling in it.

In a matter of minutes the warriors had overrun the militia.

They turned their attention inland. Soon, they came across the first village.

Ah, a collective growl rose up. *Children.*

***

Kofar was screaming. He slithered on the floor like a landed fish, but the wizards retained the spell. The King had not commanded otherwise.

Lewis, Cerniss and Trakiss had their eyes closed. They were seeing what the King was seeing. The crystal shimmered in the centre of the room, throwing off sickly green rays which infiltrated the minds of those present, King and wizard alike. It was inanimate, a thing of magic, imbued with power aeons ago — but Cerniss was certain that it revelled in what it showed. A sickness swept through him, and helplessness at the slaughter they were witnessing from a distance.

A mother and her three children, trapped in the corner of a village square by a tall thing with six arms. Each arm ended in a snake head; each head darted, snapped and chewed. The victims did not last for more than a few seconds, but in that time their terror was total.

Small things being fired from a huge pot carried under a warrior's arms. They transformed during flight into spiky balls, a tiny mouth at the base of each spike opening and closing. They impacted and twisted in the target flesh, ripping veins, tearing flesh asunder, and the mouths drank their fill.

Other things too terrible to contemplate, too strange to understand. This was a whole new language of destruction and slaughter, wrought over the land with no hope of comprehension. Each utterance meant the death of a dozen, each evil sentence doomed another village.

"Enough!" shouted the King. He had bitten his tongue. He sat up on the cold stone floor, ignoring the pain. There were some agonies greater than the physical, some pains beyond the scope of tears, or raging, or even prayer. "Enough," he said, quieter now. The wizards gratefully relinquished their hold on the spell. The green tinge vanished from the air, sucked back into the crystal with what sounded like a satisfied sigh.

"What can we do?" the King said.

"Sire, there is nothing — "

"Nothing is not a word I wish to hear. I have witnessed the deaths of my subjects. A million more will suffer their fate. 'Nothing' does not count. Tell me anything we can do."

The wizards were silent for a moment. They exchanged the mental equivalent of nervous glances, because each knew what the other was thinking. The unthinkable. The unimaginable. The forbidden.

"There is," Cerniss said, enunciating each word as if talking to a child, "nothing. We. Can. Do... Sire."

The King looked up. There had been a trace of doubt in the wizard's voice.

"Cerniss," he said, "Lewis, Trakiss. You were alchemists, were you not?"

"Of a time, yes, sire," Cerniss said. "You know that very well."

"And mages?"

Lewis nodded.

"Conjurors, warlocks, spellbinders?"

This time, the three wizards did not even react. They knew what was to come.

"Necromancers?"

"It is forbidden," Lewis gasped. "It is forgotten knowledge. It is hated. It is hatred itself. Do you know how the dead despise the necromancer?"

"It is the only way," Kofar said. He walked to the west-facing window, trying to see some sign of the carnage taking place out there. But the landscape looked just as it always did: vegetation weak and bland against the dusty ground; houses huddled around springs, each serving a family unit; other buildings, silos, a dozen graveyards.

His land.

"You *will* help," he said. "You, with your spells weakened by easy living. Your power diminished by the bland sex you indulge yourselves in. You, who came here with me to build a good place to live in this dying world. You will all help."

He turned to look into their eyes. For a moment, he was no longer a King. For these few seconds he was no more than a human being, terrified of his own demise and even more afraid of the manner he now feared that end would take. "You are our only hope."

The wizards did not move. They closed their eyes and lowered their heads in silent conference.

Now, Kofar thought, now is when they flee. Now is when they will combine whatever meagre powers they have left and take themselves away. He averted his eyes for a second and then looked back, fully expecting to be alone in the room.

The three were still there.

From the corner of Lewis' eye, a tear trickled down his cheek.

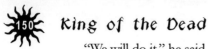

"We will do it," he said.

✳✳✳

The black tide of death had reached several miles inland. Villages lay ruined behind them, inhabitants slaughtered and left hanging from trees, impaled on spikes, spread over the ground in dismembered abandon.

The warriors were whooping, shouting and screaming, their living weapons doing likewise. The blood frenzy was upon them — the frenzy they needed to sate once every lifetime — and now the day would not be over until they had taken their fill. The land was literally awash with blood. Springs in the villages picked up human detritus, and by the time it reached the sea it was flowing red. The island was bleeding to death.

Soon, there would be no life in this place. Its past would be slowly rotting into the ground, unseen by any save the relentless sun.

That is, unless death of another sort could save it.

✳✳✳

"We have not done this for an age," Lewis said.

"Try," said the King. "Just try."

So they tried.

It did not take very long.

The King stood with his back to the window as the three wizards muttered incantations and performed impossible geometries. He could see that this was destroying them — they would surely never recover — but it was a small price to pay. If he could be there instead of them, he liked to think that he would have gladly done so.

There was a scream from outside. For a terrible moment the King thought that the invaders were here already, but when he turned he saw some activity outside a graveyard. People were fleeing in panic...

...as tombs tumbled, and graves burst open, and the dead of Blede rose up, as one, to do the wizards' bidding.

"Send them west," the King said, "send them west, now."

The mindless corpses shuffled between graves, stepping on their brethren, tripping, but still making their way as suggested by the wizards. Some were quite whole, if a little worm-eaten. Others missed limbs, or had mere scraps of dried flesh flapping from old bones, or stumbled around headless. Yet others were barely recognisable as human — single small bones shivering across the ground, an old scalp flitting like a shadow between the feet of the zombies. Soon the whole graveyard was in commotion; it looked as if the ground itself were moving.

"Send them west!"

Something terrible happened. The wizards screamed, as one, the sound of their anguish awful to behold. Kofar clapped his hands over his ears as the three men ran from the room, still screaming, eyes streaming, blood dripping from their hands where they had ground their nails through their skin.

In the wizard's wake, dust spun lazily in the sun slanting through the windows.

The King turned and watched the progress of his new army. His living subjects were in terror of the dead marching through the streets, but that could not be helped. There had been no time for an announcement. No time for consultation. And when they knew what action he had taken, and what a victory had been scored, they would forgive him his impulsiveness.

Then, something else started to happen.

The King saw movement within the palace grounds. There were herbaceous borders, heathers in rockeries growing in designed abandon, roses struggling limply to haul themselves from the poor soil, small trees growing with the aid of sticks to guide their route skyward. And between all these, the ground was shifting.

A fluttering mess of feathers, an injured bird perhaps, trying to gain flight long gone. A larger mass of spikes, an old hedgehog that the King had once watched, but had not seen for ages. It shrugged off the soil of its imprisonment and started to haul itself toward the west-facing gates. Other things too, most of them too small to be perceived properly from the balcony, all of them moving with some grotesque parody of life. Flower heads shook and dropped petals, which instantly began to flutter across the ground like dead butterflies. And dead butterflies followed in their wake, wings holed and chewed by crawling things.

How many dead things? Kofar thought. Slugs, ants, spiders, birds...

He began to be afraid.

He looked beyond the palace again, across to the square where the local market held court each morning. The place was in turmoil. A dusty trail of chopped meats dropped from a table-top and dragged itself slowly down the road. Chops, joints, brains and livers, parts of cows, half of a sheep, a dozen beheaded and plucked chickens, all following in the wake of the army of zombies. Then other tables began to vibrate and shimmer.

The King closed his eyes when he saw a leather bag drop to the ground. He did not want to believe.

He hauled the balcony doors shut, dropped the curtains, cutting out the sunlight. He could still hear, though. Still hear the scraping of dead feet across dusty ground. Still hear the moist slithering of things leaving the royal gardens, things long dead. And he could hear another noise: the rasping of sand against the palace walls; the whisper of dust taking to the air, as if picked up by a typhoon and flung about.

But there was no breeze today. Only the dust of the ancient dead, galvanised by the wizards.

The King rushed to the crystal where it lay dead and wan in its mount. He uttered the weird incantation Creetha had bestowed upon him, and instantly he could see the three wizards. They huddled in their separate chambers, crying, shaking, raging and mumbling. They held themselves, as if to give comfort.

It all came to be too much for Lewis. At a few whispered words his thumbnail grew in length, and he used it to open the arteries of his neck. As his blood pumped from his body, he smiled a smile of relief.

✳ ✳ ✳

The invading warrior hordes were unused to defeat.

It took them a while, then, to realise what was happening.

A forest of dead things sprouted from the ground before the advancing horror. People buried in mass graves during the Plagues hauled their pustulant remains up and out of the dank soil; horses, thrown into farm ditches when they died toiling on the land, found their legs and cantered at the wall of warriors; all the dead came to life, and in a land with a history as long as Blede's, the dead were the majority. People, birds, moles, horses, sheep, chickens, wasps, flies, foxes, grasses, plants, dried husks of trees, even the fossilised forms of things long vanished from the face of the world pushed themselves up from their ancient homes. And they fell upon the hordes like a wave onto a beach.

The warriors fought as they always fought, with no thought of defeat. But their living weapons had little taste for dead flesh, and the dead were stronger than the living because they had so little to lose. As each warrior died — bony fingers in brains, the dust of the ancient dead searing flesh from bones — so his or her remains were galvanised by the spell and turned upon their fellow invaders. With each success, the dead's numbers swelled.

The dead poured through the invader's ranks, leaving islands of resistance like rocks poking their heads above an incoming tide. The dusty, wet and putrid corpses continued on, smothering a warrior here, snapping the head from a weapon there, always adding to their bewitched numbers and, with every victory, ensuring even more the defeat of the invaders. In places, only the weapon of a warrior was gashed or sliced or squeezed — once dead, it would move again under a different impulse.

The air itself became animated with necromantic life. The sun darkened as clouds swept in from the island's centre, the particles the size of dead birds down. They were swept upon an unnatural wind — the breeze of the wizard's commands, even though there were now only Cerniss and Trakiss left alive. The cloud made a strange noise: first a whisper; then a hiss, as it closed in on the struggling hordes; they a scream, part friction, part unholy rage that so many had been awakened to perform such an unnatural task. The pain of the dead merged with the dust of their primordial bones, and for the first time — the first time ever, the first time since their nomadic, pillaging existence had begun — the warriors showed fear.

Those that remained turned and fled towards the sea. In their growing panic they knew that they ships were gone, victims of their own greed, laying now at the bottom of the harbour and already melting down into the silt of centuries.

But there was nowhere else to go.

* * *

The King shook in his resplendent sackcloth robes as the noise from outside grew. First it had been the sound of turning earth and opening graves. Then other things — slithering things — had added to the concerto. Now the air itself was alive, rasping at the walls, picking at the shutters with particular care. There were no more screams from his subjects.

"Send them west!" he shouted at the crystal, but of course he knew that his words would not be heard by the wizards. From what he could see, he guessed that they would not hear him were he standing directly next to them.

Cerniss moved, a flash of dark cloak. The King squinted into the crystal, because something was obscuring his vision. Then he saw that Cerniss' chambers were alive — or dead — with the dust of ages, and the wizard knew what was happening, and the King watched just long enough to see the old man strike his head against the wall, repeatedly, denying the dead their bounty.

Trakiss swallowed a potion and died.

The crystal darkened, its mission now pointless as the three wizards were dead. But the noise from outside continued to grow, and on occasion a terrified scream still found its lonely way to the King's ears.

He turned from the crystal — but glanced back once more as green light shimmered in its hazy depths. This was a sickly green, the green of marsh gas, poisonous and corrupt. He closed his eyes. He did not want to see. But see he did, when seconds later he looked again.

The three wizards — Lewis with throat still seeping, Cerniss' forehead smashed into a fluid pulp, Trakiss pale from the awful route he had taken from life — were standing in their rooms. Staring. Through the crystal, and into the eyes of their King.

❋ ❋ ❋

The invaders had never met the victims of their crimes. They had no enemies.

The dead of the villages fell upon the warriors and inflicted terrible, torturous deaths upon them. The invaders screamed for mercy and forgiveness, but this merely enraged the bloody dead more and made the torture worse.

Some survived. Managing to keep ahead of the dust clouds, the swarming zombies, the particles of enlivened bone and gristle and desiccated flesh, a handful of warriors made it back to the cliffs above the port. There they fought with the living-dead militia, and fewer still made it past. They headed down the paths to the harbour, knowing that there were still more dead to deal with down there, but also believing that it was their only way out.

They were correct in most respects, save one: there was no way out. Death is the most natural thing about living.

As the invaders swept down the hillsides back into the harbour — the stragglers being picked off by the teeming dead — there was movement ahead of them. Wet, salty movement; green-tinged with decades of algae growth; tentacles of semi-liquid flesh shifting in the dust. They ran on regardless, having no choice in the matter, and prepared to fight.

The potential invaders of old rose up, shoving aside the rotted wrecks of their ships, shrugging skeletal shoulders clad in rusted steel armour. Plucked from the sea bed by the present invaders' blood-waves, they stood on their enemies' ground aeons after originally intended. The warriors saw, and screamed their terror, but the wall of living dead drove them ever onward, into the welcoming embrace of the reanimated.

A handful made it through. They stood at the harbour-side, wandering what to do, looking back fearfully at the horrendous spectacle bearing down upon them. They raised their arms, but their weapons were sentient too, and where there is a mind there is a threshold of terror: most were now way beyond that fine line.

The sky was black with the swirling detritus of past lives, old bodies, lost times. The ground was smothered by a teeming carpet of dead things, squirming their way down the hillsides, plunging from the cliffs to be dashed on the rocks below, rising again to continue their relentless mission. Death did not differentiate between friend and foe, good and bad: civilians walked alongside the militia; bony remains stumbled into shuffling warriors. A sea of bodies swept down to meet the natural sea, the expanse of water that had kept Blede free and unconquered for too long for any living soul to remember.

The remaining warriors — killers, rapists and plunderers all — knew that they were doomed. But as was their wont they stood their ground and raised their useless, petrified weapons. There was fight left in them, if they had the chance. Defiance, and a stunned disbelief at what had happened.

Their doom, however, came from another quarter.

The dead ships of their own fleet rose as one from the harbour floor, bubbles of vile gas preceding them, and rushed at the ruined harbour wall. When the waves of water receded, eddies of undead followed. The harbour was overrun. No living thing remained, yet nowhere was still, nowhere was silent.

The dead surveyed their domain, spied no living victim, and once again turned their backs on the sea.

✳ ✳ ✳

Before his death, the King was afforded one final ignominy.

He had hurried down curving staircases to lock himself in the deep basements of the palace. They stank of stale wine and old mould smothered by new. They were still, as yet, but Kofar could not forget the eyes of his dead wizards staring at him. And now the crystal showed the King what remained of his domain.

There was nothing left worth living for.

The basements began to hum and whine with the hint of approaching chaos. The stench of rot wafted from shadowy corners. Kofar began to wonder at his reign, question whether his decisions had been the right ones, but all that was academic now. If he realised he had been wrong all along, there was no one left to apologise to. The sound increased in volume, rising from a deep rumble that shook his bones to a high pitched, ear-spiking scream. Sickly green light from the crystal filled the chambers, and though he was determined to look at it no more — the sight of the devastated Blede was too much, too much — it illuminated other things for him.

The floors, waving and creeping with dust.

The air, shimmering where vicious sand-spirals scoured their way toward his soft, thin skin.

The walls, dripping with the memory of dried blood.

Shadows slipping from doorways and solidifying into the shapes of his predecessors — the traders, sailors and farmers who had ruled this land before him, and built this palace, and laid their dead down to rest forever in its cool basements.

Never suspecting that even eternal rest can be disturbed; that death is not, necessarily, the end.

* * *

Eventually, the spell wore away. After many years, with the sun shining down sadly at the ruined isle, the walking, crawling and flowing dead became weary of their constant resurrection, and they laid down to rest once more. The land was covered with the material waste of their degrading bodies. The sea plucked bones and scraps of cloths from the shore, sucked them out, threw them back in again at hide tide, like driftwood.

The palace stood in the dry atmosphere, its joints slowly corroding, its walls eventually slumping to the ground as if in slow-motion death.

Market stalls stood for centuries, awaiting ghost traders.

And if a sea bird ever mistook the island for a place of rest and landed on its tainted soil, the poisoned atmosphere killed it within minutes. Then, just for a few hours, it would rise again, and flutter a flightless, pointless journey until it fell once more, forever.

Recipe for Disaster

You will need:

A group of people randomly linked through fate; interactions of personalities coming together to make a whole; a mix of neuroses and manias chewing at each other to make a stew of struggle and counter-struggle.

Proportions do not matter. Life is not an exact science.

Take one woman:

Like this one. A giver of keys; the key to one's soul, so that locked routes to life may be opened. A preacher to the converted, maintaining a rate of recovery for those who, so little time ago, wallowed in pits of despair. Her keys are precious, lined with a belief in the power of hope.

Her eyes are wide, because she does not want to miss anything. Mostly, she loves it all. Usually, her mind is bright and free, alight with the possibilities inherent in her vocation. To bring hope. To banish hate, and fear, and depression.

But sometimes, she is sucked into the monster she seeks to destroy. It eats her up, this monster, chewing on her flesh until it tingles with acidic twitches, gnawing at the reptilian stem of her brain and pumping in suggestion after suggestion. Fear, fear, fear. Hate, hate, hate.

That's why she does what she does. She knows what hopelessness can do to someone. She was once hopeless herself.

She leaves her flat and sings softly as she walks down the darkened staircase. She has no need of the light, because today she does not fear the dark. Today, everything is light. It is cloudy outside but her outlook is bright, and she waves gaily to the postman as he scissors over dividing walls.

"Brian," she says.

"Hope."

She sometimes thinks that her parents' choice of name could have dictated her mentality, her career, her life and, ultimately, the course and cause of her death.

Other times, it's just a sick joke.

"Nice day," she says, rattling her keys against the scabbed paint of her Mini.

"Cloudy," Brian replies from across the street.

"The sun's still there, above the clouds. Any post for me, Mr. Postman?"

Brian smiles. "Oooh yes, wait a minute." He rummages in his bag, brings out letters and bills and secret words all fused together by an elastic band. Hope often wonders what all-encompassing secret she would find, were she to receive all the mail in the world for just one day. How much despair would be there, and what proportion would it amount to? It is a depressing fact that most people communicate better when they have something to get them down.

"Thanks," says Hope as she takes the wad of letters. Bill, credit card application, bill...

Letter. With *his* scrawl across the front, words twisted together like the dregs of the nightmares he suffers, each curve cutting, each barb sharp.

She feels the kiss of despair at the nape of her neck. It nestles there for a while, massaging her skin, seeking entry to her nerve cortex. She can almost feel its teeth sink into her, and she knows that if it that happens, she is finished. But knowing is no defence. Only hope is a defence, and Hope, sometimes, loses this whenever she hears from him. He is her dark past. He is her living skeleton in the closet of her life, tucked away conveniently and sealed in with superficial imprints of happier times to come.

"Something wrong?" Brian says.

Hope shakes her head. "Nothing I can't handle." And she gets in her Mini and drives away.

Already, it is beginning to crumble.

Strange girl, Brian thinks. Lots of history behind those bright eyes. Lovely. Caring. But a strange girl, nonetheless.

Add one man:

This man. Nathan. Constantly struggling, always striving to

keep the soulbiter at bay. But the soulbiter comes all to often, in his sleep when defences are down and perceived barriers are ineffective. It is sharp, barbed, all teeth and claws and bad intent. It rips his sanity to smithereens and opens up new routes through which the bad dreams can enter. Then it locks them in.

He no longer wants to sleep.

But this is just what the soulbiter wishes, because tiredness makes Nathan all too susceptible to other suggestions. Pain. Hunger. Not a human hunger, but a primeval one, a yearning for what is not his, a quest to subsume that which eludes him. For now, it is happiness. Wherever he finds happiness, he must seek to destroy it. Because he knows he can never have it for himself.

The desires manifest themselves in lethargy. He wears clothes, but they are old and unwashed, and they provide a warning signal for those in the neighbourhood who know him. They know to get out of his way. They know that if they are smiling when he passes them by, he will bite out, strike out, claw at them as if possessed of a desire to wear their insides as a scarf.

If only they knew. It's not their slippery bits he wants. He has no use for insides hanging out. He wants their smiles.

Like a figure from ancient Greece, he pursues his nemesis. Out of his home. Through the streets.

The black gash of the post-box looms ever closer. He sees the black gash, not the bright blood-red surrounding it. He sees the nothing, the darkness, and identifies with it. He tries to squeeze up a smile from inside, but it hurts. He posts the letter, knowing it can never help, she can never be there for him because the soulbiter will always eat her, rip her from him and, when there's nothing else left, lick her essential juices from his skin. But it is the only hope he has to hang onto. He needs hope. He has always needed Hope. Even when he once had her.

A man watches him from a shop window. Poor bloke. Well and truly screwed by life. Miserable as sin. And that twitch! Like he's constantly trying to run away from something but just can't pick up the speed.

Mix in an ex-husband:

Like this one. His knuckles still congealed into broken knots from the beatings he has dished out to his wife. His face a mask of indifference, a wasted mask because it resembles him exactly. Useless as blusher applied to the cheeks of a coy virgin.

He cuddles a drink, supping frequently, replenishing his glass before it is even half-empty. He never wanted to be a glass half-empty kind of person, he had told his wife. He always wanted there to be something positive. Even while he was beating her, he was thinking positive. Perhaps, he thinks, that's why she hung around for so long. Maybe she actually believed him.

The pub is old, grim and grey. The bar is scarred and scored with decades of abuse, like his skin. Harsh words are cut into table tops. The air is dingy and hazed with smoke, hiding the room's main features, just as his long, unhindered hair obscures his face. He can see out, no one can see in. That's just what he wants.

The clientele do not talk to him. But then, neither do they speak to one another. Some would say that this is a pub for losers, but he knows better. His glass is always half-full. This is a pub for winners who simply have not yet been acknowledged. He ignores the whimpering shadows nursing empty, stained glasses in forgotten corners.

He goes to the bar. Double whiskey. He glares at the barman, and smiles; the old man looks like a fly caught in the web of his overhanging hair.

The barman serves, but does not engage the man in conversation. He does not speak to any of his customers. The only person he talks to while he's working is himself. Even then, he waits until he is alone behind the bar once more, and his customers are back on their rickety seats.

"Beat his wife, you know. Drove her mad. Then she got better. So they say."

Marinate in a far-reaching failure:

She had tried. She really had. But the golden key of her hope had failed to even dent the solid wall of despair built up around Nathan's mind. She had never thought she'd encounter a failure, and maybe that's why it bit in so hard. Clung onto her memory with tenacious cruelty. Always there.

As if she even needed to remember. He remembered for her. Sent her letters, hopeless, terrible letters begging one more chance, one more try. But she had given him a dozen 'one more tries,' and they inevitably ended up turning around and fucking her up instead. Dredged up memories. Opened portions of her mind which, she secretly wished, would remain forever locked.

She had seen in him the potential realised in her husband. Her husband had never begged redemption, and she knew that it would never come to him anyway. He was not evil and hopeless; he liked what he did. Whereas Nathan... Nathan, she kept trying to save. But however hard she tried to turn the key, the barrel of his hope had rusted shut long ago.

She tried, they would say at the hospital. She gave her all. But sometimes there's just no hope.

Maybe, they would say, she should have given up sooner.

Throw in an Extinction Level Event:

Careful on the pity, here. Not too much. Because an Extinction Level Event implies humanity moving on (at the very least), and in this unknown place pity may be as misplaced as an objective youth.

Things change. Hope mutates. It is different for different people. Often, optimism hangs around after the very worst calamity. Occasionally, it does not.

Hope has no hope. In a landscape awash with blood, the teeth are well and truly ground into her spine. Her nerves have been hijacked by her constant fear of regression, and all she can see when she closes her eyes are the fists, raising, falling, and his mad eyes staring through his long, sweat-clogged hair.

Not the scenes of devastation as the disease ravages the world.

Not the crying children, their tears blood-red as they nudge the bled-out bodies of their parents.

Not the mouths, hanging open but uttering nothing because screams are drowned in the blood dripping from pores.

Only the fists. The hatred driving them so pure and basic that they pummel down even when the fingers flop brokenly, like loose scarves in the breeze.

Two failures, she realises. One her fault, the other not. One she had forced herself away to turn away from, the other drawn to her by her weakness, grabbing on limpet-like and only letting go after it had seemingly bled her dry.

Both of them impossible to forget. All she had was a false face to hide behind, and now even that was wearing away.

Bring to the boil:

Hope is not eternal. She wanders, trying to avoid the plague. Somehow, it misses her.

Nathan goes to find the post-box, but it is overflowing. There is no longer a dark gash in its face. It is as if a dying population had tried one last time to heal differences, swap a kind word or settle old accounts.

The bad man remains in the bar; he will be there forever. His glass is half full of the black blood that gushed from his nose and eyes in the final minutes of his miserable life.

She walks the streets. There are bodies, but most of them must have remained at home, preferring to die somewhere familiar. A final act of humanity as their insides bled out.

Nathan opens some of the letters. Vitriol spills forth. In none of them does he find salvation. In his muddled mind, he already understands that this end has been inevitable from the beginning.

Hope's ex-husband's hair is stuck to the table, elbows rooted in the pool of hardened blood covering the vandalised surface. Scratched names hidden forever.

Drain off excess:

He feels bad. The soulbiter is on his trail. It has buried its teeth in all and sundry, it seems, but his panic is just as great. Inside — somewhere deep down, where reality may no longer reach — there is a whiff of contentment. Happiness has been wiped away with the wind, swept up into a little pile of smiles against a mythical hillside.

Now, he must find Hope. It is different merely writing to her: impersonal; mysterious. Now, he has to actually find her. He has so much to say that words can never express.

Simmer gently, forever:

Hope is living in an old shop. The window was smashed weeks ago, tins snatched from shelves, water bottles fought over and killed for. Shards of glass still catch sunlight, but they reflect red. Some bodies lay on the pavement, drilled with bullets into blank death. At least they died quickly.

She is eating gone-off cheese and stale bread. She fears the outside, because that is where the disease still stalks the streets. Sometimes she sees a victim, dragging themselves along the gutter, blood spewing from their body to merge underground with the blood of a city. It is ironic that as the veins of the populace purge through pores, so the arteries of the city flow red. A vampiric liaison. Another sick joke.

She has been eaten by the monster, and now she knows only fear. Her spine is crushed between its teeth. Her eyes are still wide, but only because she cannot believe what she sees inside herself. The self-deception she has been a party to.

Nathan steps in. He sees Hope in the corner, covered with old newspapers, and he shouts out in dismay.

In her sleep, the fists keep raining down. Only now, they spray blood as they go, their pores yawning, nails split and dripping.

Nathan kneels down and reaches out, aghast that a face previously so happy could now be moulded with such pain. This is one sad face he never hoped to see. His hunger should never have reached this far.

She pushes his hands away, though her eyes remain shut. Her face is bruised, blood leaking slowly from tiny splits in the skin.

He realises, as he touches her, that the soulbiter is here.

Hope opens her eyes. Her failure is there before her (a downfall borne of falling fists, two failures in one), reaching out, crying clear tears. But suddenly she sees long hair again, mad eyes, flapping fingers spraying red mist across her vision, and she lashes out.

Nathan staggers back and trips onto the shattered plate glass window. He feels the cool kiss of air as the skin of his neck parts. He panics, feeling the soulbiter drawing near. But then, as things become hazy and indistinct, he realises that he may not even be awake when the soulbiter takes its fill.

One prepared earlier:

They may be brother and sister. Part of a happy family, perhaps. Big house, friendly dog, parents both in useful jobs. Good prospects ahead of them, an interest in all things right. Full of hope for a rosy future. Young, viewing the world through filter lenses which hold back all the bad stuff until the teenage years, when it all comes flooding through. When they realise what the noises in the night may mean. When they see the tensions and stresses, where before there was only their own happiness to discern. When their perception spreads.

But even then, hope seems eternal, invincible. It is the horizon, shining through the dark with a promise of life everlasting. It manifests in the shape of a first love, a composite of a smile and a laugh and a long-remembered fumble in a forest. It is always there. Unchanging. A constant throughout their life.

If only they knew.

The Beach

"Sunday," Ray said.

I nodded. "Sunday. Day of rest." From behind us, the regular crack of rifles.

He sighed. "I'm dead beat. Stiff as a bugger. Do you think there's any hope?"

Without looking at him, I uttered something between a giggle and a sob. I'd been feeling pretty weird lately. "There's always hope. So long as we have bullets, there's always hope." I drew a shape in the dew-speckled grass, but did not know what it was meant to be.

"Cliché King strikes again."

We faced the house because it implied normality, a façade from the past. It stood alone on the plain, a supposed retreat from all that was happening. We had come here because we thought it would be safe. We though nobody else would know about it. Our complacency had marked us out.

Behind us, another cascade of rifle shots. Ammunition was running low. The snipers were using their rounds sparingly, trying to line up two or more to make the most of the shot. Each miss was another two steps closer to the end; each hit was merely one.

"I never thought it would end like this," Ray said. "When we came here, I mean. I thought it would be safe. We can see for miles around. I thought it'd be safe." He often used the word *safe;* as if repetition could imbue it with power over unrelenting reality.

I glanced at my watch, but did not know the time. The smashed face recorded forever the instant of my fleeing the city, where I had abandoned Gemma to her fate. She had been dead already, but I could have done so much more for her. I hated myself for that. I hoped she did not hate me too.

Sometimes I thought I saw her on the distant hillside, shuffling towards the house with interminable, relentless steps. I prayed every night that it would not be my shift when she arrived.

"Our shift," I said. Ray and I stood, turned from the house — the mental placebo for our sickness — and faced the real world.

I took a rifle from Dawn. I smiled encouragingly, but she had been at the barricade for two hours, and her face was moulded grim.

The gun was still hot. The rack of magazines was sadly depleted. I'd have to make every shot count.

There must have been a million of them. They seemed to be coming here from all over the world. Dead but walking, all their stagnant attention was focussed on our house. We were the centre of the world, and it was hopeless. I wished they would all turn around and walk back the way they had come, but eventually, I knew, they would simply travel around the globe and reach us from the opposite direction.

I took aim and fired. A head exploded into dry brains and shattered skull.

We were an island in a sea of moving dead. They walked over the pathetic corpses of those we had already shot. They came slowly, like a glacier of doom, guaranteed to sweep us away eventually but content in the knowledge that they need not rush things.

I took aim and fired. One went down with half a head, the bullet ricocheting and punching through the spine of another. A bullet well spent.

In the distance, flaming red hair. A smile borne of decomposition, not love. Gemma.

It would be another hour or so before she was near enough to be worth shooting. It was an hour I spent reliving our time together, like an extended flashback experienced by a drowning man. And I was drowning. Choking on the inevitability of things. Putting off the end, as mankind had for decades, the difference being that I had no faith in redemption. I was not waiting for God to intervene; I simply wanted a few more hours of life.

At the end of the hour, when she was close enough for me to see the empty sockets where once resided the eyes I loved, I took aim and pulled the trigger. But there were no more bullets left.

Reconstructing Amy

Sometimes life changes without letting anyone know. It's said that a child becomes an adult when he or she recognises the fact of their inevitable death. And perhaps the process of death begins when the realisation that a partner is never, ever coming back first strikes home.

Jake had been dying for months. Amy had gone, but it was only now — in cold, dark nights haunted by 'mares and nail-torn sheets — that he had begun to accept that she was gone for good.

He avoided sleep, just as a drug addict on the mend will try to steer clear of all their old haunts. But Jake's drug was contained within: Amy, injected through recollection, snorted with each fleeting image of her face. However far he walked — through streets pocked with violent rain and parks teeming with invisible night life — his addiction held on to him. It wasn't that he did not want to remember his darling wife; it was just that he could not bear the awful, final truth of her death.

In a village like this traces of Amy were everywhere, not only in memory, but in reality too. With each breath he might inhale a part of her final sigh; any speck of dust on a café window could be a part of her skin. In pubs where they had drunk together, her fingerprints may still mark a glass, or an ashtray, or the underside of a table where she had always checked for rogue chewing-gum.

If he saw a friend across the street, and they came over to see how he was doing, their first thoughts were always of Amy. He knew this because he could see her reflected in their eyes, as though she were standing just behind him.

He chose nightime to walk the streets; there were fewer people to hide his grief from. There was also less to see, so his mind turned inward, which he liked.

Until he saw the ragged little mess in the gutter.

At first, he thought it was a child. He stopped, looked around with a sudden, irrational guilt, certain that accusing eyes would fall on him and mark him forever as the killer. Then concern took over, and Amy's voice came from memory. *You're a good man, Jake.* He hurried along the wet pavement, trying to see further than he could, attempting to make out the truth before he was close enough to do so.

It was a rag doll. He picked it up. It did not belong in the gutter and although he would never want it, he felt the need to put it somewhere dry. It was heavy with water and he recalled reading somewhere that dead bodies appeared to put on weight. Its original eyes had been lost and replacements painted on. In the rain the paint had run, and now it cried blue and black tears.

It had Amy's nose. Small, slight, upturned, a dainty baby's nose, he had always told her.

He sits next to her in their back garden, running a blade of grass up and down her top lip, trying not to laugh and wake her. Her hand comes up and waves him away, but her eyes remain closed. The sun has dipped noticeably before she stirs and swats him across the head, and he eats the blade of grass, straddles her on the seat and tickles until her cheeks turn red with backed-up laughter.

Night and rain closed in, and this time his look of guilt was different. What if the doll's owner was sitting at a window, looking out to see if anyone would be cruel enough to steal their favourite toy?

He shoved it inside his coat and walked home. The dampness felt comfortable against his skin, like the tears of someone familiar.

✳✳✳

"How're you doing?" Jamie said.

Jake knew what he meant. "Learning to live without her." The bar was noisy and smoky, just how he liked it. That way, nobody could hear him breathing. He may as well have not been there.

He had met up with Jamie after work and now they were half way through a bottle of good Irish whiskey. *I've kissed the Blarney Stone,* Jamie said before every swig of the potent brew. Amy had always said he was good value; undemanding, intelligent, entertaining company. He had also been a very good friend to both of them, and a rock since Amy's death. Tonight, Jake could hardly wait for him to go home.

"Move on, Jake," Jamie said.

The wrong thing, always the wrong thing. People told him to move on, place Amy in the fond shadow of memory, don't worry about things, everything would be all right. But none of them had lost her. None of them had held her one night, then held only cold air the next, not even able to find warmth because their shuddering loss drove away everything but misery.

"I'm moving on all the time," Jake said, not angry. "There's a difference between moving on and forgetting. Time moves me on, but it also makes me remember. Every minute of the day is another minute I spend on my own. Without Amy." He took a slug of whiskey and grinned. He laughed at the foolishness of those who drank to forget. How could he ever forget Amy, ever, for even a second? It would be like missing a breath.

One day that would happen. No more breaths. All he had to do was to find a way to fill the days between then, and now.

"More Scotch!" he quipped, his playful tone fooling Jamie.

"It's Irish, you fool!" Jamie shouted, clapping Jake on the back, slamming his palm down on the bar. "Barman! Bring a further bottle of Ireland's finest, if you would be so kind."

Jake smiled and sipped and Jamie talked and poured. Jake had placed the rag doll on the landing; it had seemed the right location, there was no other reason. A wet patch had appeared around it after the first hour as collected rain fled the body, but the heating soon dried it into a vague stain. Every time he walked by, he bent down and tweaked its nose. Last night, when the past shouldered him from sleep and the unbearable present slapped him around the face, he went out onto the landing and tickled the doll's nose, careful not to wake it, smiling as he recalled the smell of Amy's breath.

Then he had gone back to sleep. Dawn had come without another nightmare.

"Jamie, I'm going," he said, slipping from his stool and twisting his ankle as he hit the deck. There was a muffled rustle of interest from around the bar — the squeal of moved chairs, sniggers, a high laugh — then Jamie was pulling him to his feet and guiding him from the smoky room.

"Moved on," Jake said, laughing through tears he did not even know he was crying. "I've moved on, eh, Jamie? Moved on. Amy? Amy who?" But it was a sad display, not humourous, and somehow the other patrons knew this. Eyes were averted as Jamie dragged his crying, slurring friend out into the night.

***

There was something in his jacket pocket. It had hard angles and uncomfortable edges, but when it hit daylight it took form. A doll, all pink plastic, cherubic cheeks, knotted hair and grotesque lipstick smile. How the fuck it had got there he had no idea, but the nuclear hangover which was just kicking in hinted that anything, truly anything was possible. He sat up slowly and the doll let out a long, painful groan.

Jake shouted, hurting his head and shocking himself even more. The doll bounced from his knees and hit the floor, groaning again. Things went fuzzy for a while as his blood found its own level. Time seemed to dilute his foolish fears, for when he picked up the doll once more he could see that it was one of those fancy ones — sold via mail order, no doubt — with its own tilt-action voice. Conversations would be sparse, Jake knew.

"Who are you, then?" he asked softly.

Tilt. "Woorrgghhh."

"And what were you doing in my pocket?"

Tilt. "Woorrgghhh."

"And look at your…" The doll's eyes were big and green. Just like Amy's. Clover eyes, his mother-in-law had called them, gained from her supposed Irish ancestry which Amy had maintained was a complete myth, made up by her mother to give their family some glamour. It's not that her mother found Ireland in particular glamorous, but the fact that it was somewhere she'd never been was enough.

Jake had never realised just how deep a doll's eyes could be.

Amy glances at him as they drive through country lanes, raising one eyebrow and smiling sexily. Jake feels so content sitting with his arm resting out of the open passenger window, smelling the air blasting through the car: cut grass; the tang of a summer shower; fields of rape casting yellow shadows across the landscape. Amy slows the car and pulls into a lane leading to an open gate, the field beyond standing fallow. *What?* he says, but she smiles and does not reply. Instead she shrugs her blouse off her shoulders and unhooks her bra, freeing her breasts to the warm air. She says nothing, but her eyes tell him everything. *I love you,* they say. Let's have fun, let's be daring, like when we were courting, they say. Jake loves Amy. He is never one to argue with her. They make hay.

Jake stumbled from his bed and walked slowly across the landing to the toilet. The rag doll was still there, still sniffing the air with Amy's nose. He put the new plastic doll down next to the bath while he pissed and it ended up staying there. It watched him strip and shower, and even though his head felt fit to burst his cock twitched and stood to attention under the doll's gaze.

Later he went out for a walk to clear the cobwebs, tickling the rag doll under its nose as he passed by. The scratching of his fingernail sounded like a dry giggle. Jamie rang just as he was opening the door. "Jake, let's get away for a while," he said. "Let's up and leave. You could do with a break, and I'd like to go with you. Let's go to the New Forest, or something. Do some tree climbing."

Jake said no thanks and went on his way. He put his head down and smoked so that nobody would want to talk to him.

***

Amy had loved the woods. Jake had always hated them — they made him itch and the birds spooked him because they were always out of sight — but today he needed to be there. They were quiet. No one would tap him on the back and ask how he was doing.

Amy had always been one for larking around when they came for a walk, as if to pass the threshold between field and wood was to shrug off adulthood and rediscover the careless, aimless abandon of youth. Jake had never been able to do this — Amy always mocked that he'd never even been a kid — and so he'd used to watch as she ran and rolled and climbed, exploring shadowy holes in the ground, peering between old trees to find something older, running away and hiding from him until he passed from angry to unsettled. And she climbed. She loved to climb. She'd been a tomboy when she was young, she said, and Jake could well believe it. She was thin and wiry, and when she swung herself up into the trees he just stood and gazed in marvel at her athleticism. He had never really liked these trips. But he put up with them because he knew Amy would always come home invigorated, and the first thing she'd want to do is make love hard and fast in the shower. So, the woods weren't all that bad.

Today they seemed even quieter than usual. There was the occasional twitter of a bird hidden somewhere high in the canopy, a rustle and scratch as some small mammal scampered through the undergrowth, but other than that all was silent. Jake followed the well-worn path which came out on the other side of the woods by the village shops. He'd buy a paper and some orange juice, try to dilute his hangover with vitamin C while reading about all the woes of the world.

He recognised parts of the wood, even though he had not been here since Amy's death. A place where they had laughed and shouted and been bitten by wood ants as they watched the thousands of little creatures hurry about on their huge nest. Jake had wanted to throw a caterpillar in there to see what happened, but Amy hadn't let him. She said it was cruel, and how would he like it. A small bridge spanned a dry stream. Their initials were carved here somewhere, another youthful antic Amy had been guilty of one summer day several years ago.

Jake shut his eyes. He did not want to see their names. He hated the thought that a scar in old wood still existed, while the person who had whittled it there was little more than dust in his own frequent tears.

He reached the shops and tried to buy some orange juice, but there were several people in there and they assaulted him with their pitying gaze. He turned around and walked out, back strafed by sibilant compassion. He went to the baker's instead and bought a fresh loaf without looking up from the display case. "Forty pence," the baker said, but Jake could hear the undertones: *My God, his wife died, how can he handle that, poor bastard, what could I say, should I say anything, maybe best to just let him go ...*

Back in the woods again, because the roads were busier now and there was always the chance of someone stopping and offering him a lift, and by the way how are you coping now that you're on your own...

Besides, from this end the woods looked nice. Welcoming. And even though memories of Amy made him sad, still he needed to remember.

As he passed the tree where she'd had her accident he saw something propped against the trunk. *A doll,* he thought, even before he got close enough to see properly. Why he would think that he did not know, but he was right, it was a doll, though of a sort he had never seen. This one was made of the woods, a construct of twigs and leaves and wet bark and dried plant tendrils. It stared at him with acorn eyes and its fingers pointed with palm-frond dexterity. And its legs... its legs...

Amy climbs the tree, swinging herself from branch to branch, higher and higher. Jake stays below, smiling up at her and bending and twisting so he can see up her skirt. "Great views from up here," she says. "Down here, too," he says. She does a forward roll across a branch to flash her knickers at him, then she slips and falls. "Oh," is all she says as one branch pushes her into another. She hits the ground with a whoosh of air from her lungs, a fart and a crack as something breaks. Jake is there immediately, terrified at what he will see. Her leg is broken badly. She's looking up at him with tears in her

eyes. "Sorry, hon," she says. She spends three weeks in hospital.
He never knew exactly what she'd apologised for.

The doll had a twisted left leg. It was knotted at the knee, just as
Amy's had been, and it was actually a thumbnail shorter that the
other. Just like Amy.

Jake carried the doll home, buzzed all the way by fresh memories he had thought lost forever, each one vibrant and surprising like
a dream recalled after twenty years. The doll sat in the crook of his
arm as if watching the way they were going, ready to object should
he take a wrong turn.

***

It went in the dining room, which only seemed right. Small
insects and dried bark fell from its innards for the first few hours, but
Jake sucked them up with a vacuum cleaner and soon it sat on its
own clean, dry table. He looked at it and remembered Amy's legs
kicking in the tree, curled beneath her as she watched television,
wrapped around his neck as he nuzzled where she loved to be
nuzzled.

He tickled the rag doll's nose on the landing and smiled at the
green eyes in the bathroom.

Later he rang Jamie and suggested a meal. His friend accepted
willingly. Locking the front door behind him he whispered: "Be back
soon." He did not know to whom exactly he was talking, but they
seemed to hear anyway.

***

Jake and Jamie went to a small bistro in a neighbouring village,
intended for tourists but frequented mostly by the bored youths of
the area. Some of them were there now, smoking and looking hard
and flashing tattoos and earrings.

"I've found some things," Jake said, but suddenly he did not feel
like telling. There was something secret about the dolls, a sense of
mystery which felt fresh and naïve but, if revealed, it would take on
a dangerous quality. He glanced at the chair beside him, sure for an
instant that Amy was there. But there was only hazy smoke from the
kid's cigarettes.

"I'll get us a coffee," Jamie said, "then we can order."

Not, *so what have you found, Jake?*. Not, *what were you going to say,
Jake?* He watched Jamie walk to the counter, pick up a menu and
order a couple of coffees. When his friend sat back down he was

taking something from his pocket.

"What did Amy always call me?" Jamie asked suddenly. He barely mentioned her by name since her death, as if to do so would aggravate Jake's grief. "Do you remember?"

"What do you mean?" Jake asked. He felt the sting of tears threatening, coughed as if to blame it on the smoke. Even the mention of her name...

"You remember," Jamie said. He'd taken a small phial from his pocket, clear as glass but apparently flexible. He placed it gently on the table and it sounded like a feather hitting water. "All those times we went out together. All those intimate moments when there was just the three of us, drinking whiskey, talking about books and holidays and God and sex and food."

Jake did recall; those times were often all he thought of, because they were the best they'd had. The times before Amy had gone and walked in front of a car.

"What did Amy call me at the end of those long nights, Jake? When I kissed you both goodbye with the innocence of good friends. When you watched me down the garden path and waved from your doorway as I went out into the night." As Jamie talked he stroked the thing he'd taken from his pocket. It opened slowly, like the accelerated film of a flower turning and facing the sun, and a splash of white light leapt from it and drowned itself in Jake's coffee. "Do you remember?"

"She called you Jamie," Jake said, but even as he spoke he could not picture Amy saying that name. No, not Jamie, something else. She'd called him something else.

They sat in silence for a while until the waiter came to take their order, then Jamie reached across the table and grabbed one of Jake's hands in both of his. There were sniggers from the group of kids; Jamie glanced at them and they were silent.

"Jake," he said, "drink your coffee. Then go to some places." He told him which places.

Jake did not question what he was being told, or even why. After the first whiff of coffee everything seemed to fall into place, and what Jamie was telling him made perfect sense even though the sense was yet to be made. The kids smoking cheap cigarettes glanced over and smiled, the smoke drifting in haloes around their shaven heads. At the first sip — hot, acidic, a tantalising touch to his throat — Amy kissed him on the back of the neck, though when he turned around there was only a man opening a door. The man had a bag over his shoulder which twitched with hidden lives, and Jake only realised as the door closed behind him that it was Jamie.

What did Amy call me? He had asked. *What name did she use?*

Tired, confused and completely rid of his hangover, Jake left the bistro and went to the first of the places Jamie had told him to visit.

✻✻✻

In the public toilet there were three cubicles, two of which were occupied. Jake went into the third and, without locking the door, stuck his hand into the pan. He curved his fingers and felt further around the bend until something solid brushed his fingertips.

It was a beanie doll, clownish colours faded, one eye missing, leaving only the memory of stitches behind. It had Amy's hair — long, dark, wild and yet always right, always perfect.

Amy steps from the shower and shakes her head, hair splaying out and water spraying further still. Jake curses as his clean shirt is spotted and stained. They are going out tonight and they should have left already. Amy giggles at his anger, chases him into the bedroom and squeezes him tight, leaving two large breast-shaped patches on the front of his shirt. It is impossible to be angry with her.

The beanie went in the living room.

✻✻✻

The second-hand shop looked like an explosion in a devout Christian's parlour. Every tacky, exploitive and offensive items of religious paraphernalia ever thought of was for sale here: plastic Christs with glowing eyes; a hundred crosses, all certified portions of the one true cross; self-exorcism kits with warnings on the labels about having to be an adult to buy one. And a Jesus doll, poseable arms frozen by ignorance into a welcoming embrace, one leg missing, the crown of thorns missing too. Jake had felt uncomfortable in the shop until now, because Jesus had Amy's ears. Big ears, hidden beneath flowing locks (or, in this case, stringy horse's hair).

Amy prepares tea in their caravan on the Cornish coast, and the smell tells Jake that the meal will discredit her claim of not being able to cook with the first mouthful. She's often like that, not so much putting herself down as hiding obvious talents in order to produce surprises every now and then. When he opens the door and sees that she is wearing nothing but an apron things get out of hand, and they have pudding first.

The Jesus doll went in the kitchen, ears exposed by a hasty and decidedly unholy haircut.

***

By the end of the day there were no more places to go. So Jake went home.

***

Jake sat on their bed and watched the sun rise over the wooded hills to the east. He had not slept all night. He'd wandered the house, tending the dolls and letting them inspire memories long since forgotten. And all the time he'd been thinking of what Jamie had said the previous day, wondering where all these dolls had come from. Wondering also why it felt as though Amy were strolling around the house with him. Not only did the beanie have her hair, but he could smell her breath when he walked by. The doll with Amy's nose inspired a discorporated giggle as Jake squatted before it, the sort of laugh she'd utter before playing some joke on him. Everywhere in the house reminded him more and more of his dead wife, and yet it was all still memory. Somehow, after the strangeness of yesterday, he had expected a little more.

Then, as the sun rose fully, he remembered what Amy had used to call Jamie.

Angel. Not my angel, or our angel, just plain angel. *See you, angel,* she'd say after a night on the town, and she'd peck him on the cheek. *Hey, angel,* she'd greet him as he stood on their doorstep, a bottle of wine in one hand and a recommended book in the other.

"She called him angel," Jake said. And the house began to breathe.

The Unfortunate

"Oh look," said Adam, "a four-leafed clover." He stroked the little plant and sighed, pushing himself to his feet, stretching his arms and legs and back. He had been lying on the grass for a long time.

He walked across the lawn and onto the gravelled driveway, past the Mercedes parked mock casual, through the front door of the eight-bedroom house and into the study.

Two walls were lined with books. Portraits of the people he loved stared down at him and he should have felt at peace, should have felt comforted... but he did not. There was a large map on one wall, a thousand intended destinations marked in red, half a dozen places he had already visited pinned green. Travel was no longer on his agenda, neither was reading, because his family had gone. He was still about to make a journey, however, somewhere even stranger than the places he had seen so recently. Stranger than anyone had ever seen to tell of, more terrifying, more final. After the past year he was keener than ever to find his own way there.

And he had a map. It was in the bureau drawer. A .44 Magnum, gleaming snake-like silver, slick to the touch, cold, impersonal. He warmed it between his legs before using it. May as well feel comfortable when he put it in his mouth.

Outside, the fourth leaf on the clover glowed brightly and disappeared into a pinprick of light. Then, nothing.

"Well," Adam said to the house full of memories, "it wasn't bad to begin with... but it could have been better."

He heard footsteps approaching along the gravelled driveway, frantic footsteps crunching quickly towards the house.

"Adam!" someone shouted, panic giving their voice an androgynous lilt.

He looked around the room to make sure he was not being observed. He checked his watch and smiled. Then he calmly placed the barrel of the gun inside his mouth, angled it upwards and pulled the trigger.

✸✸✸

He had found them in the water.

At least he liked to think he found them but later, in the few dark and furtive moments left to him when his mind was truly his own, he would realise that this was not the case. *They* found *him*. Gods or fairies or angels or demons — mostly just one or another, but sometimes all four — they appeared weak and delicate.

It was not long, however, before Adam knew that looks count for nothing.

Put on your life jackets, the cabin crew had said. *Only inflate them when you're outside the aircraft. Use the whistle to attract attention, and make for one of the life rafts.* As if disaster had any ruling factor, as if control could be gained over something so powerful, devastating and final.

As soon as the 747 hit the water, any semblance of control vanished. This was no smooth crash landing, it was a catastrophe, the shell splitting and the wings slicing through the fuselage and a fire — brief but terrible — taking out first class and the cockpit. There was no time even to draw away from the flames before everything fell apart, and Adam was ditched into a cool, dark, watery grave. *Alison,* he thought, and although she was not on the flight — she was back at home with Jamie — he felt that she was dead already. Strange, considering it was he who was dying.

Because in the chaos, he *knew* that he was about to die. The sounds of rending metal and splitting flesh had been dampened by their instant submersion in the North Atlantic, but a new form of blind panic had taken over. Bubbles exploded around him, some of them coming from inside torn bodies, and sharp, broken metal struck out at him from all around. The cold water masked pain for a while, but he could still feel the numbness where his leg had been, the ghostly echo of a lost limb. He wondered whether his leg was floating above or below him. Then he realised that he could not discern up or down, left or right, and so the idea was moot. He was blinded too, and he did not know why. Pain? Blood? Perhaps his eyes were elsewhere, floating around in this deathly soup of waste and suffering, sinking to the seabed where unknown bottom-crawlers would snap them up and steal everything he had ever seen with one dismissive *clack* of their claws.

He had read accounts of how young children could live for up to an hour submerged in freezing water. They still retained a drowning reflex from being in the womb, their vocal chords contracted and drew their throats shut, and as long as they expelled the first rush of water from their lungs they could survive. Body temperature would drift down to match their surroundings, heart rate would halve, oxygen to the brain would be dramatically lessened, brain activity drawn in under a cowl of unconsciousness... so why, then, was he thinking all this now? Why panic? He should be withdrawing into himself, creating his own mini-existence where the tragedies happening all around him, here and now, could not break in.

Why not just let everything happen as it would?

Adam opened his eyes and finally saw through the shock. A torn body floated past him, heading down, trailing something pale and fleshy behind it. It had on a pair of shorts and Bart Simpson socks. No shoes. Most people kicked off their shoes in a long-haul flight.

The roaring sound around him increased as everything began to sink. Great bursts of bubbles stirred the horrid brew of the sea, and Adam felt a rush of something warm brushing his back. A coffee pot crushed and spewing its contents, he thought. That was all. Not the stewardess holding it being opened up by the thousands of sharp edges, gushing her own warm insides across his body as they floated apart like lost lovers in the night...

And then he *really* opened his eyes, although he was so far down now that everything was pitch black. He opened them not only to what was happening around him, but to what was happening *to* him. He was still strapped in his seat. One of his legs appeared to be missing... but maybe not, maybe in the confusion he had only dreamed that he had lost a leg. Perhaps he'd been dreaming it when the aircraft took its final plunge, and the nightmares — real and imagined — had merely blended together. He thought he felt a ghost ache there, but perhaps ghosts can be more real than imagination allows... and he held out his hands and felt both knees intact.

Other hands moved up his body from his feet, squeezing the flesh so that he knew it was still there, pinching, lifting... dragging him up through the maelstrom and back towards the surface. He gasped in water and felt himself catch on fire, every nerve end screaming at the agony in his chest. His mind began to shut down —

yes, yes, that's the way, go to sleep, be that child again.

— and then he broke surface.

The extraordinary dragged his sight from the merely terrifying. He was aware of the scenes around him — the bodies and parts of bodies floating by, the aircraft wreckage bobbing and sinking and still smouldering in places, the broken-spined books sucking up water, suitcases spilling their insides in memory of their shattered owners — but the shapes that rose out of the water with him were all he really registered, all he really comprehended. Although true comprehension... that was impossible.

They were fairies.

Or demons.

Or angels.

Or gods.

There were four of them, solid yet transparent, strong yet unbelievably delicate. Their skin was clear, but mottled in places with a darker light, striped like a glass tiger. They barely seemed to touch him, yet he could feel the pinch of their fingers on his legs and arms where they held him upright. The pain seemed at odds with their appearance. He closed his eyes and opened them again. The pain was still there, and so were the things.

They were saving him. He was terrified of them. For one crazy moment he looked around at the carnage and wished himself back in the water, struggling against his seat restraint as it dragged him down, feeling his ears crunch in and his eyeballs implode as awful pressures took their toll, sucking out the last of his air and flooding him and filling him. Perhaps he would see Alison again —

she's dead!

— love her as he had always loved her, feel every moment they had shared. He thought it was a fallacy that a drowning man's life flashes before him. But it was a romantic view of death, and if he had to die then a hint of romance...

"You're not going to die," a voice said. None of the things seemed to have spoken and the voice appeared in his head, unaccented, pure, like a playback of every voice ever saying the same thing.

He looked around at them. He could see no expressions because their faces were ambiguous, stains on the air at best. He reached out and touched one, and it was warm. It was *alive*. He laid his palm flat against its chest.

"That's alright," the same voice intoned, "feel what you must. You have to trust us. If you have to believe we're here in order to trust us, make sure you do. Because we have a gift for you. We can save you, but... you must never forget us or deny us."

Adam held out his other hand. "You're there," he whispered as he felt a second heartbeat beneath his palm. For some reason, it was disgusting.

"So pledge."

He was balanced on a fine line between life and death. He was in no condition to make such a decision. That's why all that happened later was so unfair.

He nodded. And then he realised the truth.

"I'm dead." It was obvious. He'd been drifting down, down, following the other bodies deep down, perhaps watched by some of them as he too had watched. He'd known his leg had gone, he'd felt the water enter him and freeze him and suck out his soul... he was dead.

"No," the voice said, "you're very much alive." And then one of the things scraped its nails across his face.

Adam screamed. The pain was intense. The scratches burnt like acid streaks, and he touched his cheek and felt blood there. He took his hand away and saw its red smear. He looked down at his legs; still whole. He looked back up at the four things that were holding him and his wrecked seat just out of reach of the water. Their attitude had not changed, their unclear faces were still just that.

He saw a body floating by, a person merged somehow with a piece of electrical panelling, metallic and biological guts both exposed.

"We have something to show you," the voice said.

And then he was somewhere else.

✳✳✳

He actually felt the seat crumple and vanish beneath him, and he was suddenly standing in a long, wide street. His clothes were dry and whole, not ripped by the crash and soaked with sea-water and blood. His limbs felt strong, he was warm, he was invigorated. His face still hurt...

The four things — the demons, the angels, whatever they were — stood around him, holding out their hands as if to draw his attention to this, to that. They gave the impression that they lived there, but to Adam they did not seem to feel at home.

"Where is this place?" Adam said. "Heaven?"

"How is your face?"

"It still hurts." Adam touched the scratches on his cheek, but the blood had almost ceased flowing now, and already he could feel the wounds scabbing over. They were itching more than burning. He wondered just how long ago the crash had been.

"You're alive, you see," the voice said, "but we brought you here for a while to show you some things. And to give you a gift. Come with us."

"But who are you. *What* are you?"

The things all turned to look at him. They were still transparent but solid, shapes made of flowing glass. Try as he might, he could not discern any features with which to distinguish one from another, yet they all acted in slightly different ways. The one on his far left tilted its head slightly as it watched him, the one to his right leaned forward with unashamed curiosity whenever he spoke.

"Call us Amaranth," the voice said, "for we are eternal."

Adam thought to run, then. He would turn and sprint along the street, shout for help if the things pursued him, slap off their hands if they chose to grasp at him. He would escape them. He *wanted* to escape them... even though, as yet, they had done him only good.

Am I really here, he thought, *or am I floating at the bottom of the sea? Fishes darting into my mouth. Crustaceans plucking at my brain as these final insane thoughts seek their escape.*

"For the last time," Amaranth said, and this time two of them attacked him. One held him down, the other reached into his mouth and grasped his tongue. Its hand was sickly warm, the skin — or whatever surface sheen it possessed — slick to the touch. It brought his tongue forward and then pricked at it with an extended finger.

The pain was bright, explosive, exquisite. Blood gushed into Adam's throat and he struggled to stand. The things moved aside to let him up and he spat a gob of blood, shaking with shock and a strange, subdued fury.

"You are alive," Amaranth said, "and well, and living here for now. We shan't keep you long because we know you wish to return to your world... to your Alison and Jamie... but the price of our saving you is for you to see some things. Follow us. And don't be afraid. You're one of the lucky ones."

Adam wanted nothing more than to see his family. His conviction that Alison was dead had gone, had surely been a result of his own impending death. And Jamie... sweet little Jamie, eighteen months old and just discovering himself... how cruel for him to suddenly be without a father. How pointless. Yes, he needed to see them soon.

"Thank you," Adam said. "Thank you for saving me."

Amaranth did not reply. Adam was truly alive, the pain in his tongue told him that. This was unreal and impossible, yet he felt completely, undeniably alive. As to whether he really had been saved... time would tell.

One of the things gently took his hand and guided him along the street.

At first Adam thought he could have been in London. The buildings on either side presented tall, grubby facades, with their shopfronts all glazing and posters and flashing neon. A bar spewed music and patrons into the street on one corner, some of them sitting at rickety wooden tables, others standing around, mingling, chatting, laughing. They were all laughing. As he watched, a tall man — hair dyed a bright red, body and legs clad in leather, and sporting a monstrous tattoo of a dragon across his forehead, down the side of his neck and onto his collarbone — bumped into a table and spilled several drinks. Glass smashed. Beer flowed and gurgled between brick paviours. The couple at the table stood, stared at the leather-clad man and smiled. He set his own drinks down on their table, sat and started chatting to them. Adam heard them introducing themselves, and as he and Amaranth passed the bar, the three were laughing and slapping each other's shoulders as if they had been friends forever.

The tall man looked up and nodded at Adam, then again at each of the things with him. His eyes were wide and bright, his face tanned and strong, and it shone. Not literally, not physically, but his good humour showed through. He was an advert for never judging people by their appearances.

Within a few paces the street changed appearance, so quickly that Adam felt as though it was actually shifting around him. He could see nothing strange, but suddenly the buildings were lower, the masonry lighter, eaves adorned with ancient gargoyles growling grotesquely at the buildings opposite, old wooden windows rotting in their frames, pigeons huddling along cills. He could have moved from London to Italy in the space of a second. And if anything the street felt more real, more meant to be than he had ever experienced. It was as if nature itself had built this place specifically for these people to inhabit, carving it out of the landscape as perfectly as possible, and even though the windows were rotting and the buildings had cracks scarring their surfaces like old battle wounds, these things made it even more perfect.

"It's like a painting," Adam said.

"It's art, true." The thing holding his hand let go and another took its place, this one warmer, its flesh more silky. "This way."

The sudden music of smashing glass filled the street, followed by a scream and a sickening thud as something hit the road behind them. Adam spun around, heart racing, scalp stretching as he tried not to imagine what he was about to see.

What he did see was certainly not what he expected.

A woman was lying stretched over the high gutter, half on the pavement, half on the road. As he watched she stood and brushed diamond-shards of broken glass from her clothes. She picked them from her face, too, but they had not torn the skin. Her limbs had not suffered in her tumble from the second-storey window, her suit trousers and jacket were undamaged, her skull was whole. In fact, as she ruffled up her hair, stretched her back with a groan and glanced up at where she had fallen from, she looked positively radiant. An extreme sports fan perhaps. Maybe this was just a stunt she was used to doing day in, day out.

She saw Adam watching her and threw him a disarmingly calm smile. "That was lucky," she said.

"What the hell's lucky about falling from a window?"

She shrugged. Looked around. Waved at someone further along the street. "I didn't die," she said, not even looking at Adam anymore. And without saying another word she walked past him and Amaranth to a small Italian café.

Amaranth steered Adam past the café and into a side alley. Again, scenery changed without actually shifting, as if flickering from place to place in the instant it took him to blink. This new setting was straight out of all the American cops and robber television shows he had ever seen. There was a gutter running down the centre of the alley overflowing with rubbish and shit, boxes piled high against one wall just begging a speeding car to send them flying, pull-down fire escapes hanging above head-height, promising disaster. Doorways hid back under the shadows of walls, and in some of these shadows darker shadows shifted.

Someone rolled from a doorway into their path. Adam stopped, caught his breath, ready for the gleam of metal and the demand for money.

Amaranth paused as well. Were they scared?

And then he realised something else. People had seen him and Amaranth, he had noticed them looking... looking and smiling... and they were not out of place.

"This isn't real," he said, and a shape stood before him.

The man wore a long coat. His hair was an explosion of dirt and fleas and insects, his shoes were burst and his toes struck out, as if seeking escape from the wretched body they belonged to.

He looked up.

"My friend!" he said, though Adam had never seen him before. "My friend, how are you? Welcome here, welcome everywhere, I'm sure. Oh, so I see they've found you too?" He nodded at the shapes around Adam and they shifted slightly, as if embarrassed at being noticed. "They're angels, you know," the man said quietly. "Look at me. Down and out, you guess? Ready to blow you or stab you for the money to buy a bottle of paint stripper."

"The thought had crossed my mind," Adam said, but only because he knew, already, that he was wrong. There was something far stranger, far more wonderful at work here.

"Maybe years ago," the man nodded, "but not any more. See, I'm one of the lucky ones. Take a look!" He opened up his coat to display a glimmering, golden suit. It looked ridiculous, but comfortable. The man *himself* looked comfortable. In fact, Adam had rarely seen anyone looking so contented with their lot, so at home with where and what they were.

"It's... nice," Adam said.

"It's fucking awful! Garish and grotesque, but if that's what I want to be sometimes, hey, who's to deny me that? Nobody, right? In the perfect world, nobody. In the perfect world, I can do and be what I want to do and be, whenever I want. Yesterday I was making love with a princess, tomorrow I may decide to crash a car. Today... today I'm just reliving how I used to be. I hated it, of course; who wouldn't? Today, here... in the perfect world, it's not so bad."

"But just where are we?" Adam asked, hoping — realising — that perhaps this man could tell him what Amaranth would not. "I was in a plane crash, I was sinking, I was dying — "

"Right," the man said, nodding and blinking slowly. "And then you were rescued. And they brought you here for a look around. Well... you're one of the lucky ones. We're all lucky ones here."

There was a noise of something moving quickly down the alley, still hidden by shadows but approached rapidly. For an instant Adam thought it was gunfire and he went to dive for cover... but then he saw the magnificent shape emerge into the sunlight.

"Hold up!" the man said with a distinctly Cockney accent, "'ere comes my ride."

Adam and Amaranth stood aside, and Adam watched aghast as the unicorn galloped along the alley. It did not slow down — did not even seem to notice the man — but he grasped its mane as it ran, swung himself easily up onto its back and rode it out into the street. It paused for a moment and reared up, and Adam was certain it was a show just for him. The man in the golden suit waved an imaginary hat back at Adam, then he nudged the unicorn with his knees and they disappeared out of sight along the street.

He heard the staccato of hooves for a long time.

For the first time he wondered whether it was *all* a display put on for him, and him alone. The red-haired man... the jumper... the down and out. They had all looked at him. Somehow, it was all too perfect.

He pressed his sore tongue against the roof of is mouth.

"Do you get the idea?" Amaranth asked.

"What idea?"

The things milled around him, touching him, and now their touch was more pleasant than repulsive. His skin jumped wherever they made contact. He found himself aroused and he went with the feeling. It did not feel shameful or inappropriate. It felt just right. While he was here, why not enjoy it?

"The idea that good luck is a gift," Amaranth said.

A talent or a present? Adam wanted to ask, but already they were pulling him further along the alley towards whatever lay beyond its far end.

He smelled the water before he saw it, rich and cloying, heavy with effluent and rubbish. As they emerged from the mouth of the alley and turned a corner, the lake came into view. It was huge, not just a city lake, more a sea. Adam was reminded briefly of Venice, but there were no gondoliers here, and the waters were rougher and more violent than Venice ever experienced. And there were things in there, far out from the shore, shiny grey things breaking the surface and screeching before heading back down to whatever depths they came from.

A woman walked past them whistling, nodded a hello, indicated the lake with a nod of her head and looked skyward, as if to say: *oh dear, that lake, huh?* She wore so much jewellery on her fingers and wrists that Adam was sure she'd sink, were she to enter the waters. But she never would, no one in their right mind would, because to go in here would be to die.

Things in there, Adam thought. *Shattered aircraft, perhaps? Bodies of passengers I chatted with being ripped and torn and eaten? Where am I now? Where, really, am I?*

"We stand on the shore of bad luck," Amaranth said. "Out there... the island, do you see?... there live the unlucky ones."

Now that it had been pointed out to him Adam could see the island, though he was sure it had not been there before. *You never notice a damn thing until it's pointed out to you,* Alison would say to him, and he agreed, he was not very observant. But this island was huge... growing larger... and eventually, even though nothing seemed to have actually moved, the lake was a moat and the island filled most of his field of vision.

Sounds reached him then, and they were dulled and weary with distance. Screams, shouts, cries, the rending crunch of buildings collapsing, an explosion, the roar of flames taking hold somewhere out of sight. Adam edged closer to the shore of the moat, straining to see through the hazy air, struggling to make out what was happening on the island. There were signs erected all along its shore. Some of them seemed to be moving. Some of them...

They were not signs. They were crucifixes, and most of them were occupied. Heads lolled on shoulders, knees moved weakly as the victims tried to shift their weight, move the pain around their bodies so that it did not burn its way through their flesh.

Beneath some of the crosses, fires had been set.

"It's hell!" Adam gasped, turning around to glare at the four things with him.

"No," Amaranth said, "we have explained. Those over there are the unlucky one, but they are not dead. Not yet. Many of them will be soon... unlucky ones always die... but first, there is pain and suffering."

Adam felt tears burning behind his face. He did not understand any of this. Sinking into the Atlantic, dying, being a nameless statistic on an airline's list of victims, that he understood. Losing Alison and Jamie, even... never seeing them again... that he could understand.

But not this.

"I want my family," he said. "If you've saved me like you say, I want my family. I don't want to be here. I don't know where here is."

"Do you ever, truly?"

"Oh Jesus," Adam gasped in despair, dropping to his knees and noticing as he did so that the shore was scattered with pale white bones. Washed up from the island of the unlucky ones, no doubt.

He closed his eyes.

And fell into the moat.

❋❋❋

He'd been expecting fresh water — polluted by refuse perhaps, rancid with death — but inland water nonetheless. His first mouthful was brine.

Beneath him, the aircraft seat. Around his waist the seatbelt, which would ensure that he sank to his death. Above him, the wide blue sky he had fallen from.

Under his arms and around his legs, hands lifting him to safety.

"Here's a live one!" a voice shouted, and it was gruff and excited, not like Amaranth or the people he had heard back there in the land of the lucky. This one held a whole range of experience.

"Unlucky," Adam muttered, spitting out sea water and feeling a dozen pains bite into him at the same instant. "Bad luck... "

"No, mate," said a voice with an Irish lilt from somewhere far away. "You're as lucky as fuck. Everyone else is dead."

Adam tried to speak, to ask for Alison and Jamie because he knew he was about to die, he'd already visited Heaven and slipped back again for his final breath. But the bright sunlight faded to black and the voices receded. Already, he was leaving once more...

As he passed out he fisted his hands so that no one or nothing could hold onto them.

❋❋❋

The next time he woke, Alison was staring down at him. There had been no dreams, no feelings, no sensations. It felt as if a second had passed since he had been in the sea, but he knew instantly that it was much longer. There was a ceiling and fluorescent lights, and the cloying stench of antiseptic, and the metallic grumble of trolley wheels on vinyl flooring.

And there was Alison leaning over him, hair haloed by a bright light. "Honey," she said. She began to cry.

Adam reached up to her and tried to talk, but his throat was dry and rough. He rasped instead, just making a noise, happy that he could do anything to let her know he was alive.

"Alive," he croaked eventually. "You're alive."

She looked down at him and frowned, but the tears were too powerful and her face took on the shine of relief once more. "Yes, you're alive. Oh honey, I was so terrified, I saw the news and I knew you were dead, I just *knew*... and I came here, Mum didn't want me to but I just had to be here when they started... when they started bringing in the bodies. And the worst thing," she whispered, touching his cheek, "...I *wanted* them to find your body. I couldn't live knowing you were still out there, somewhere. In the sea." She buried her face in the sheets covering him and swung her arm across his stomach, hugging him tight, a hug *so* tight that he would never forget it.

This is what love is, he thought to himself. *Never wanting to let go.* He put his hand behind her head and revelled in the feel of her hair between his fingers.

"Come on," he said, "it's alright now. We're both alright now." A terrible thought came out of nowhere. In seconds, it became a certainty. *My leg!*

"I am alright, aren't I? Alison, am I hurt? Am I damaged?"

She looked up and grinned at him, red-rimmed eyes and snotty nose giving her a strange child-like quality. "You're fine! They said it was a miracle, you're hardly touched. Bruises here and there, a few scratches on your face and you bit your tongue quite badly. But you escaped... well, you're on the front page of the papers. I kept them! Jamie, he's got a scrap book!"

"Scrapbook? How long have I been here?"

"Only two days," Alison said. She stood and sat on the bed, never relinquishing contact with him, eye or hand. He wondered whether she'd ever let go again.

"Two days." He thought of where he had been and the things that had taken him there. As in all particularly vivid dreams, he retained some of the more unusual sensory data from the experience... he could smell the old back-alley, the piss and the refuse... he could hear the woman hitting the street, feel the jump in his chest as he realised what had happened. He could taste the strange fear he had experienced every second of that waking dream, even though Amaranth had professed benevolence.

A nightmare, surely. A sleeping, verge-of-death nightmare.

"Where's Jamie?"

Alison started crying again because they were talking about their son, their son who still had his father after all. "He's at home with Mum, waiting for you. Mum's told him you fell out of the sky but were caught by angels. Bless him, he — "

"What does she mean by that?" Adam whispered. His throat was burning and he craved a drink. He felt as if someone was strangling him slowly. *Angels, demons, who can tell?*

Alison shrugged. "Well, you know Mum, she's just telling Adam stories. Trying to imbue him with her religion without us noticing."

"But she actually said angels?"

His wife frowned and shrugged and nodded at the same time. This was obviously not how she had expected him to react after surviving crashing into the sea in a passenger jet. "Why, hon? You really see some?"

What would you think if I said yes, he thought.

Alison brought him some iced water. Then she kissed him.

Three days later they let him go home.

✳✳✳

In the time he had been in hospital, several major newspapers and magazines had contacted Alison and offered her five-figure payments for Adam's exclusive story. He was a star, a survivor amongst so much death, a miracle man who had lived through a thirty-nine thousand foot plunge into the North Atlantic and come out of it with hardly a scratch.

Hardly. The three parallel lines on his cheek had scarred. *You were lucky,* the doctors had said. *Very lucky.*

Lucky to be scarred for life? Adam had almost asked, but thankfully he had refrained. At least he hadn't died.

On his first full day back at home the telephone rang twice before breakfast. Alison answered and calmly but firmly told whoever was on the other end to go away and spend their time more productively. On the third ring she turned the telephone off altogether.

"If anyone wants us badly enough, they can come to see us. And if it's family, they have my mobile number."

"Maybe I should do it," Adam said, sipping from a cup of tea. Jamie was playing at his feet, building complex Lego constructions and then gleefully smashing them down again. A child's appetite for creation and destruction never ceased to amaze Adam. His son had refused to move from his feet since they had risen from bed, even when tempted to the breakfast table with the promise of a yoghurt. He loved that. He loved that his wife wanted to hold him all the time, he loved that Jamie wanted to be close in his personal space. Even though his son barely looked up at

The Unfortunate

him — he was busy with blocks and cars and imaginary lands — Adam felt himself at the centre of his attention.

"You sure you want to do that?" Alison asked. She sat down and leant against him, snuggling her head onto his shoulder. He felt her breath on his neck as she spoke. "I mean, they're after sensation, you know that. They're after miracle escapes and white lights at the end of tunnels. They don't want to hear... well, what happened to you. The plane fell. You passed out. You woke up in the fishing boat."

Adam shrugged. "Well, I could tell them... I could tell them more."

"What more is there?"

He did not elaborate. How could he? *I dreamt of angels. I dreamt of demons scratching my face when I did not believe in them, of a place where good luck and bad luck were distilled into very refined, pure qualities. I dreamt that I gave a pledge.*

"You need time at home. Here, with us. Time to get over it."

"To be honest, honey, I don't feel too bad about it all." And that was shockingly true. He was the sole survivor of a disaster that had killed over three hundred people, but all of the guilt and anger and frustration he thought he should feel was thankfully absent. Perhaps in time... but he thought not. After all, he was one of the lucky ones. "Besides," he said quietly, "think of the money. Think what we could do with twenty grand."

Alison did not respond.

He could hear her thinking about it all.

They sat that way for half an hour, relishing the contact and loving every sound or motion Jamie made. He joined them on the settee several times, hugging them and pointing at Adam's ears and eyes, as if he knew what secrets lay inside. Then he was back on the floor, back in make-believe. They both loved him dearly and he loved them too, and what more could a family ask? Really, Adam thought, what more?

There *was* more. The ability to pay the mortgage each month without worrying about going overdrawn. The occasional holiday, here and there. Adam's job as a publishing representative paid reasonably well, and he did get to travel, but Alison's previous marriage had damaged her financially, and they were both still paying for her mistakes. Money was not God... but there really was so much more they could ask.

After lunch, Adam took a look at the numbers and names Alison had been noting down over the past week. He chose a newspaper which he judged to be more serious than most, selling merely glorified news, not outright lies. He rang them, told them who he was and arranged for a reporter to visit the house.

That afternoon they decided to visit the park. It was only a short stroll from their home so they held Jamie's hands and let him walk. The buggy was easier, but Adam liked his son walking alongside him, glancing up every now and then to make sure his dad was still there. Their neighbours said a friendly hello and greeted Adam with honest joy. Other people they did not know smiled and stared with frank fascination. On that first trip out, Adam truly came to realise just how much he had been the subject of news over the past week. The last time these people had seen him he'd been on a television screen, a pixellated victim of a distant disaster, bloodied face stark against the white hospital pillows. Now that he was flesh and blood once more, they did not quite know how to take it.

Just before the park an old stone bridge crossed a stream. Adam loved to sit on the parapet and listen to the water gurgling underneath. Sometimes Alison and Jamie would go on to the park and leave Adam to catch up, but not today. Today she refused to leave his side, and she held their son in her arms as they both sat on the cold stone.

"We'll get moss on our arses," she said, glancing over her shoulder.

"I'll lick it off when Jamie's in bed."

"You! Saucy sod."

"You don't know what surviving a fatal air crash does for one's libido," Adam said, and he realised it was true. He could feel the heat of Alison's arm through his shirt sleeve, feel her hip nudging against his. He felt himself growing hard so he turned away and looked at the opposite parapet. There was a date block in there, testifying that the bridge had been built over a hundred years ago. He tried to imagine the men who had built it, what they had talked about as they were pointing between the stones, whether they considered who would cross the bridge in the future. Probably not. Most people rarely thought that far ahead.

Something glittered in the compressed leaves at the base of the wall. He frowned, squinted, leant forward for a closer look. Something metallic, perhaps, but glass as well. He crossed the quiet road and bent down to see what it was.

"Adam? What have you found, honey?"

Adam could only shake his head.

"Honey, we should go, young rascal's getting restless. He needs his slide and swing fix."

"I'll be damned," Adam gasped.

"What is it?"

He took the watch back to Alison, gently wiping dirt from its face and picking shredded leaves from the expanding metal strap. He showed it her and watched her face.

"Does it work?"

He looked, tapped it against his palm, looked again. The second hand wavered and then began to move, ticking on from whatever old time it had been stuck in. Strangely, the time was now exactly right.

"Looks quite nice," she said, cringing as Jamie twisted eel-like in her arms.

"Nice? It's priceless. It's Dad's. You remember Dad's old watch, the one he left me, the one we lost in the move?"

Alison nodded and stared at him strangely. "We moved here six years ago."

Adam nodded, too excited to talk.

It told the right time!

"Six years, Adam. It's not your dad's watch, just one that looks a bit — "

"Look." He flipped the strap inside out and showed his wife the backside of the watch casing. *For Dear Jack, love from June,* it said. Jack, his father. June, his mother.

"Holy shit."

"Shit, shit, shit," Jamie gurgled, and they looked at each other and laughed because their swearing son took their attention for a moment, stole it away from this near-impossibility.

They walked in silence, Adam studiously cleaning dirt from the watch, checking its face for cracks, winding it, running his fingers over the faded inscription.

At the entrance to the park Alison let Jamie run to the playground and took the timepiece from Adam. "What a stroke of luck," she said. "Oh, you've put it right."

Adam did not say anything. He accepted the watch back and slipped it into his pocket. Maybe this was something that would make a nice end to his interview with the newspaper… but straight away he knew he would never tell them.

With Jamie frolicking on the climbing frame and Alison hugging him, Adam silently began to get his story straight.

✸✸✸

Nobody is news forever, even to the ones they love. Stories die down, a newer tragedy or celebrity gossip takes first place, family problems beg attention. It's something to do with time, and how it heals and destroys simultaneously. And luck, perhaps. It's a lot to do with luck.

Three weeks after leaving hospital Adam's name disappeared from the papers and television news, and he was glad. Those three weeks had exhausted him, not only because he was still aching and sore and emotionally unhinged by the accident — although he did not feel quite as bad as everyone seemed to think he should — but because of the constant, unstinting attention. He had sat through that painful first interview, the paper had run it, he and Alison had been paid. Days later a magazine called and requested one interview per month for the next six months.

The airline wrote to ask him to become involved with the investigation, and to perhaps be a patron of the charity hastily being set up to help the victims' families. A local church requested that he make a speech at their next service, discussing how God has been involved in his survival and what it felt like to be cradled in the Lord's hand, while all those around him were filtering through His divine fingers. The suggestion was that Adam was pure and good, and those who had died were tainted in some way. The request disgusted him. He told them so. When they persisted he told them to fuck off, and he did not hear from them again.

His reaction was a little extreme, he knew. But perhaps it was because he did not know exactly what *had* saved him

He turned down every offer. He'd been paid twenty thousand pounds by the newspaper, and nobody else was offering anywhere near as much. Besides, he no longer wanted to be a sideshow freak: *Meet the miracle survivor!*

The telephone rang several times each night — family, friends, well-wishers, people he hadn't spoken to for so long that he could not truly even call them friends anymore — and eventually he stopped answering. Alison became his buffer, and he gave her carte blanche to vet the calls however she considered appropriate.

This is how he came to speak to Philip Howards.

Jamie was in bed. Adam had his feet up on the settee, a beer in his hand and a book propped face-down on his lap. He was staring at the ceiling through almost-closed eyes, remembering the crash, his thoughts dipping in and out of dream as he catnapped. On the waking side, there was water and the nudge of dead bodies; when he just edged over into sleep, transparent shapes flitted behind his eyes and showed him miracles. Sometimes the two images mixed and merged. He'd been drinking too much that evening.

Alison went straight to the telephone when it rang, sighing, and Adam opened one eye fully to follow her across the room. They had been having a lot of sex since he came home from hospital.

"Hello?" she answered, and then she simply stood there for a full minute, listening.

Adam closed his eyes again and thought of the money. Twenty thousand. And the airline would certainly pay some amount in compensation as well, something to make them appear benevolent in the public eye. He could take a couple of years off work. Finish paying the mortgage. Start work on those paintings he had wanted to do for so long.

He opened his eyes again and appraised his artist's fingers where they were curved around the bottle. He was stronger there, more creative. He felt more of an emotional input to what he was doing. The painting he had started two weeks ago was the best he had ever done.

The Unfortunate

All in all, facing death in the eye had done wonders for his life.

"Honey, there's a guy on the 'phone. He says he really has to talk to you."

"Who is it?" The thought of having to stand, to walk, to actually talk to someone almost drove him back to sleep.

"Philip Howards."

Adam shrugged. He didn't know him.

"He says it's urgent. Says it's about the angels." Alison's voice was in neutral, but its timbre told Adam that she was both intrigued, and angry. She did not like things she could not understand. And she hated secrets.

The angels! Adam's near-death hallucination flooded back to him. He reached up to touch the scars on his cheek and Alison saw him do it. He stood quickly to prevent her asking him about it, cover up the movement with motion.

She looked at him strangely as he took the receiver from her. He knew that expression: *We'll talk about it later.* He also knew that she would not forget.

"Can I help you?"

There was nothing to begin with, only a gentle static and the sound of breathing down the line.

"Hello?"

"You're one of the lucky ones," the voice said. "I can tell. I can hear it in your voice. The unlucky ones — poor souls, poor bastards — whatever they're saying, they always sound like they're begging for death. Sometimes they do. One of them asked me to kill her once, but I couldn't do it. Life's too precious for me, you see."

Adam reeled. He recalled his dream again, the island of unlucky souls surrounded by the stinking moat. He even sniffed at the receiver to see whether this caller's voice stank of death.

"Has something happened?" the man continued. "Since you came back, has something happened which you can't explain? Something wonderful?"

"No," Adam spoke at last, but then he thought, *the watch, I found Dad's watch!*

"I'm not here to cause trouble, really. It's just that when this happens to others, I always like to watch. Always like to get in touch, ask about the angels, talk about them. It's my way of making sure I'm not mad."

The conversation dried for a moment, and Adam stood there breathing into the mouthpiece, not knowing what to say, hearing Philip Howards doing the same. They were like two duelling lovers who had lost the words to fight, but who were unwilling to relinquish the argument.

"What do you know about them?" Adam said at last. Alison sat up straight in her chair and stared at him. He diverted his eyes. He could not talk to this man and face her accusing gaze, not at the same time. *What haven't you told me*, her stare said.

The man held his breath. Then, very quietly: "I was right."

"What do you know?"

"Can we meet? Somewhere close to where you live, soon?"

Adam turned to Alison and smiled, trying to reassure her that everything was all right. "Tomorrow," he said.

Howards agreed, they arranged where and when, and the strangest phone call of Adam's life ended.

"What was that?" Alison asked.

He did not know what to say. What could he say? Could he honestly try to explain? Tell Alison that her mother had been right in what she'd told Jamie, that angels really had caught and saved him?

Angels, demons, fairies... gods.

"Someone who wants to talk to me," he said.

"About angels?"

Adam nodded.

Alison stared at him. He could see that she was brimming with questions, but her lips pressed together and she narrowed her eyes. She was desperately trying not to ask any more, because she could tell Adam had nothing to say. He loved her for that. He felt a lump in his throat as he stooped down, put his arms around her shoulders and nuzzled her neck.

"It's alright," he said. Whether she agreed or not, she loved him enough to stay silent. "And besides," he continued, "you and Jamie are coming too."

He never could keep a secret from Alison.

✹✹✹

Later than night, after they had made love and his wife drifted into a comfortable slumber with her head resting on his shoulder, Adam had the sudden urge to paint. This had happened to him before but many years ago, an undeniable compulsion to get up in the middle of the night and apply brush to canvas. Then, it had resulted in his best work. Now, it just felt right.

He eased his arm out from beneath Alison, dressed quickly and quietly and left the room. On the way along the landing he looked in on Jamie for inspiration, then he carried on downstairs and set up his equipment. They had a small house — certainly no room for a dedicated studio, even if he was as serious about his art now as he had been years ago — so the dining room doubled as his work room when the urge took him.

He began to paint without even knowing what he was going to do.

By morning, he knew that they had lost their dining room for a long, long time.

✻✻✻

"You're a very lucky man," Philip Howards said. He was sitting opposite Adam, staring over his shoulder at where Alison was perusing the menu board, Jamie wriggling in her arms.

Adam nodded. "I know."

Howards look at him intently, staring until Adam had to avert his gaze. Shit, the old guy was a spook and a half! Fine clothes, gold weighing down his fingers, a healthy tan, the look of a travelled man about him. His manner also gave this impression, a sort of weary calmness that came with wide and long experience, and displayed a wealth of knowledge. He said he was seventy, but he looked fifty

"You really are. The angels, they told you that didn't they?"

Adam could not look at him.

"The angels. Maybe you thought they were fairies or demons. But with them, it's all the same thing really. How did you get those scars on your cheek?"

Adam glanced up at him. "You know how or you wouldn't have asked."

Howards raised his head to look through the glasses balanced on the tip of his nose. He was inspecting Adam's face. "You doubted them for a while."

Adam did not nod, did not reply. To answer this man's queries — however calmly they were being put to him — would be to admit to something unreal. They were dreams, that was all, he was sure. Two men could share the same dreams, couldn't they?

"Well, I did the same. I got this for my troubles." He pulled his collar aside to display a knotted lump of scar tissue below his left ear. "One of them bit me."

Adam looked down at his hands in his lap. Alison came back with Jamie, put her hands on his shoulders and whispered into his ear. "Jamie would prefer a burger. We're not used to jazzy places like this. I'll take him to McDonald's — "

"No, stay here with me."

She kissed his ear. "No arguing. I think you want to be alone anyway, yes? I can tell. And later, *you* can tell. Tell me what all this is about."

Adam stood and hugged his wife, ruffled Jamie's hair. "I will," he said. He squatted down and gave his son a bear-hug. "You be a good boy for Mummy."

"Gut boy."

"That's right. You look after her. Make sure she doesn't spend too much money!"

"Goodbye, Mr Howards," Alison said.

Howards stood and shook her hand. "Charmed." He looked sadly at Jamie and sat back down.

Alison and Jamie left. Adam ordered a glass of wine. Howards, he knew, was not taking his eyes from him for a second.

"You'll lose them," he said.

"What?"

Howards nodded at the door, where Alison and Jamie had just disappeared past the front window. "You'll lose them. It's part of the curse. You do well, everyone and everything else goes."

"Don't you talk about my family like that! I don't even know you. Are you threatening me?" He shook his head when the old man did not answer. "I should have fucking known. You're a crank. All this bullshit about angels, you're trying to confuse me. I'm still not totally settled, I was in a disaster, you're trying to confuse me, get money out of me — "

"I have eight millions pounds in several bank accounts," Howards said. "More than I can ever spend... and the angels call themselves Amaranth."

Adam could only stare open-mouthed. Crank or no crank, there was no way Howards could know that. He had told no one, he had never mentioned it. He hadn't even hinted at the strange visions he experienced as he waited to die in the sea.

"I'll make it brief," Howards said, stirring his glass of red wine with a finely manicured finger. "And then, when you believe me, I want you to do something for me."

"I don't know — "

"I was on holiday in Cairo with my wife and two children. This was back in fifty-nine. Alex was seven. Sarah was nine. There was a fire in the hotel and our room was engulfed. Alex... Alex died. Sarah and my wife fled. I could not leave Alex's body, not in the flames, not in all the heat. It just wasn't right. So I stayed there with him, fully expecting rescue. It was only as I was blinded by heat and the smoke filled my lungs that I knew no rescue was going to come.

"Then something fell across me — something clear and solid, heavy and warm — and protected me from the flames. It took the smoke from inside me... I can't explain, I've never been able to, not even to myself. It just sucked it out, but without touching me.

"Then I was somewhere else, and Amaranth was there, and they told me what a lucky man I was."

Adam shook his head. "No, I'm not hearing this. You know about me, I've talked in my sleep or… or… "

"Believe me, I've never been to bed with you." There was no humour in his Howards' comment.

How could he know? He could not. Unless…

"Amaranth saved you?"

Howards nodded.

"From the fire?"

"Yes."

"And they took you… they took you to their place?"

"The streets of Paris and then a small Cornish fishing village. Both filled with people of good fortune."

Adam shook his head again, glad at last that there was something he could deny in this old man's story. "No, no, it was London and Italy and then America somewhere, New York I've always thought."

Howards nodded. "Different places for different people. Never knew why, but I suppose that's just logical really. So where were the damned when you were there?"

"The damned… " Adam said quietly. He knew exactly what Howards meant but he did not even want to think about it. If the old man had seen the same thing as he, then it was real, and people truly did suffer like that.

"The unlucky, the place… You know what I mean. Please, Adam, be honest with me. You really must if you ever want to understand any of this or help yourself through it. Remember, I've been like this for over forty years."

Adam swirled his wine and stared into its depths, wondering what he could see in there if he concentrated hard. "It was an island," he said, "in a big lake. Or a sea, I'm not sure, it all seemed to change without moving."

Howards nodded.

"And they were crucified. And they were burning them." Adam swallowed his wine in one gulp. "It was horrible."

"For me it was an old prison," Howards said, "on the cliffs above the village. They were throwing them from the high walls. There were hundreds of bodies broken on the rocks, and seagull and seals and crabs were tearing them apart. Some of them were still alive."

"What does this mean?" Adam said. "I don't know what to do with this. I don't know what to tell Alison."

Howards looked down at his hands where they rested on the table. He twirled his wedding band as he spoke. "I've had no family or friends for thirty years," he said. "I'm unused to dealing with such… intimacies."

"But you're one of the lucky ones, like me? Amaranth said so. What happened to your family? What happened to your wife and your daughter Sarah?"

Howards looked up, and for an instant he appeared much older than he had claimed, ancient. It was his eyes, Adam thought. His eyes had seen everything.

"They're all dead," Howards said. "And still those things follow me everywhere."

Adam was stunned into silence. There was chatter around them, the sound of Howards' rings tapping against his glass as he stirred his wine, the sizzle of hot-plates bearing steaks and chicken. He looked at Howards' downturned face, trying to see if he was crying. "They follow you?" he gasped.

Howards nodded and took a deep breath, steeling himself. "Always. I see them from time to time, but I've known they're always there for years now. I can feel them… watching me. From the shadows. From hidden corners. From places just out of sight." His demeanour had changed suddenly, from calm and self-assured to nervous and frightened. His eyes darted left and right like a bird's, his hands closed around his wineglass and his fingers twisted against each other. Someone opened the kitchen door quickly and he sat up, a dreadful look already on his face.

"Are they here now?" Adam asked. He couldn't help himself.

Howards shrugged. "I can't see them. But they're always somewhere."

"I've not seen them. Not since I dreamt them."

The old man looked up sharply when Adam said *dreamt*. "We're their sport. Their game. I can't think why else they would continue to spy… "

"And your family? Sport?"

Howards smiled slightly, calming down. It was as if casting his mind back decades helped him escape the curse he said he lived under in the present. "You ever heard Newton's third law of motion? To every action, there is an equal and opposite reaction."

Adam thought of Alison and Jamie, and without any warning he began to cry. He sobbed out loud and buried his face in his napkin, screwing his fingers into it, pressing it hard against his eyes and nose and mouth. He could sense a lessening in the restaurant's commotion as people turned to look, and soon after a gradual increase in embarrassed conversation.

"And that's why I have to ask you something," Howards said. "I've been asking people this for many years now, those few I meet by chance or happen to track down. Amaranth doesn't disturb me; they must know that no one will agree to what I ask. My asking increases their sport, I suppose. But I continue to try."

"What?" Adam gasped. He remembered the certainty, as he floated in the sea, that Alison was dead. It brought a fresh flow of tears but these were silent, more heartfelt and considered. He could truly imagine noth-

The Unfortunate

ing worse... except for Jamie.

"Deny them. Take away their sport. They've made you a lucky man, but you can reject that. If you don't... your family will be gone."

"Don't you fucking threaten me!" Adam shouted, standing and throwing his napkin, confused, terrified. The restaurant fell completely silent this time, and people stared. Some had a look in their eyes... a hungry look... as if they knew they were about to witness violence. Adam looked straight at Howards, never losing eye contact, trying to see the madness in his face. But there was none. There was sorrow mixed with contentment, a deep and weary sadness underlying healthy good fortune. "Why don't you do it yourself! Why, if it's such a good idea, don't you deny them!"

"It's too late for me," Howards said quietly, glancing around at the patrons watching him. "They were dead before I knew."

"Fuck you!" Adam shouted. "You freak!" He turned and stormed from the restaurant, a hundred sets of eyes scoring his skin. He wondered if any of the diners recognised him from his fifteen minutes of fame.

As the door slammed behind him and he went out into the street the sun struck his tearful eyes, blinding him for a moment. Across the pedestrianised area, sandwiched between a travel agent's and a baker's shop, a green door liquefied for a second and then reformed. Its colour changed to deep-sea blue.

Before his sight adjusted, Adam saw something clear and solid pass through it.

***

"So?" Alison asked.

"Fruitcake." He slid across the plastic seat and hugged his son to him. Then he leaned over the food-strewn table and planted a kiss squarely on his wife's mouth. She was unresponsive.

"The angels, then?" She was injecting good cheer into her voice but she was angry, she wanted answers, he knew that. He had never been able to lie to his wife. Even white lies turned his face blood-red.

Adam shook his head and sighed, stealing a chip from Jamie's tray and fending off his son's tomato sauce retribution. He looked up, scanned the burger bar, searching for strange faces he could not explain.

"Adam," Alison said, voice wavering, "I want to know what's going on. I saw the look on your face when you were on the phone to him yesterday. It's like you were suddenly somewhere else, seeing something different, feeling something horrible. You turned white. Remember that time, you tried some pot and couldn't move for two hours and felt sick?

You looked worse than you did then."

"Honey, it's just that what he said reminded me of the crash."

Alison nodded and her face softened. She wanted to keep on quizzing, he could tell, but she was also a wonderful wife. She didn't want to hurt him, or to inspire thoughts or memories which might hurt him.

"And what your mum said to Jamie about the angels saving me. When Howards mentioned angels, it brought it all back. I was sinking, you know? Sinking into the sea. Bodies around me. Then I floated back up, I saw the sunlight getting closer. And... he just reminded me of when I broke the surface." He was lying! He was creating untruths, but he was doing it well. Even so he felt wretched, almost as if he were betraying Alison, using her supportive nature against her. He looked outside and wondered whether those things were enjoying his lies. He felt sick

"Park!" Jamie shouted suddenly. "Go to park! Swing, swing!"

"Alright tiger, here we go!" Adam said, pleased to be able to change the subject. Tears threatened once more as he wrestled with Jamie and stole his chips and heard his son squeal with delight as he tickled him.

Deny them, Howards had said. *If you don't... your family will be gone.*

He thought of the watch, and the interview money, and his painting, and the newfound closeness that surrounded he and Alison and Jamie like a sphere of solid crystal, fending off negative influences from outside, reflecting all the badness that bubbled in the world around them.

How could he give any of this up? Even if it were possible — even if Howards was not the madman Adam knew him to be — how could he possibly turn his back on this?

In the park, he and Alison sat on a bench and hugged each other. Jamie played on a toddler's climbing frame, occasional tumbles making him giggle, not cry. He was an adventurous lad and he wore his grazed knees and bruised elbows as proud testament to this. Adam kissed Alison. It turned from a peck on the lips to a long, lingering kiss, tongues meeting, warmth flooding through him as love made itself so beautifully known.

Then the inevitable shout from Jamie as he saw his parents involved in each other for a moment, instead of him.

"I could have lost you both," Adam said, realising as he spoke how strange it sounded.

"We could have lost you."

He nodded. "That's what I meant." He looked across to the trees bordering the park, but there were no flitting shadows beneath them. Nobody was spying on them from the gate. The hairs on the back of his neck stayed down.

They watched Jamie for a while, taking simple but heartfelt enjoyment in every step he climbed, each little victory he won for himself.

"I started a painting this morning," Adam said.

"I know. I saw you leave the room and heard you setting up."

"It's… incredible. It's already painted it in here," he said, tapping his head, "and it's coming out exactly how I envisaged it. No imperfections. You know the quote from that Welsh writer, *I dream in fire* — "

"— *and work in clay.* Of course I know it, you've spat it out every month since I've known you."

Adam smiled. "Well, this morning I was working in fire. Dreaming and working in fire. I'm alight… my fingers and hands are doing the exact work I want of them. I can't explain it, but… maybe the crash has given me new insight. New vigour."

"Made you realise how precious life is," Alison mused, watching Jamie slip giggling down the slide.

Adam looked at her and nodded. He kissed her temple. He worshipped her, he realised. She was his bedrock.

He could smell the rich scent of flowers, hear birds chirping in the trees bordering the park, feel the warmth of the wooden bench beneath him, taste the sweetness of summer in the air. He truly was alight.

He finished the painting the following morning. That afternoon he called Maggie, his old art agent, and asked her to come up from London, take a look. Two days later he had placed it in a major exhibition in a London gallery.

The painting was entitled *Dreaming in Fire and Ice.* Only Alison saw it for what it really was: an affirmation of his love, and a determination that nothing — *nothing* — would ever rip their family apart. He was a good man. He would never let that happen.

On the first day of the exhibition he sold the painting for seven thousand pounds. That same evening, Alison's elderly mother slipped and fell downstairs, breaking her leg in five places.

✳✳✳

"How is she?"

Alison looked up from the magazine she was not reading and Adam's heart sank. Her eyes were dark, her skin pale, nose red from crying. "Not too good. There's a compound fracture, and they're sure her hip's gone as well. She's unconscious. Shock. In someone so old, they said… well, I told them she was strong."

He went to his wife and hugged her, wondering whether he was being watched by Amaranth even now. He'd seen one of them on the way to the hospital, he was certain, hunkered down on the back of a flatbed truck, raising its liquid head as he motored the other way. He'd glanced in the rearview mirror and seen something… but he could not be sure. The car was vibrating, the road surface uneven. It could have been anything. Maybe it was light dancing in his eyes from the panic he felt.

"Oh honey," he said, "I'm so sorry. I'm sure she'll be alright, she'll pull through. Stubborn old duck wouldn't dream of doing anything otherwise, you know that."

"I just don't want her to meet her god that quickly," Alison said, and she cried into his neck. He felt her warm tears growing cold against his skin, the shuddering as she tried to stop but failed, and he started to cry as well.

"The angels will save her," Adam said without thinking, for something to say more than anything, and because it was what Molly would have said. He didn't mean it. He felt Alison stiffen and held his breath. *They won't*, he thought. *They won't save her. They've got their sport in me.*

Something ran a finger down his spine, his balls tingled, and he knew that there were eyes fixed upon him. He turned as best he could to look around, but the corridor was empty in both directions. There were two doors half open, a hosereel coiled behind a glass panel, a junction two dozen steps away, a tile missing from the suspended ceiling grid. Plenty of places to hide.

"I wonder if she's scared," Alison said instead. "If she's still thinking in there, if she's dreaming. I wonder if she's scared? I mean, if she dies she goes to Heaven. That's what she believes."

"Of course she is, but it doesn't matter. She'll come around. She will." Adam breathed into his wife's hair and kissed her scalp. A door snicked shut behind him. He did not even bother turning around to look.

He knew that Howards was right, purely because his senses told him so.

He was being watched.

✸✸✸

Maggie's call came three days later. A major London gallery wanted to display his paintings. And more than that, they were keen to commission some work for the vestibule of their new wing. They had offered twenty-five thousand for the commission. Maggie had already accepted. They wanted to meet Adam immediately to talk the projects through.

Alison's mother had not woken up, other than for a few brief moments during the second night. No one had been there with her, but a nurse had heard her calling in the dark, shouting what appeared to be a plea: *Don't do it again, don't, please don't!* By the time the nurse reached the room Molly was unconscious once more.

"You have to go," Alison said. "You simply have to. No two ways about it." She was washing a salad while Adam carved some ham. Jamie was playing in their living room, building empires in Lego and then cheerfully aiding their descent.

Adam felt woeful. There was nothing he wanted more than to travel to London, meet with the gallery, smile and shake hands... and to see himself living the rest of his life as what he had always dreamt of becoming: an artist. It was so far-fetched, too outlandish. But he was a lucky man now. The faces at distant windows told him so. He was lucky, and he was being watched.

Deny them, Howards had said. *If you don't... your family will be gone.*

He could still say no. Maggie had accepted but there was no contract, and she really should have consulted him before even commencing a deal of such magnitude. He could say no thank you, I'm staying here with my family because they need me, and besides, I'm scared of saying yes, I'm scared of all the good luck. Every action has an equal and opposite reaction, you know.

There was still money left from the interview. They didn't really *need* the cash.

And he could always go back to work... they'd been asking for him, after all.

"I'm doing some of the best work of my life," he said, not sure even as he spoke whether he had intended to say it at all. "It's a golden opportunity. I really can't turn it down."

"I know," Alison replied. She was slicing cucumber into very precise, very regular slices. It was something her mother always did. "I don't *want* you to turn it down. You have to go, there's no argument."

Adam popped a chunk of ham into his mouth and chewed. "Yes there is," he said around the succulent mouthful. "The argument is, your mum is ill. She's very poorly. You're upset and you need me here. And there's no one else who baby-sits Jamie for us on such a regular schedule. I could ask my parents down from Scotland... but, well, you know."

"Not baby types."

"Exactly."

Alison came to him and wrapped her arms around his waist. She nuzzled his ear. When she did that, it made him so glad he'd married someone the same height as him. "I know how much you've been aching for this for years," she said. "You remember that time on holiday in Cornwall... the time we think we conceived Jamie in the sauna... remember what you said to me? *We'll have a big posh car, a huge house with a garden all the way around and a long gravel driveway, a study full of books, you can be my muse and I'll work by day in the rooftop studio, and in the evenings I'll play with my children.*"

"What a memory for words you have," Adam said. He could remember. It used to be the only thing he ever thought of.

"Go," his beautiful wife said. "I'll be fine. Really. Go and make our fortune. Or if you don't, bring a cuddly toy for Jamie and a bottle of something strong for me."

Good fortune, he thought. *That's what I have. Good fortune.*

Deny them, Howards had said. But Howards was a crank. Surely he was.

"Fuck it," he whispered.

"What?"

"I'll go. And I promise I'll be back within two days. And thanks, honey."

Later that night they tried to make love but Alison began to cry, and then the tears worsened because she could not forget about her mother, not even for a moment. Adam held her instead, turning away so that his erection did not nudge against her, thinking she may find it horrible that he was still turned on when she was crying, talking about her injured mother, using his shoulder as a pain-sink.

When she eventually fell asleep he went to look in on Jamie. His son was snoring quietly in the corner of his cot, blankets thrown off, curled into a ball of cuteness. Adam bent over and kissed his forehead. Then he went to visit the bathroom.

Something moved back from the frosted glass window as he turned on the light. It may have been nothing... as substantial as a puff of smoke, there for less than a blink of an eye... but he closed the curtains anyway. And held his breath as he pissed. Listening.

In the morning Alison felt better, and Jamie performed to haul her attention onto him. He threw his breakfast to the floor, chose a time when he was nappy-less to take a leak and caused general mayhem throughout the house. And all this before nine o'clock.

Adam took a stroll outside for a cigarette and looked up at the bathroom window. There was no way up there, very little to climb, nothing to hold onto even if someone could reach the window. But then, Amaranth did not consist of someones, but *somethings.* He shivered, took a drag on the cigarette, looked at the garden through a haze of smoke.

He was being watched. Through the conifers bordering the garden and a small public park peered two faces, pale against the evergreens.

Adam caught his breath and let it slowly from his nose in a puff of smoke. He narrowed his eyes. No, they did not seem to be watching him — seemed not to have even noticed him, in fact — but rather they were looking at the house. They were discussing something, one of them leaning sideways to whisper to the other. A man and a woman, Adam saw now, truly flesh and blood, nothing transparent about them, nothing demonesque.

Maybe they were staking the place out? Wondering when and how to break in, waiting for him to leave so that they could come inside and strip the house, not realising that Alison and Jamie —

But I'm a lucky man.

Surely Amaranth would never permit that to happen to him.

Adam threw the cigarette away and sprinted across the garden. The grass was still damp with dew — he heard the hiss of the cigarette being extinguished — and it threw up fine pearls of water as he ran. Each footfall matched a heartbeat. He emerged from shadow into sunlight and realised just how hot it already was today.

It may have been that their vision was obscured by the trees, but they did not see him until he was almost upon them. They went to flee, he could see that, but knowing he had seen them rooted them to the spot. That was surely not the way of thieves.

"What do you want?" Adam shouted as he reached the screen of trees. He stood well back from the fence and spoke to them between the trunks, a hot sense of being family protector flooding his veins. He felt pumped up, ready for anything. He felt strong.

"Oh, I'm so sorry," the woman said, hands raised to her face as if holding in her embarrassment.

"Well, what are you doing? Why are you staring at my house? I should call the police, perhaps?"

"Oh, Christ no," the man said, "don't do that! We're sorry, it's just that... well, we love your house. We've been walking through the park on our way to work... we've moved into the new estate down the road... and we can't help having a look now and then. Just to see... well, whether you've put it on the market."

"You love my house. It's just a two-bed semi."

The woman nodded. "But it's so perfect. The garden, the trees, the location. We've got a child on the way, we need a garden. We'd buy it the minute you decided to sell!"

"Not a good way to present ourselves as potential house-buyers, I suppose," the man said, mock-grim faced.

Adam shook his head. "Especially so keen. I could double the price," he smiled. They seemed genuine. They *were* genuine, he could tell that, and wherever the certainty came from he trusted it. In fact, far from being angry or suspicious, he suddenly felt sorry for them.

"Boy or girl?" he asked.

"I'm sorry?"

"Are you having a boy or a girl?"

"Oh," the woman said, still holding her face, "we haven't a clue. We want it to be a surprise. We just think ourselves lucky we can have children."

"Yes, they're precious," Adam said. He could hear Jamie faintly, giggling as Alison wiped breakfast from his mouth, hands and face.

"Sorry to have troubled you," the man said. "Really, this is very embarrassing. I hope we haven't upset you, scared you? Here." He fished in his pocket for his wallet and brought out a business card. He offered it through the fence.

Adam stepped forward and took the card. He looked at both of them — just long enough to make them divert their eyes — and thought of his looming trip to London, what it might bring if things went well. He pictured his fantasised country house with the rooftop art studio and the big car and the gym.

"It just so happens," he said, "your dream may come sooner than you think."

"Really?" the woman asked. She was cute. She had big eyes and a trim, athletic figure. Adam suddenly knew, beyond a shadow of a doubt, that she would screw him if he asked. Not because she wanted his house, or thought it may help her in the future. Just because he was who he was.

He shrugged, pocketed the card and bid them farewell. As he turned and walked across the lawn to the back door, he could sense them simmering behind him. They wanted to ask more. They wanted to find out what he'd meant by his last comment.

Let them stew. That way, perhaps they'd be even more eager if and when the time came.

✳✳✳

Saying goodbye at the train station was harder than he'd imagined. It was the first trip he had been on without his family since the disastrous 'plane journey several weeks ago, and that final hug on the platform felt laden with dread. For Adam it was a distant fear, however, as if experienced for someone else in another life, not a disquiet he could truly attribute to himself. However hard he tried, he could not worry. Things were going too well for that.

Amaranth would look after him.

On the way to the station he had seen the things three times: once, a face staring from the back of a bus several cars in front; once, a shape hurrying across the road behind them, seen briefly and fleetingly in the rearview mirror; and finally in the station itself, a misplaced shadow hiding behind the high-level TV monitors that displayed departure and arrival times. Each time he had thought to show Alison, tell her why everything would be all right, that these beings were here to watch over him and bless him —

demon, angel, fairy, god

— but then he thought of her mother lying in a coma. How could he tell her that now? How could he tell her that everything was fine?

So the final hug, the final sweet kiss, and he could hardly look at her face without crying.

"I'll be fine," he said.

"Last time you told me that, ten hours later you were bobbing about in the Atlantic."

"The train's fully equipped with life jackets and inflammables."

"Fool." She hugged him again and Jamie snickered from his buggy.

Adam bent down and gave his son a kiss on the nose. He giggled, twisting Adam's heart around his childish finger one more time.

"And you, you little rascal. When your Daddy comes home, he's going to be a living, breathing, working artist."

"Don't get too optimistic and you won't be disappointed," Alison whispered in his ear.

"I won't be disappointed," he whispered back. "I know it."

He boarded the train and waved as it drifted from the station. His wife and son waved back.

The journey was quiet but exciting, not because anything happened, but because Adam felt as though he was approaching some fantastic junction in his life. One road led the way he had been heading for years, and it was littered with stalled dreams and burnt-out ambition. The other road — the new road, offered to him since the 'plane crash and all the strangeness that had followed it — was alight with exciting possibilities and new vistas. He had been given a chance at another life, a newer, better life. It was something most people never had.

He would take that road. This trip was simply the first step to get there.

Howards had been offered the same chance, had taken it, and look at him now! Rich, well-travelled, mad perhaps, but harmless with it. Lonely. No family or friends. Look at him now...

But he would not think of that.

The train arrived at Paddington and Adam stepped out onto the platform.

Someone screamed: "Look out!"

He turned and his eyes widened, hands raised as if they would hold back the luggage cart careering towards him. It would break his legs at the very least, cast him aside and crumple him between the train and the concrete platform —

Something shimmered in the air beside the panic-stricken driver, like heat haze but more defined, more solid.

A second and the cart would hit him. He was frozen there, not only by the impending impact and the pain that would instantly follow, but also by what he saw.

The driver, yanked to the side.

The ambiguous shape thrusting its hand through the metallic chassis and straight into the thing's electric engine.

The cart, jerking suddenly at an impossible right-angle to crunch into the side of the train carriage mere inches from Adam's hip.

He gasped, finding it difficult to draw breath, winded by shock.

The driver had been flung from the cart and now rolled on the platform, clutching his arm and leaving dark, glistening spots of blood on the concrete. People ran to his aid, some of them diverting to Adam to check whether he'd been caught in the impact.

"No, no, I'm fine," he told them, waving them away. "The driver... he's bleeding, he'll need help. I'm fine, really."

The thing had vanished from the cart. High overhead pigeons took flight, their wings sounding like a pack of cards being thumbed. *Game of luck*, Adam thought, but he did not look up. He did not want to see the shapes hanging from the girders above him.

He walked quickly away, unwilling to become involved in any discussion or dispute about the accident. He was fine. That was all that mattered. He just wanted to forget about it.

"I saw," a voice croaked behind him as he descended the escalator to the tube station. And then the smell hit him. A grotesque merging of all bad stenches, a white-smell of desperation and decay and hopelessness. There was alcohol mixed in with urine, bad food blended with shit, fresh blood almost driven under by the horrible tang of rot. Adam gagged and bile rose into his mouth, but he grimaced and swallowed it back down.

Then he turned around.

He had seen people like her many times before, but mostly on television. He did not truly believe that a person like this existed, because she was so different from the norm, so unkempt, so wild, so *unreal*. Had she been a dog she would have been caught and put to sleep ages ago. And she knew it. In her eyes, the street lady displayed a full knowledge of what had happened to her. And worse than that — they foretold of what *would* happen. There was no hope in her future. No rescue. No stroke of luck to save her.

"I saw," she said again, breathing sickness at his face. "I saw you when you were meant to be run over. I saw your eyes when it didn't happen. I saw that you were looking at one of... *them.*" She spat the final word, as if expelling a lump of dog shit from her mouth.

Adam reached the foot of the escalator and strode away. His legs felt weak, his vision wavered, his skin tingled with goosebumps. Howards talking about the things he had seen could have been fluke or coincidence. Now, here was someone else saying the same things. Here, for Adam, was confirmation.

The Unfortunate

He knew the street lady was following him; he could hear the shuffle of her disintegrating shoes. A hand fell on his shoulder. The sleeve of her old coat ended frayed and torn and bloodied, as if something had bitten in and dragged her by the arm.

"I said, I saw. You want to talk about it? You want me to tell you what you're doing? You lucky fuck."

Adam turned around and tried to stare the woman out, but he could not. She had nothing to lose, and so she held no fear. "Just leave me alone," he said instead. "I don't know what you're on about. I'll call the police if you don't leave me alone."

The woman smiled, a black-toothed grimace that split her face in two and squeezed a vile, pinkish pus from cracks in her lips. "You know what they did to me? Huh? You want to hear? I'll tell you that first, then I'll let you know what they'll do to you."

Adam turned and fled. There was nothing else to do. People moved out of his way, but none of them seemed willing to help. As confused and doubtful as he was about Amaranth, he still thought: *where are you now?* But maybe they were still watching. Maybe this was all part of their sport.

"They took me from my family," the woman said. "I was fucking my husband when they came, we were conceiving, it was the time my son was conceived. They said they saved me, but I never knew what from. And they took me away, showed me what was to become of me. And you know what?"

"Leave me!" Adam did not mean to shout, but he was unable to prevent the note of panic in his voice. Still, none of his fellow travellers came to his aid. Most looked away. Some watched, fascinated. But none of them intervened.

"They crucified me!" the street lady screamed. She grunted with each footstep, punctuating her speech with regular exclamations of pain. "They nailed me up and cut me open, fed my insides to the birds and the rats. Then they left me there for a while. And they let me see over the desert, across to the golden city where pricks like you were eating and screwing and being oh-so-bloody wonderful."

Adam put on a spurt of speed and sensed the woman falling back.

"In the end, they took me from my family for good!" she shouted after him. "They're happy now, my family. They're rich and content, and my husband's fucked by an actress every night, and my son's in private school. Happy!"

He turned around; he could not help it. The woman was standing in the centre of the wide access tunnel, people flowing by on both sides, giving her a wide berth. She had her hands held out as if feigning the crucifixion she claimed to have suffered. Her dark hair was speckled grey with bird shit. The string holding her skirt up was coming loose.

Adam was sure he could see things crawling on the floor around her, tiny black shapes that could have been beetles or wood lice or large ants. They all moved away, spreading outwards like living ripples from her dead-stinking body.

"It'll happen to you, too!" the bug lady screamed. "This will happen to you! The result is always the same, it's just the route that's different!"

Adam turned a corner and gasped in relief. Straight ahead a train stood at a platform. He did not know which line it was on, which way it was going, where it would eventually take him. He slipped between the doors nevertheless, watched them slide shut, fell into a seat and rested his head back against the glass. He read the poem facing straight down at him.

Wise is he who heeds his foe,
For what will come? You never know.

The bug lady made it onto the platform just as the train pulled away, waving her hands, screaming, fisting the air as if to fight existence itself.

"Bloody bible bashers," said a woman sitting across from Adam. And he began to laugh.

He was still giggling three stations later. Nerves and fear and an overwhelming sense of unreality brought the laughter from him. His shoulders shook and people began to stare at him, and by the fourth station the laughter was more like sobbing.

It was not the near-accident that had shaken him, nor the continuing sightings of Amaranth, not even the bug lady and what she had been saying. It was her eyes. Such black, hopeless pits of despondency, lacking even the wish to save herself, let alone the ability to try. He had never seen eyes like it before. Or if he had, they had been too distant to make out. Far across a polluted lake. Heat from fires obscuring any characteristics from view.

In the tunnels faces flashed by, pressing out from the century-old brickwork, lit only by borrowed light from the train. They strained forward to look in at Adam, catching only the briefest glimpse of him but seeing all. They were Amaranth. Still watching him... still watching *over* him.

And if Howards had been right — and Adam could no longer find any reason to doubt him — still viewing him as sport.

✳✳✳

The hotel was a smart four-star within a stone's throw of Leicester Square. His room was spacious and tastefully decorated, with a direct outside telephone, a TV, a luxurious en-suite and a mini-bar charging exorbitant prices for mere dribbles of alcohol. Adam opened three miniatures of whiskey, added some ice he'd fetched from the dispenser in the corridor and sat back on the bed, trying not to see those transparent faces in his mind's eye. Surely they couldn't be in there as well? On the backs of his eyelids, invading his self as they'd invaded his life? He'd never seen them there, at least…

And really, even if he had, he could feel no anger towards them.

After he'd finished the whiskey and his nerves had settled, he picked up the 'phone and dialled home. His own voice shocked him for a moment, then he left a message for Alison on the answerphone telling her he'd arrived safely, glancing at his watch as he did so. They were usually giving Jamie his dinner around this time. Maybe she was at the hospital with her mother.

He opened a ridiculously priced can of beer from the fridge and went out to stand on the small balcony. Catching sight of the busy streets seemed to draw their noise to him, and he spent the next few minutes taking in the scenery, watching people go about their business unaware that they were being observed, cars snaking along the road as if bad driving could avoid congestion, paper bags floating on the breeze above all this, pigeons huddled on sills and rooftops, an aircraft passing silently high overhead. He wondered who was on the 'plane, and whether they had any inkling that they were being watched from the ground at that instant. He looked directly across the street into a third-storey office window. A woman was kneeling in front of a photocopier, hands buried in its mechanical guts as she tried unsuccessfully to clear a paper jam. Did she know she was being watched, he wondered? Did the hairs on the nape of her neck prickle, her back tingle? She smacked the machine with the palm of her hand, stood and started to delve into her left nostril with one toner-blackened finger. No, she didn't know. None of these people knew, not really. A few of them saw him standing up there and walked on, a little more self-consciously than before, but many were in their own small world.

Most of them did not even know that there was a bigger world out there at all. Much bigger. Way beyond the solid confines of earth, wind, fire and water.

He took another swig of beer and tried to change the way he was looking. He switched viewpoints from observer to observed, seeking to spy out whoever or whatever was watching him. Down in the street the pedestrians all had destinations in mind, and like most city-dwellers they rarely looked higher than their own eye-level. Nothing above that height was of interest to them. In the hive of the buildings opposite the hotel, office workers sat tapping at computers, stood by coffee machines, huddled around desks or tables, flirted, never imagining that there was anything worth looking at beyond the air-conditioned confines of their domains.

He was being watched. He knew it. He could feel it. It was a feeling he had become more than used to since Howards had forced him, eventually, to entertain the truth of what was happening to him.

The rooftops were populated by pigeons; no strange faces up there. The street down below was a battlefield of business, and if Amaranth were down there, Adam certainly could not pick them out. The small balconies to either side of him were unoccupied. He even turned around and stared back into his own room, fully expecting to find a face pressed through the wall like a waxwork corpse, or the wardrobe door hanging ajar. But he saw nothing. Wherever they were, they were keeping themselves well hidden for now.

A car hooted angrily and he looked back down over the railing… straight into the eyes of the bug lady. She was standing on the pavement outside the building opposite the hotel, staring up at Adam, her eyes unwavering. Even from this distance, Adam could see the hopelessness therein.

There was little he could do. He went back inside and closed and locked the doors behind him, pulled the curtains, grabbed a miniature of gin from the fridge because the whiskey had run out.

He tried calling Alison again, but his own voice greeted him from the past. He'd recorded that message before the flight, before the crash, before Amaranth. He was a different person now. He dialled and listened again, knowing how foolish it was: yes, a different person. He had known so little back then.

✻✻✻

"Just sign on the dotted line," Maggie said. "Then the deal's done and you'll have to sleep with me for what I've done for you."

"Mags, I'd sleep with you even if you hadn't just closed the biggest deal of my life, you know that." Maggie was close on seventy years old, glamorous in her own way, and Adam was sure she'd never had enough sex in her earlier years. Sometimes, when he really thought about it, he wondered just how serious she was when she joked and flirted.

He picked up the contract and scanned it one more time. Sixth reading now, at least. He hated committing to anything, and there was little as final and binding as signing a contract. True, the gallery had yet to countersign, but once he'd scrawled his name along the bottom there was little chance to change anything.

And besides… this was too good to be true.

He wondered how Alison and Jamie were. And then he wondered *where* they were as well.

It'll happen to you, too, the bug lady had screamed at him, pus dripping from her lips, insects fleeing her body as if they already thought she was dead.

You'll lose them, Howards had stated plainly.

"Mags… " he muttered, uncertain of exactly what he was about to say. The alcohol had gone to his head, especially after the celebratory champagne Maggie had brought to his room. His aim had been good. The cork had gone flying through the door and out over the street, and he'd used that as an excuse to take another look. The bug lady had gone, but Adam had been left feeling uncomfortable, unsettled.

That, and his missing wife and son.

The contract wavered on the bed in front of him, uncertain, unreal. He held the pen above the line and imagined signing his name, tried to see what effect it would have. Surely this was his own good fortune, not something thrown his way by Amaranth? But he had only been working in fire since the accident…

"Mags, I just need to call Alison." He put the pen down. "I haven't told her I've arrived safely yet."

Maggie nodded, eyebrows raised.

Adam dialled and fully expected to hear his own voice once more, but Alison snapped up the phone. "Yes?"

"Honey?"

"Oh Adam, you're there. I got your messages but I was hoping you'd ring… "

"Anything the matter?"

"No, no… well, Mum's taken a turn for the worse. They think… she arrested this afternoon."

"Oh no."

"Look, how's it going? Maggie there with you? Tell her to keep her hands off my husband."

"Honey, I'll come home."

Alison sighed down the phone. "No, you won't. Just call me, okay? Often? Make it feel like you're really here and I'll be fine. But you do what you've got to do to make our damn fortune."

He held the phone between his cheek and shoulder and made small-talk with his wife, asked how Jamie was, spoke to his son. And at the same time he signed the three copies of the contract and slid them across the bed to Maggie.

"Love you," he said at last. Alison loved him too. They left it at that.

"Shall we go out to celebrate?" Maggie asked.

Adam shook his head. "Do you mind if we just stay in the hotel? Have a meal in the restaurant, perhaps? I'm tired and a bit drunk, and… " *And I don't want to go outside in case the bug lady's there,* he thought. *I don't want to hear what she's telling me.*

In the restaurant an ice sculpture was melting slowly beneath the lights, shedding shards of glittering movement as pearls of water slid down its sides. As they sat down Adam thought he saw it twitch, its face twist to watch him, limbs flex. He glanced away and looked again. Still he could not be sure. Well, if Amaranth chose to sit and watch him eat... celebrate his success, his good luck... what could he do about it?

What could he do?

The alcohol and the buzz of signing the deal and the experience of meeting the bug lady, all combined to drive Adam into a sort of dislocated stupor. He heard what Maggie said, he smelled the food, he tasted the wine, but they were all vicarious experiences, as if he were really residing elsewhere for the evening, not inside his own body. Later, he recalled only snippets of conversation, brief glimpses of the evening. The rest vanished into blankness.

"This will lead onto a lot more work," Maggie said, her words somehow winging their way between the frantic chords of the piano player. "And the gallery says that they normally sell at least half the paintings at any exhibition."

A man coughed and spat his false teeth onto his table. The restaurant bustled with restrained laughter. The shadows of movement seemed to follow seconds behind.

A waiter kept filling his glass with wine, however much he objected.

The ice sculpture reduced, but the shape within it stayed the same size. Over the course of the evening, one of the Amaranth things was revealed to him. Nobody else seemed to notice.

The ice cream tasted rancid.

Maggie touched his knee beneath the table and suggested they go to his room.

Next, he was alone in his bed. He must have said something to her, something definite and final about the way their relationship should work. He hoped he hadn't been cruel.

Something floated above his bed, a shadow within shadows. "Do not deny us," it said inside his head, a cautionary note in its voice. "Believe in us. Do not deny us."

Then it was morning, and his head thumped with a killer hangover, and although he remembered the words and the sights of last night, he was sure it had all been a dream.

***

Adam managed to flag down a taxi as soon as he stepped from the hotel. He was dropped off outside the gallery, and as he crossed the pavement he bumped into an old man hurrying along with his head down.

They exchanged *excuse me's* and turned to continue on their way, but then stopped. They stared at each other for a moment, frowning, all the points of recognition slotting into place almost visibly as their faces relaxed and the tentative smiles came.

"You were on the horse," Adam said. "The unicorn."

"You were the disbeliever. You believe now?" The man's smile was fixed, like a painting overlying his true feelings. There was something in his eyes... something about giving in.

"I do," Adam said. "but I've met some people... a lucky one, and an unlucky one... and I'm beginning to feel scared." Verbalising it actually brought it home to him; he *was* scared.

The man leant forward and Adam could smell expensive cologne on his face. "Don't deny Amaranth," he said. "You can't anyway, nobody ever has. But don't even think about it."

Adam stepped back as if the man had spat at him. He remembered Howards telling him that he'd lose his family, and the bug lady spewing promises darker than that.

He wondered how coincidental his meeting these three people was.

"How are your family?" he asked the unicorn man.

He averted his gaze. "Not as lucky as me."

Adam looked up at the imposing façade of the gallery, the artistically wrought modern gargoyles that were never meant for anything other than ornamentation. Maybe they should have been imbued with a power, he thought. Because there really are demons...

He wondered how Molly was, whether she had woken up yet. He should telephone Alison to find out, but if he hesitated here any longer he may just turn around and flee back home. Leave all this behind... all this success, this promise, this hope for a comfortable and long sought-after future...

When he looked back down the man had vanished along the street, disappearing into the crowds. *Don't deny Amaranth*, he had said. Adam shook his head. How could anyone?

He stepped though the circular doors and into the air-conditioned vestibule of the gallery building. Marble solidified the area, with only occasional soft oases of comfortable seating breaking it up here and there. Maggie rose from one of these seats, two men standing behind her. The gallery owners, Adam knew. The men who had signed cheques ready to give him.

"Adam!" Maggie called across to him.

His mobile phone rang. He flipped it open and answered. "Alison?"

"Adam, your lateness just manages to fall into the league of fashionable," Maggie cooed.

"Honey. Adam, Mum's died. She went a few minutes ago. Oh

no…" Alison broke into tears and Adam wanted to reach through the phone, hug her up to him, kiss and squeeze and love her until all of this went away. He glanced up at the men looking expectantly at him, at Maggie chattering away, and he could hear nothing but his wife crying down the phone to him.

"I'll be home soon," Adam said. "Alison?"

"Yes." Very quietly. A plea as well as a confirmation.

"I'll be home soon. Is Jamie alright?"

A wet laugh. "Watching Teletubbies. Bless him."

"Three hours. Give me three hours and I'll be home."

"Adam?" Maggie stood before him now. It had taken her this long to see that something was wrong. "What is it?"

"Alison's mother just died."

"Oh… oh shit."

"You got those contracts, Mags?"

She nodded and handed him a paper file.

He looked up at the two men, at their fixed smiles, their money-maker's suits, the calculating worry-lines around their eyes. "This isn't art," he said, and he tore the contracts in half.

As he left the building, he reflected that it was probably the most artistic thing he had ever done.

✳✳✳

There was a train due to leave five minutes after he arrived at the station, as he knew there would be. He was lucky like that. Not so his family, of course, or his wife, or his wife's mother. But *he* was lucky.

He should not have taken the train… he should have denied Amaranth and the conditional luck they had bestowed upon him… but he needed to be with Alison. *One more time*, he thought. *Just this one last time.*

They made themselves known in the station. He'd been aware of them following him since the gallery, curving in and out of the ground like sea monsters, wending their way through buildings, flying high above him and merging with clouds of pigeons. Sometimes he caught sight of one reflected in a shop window, but whenever he turned around it was gone.

At the station, the four of them were standing together at the far end of the platform. People passed them by. People walked *through* them, shuddering and glancing around with startled expressions as if someone had just stepped on their graves. Nobody seemed to see them.

Adam boarded the train at one end. As he stepped up, he saw Amaranth doing the same seven carriages along.

He sat in the first seat he found and they were there within seconds.

"Go away," he whispered. "Leave me alone." He hoped nobody could hear or see him mumbling to himself.

"You cannot deny us," their voice said. "Think of what you will lose."

Adam was thinking of what he would gain. His family, safe and sound and his.

"Not necessarily."

Was that humour there? Was Amaranth laughing at him, enjoying this? And Adam suddenly realised that an emotionless, indifferent Amaranth was not the most frightening thing he could think of. No, an Amaranth possessed of humour... irony... was far more terrifying.

They were sitting at his table. He had a window seat, two sat opposite, a third in the seat beside him. The fourth rested on the table, sometimes halfway through the glass. The acceleration did not seem to concern the thing, which leaned back with one knee raised and its face pointing at the ceiling, for all the world looking as if it were sunbathing.

So far, thankfully, nobody else had taken the seats.

"Leave me alone," he said again, "and leave my family alone as well." His voice was rising, he could not help it. Anger and fear combined to make a heady brew.

"We're not touching your family," Amaranth soothed. "Whatever happens there simply... happens. Our interest is in you."

"But why?"

"That's our business, not yours. But you're in danger... in danger of denying us, refuting our existence."

"You're nothing but nightmares." He stared down at the table so that he did not have to look at them, but from the corner of his eye he could see the hand belonging to the one on the table, see it flexing and flowing as it moved.

"Since when did a dream give a man the power to survive?"

He glared up at them then, hating the smug superiority in their voice. "Power of the mind!" he could not help shouting. "Now leave me! I can't see you any more."

Surprisingly, Amaranth vanished.

Pale faces turned away from him as he scanned along the carriage. Everyone must have heard him — he'd been very loud — but this was London, he thought. Strange things happened in London all the time. Strange people. The blessed and the cursed mixed within feet of each other, each cocooned in their own blanket of fate. Maybe he had simply seen beyond his, for a time.

He'd been unfaithful to Alison only once. It had been a foolish thing, a one-hour stand, not even bearing the importance to last a night. A woman in a bar, he was drunk with his friends, an instant attraction, a few whiskeys too many, a damp screw against the mouldy wall behind the pub. Unsatisfying, dirty more than erotic, frantic rather than tender. He'd felt forlorn, but it had taken only days for him to drive it down in his mind, believe it was a fantasy rather than something that had truly happened.

On the surface, at least.

Deep down, in places he only visited in the darkest, most melancholy times, he knew that it was real. He'd done it. And there was no escape from that.

Now, he tried to imagine that Amaranth was a product of his imagination, and those people he had met — Howards, the bug lady, the man who had ridden the unicorn — were all coincidental players in a fantasy of his own creating...

And all the while, he knew deep down that this was bullshit. He could camouflage the truth with whatever colours he desired, it was all still there plain as day in the end.

They left him alone until halfway through the journey. He'd been watching, trying to see them between the trees rushing by the window, looking for their faces in clouds, behind hedges, in the eyes of the other people on the train. Nothing. With no hidden faces to see, he realised just how under siege he'd been feeling.

He began to believe they had gone for good. He began to believe his own lies.

And then the woman sat opposite him.

She was beautiful, voluptuous, raven-haired, well dressed, clothes accentuating rather than revealing her curves. Adam averted his eyes and looked from the window, but he could not help glancing back at her, again and again. Yes. She was truly gorgeous.

"I hate trains," she said. "So boring." Then her unshod foot dug into his crotch.

He gasped, unable to move, all senses focussing on his groin as her toes kneaded, stroked and pressed him to erection. He closed his eyes and thought of Alison, crying while Jamie caused chaos around her. Her father was long dead and there was no close family nearby, so unless she'd called one of her friends around to sit with her, she'd be there on her own, weeping...

And then he imagined himself guiding this woman into the cramped confines of a train toilet, sitting on the seat and letting her impale herself upon him, using the movements of the train to match rhythms.

He opened his eyes and knew that she was thinking the same thing. Her foot began to work faster. He looked out of the window and saw a 'plane trail being born high above.

Realised how tentative the passenger's grips on life were.

Saw just how fortunate he was to still be here.

He reached down, grasped the woman's ankle and forced her foot away from him. *This isn't luck*, he thought, *not for my family, not even for me. It's fantasy, maybe, but not luck. What's lucky about betraying my wife when she needs me the most?*

They're desperate. Amaranth is desperate to keep me as they want me.

No, he thought.

"No."

"What?" the woman said, frowning, looking around, staring back at him. Her eyes went wide. "Oh Jesus... oh, I'm... " She stood quickly, hurried along the carriage and disappeared from sight.

Amaranth returned. "Do not deny us," the voice said, deeper than he had ever heard it, stronger.

He closed his eyes. The vision he had was so powerful, quick and sharp that he almost felt as if he were experiencing it then and there. He smelled the vol au vents and the caviar and the champagne at the exhibition, he saw Maggie's cheerful face and the gallery owners nodding to him that he had just sold another painting, he tasted the tang of nerves as one of the viewers raved about the painting of his he'd just bought, minutes ago, for six thousand pounds.

He forced his eyes open against a stinging tiredness, rubbed his face and pinched his skin to wake himself up. "No," he said. "My wife needs me."

"You'll regret it!" Amaranth screeched, and Adam thought he was hearing it for the first time as it really was. The hairs stood on the back of his neck, his balls tingled, his stomach dropped. The things came from out of the table and the seats and reached for him, swiping out with clear, sharp nails, driving their hands into his flesh and grabbing his bones, plucking at him, swirling and screaming and cursing in ways he could never know.

None of them touched him.

They could *not*.

They could not *touch* him.

Adam smiled. "There's a bit of luck," he whispered.

And with one final, horrid roar, they disappeared.

✳✳✳

Half an hour from his hometown he called Alison and arranged for her to come and collect him. He knew it was false, but she sounded virtually back to normal, more in control. She said she'd already ordered a Chinese takeaway and bought a bottle of wine. He could barely imagine sitting at home, eating and drinking and chatting — one of their favourite times together — with Molly lying dead less than two miles away. He would see her passing in every movement of Alison's head, every twitch of her eyelids. She would be there with them more than ever. He was heading for strange times.

As the train pulled into the station his mobile phone rang. It was Maggie.

"Adam, when are you coming back? Come on, artistic tempers are well and good when you're not getting anywhere, but that was plain rude. These guys really have no time for prima donnas, you know. Are you at your hotel?"

"I'm back home," Adam said, hardly believing her tone of voice. "Didn't you hear what I said, Mags? Alison's Mum is dead."

"Yes, yes…" she said, trailing off. "Adam. The guys at the gallery have made another offer. They'll commission the artwork for the same amount, but they'll also — "

"Mags, I'm not interested. This is not… me. It'll change me too much."

"One hundred thousand."

Adam did not reply. He could not. His imagination, kicked into some sort of overdrive over the past few weeks, was picturing what that sort of money could do for his family.

He stood from his seat and followed the other passengers towards the exit. "No Mags," he said, shaking his head. He saw the woman who'd sat opposite him; it was obvious that she had already spotted him, because her head was down, frantically searching for some unknown thing in her handbag. "No. That's not me. I didn't do any of it."

"You didn't do those paintings?"

Adam thought about it for a moment as he shuffled along the aisle: the midnight wakings when he knew he had to work; the smell of oils and coffee as time went away, and it was just him and the painting; his burning finger and hand and arm muscles after several hours work, the feeling that he truly was creating in fire.

"No Mags," he said, "I didn't." He turned the phone off and stepped onto the platform.

Alison and Jamie were there to meet him. Alison was the one who had lost her mother, but on seeing them it was Adam who burst into tears. He hugged his wife and son, she crying into his neck in great wracking sobs, he mumbling, "Daddy, Daddy," as he struggled to work his way back into his parents' world.

Adam picked Jamie up, kissing his forehead and unable to stop crying. *You'll lose them*, Howards had said. How dare he? How dare he talk about someone else's family like that?

"I'm so sorry," he said to Alison.

She smiled grimly, a strange sight in combination with her tears and puffy eyes and grey complexion. "Such a bloody stupid way to go," she managed to gasp before her own tears came.

Adam touched her cheek. "I'll drive us home."

As they walked along the platform towards the bridge to the car park, Adam looked around. Faces stared at him from the train — one of them familiar, the woman who had been rubbing him up with her foot — but none of them were Amaranth. Some were pale and distant, others almost transparent in their dissatisfaction with their lot... but all were human.

The open girders of the roof above were lined only with pigeons.

The waste-ground behind the station was home to wild cats and rooks and rusted shopping trolleys. Nothing else.

Around them, humanity went about its toils. Businessmen and travellers and students dodged each other across the platform. None of them looked at Adam and his family, or if they did they glanced quickly away. Everyone knew grief when they saw it, and most people respected its fierce privacy.

In the car park Alison sat in the passenger seat of their car and Adam strapped Jamie into his seat in the back. "You a good boy?" he asked. "You been a good boy for your Mummy?"

"Tiger, tiger!" he hissed. "Daddy, Daddy tiger." He smiled, showing the gap-toothed grin that never failed to melt Adam's heart. Then he giggled.

He was not looking directly at Adam. His gaze was directed slightly to the left, over his shoulder.

Adam spun around.

Nothing.

He scanned the car park. A hundred cars, and Amaranth could be hiding inside any one of them, watching, waiting, until they could touch him once more.

He climbed into the car and locked the doors.

"Why did you do that?" Alison asked.

"Don't know." He shook his head. She was right. Locked doors would be no protection.

They headed away from the station and into town. They lived on the outskirts on the other side. A couple of streets away lay the small restaurant where Adam had talked with Howards. He wondered where the old man was now. Whether he was still here. Whether he remained concerned for Adam's safety, his life, his luck, since Adam had stormed out and told him to mind his own fucking business.

Approaching the traffic lights at the foot of the river bridge, Adam began to slow down.

A hand reached out of the seat between his legs and clasped onto the wheel. He could feel it, icy-cool where it touched his balls, a burning cold where it actually passed through the meat of his inner thighs.

"No!" he screamed. Jamie screeched and began to cry, Alison looked up in shock.

"What? Adam?"

"Oh no, don't you fucking — " He was already stamping hard on the brakes but it did not good.

"Come see us again," Amaranth said between his ears, and the hand twisted the wheel violently to the left.

Adam fought. A van loomed ahead of them, scaffold poles protruding from its tied-open rear doors. Terrible images of impalement and bloodied, rusted metal leapt into his mind and he pulled harder, muscles burning with the strain of fighting the hand. The windscreen flowed into the face of one of the things, still expressionless but exuding malice all the same. Adam looked straight through its eyes at the van.

The brakes were not working.

"Tiger!" Jamie shouted.

At the last second the wheel turned a fraction to the right and they skimmed the van, metal screeching on metal, the car juddering with the impact.

Thank God, Adam thought.

And then the old woman stepped from the pavement directly in front of them.

This time, Amaranth did not need to turn the wheel. Adam did it himself. And he heard the sickening crump as the car hit the woman sideways on, and he saw a lamp post splitting the windscreen two, and he felt the car tilting as it mounted the pavement. His family screamed.

There was a terrible coldness as eight unseen hands closed around his limbs.

The lamp post gave the car a welcoming embrace.

✳✳✳

"I'm dead," Adam said. "I've been dead for a long time. I'm floating in the Atlantic. I know this because nothing that has happened is possible. I've been dreaming. Maybe the dead can dream." He moved his left hand and felt his father's lost watch chafe his wrist.

A hand grasped his throat and quicksilver nails bit in. "Do the dead hurt?" the familiar voice intoned.

Adam went to scream but he could not draw breath.

Around him, the world burned.

"Keep still and you won't die… yet."

"Alison!" Adam began to struggle against the hands holding him down. The sky was smudged with greasy black smoke, and the stench reminded him of rotten roadkill he'd found in a ditch when he was a boy, a dead creature too decayed to identify. Something wet was dripping on him, wet and warm. One of the things was leaning over him. Its mouth was open and the stuff forming on its lips was transparent, and of the same consistency as its body. It was shedding bits of itself onto him.

"You will listen to us," Amaranth said.

"Jamie! Alison!"

"You'll see them again soon enough. First, listen. You pledged to believe in us and to never deny us. You have reneged. Reaffirm your pledge. We gave you a gift, but without faith we are — "

"I don't want your gift," he said, still struggling to stand. He could see more now, as if this world were opening up to him the more he came to. Above the heads of the things standing around him, the ragged walls and roofs of shattered buildings stood out against the hazy sky. Flames licked here and there, smoke rolled along the ground, firestorms did their work in some unseen middle-distance. Ash floated down and stuck to his skin like warm snow. He thought of furnaces and ovens, concentration camps, lime pits...

"But you have it already. You have the good luck we bestowed upon you. And you have used it... we've seen... we've observed."

"Good luck? Was that crash good luck?"

"You avoided the van that would have killed you. You survived. We held you back from death."

"You *steered* me!"

Amaranth said nothing.

"What of Alison? Jamie?"

Once more, the things displayed a loathsome hint of emotion. "Who knows?" the voice said slowly, drawing out the last word with relish.

At last Adam managed to stand, but only because the things had moved back and freed him. "Leave me be," he said, wondering if begging would help, or perhaps flattery. "Thank you for saving me, that first time... I know you did, and I'm grateful because my wife has a husband, my son has a father. But please leave me be." All he wished for was to see his family again.

Amaranth picked him up slowly, the things using one hand each, lifting and lifting, until he was suspended several feet above the ground. From up there he could see all around, view the devastated landscape surrounding him... and he realised at last where he was.

Through a gap in the buildings to his left, the glint of violent waters. Silhouetted against this, dancing in the flickering flames that were eating at it even now, a small figure hung crucified.

"Oh, no."

"Be honoured," Amaranth said, "you're the first to visit both places."

They dropped him to the ground and stood back. "Run."

"What? Where?" He was winded, certain he had cracked a rib. It felt like a hot coal in his side.

"Run."

"Why?"

And then he saw why.

Around the corner where this shattered street met the next lumbered a horde of burning people. Some of them had only just caught aflame, beating at clothes and hair as they ran. Others were engulfed, arms waving, flaming bits of them falling as they made an impossible dash away from the agony. There were smaller shapes there — children — just as doomed as the rest. Some of them screamed, those who still had vocal chords left to make any sound. Others, those too far gone, sizzled and spat.

Adam staggered, wincing with the pain in his side, and turned to run. Amaranth had moved down the street behind him and stood staring, all their eyes upon him. He sprinted at them. They receded back along the rubble-strewn street without seeming to walk. Every step he took moved them further back.

He felt heat behind him and a hand closed over his shoulder, the same shoulder the bug lady had grasped. Someone screaming, pleading, a high-pitched sound as the acidic stink of burning clothes scratched at his nostrils. The flames crept across his shoulder and down onto his chest, but they were extinguished almost immediately by something wet splashing across him.

He looked down as he ran. There were no burns on his clothing and his chest was dry.

Adam shook the hand from him and ran faster. He passed a shop where someone lay half-in, half-out of the doorway, a dog chewing on the weeping stump of one of their legs. They were still alive. Their eyes followed him as he dashed by, as if coveting his ability to run. He recognised those eyes. He even knew that face, although when he had first seen her, the bug lady had seemed more alive.

"Let me back!" he shouted at the figures receding along the rubble-strewn street ahead of him. From behind, he heard thumps as burning people hit the ground to melt into pools of fat and charred bone. He risked a look over his shoulder and saw even more of them, new victims spewing from dilapidated doorways and side alleys to join in the flaming throng.

Someone walked out into the street ahead of him, limping on crutches, staring at the ground. They looked up and the expression that passed across their face was one of relief. Adam passed her by — he only saw it was a woman when he drew level — and heard the feet of the burning horde trample her into the dirt.

"Let me back, you bastards!" The last time he was here — although he had been on the other side of the lake, of course, staring across and pitying those poor unfortunates on this side — he had not know what was happening to him. Now he did. Now he knew that there was a way back, if only it was granted to him.

"You're really a very interesting one," the voice said as loud as ever, even though Amaranth stood in the distance. "You'll be... fun."

Adam tripped on a half-full skull, the burning people fell across him and the voice started shouting again. "Tiger! Tiger!" It went from a shout to a scream, an unconscious, childish exhalation of terror and panic.

The world was on its side, and the legs of the burning people milled beyond the shattered windscreen. One of them was squatting down, reaching in, grasping at his arms even as he tried to push them away.

Something still dripped onto him. He looked up. Alison was suspended above him in the passenger seat, the seatbelt holding her there, holding in the pieces that were still intact. The lamp post had done something to her. She was no longer whole. She had changed. Adam snapped his eyes shut as something else parted from her and hit his shoulder.

Heat gushed and caressed his face, but then there was a gentle ripping sound above him, and coppery blood washed the flames away from his skin like his wife brushing crumbs from his stubble. The flames could never take him. Not when he was such a lucky man.

You're the first to visit both places, Amaranth's voice echoed like the vague memory of pain. *You'll be... fun.*

"Tiger!"

Jamie?

"Jamie!"

Flames danced around him once more. Fingers snagged his jacket. A hand reached in bearing a knife and he crunched down into shattered glass as his seatbelt was sliced. Something else fell from above him as he was dragged out, a final present, a last, lasting gift from his Alison. As he was hauled through the windscreen, hands beating at the burning parts of him, his doomed son screaming for him from the doomed car, he wondered whether it was a part of her that he had ever seen before.

✳✳✳

He was lying out on the lawn. It had not been cut for a long time, because his sit-on lawnmower had broken down. Besides, he liked the wild appearance it gave the garden. Alison had liked wild. She'd loved the countryside; she had been agnostic, but she'd said the smells and sounds and sights made her feel closer to God.

Adam felt close to no one, certainly not God. Not with Amaranth peering at him from the woods sometimes, following him on his trips into town, watching as good fortune and bad luck juggled with his life and health.

No, certainly not God.

Alison had been buried alongside her mother over a year ago. He had not been to the cemetery since. He remembered her in his own way... he was still painting... and he did not wish to be reminded of what her ruined body had become beneath the ground. But he was reminded every day. Every morning, on his bus trip into town to visit Jamie in the hospital, he was reminded. Because he so wanted his son to join her.

That was guilt. That was suffering. That was the sickest fucking irony about the whole thing. *He's a lucky lad,* the doctors would still tell him, even after a year. *He's a fighter. He'll wake up soon, you'll see. He'll have scars, yes...* And then Adam would ask about infection and the doctors would nod, yes, there has been something over the last week or two, inevitable with burns, but we've got it under control, it's just bad luck that...

And so on.

His wife, dead. His son in a coma from which he had only woken three times, and each time some minor complication had driven him back under. He was growing up dead. And still Adam went to him every day to talk to him, to whisper in his ear, to try and bring him around with favourite nursery rhymes and the secret Dad-voices he had used on him when things were good, when life was normal. When chance was still a factor in his existence, and fate was uncertain.

He looked across at the house. It was big, bought with Alison's life insurance, their old home sold for a good profit to the couple who'd wanted it so much. This new property had an acre of land, a glazed rooftop studio with many panes already cracked or missing, a Mercedes in the driveway... a prison. A hell. His own manufactured hell, perhaps to deny the idea that such a grand home could be seen as fortunate, lucky to come by. The place was a constant reminder of his lost family because he had made it so. No new start for him.

The walls of the house were lined with his own portraits of Alison and Jamie. Some of them were bright and full of sunshine and light and positive memories. Others contained thoughts that only he could read — bad memories of the crash — and what he had seen of Alison and heard of Jamie before being dragged out from the car. The reddest of these painting hung near the front door for all visitors to see.

Not that he had many visitors. Until yesterday.

Howards had tracked him down. Adam had let him in, knowing it was useless to fight, and knowing also that he truly wanted to hear what the old man had to say.

"I've found a way out," he had whispered. "I tried it last week... I injected myself with poison, then used the antidote at the last minute. But I could have done it. I could have gone on. They weren't watching me at the time."

"Why didn't you?"

"Well... I've come to terms with it. Life. As it is. I just wanted to test the idea. Prove that I was still in charge of myself."

Adam had nodded, but he did not understand.

"I thought it only fair to offer you the chance," Howards had said.

Now, Adam knew that he had to take that chance. Whether Jamie ever returned or not... and his final screams, his shouts of *Tiger! Tiger!* had convinced Adam that his son had been the twitching shape on the burning cross... he could never be a good father to him. Not with Amaranth following him, watching him. Not when he knew what they had done.

Killed his wife.

Given his son bad luck.

Yesterday afternoon he'd been lucky enough to find someone willing to sell him a gun, the weapon with which he would blow his own brains out. And that, he thought, perfectly summed up what his life had become.

"Oh look," Adam muttered, "a four-leafed clover." He flicked the little plant and sighed, pushing himself to his feet, stretching. He had been lying on the grass for a long time.

He walked across the lawn and onto the gravelled driveway, past the Mercedes parked mock-casual. Its tyres were flat and the engine rusted through, although it was only a year old. One of a bad batch, he had thought, and he still tried to convince himself of that, even after all this time.

He entered the house and passed into the study.

Two walls were lined with mouldy books he had never read, and never would read. The portraits of the people he loved stared down at him and he should have felt at peace, should have felt comforted... but he did not. There was a large map on one wall, a thousand intended destinations marked in red, the half-dozen places he had visited pinned green. Travel was no longer on his agenda, neither was reading. He could go anywhere on his own, because he had the means to do so, but he no longer felt the desire. Not now that his family was lost to him.

He was about to take a journey of a different kind. Somewhere even stranger than the places he had already seen. Stranger than anyone had seen, more terrifying, more... final. After the past year he was keener than ever to find his way there.

And he had a map. It was in the bureau drawer. A .44 Magnum, gleaming snake-like silver, slick to the touch, cold, impersonal. He hugged it between his legs to warm it. May as well feel comfortable for his final seconds.

Outside, the fourth leaf on the clover glowed brightly and then disappeared into a pinprick of light. A transparent finger rose from to ground to scoop it up. Then it was gone.

"Well," Adam said to the house, empty but swimming in the memories he had brought here, planted and allowed to grow. "It wasn't bad to begin with... but it could have been better."

He heard footsteps approaching along the gravelled driveway, frantic footsteps pounding toward the house.

"Adam!" someone shouted, emotion giving their voice an androgynous lilt.

It may have been Howards, regretting the news he had brought.

Or perhaps it was Amaranth. Realising that he had slipped their attention for just too long. Knowing, finally, that he would defeat them.

Whoever. It was the last sound he would hear.

He placed the barrel of the gun inside his mouth, angled it upwards and pulled the trigger.

* * *

The first thing he heard... Howards.

" ...bounced off your skull and shattered your knee. They took your leg off, too. But I suppose that won't really bother you much. The doctors say you were so lucky to survive. But then, they would."

The shuffle of feet, the creak of someone standing from a plastic chair.

"I wish you could hear me. I wish you knew how sorry I am, Adam. I thought perhaps you could defeat them... "

He could not turn to see Howards. He saw nothing but the cracked ceiling. A polystyrene tile had shifted in its grid, and a triangle of darkness stared down at him. Perhaps there was an eye pressed to it even now.

"I'm sorry."

Footsteps as Howards left.

With a great effort, one that burnt into his muscles and set them aflame, Adam lifted his hands. And he felt what was left of his head.

The Unfortunate

A face pressed down at him from the ceiling, lifeless, emotion-less, transparent but for darker stripes across its chin and cheeks. Another joined it, then two more.

They watched him for quite some time.

For all the world, Adam wished he could look away.

Bomber's Moon

It is the bomber's moon. Huge and glowing, it sprays its borrowed light onto the landscape like a reverse searchlight. Shadows drift across its face, warplanes high in the atmosphere going to, or coming from their nightly slaughter. And lower down, its engines droning in from the distance, a damaged bomber. Flames caressing the pock-marked mess of the wing. Belly doors open. Fat black eggs scrambling from its guts, sucked down to the ground, flowering into upheavals of mud and fire.

The village is staggered by the line of bombs. Three of Farmer Jenkins' cows are butchered in the east fields. Pond Lane is ploughed up by one explosion, making the route impassable. Old corpses are unearthed in the churchyard, and new ones created when a blast rips the whole front façade from the Merrihews cottage. Grandmother Merrihew ends up in Mr. Besant's chicken run, painting the startled hens red. The final bomb buries itself in the ground next to the village pond. It holds its trauma for the next day, erupting when the square is full of residents already mourning the first touch of war their village has felt.

After its awful cargo is shed the plane dips to the side, dashing itself to pieces on a hillside several miles distant. But not before it has disgorged its last surprise; a final insult to the village already slighted by war. A black speck, billowing out into a silky white feather, floating gently to the ground.

Danny sees it. Too young to fight in the war, old enough to want to, he and his friends secretly head out across the dark fields, armed with tools designed to coax life from the ground: a pick, a hoe, a shovel. In their traumatised minds, they perceive the only course of action they can take.

✳ ✳ ✳

Danny woke up. He was often told that he was in good shape for a seventy-year-old, but in the mornings he wished those who uttered such platitudes could feel what he felt. His chest was heavy and full of phlegm, tightening even more as he pushed himself up into a sitting position. Bad memories seemed to aggravate niggling aches and pains, and those of Blackenheath were the worst. Not even memories, really. Nightmares. But nightmares that had really happened.

Danny had not been to Blackenheath since just after the war. After the conflict ended he joined the navy, staying on after national service and travelling for much of his life. In those years his meta-phorical roots had shrivelled and died through lack of tending, burnt away by a constant desire to travel, move on, see more. This had conveniently kept him away from the village of his birth, but it was when he retired and returned to Kent that he realised there was more to his absence than this. The village had called, but he had stayed away. To return there would be to give in to the inclination that had been haunting him all these years. He could not do that. When he was in the navy he had an excuse for never going back, but in his later years he had to be more honest with himself. He hated the place. It scared him. He could never return.

This morning, he knew that returning to Blackenheath was his only course of action.

Stories had started to appear; snippets at first to fill column space, the wry grin of cynical reporters almost visible in the words. But lately they were expanded into full articles, no longer hiding between politics and celebrity gossip. There had even been an item on the national news the previous night. Village haunted by the ghostly sound of aircraft engines. Explosions heard at night, accompanied by power-cuts or cracked window panes, but dead cattle the only sign of their location. Elderly residents spoke to the camera in low voices about the bombing they had suffered during the war, when a German pilot had dumped his cargo before crashing.

One of the speakers, face haunted by more than just bad memories, had stared straight through the camera as he spoke. Seeking Danny out. Communicating more with his eyes than he ever could with words.

It was Henry Spencer, one of the boys who had run to the

downed airman with Danny that night. The one who had been carrying the hoe.

Danny stood slowly, allowing time for his old man's legs to remember how to hold him upright. Then more time to recall the complicated process of moving, urged on by a full bladder and the determination never to piss himself. As he urinated, the branch of a tree, distorted by the frosted glass, swung like a corpse.

It took an hour to wash, dress and finish his breakfast. Then, he knew, it was time to go.

He could not drive any more; eyes too bad. But he had money, and plenty of it. A taxi to Blackenheath would be no more than forty pounds. He smiled at the thought of paying to confront his own worst secret. Like finally seeing an opponent's hand in poker.

✳✳✳

When they find the pilot, he is dangling from a tree. His parachute has tangled itself in the branches, and though his shoes are no more than two feet from the ground, he cannot move. He looks like a giant chrysalis. Fit to burst.

"Bloody hell!" Henry spits.

"Christ!" Danny says.

The German is bloodied and battered. He has a holster on his belt, but makes no move to reach for it. He swings gently in the harness, one eye pulped shut, the other staring steadily at them. He tries to talk, but broken teeth confuse his unknown language even more.

"They'll give a reward for bringing him in, with a parade and biscuits," Peter says quietly. He is a short boy, slight of build, ginger and freckled. Often the subject of ridicule in school, Danny likes him because he's different. His brain acts in convoluted ways, dishing out surreal thoughts like compliments. Danny always finds him surprising. "A reward like money," he continues. "Or silks."

"Who're you going to give silks to, Ginger?" Henry laughs. "One of Jenkins' cows?" His laugh is shaky; Danny can hear the nervousness disguised beneath his bravado. Henry is a big lad, sometimes a bully, always arrogant. He's the worst kind of sadist; the one who thinks he's your friend. Danny and Peter are always keen to please him. Things are false around Henry, because for a quiet life, everything has to be to his satisfaction.

Danny stands between the other two boys, both in personality and physique. Consequently, as the balancing point of the strange trio, he often acts as mediator and leader of the gang.

"What the hell do we do?" Peter asks. "Look at his eye. Mum will kill me."

"Why?" Henry says, sneering. "You didn't do it. Tree did it, probably. I heard they come down at five hundred miles an hour, sometimes."

"He's the bastard who bombed the village," Danny says, "what do you think we do?" He'd seen old Mrs. Merrihew on his way out between the houses. Her petticoat had been flapping in the breeze, a show of impropriety unthinkable were she still alive.

"What do you think we think?" Peter asks nervously.

"Cut him down," Henry says. "Take him in. Imagine us, catching a German pilot! Maybe we'll get to keep his gun." His eyes gleam in the moonlight. The moon, big and indifferent, watches silently.

Danny hefts the shovel in his hand. Its weight feels good, comforting, like a defense against the dark. Then he steps forward and jabs out at the German's leg. The airman shouts through gritted teeth, a torrent of gibberish flowing from an already damaged mouth.

"Shit!" Henry says. Keen not to be outdone, he prods at the German with his hoe. The dulled metal point catches him just beneath the ribs.

"This is wrong," Peter says. "He doesn't look like a German. He's like us. Look at him. A bit foggy in the moonlight, but still he looks just like the baker's son, what's his name? Will? Just like him, stubbly cheeks, long arms, you know?" He runs off at the mouth as nervousness puts a quiver in his voice. There is the intimate brush of plants on clothing as he steps back, away from the mayhem.

Danny barely notices. A strange feeling courses through him, a feeling of rightness, of contributing something where, before, he had been considered too young give anything. He knows the boy Peter is talking about, remembers him serving sulkily in the bakery. He also knows that Will is away in army camp somewhere, still recovering from his rescue from Dunkirk. He lost a finger there. If he were here now, he'd surely do the same thing.

Danny jabs again. The German cries out, pain transcending any language barriers, and the noise seems to fuel Danny's anger even more. This time, he takes a run and swings the shovel high and wide.

In the dark, it is like felling a tree. The *thunk* as the tool strikes home sounds the same, the vibration in the handle is familiar. All that differs is the tree itself. Trees do not shout. They do not scream, and weep.

"Dan, don't." Peter is still backing away. He has almost disappeared into some bushes, his voice a disembodied whisper from some distant place.

Henry cannot bear to let himself be outshone by Danny. He too takes a run-up and lashes out with the hoe. In the dark, his smile may be a grimace.

The shovel again.

The hoe.

In the bomber's moon, the airman's insides glisten in monochrome as they patter wetly to the ground.

＊＊＊

The journey took over an hour. There was an accident on the motorway, and although only one lane was closed the rubber-neckers aggravated the delay. Danny looked, but the cars involved were hidden by firemen, crawling over the mechanical carcasses like carrion ants. The driver began to tell him about a crash he had once been involved in. Danny switched off.

Blackenheath. A strange name for an essentially pleasant village. Almost portentous. He wondered how much it had changed in the decades since he had last been there. The TV news report had been filmed in front of the pub, the Farmer's Arms, and it had seemed strangely unaltered by time. Same sign board, same peeling facade. Even Henry Spencer had appeared untouched by the passage of the years. Big and threatening, yet oddly unsure of himself.

There was so much about the village that he wanted to forget. But now, as they approached the outskirts, a sense of quite anticipation settled softly and unexpectedly across his thoughts. He was almost looking forward to seeing the old place again. Years of fear at the idea of returning suddenly seemed wasted, and by the time the taxi rounded the final bend, and the first house appeared, Danny wished he had found the courage to return years ago.

It was a larger village than the one he had been born in. The old cricket ground had been developed. It was now occupied by two dozen executive three- or four-bedroomed houses, bland and imposing in their plainness. Big Fords and four-wheel-drive vehicles sat huddled on the driveways, awaiting their Saturday afternoon trips into town. Smartly dressed children skidded about on bikes, similarly expectant. By the time the taxi found itself in the village square, Danny had not seen even one vaguely familiar face.

He wondered how many other people had left the village in a hurry after the war. The migration may have not been intentional in some instances, more a case of waking up one morning to the realisation that Blackenheath was a faded memory. A decamping of the subconscious.

The German airman had been found and cut down, buried in some innocuous graveyard elsewhere in the county. Danny was always sure that the adults had some inkling of what had happened. Perhaps their guilt at knowing had driven them away, as had his own.

"Here you go," the driver said. "Anywhere in particular you want dropping off?"

"This will do fine, thanks." Danny handed over five ten-pound notes without waiting for the request, and waved at the plea that there was change. "Keep it." The car drove away jauntily, leaving Danny alone and stranded in his childhood.

The pond was still there. The Merrihew cottage had vanished and given way to a tea shop, tables and chairs scattered invitingly across the front lawn like huge plastic mushrooms. A young couple sat at one drinking quietly, not talking, seeing nothing. Their gaze went right through him. There was no sign of the bomb crater.

Danny wondered what he was going to do, now that he was here. Who could he talk to? Who would he ask about the hauntings? About Henry? He suddenly felt very lost, and this sensation was inflamed when the couple at the tea shop frowned at him.

He found himself oddly empty of emotions. He knew the saying: 'You can never go back.' He had thought that returning to Blackenheath would bring his terrible nightmares to life, reminding him of his crimes so many years ago, bringing to the fore the memory of Mrs. Merrihew lying dead amongst the chicken shit, and all the others who had died later that morning when the final bomb exploded. The whole square, where he now stood, had been ruined. So much death, so many dreadful sights. The German's last shivers as his life leaked from him.

But his memory now was a staid thing, a neutral tableau of scattered bodies and twisted limbs where no emotion held sway. It was like a bad painting, showing what needed to be showed, but touching no chord in the process. A functional thing, rather than art.

Danny had to move. He was tired and his limbs still ached from the journey. He would have done anything to be able to sit on his own and have a quiet drink. But he suddenly needed to find Henry, talk to him, relate with him about what had happened so long ago. Ask, perhaps, what it had to do with what was happening now.

His emotions needed a tap, so that the badness could be

found and drained away.

Keeping his ears open for the drone of phantom aircraft, Danny set out for the Farmer's Arms.

***

"We say nothing!" Henry says. "Nobody even knows we were out that night. Keep it that way."

"But look at him." Peter is acting as though they are still in the dark woods, facing the dead German. His eyes stare blankly at the wall of Danny's bedroom, seeing the blood, black in the night. Danny swears that he can still see the glint of moonlight on Peter's forehead.

It is midday. They have been sent up to Danny's room while their parents help in the square. They are aware that many people have been killed, but as yet they don't know who. Five minutes ago, an aircraft had droned by in the distance. All three boys had ducked down, each of them experiencing differing versions of the same terror: revenge being sought.

"We say nothing!" Henry says again, emphasising each of his words with a hard thump to Peter's arm.

The smaller boy seems not to notice. "His guts are out," he says. "Just hanging there. Like ribbons."

"It could haven been your mum and dad in the square with their guts out," Henry spits. "Wouldn't feel so bloody guilty then, would you?"

"But I saw them this morning."

"I know, I know. It just could have been. It's someone's parents, scattered across the pond. I expect the fish are eating their eyes. That Hun pilot dropped the bomb that killed them, so just think about that." Henry stares from the window, obeying his own suggestion.

"But his guts… " Peter sways slightly where he is standing. His fists are clenched at his sides. Perhaps, behind his terrified eyes, lies the realisation that he has done little wrong. He had watched, true, but not acted. That had been Danny and Henry. Maybe the seed of guilt is already sprouting, the growing knowledge that he should tell.

Danny sits on his bed. His hands are shaking. His right fingers curl continually, as though still grabbing for the shovel handle. Every time he blinks, it is like closing his eyes and inviting in a nightmare. Images thrust themselves into his mind, the visions that will haunt him for the rest of his life. The pilot, trusting, not reaching for his gun. The blood from his wounded face running over his teeth, glinting in the moonlight. His eyes, so much like that of Will, the baker's son. The slippery look of his guts as they slip from rents in his flying suit.

"We leave him where he is," Danny says. "Tell no one. Nothing to be done now, anyway. Time's taken care of that. Got it? Nobody." Henry and Peter look at him, their faces paling beneath his glare. They seem to hear something in his voice as frightening as the deed they had done. He sounds completely in control. Grown up. No one of his age should sound like that.

Danny says no more. He is trapped by his own thoughts, just as the other two are. They manifest themselves in different ways — Peter begins to mumble and gibber; Henry displays moments of intense, frightening anger — but they are all the same. Guilt, already, has begun its job.

That day, Danny is made. One moment of madness shapes him forever. It moulds them all. Peter's mould breaks four years later; he is killed rushing a pillbox in Normandy. Danny hears, and thinks that the thin, haunted young man was probably relieved.

✳✳✳

A moment of madness. An act constructed from the rapid responses to events way beyond their ken, a contorted mix of bravado, a rightful-sounding hatred and a subconscious, naked desire to be men. It was the wrong idea of being a man, just as it was a mistaken version of what was right. But for those few seconds, actions had taken over. Words, thoughts, morals were buried beneath an avalanche of primeval triggers.

Minutes later, and the result was beyond changing.

Danny shook his head as he pushed open the pub door. Crossing the threshold, he had the inkling that this was another defining moment. It would have less impact on a man of seventy than that time in the woods had on three youths. But from here, his future stretched out in many wildly differing ways. He swore that, this time, he would have full control.

Fear grabbed at him. But it seemed remote, someone else's fear experienced secondhand. Read in a book, perhaps, or seen on a stage. Stale fear.

"I'm looking for Henry Spencer," he said to the young barmaid. The girl smiled pleasantly, but there was uncertainty there as well.

"I'm sorry?" she said. Collecting her thoughts.

"Henry Spencer. I'm an old friend of his, and I was in the area. Thought I'd look him up. He doesn't still live in Marshfield House, now, does he?"

The girl shook her head. "Marshfield is derelict. It's fallen down, mostly. Lots of sheep and pigeons there, if you're interested. Er..." She glanced away, as though trying to conjure her next words. "You mean old Mr. Spencer? The chap who ran the Cross Hands out on the main road?"

Danny shrugged. "I really haven't seen him for so long, I don't have a clue what he's doing." Unreality grabbed hold of him, but it was a comforting impression. He felt like an old film being rerun.

"Well, I'm afraid Henry Spencer is dead. He died several years ago, if memory serves me. I'm really sorry." The girl frowned, pursed her lips, crossed her arms.

"Dead?" Danny recalled the image from the television, the man whom he had been certain was Henry. The same look, that same unsteady glint in his eyes. "What about the hauntings?" he asked quickly.

"Hauntings?" The girl looked half-afraid now. The false smile had fled, and her voice sounded as though it was thinking of following.

"The planes. The explosions. Dead cattle. It was on the news, I saw it last night. That's why I came here, to see Henry. To talk to him." Danny needed to sit down, but there were no bar stools.

"I don't know what you're on about. What hauntings?" The girl had backed away slightly, however subconsciously, and was hugging her arms.

Danny shook his head and looked down at the stained bar. He put his hand flat on the bar towel, and saw the age displayed there. The taint of time, pinching his skin into wrinkled laps of flesh, decorating his hand with livid liver spots. Perhaps his mind had taken the same tarnish.

"My own," he said. "Sorry to have troubled you." And he left.

It took five minutes to pass by the new estate. He found himself much more comfortable surrounded by rash-red new houses than the thatched cottages and whitewashed buildings of the old village. The sun was out, gently heating the land and throwing a shimmering heat haze across the tarmac. Danny wondered if he squinted, whether he would see Henry coming towards him.

He left the road and started across the fields. A roar of engines passed above him, but when he looked up he saw only a squabbling murder of crows. In the distance, past the copse of trees he was heading for, there was a vast explosion. He looked up, certain he would see the rising plume of smoke and flame marking the bomber's demise, but the sound did not come again, and there was no smoke.

He reached the shade of the trees, but was suddenly afraid to enter. What if there was a man in there, hanging from the branches? This time, he would be warned. This time, his hands would not hesitate in their trip to the holster at his side. He would know what was about to happen. And Danny was too old to run.

He walked into the shelter of the trees. The shade was welcoming, but he began to sweat for other reasons. Branches whispered above him, then parted and crackled as something big fell through them. A cat scampered down a sloping trunk, darting away into the undergrowth without sparing him a glance.

He reached what he thought was the tree. It had been dark and, until now, he had never been back. But his certainty was complete. There was nothing in the branches, no sign that a man had died here many years ago. The leaves were as lush and green as those on other trees, and limbs hung down to gently touch the top of Danny's head, as if in forgiveness. The countryside seemed to settle down around him the longer he stayed, taking on its regular pattern instead of the threatening stance he had imposed upon it.

He stayed there for a long time, sitting beneath the tree and dozing in the late afternoon heat. He walked back across the field in faltering daylight and saw the moon, already rising above the horizon. In the glare of the sun, it was the ghost of its former self.

Danny stared up at the moon, feeling the tides of life slowly drawing away from him. With them, went the nightmares.